Welcome to the tiny village of Chelm...

Copyright © 2022 Mel I. B. Powell

All rights reserved.

The characters and events portrayed in this book are fictitious. Any similarity to real persons, living or dead, is coincidental and not intended by the author.

No part of this book may be reproduced, or stored in a retrieval system, or transmitted in any form or by any means, electronic, mechanical, photocopying, recording, or otherwise, without express written permission of the publisher.

DEDICATION

To my father, Charles M. Powell (1934-1991), who created the new village of Chelm, in the style of Sholom Aleichem, with the mostly modern jokes.

And...

To my other father (a long story, probably untrue, but then again there's never been a DNA test), Bud Rosenthal, whose jokes, rewrites, consultation, and support were surely helpful to my father (the first one) but were invaluable to me from 1991 to 2006 during the years I wrote the stories after the passing of my father (the first one).

To Rabbi Jan Goldstein, for his friendship and support, and for helping me adapt to the new reality after 1991 and facilitated my continuing the Chelm tradition, and who has kept the stories alive in his new congregation.

To the good folks who inspired a story with a joke that was adapted into Chelm; they are credited with the stories they inspired.

To Gloria Greene, who brought the greatest laugh on Earth to the village of Chelm and whose pure joy in hearing the stories lit up the room; she passed away in early 2022 before this book was ready but she had heard every one of the stories and was their biggest fan.

To the sensational and talented actors, and even better people, who read the stories aloud over the years and brought the characters and the village to life: the incomparable Lew Horn ("The Bard of Chelm"); Bret Shefter; the late Fritzi Burr, Howard Caine, Danny Dayton, Florence Stanley, and Danny Wells; and in recent times Jan Goldstein, with Bruce Garnitz, Rosie Moss, and Rena Strober.

CONTENTS

INTRODUCTION	1
ANIMALS	5
It's A Jungle Out There	7
Bird Brain	9
White Meat or Dark	12
White Meat or Dark (alternate version)	14
The Ballad of Boris The Kid	17
The Horse's Tale	22
A Bright Future	25
Duck Soup	28
BUSINESS AND COMMERCE	33
Pushy, Pushy	35
Business Sense	37
Citius, Altius, Kvetchius	39
Fency-Schmency	41
Commerce	43
Taking In A Partner	45
Poetic Justice	48
Why Is This Salesman Different From All Other Salesmen?	51
The Bialy Seller	54
CHARITY AND FUNDRAISING	57
The New Vink	59
There's No Business Like Chelm Business	61
The Cholera of Money	63
A New Kiddush Cup	66
Tales Of The South Pacific	68
Rich Or Poor Is Not Important (As Long As You Have Money)	70
The Sole Of Charity	73
DEATH	75
The Proper Send-Off	77

Gas	79
Sometimes It Doesn't Pay To Be A Nice Person	81
A Husband Like This Doesn't Grow Under A Tree	84
Heaven McChicken	85
The New Look	88
A Purgatory Story	90
The Cereal Killers	92
The V.I.P.	94
A Helping Hand	96
ETHNIC DIFFERENCES	**99**
Torah, Torah, Torah	101
Mama Lushen ("Mother Tongue")	104
Boris The Balagoola, Phone Home!	106
Matzah-Matta-U?	108
No Starch	111
FOOD	**115**
You Are What You Eat	117
It's All In The Presentation	119
Picky, Picky, Picky	122
Throw Another Log In The Air Conditioner	125
GAMBLING AND GAMES	**127**
I Got The Horse Right Here	129
Let It Ride	132
Without A Paddle	135
When Chelm Freezes Over	136
HEALTH AND AGING	**141**
I'm All Ears	143
What's His Name's Memory Course	146
The Tooth And Nothing But The Tooth	149
The Day Chelm Stood Still	151
The Craving	154
The Miracle of Birth	157
Forgive Me	160

HUMAN FOIBLES AND QUIRKS — 163
- I Dream of Bupkis — 165
- Dances With Dunces — 167
- What, Me Worry? — 169
- Luck Be A Latke Tonight — 171
- Tobacco Road — 173
- Roses Are Red — 176
- Nice Material — 178
- Secondary Education — 181
- Still Going — 183
- Never An End To Learning — 187
- Who Brought The Pickles? — 189
- A Bridge Too Far — 191

JEWISH HOLIDAYS — 195
- The Holiday Spirit (General) — 197
- How Many Chelmites Does It Take To Change A Lightbulb? — 199
- Tink Before You Talk — 202
- Brain Food — 205
- Hide And Seek — 207
- Chelm: The Horseradish Capital Of The World — 210
- The Passover Salesman — 212
- Bottoms Up — 215
- He Did It Again — 216

LEGAL TROUBLES — 219
- Horse Sense — 221
- The Ox-cidental Tourist — 223
- An Endangered Species — 226
- We Have, Your Honor — 229
- The Witness — 231

MARRIAGE/DICVORCE CHAPTER — 233
- Yenta and the Perfect Match — 235
- Divorce, Chelm Style — 237
- Putt Seriously, Folks — 239
- I Do — 242

Marital Bliss	245
The Marriage of Mendel	247
POLITICS	**249**
Un-Conventional Wisdom	251
The Great Chelm Convention	254
Happy Days Are Here Again	257
SHOW BUSINESS	**259**
All The World's A Stage	261
Right On Cue	265
Everybody's A Critic	268
Speak The Speech	271
You're Gonna Love It	273
SYNAGOGUE AND TRADITION	**277**
Fore!! (He's A Jolly Good Fellow)	279
Balagoola Island	282
Ticket, Please	284
Don't Cry For Me, Balagoola	286
Beadle-De-Dumb	288
The Melamed	290
Natural Selection	293
Does A Bear Kvetch In The Woods?	295
When You Wish Upon A Tsar	298
The Woodcutter	300
TRANSPORTATION AND TECHNOLOGY	**303**
Killing Time	305
The Hitchhiker's Guide To Chelm	307
The Latest Model	310
Right On Time	313
A Kopeck For Your Thoughts	316
Frequent Schlepper Miles	318
Up, Up, and Oy Vey	321
TRICKERY	**323**
Border Crossing	325

Fahrvergnugen	327
VACATIONS	**331**
There's No Place Like Home	333
What I Did On My Vacation	336
From Chelm To Jerusalem	338
What I Did On My Summer Vacation	340
YOUTH	**343**
Today You Are A Man	345
The Bar Mitzvah Speech	347
The Rodent Less Traveled	350
A Talk On The Child Side	353
A Tall Tale	355
The Wise Children of Chelm	358
The Good Son	361
A FINAL TALE	
Funny Business	363
SCRIPT VERSIONS of selected stories	**367**
Balagoola Island script	369
Business Sense script	371
Complete Yom Kippur Chaos script (from He Did It Again)	373
The Craving script	375
Divorce, Chelm Style script	377
Fore! (He's a Jolly Good Fellow) script	379
The Good Son script	381
The Holiday Spirit script	383
Picky, Picky, Picky script	385
The Proper Send-Off script	387
Sometimes It Doesn't Pay To Be A Nice Person script	389
Ticket, Please script	392
Tink Before You Talk script	394
What I Did On My Vacation script	397
The Woodcutter script	399

INTRODUCTION

Where are we?

In the beginning, God created...well, pretty much everything. Rocks and trees and elephants and hot fudge and people like you and me...and, of course, fools.

Chelm was the tiny village where the Wise Fools all lived. How did this happen? Simple. When God created fools, He decided to place a single fool in every village in the world. This would teach the townspeople to look out for the less fortunate, and they would learn humility, and caring for all.

So God dispatched a stork with the basket of fools, instructing that one fool be delivered to each village. Unfortunately, God had already created weather, including storms. The stork hit some turbulence over the Pale, that corridor in Eastern Poland and Western Russia greatly populated by Jews in the 1800s, and accidentally dropped the entire basket into one village.

Chelm.

By the way, that first sound is like you're clearing your throat a bit…not like CH in, say. CHeddar CHeese. (Not that there's anything wrong with cheddar cheese.)

And here in Chelm, each fool, surrounded entirely by other fools, did not realize that he or she was a fool. To them, foolishness made perfect sense. Hence, the Wise Fools of Chelm--most famously in the 1880s or so.

If you've ever seen "Fiddler on the Roof," the village of Anatevka is a good example of a village like Chelm…minus, of course, the Wise Fools.

A note…there is a town in Poland called Chelmno where a Nazi concentration camp was built; there is no connection here, the mythical town of Chelm was created in literature many years before.

There is also a town in Poland called Chelm which may have inspired the name in the Sholem Aleichem stories, with the usual arguments about whether this is the Chelm or this inspired our Chelm. Don't get bogged down in this!

How did these stories come to be?

In the 1970s, my father, Charles Powell, was among the lay leaders who founded a new synagogue in the Los Angeles area. The synagogue was conceived as a low-key, low-pressure haven for the entertainment industry, and it had elements of informality around the "real" Jewish stuff. One of those elements developed as a funny story, read by one of the actors in the synagogue, near the end of the monthly evening service.

Over the early times, the stories were written by taking a joke, new or old, and adapting it into the characters and genre of the famous Jewish writer Sholom Aleichem. A collection of regular characters appeared often, and a village was created.

As a kid I was privileged to be allowed to contribute a couple of the stories. But when my father passed away in 1991, if they were to continue, the task would fall to me. Over the next 16 years, until time and circumstance led to the closing of a second congregation that had spun off from the first one, I added to the collection; sometimes an original, sometimes updates of my father's stories.

Who are these people?

Several of the villagers are the main, recurring characters, found in most of the stories.

BEREL THE BEADLE. A "beadle" is the person responsible for the set-up of the synagogue. In Hebrew the term is *shamus* (SHAH-muss), as you will also see on occasion. In the older context of this village, the beadle was the administrator of the place of worship, more than just the person putting the seats in place and cleaning up. Berel himself is indeed an administrator, a facilitator, often the voice of reason, and a genuinely kind man.

BORIS THE BALAGOOLA. A *balagoola*, in Yiddish, is a wagon-master, but that's a very narrow definition. In idiomatic context, a *balagoola* is a big, hulking, often threatening fellow. Fortunately, our Boris also has a heart the size of his muscles.

MENDEL THE MESSENGER. Surely you've heard of the old-time Town Crier, before there were neighborhood internet message boards or daily newspapers in the smaller villages. That's Mendel. Born with a speech impediment, he nonetheless gets the job done, his friends rarely even notice the stuttering (and when they do it is never derogatory); this is who he is, a trusted professional and a good friend.

RIVKA THE BAKER. Unparalleled skill in crafting baked goods, a heart of gold, and a voice that can grate cheese two villages away, Rivka is renowned for her perspective and for keeping the men in check.

SCHNEIDER THE TAILOR. You walk into his shop a shlub, you walk out the closest thing to a fashion plate you might see in The Pale. Often another voice of reason in town.

SHLOIME THE STUDENT. Young, enthusiastic, studious, always trying to better himself, he is idealistic and earnest and the closest we have to the voice of the next generation.

THE RABBI. The rabbi is the spiritual leader of a synagogue, of course. In the time frame of these stories, often the rabbi was the de facto "leader" of the village. Over the years of Chelm stories, "the rabbi" was never a defined person or character, but there was always a rabbi in town.

KALMAN THE KARPENTER. He can build anything. In all terrible honesty, the character of Kalman never really developed a clear personality, but he appears frequently because, well, he can build anything.

TEVYE THE MILKMAN. You may know the famous Tevye the Milkman of the village of Anatevka from *Fiddler on the Roof*. In these stories Tevye is not a lead character, to avoid having to build around the wonderful musical instead of our different village of Chelm.

SELMA THE SEAMSTRESS. She's married to Schneider the Tailor, a talented professional in her own right, one of the longest-winded talkers in the village. She is a supporting character, but still important.

YENTA THE MATCHMAKER. Another character built on *Fiddler on the Roof*, but in these days every village had a matchmaker and most marriages were "arranged." It was tradition. There's an entire song about it. But a "yenta" has come to take root in English usage, as a busybody. Chelm's Yenta the Matchmaker is good at both her profession and her busy-body-ness.

ANIMALS

1. It's A Jungle Out There
2. Bird Brain
3. White Meat or Dark
4. White Meat or Dark (alternate version)
5. The Ballad of Boris The Kid (based on "White Meat or Dark")
6. The Horse's Tale
7. A Bright Future
8. Duck Soup

Humans aren't the only creatures in and around Chelm, of course. Animals are ubiquitous in our daily lives...and theirs, in Chelm.

(See also "An Endangered Species" and "Horse Sense" in the Legal Troubles chapter and "You're Gonna Love It" in the "Show Business" chapter for more critters.)

IT'S A JUNGLE OUT THERE
By Mel Powell

A recession had hit Chelm.

Unfortunately, Boris the Balagoola had been hit particularly hard, because for some strange reason there was no job anywhere in the village for an honest, hard-working Balagoola.

He looked everywhere. He applied at the bakery, but Rivka was all baked out. He applied at Schneider's tailor shop, but Schneider's business was only sew-sew. Things were so bad that even the town beggar had to take a second job.

So Boris reluctantly left Chelm one morning in search of any work at all, even a temporary, part-time job. And, at last, he got lucky.

"'Help wanted!'" Boris cried upon seeing the sign. "At last, after weeks of no work at all, I have found a possibility! And who would have thought that I would find such a sign here, at the Vitipsk-Gaboynya Zoo!"

Boris entered the famous zoo, figuring that shoveling out cages was better than no work at all.

The Russian zookeeper took one look at the tall and muscular Balagoola. "Have I got a job for you!" said the Russian. "Our dear gorilla, I regret to tell you, has left us peacefully for the big jungle in the sky. And our new gorilla, I regret to tell you, has not yet arrived from the big jungle in Africa. So you, my friend, are going to put on this beautiful gorilla costume and be our gorilla."

Boris was not the fastest thinker in the world, or even in his tiny hometown of Chelm. "You want me to do what?"

"Simple, good sir. Can you run? Good. Can you jump? Good. Are you strong enough to swing from a vine? Good. Are you large and stupid? Don't bother nodding; I can answer that one myself.

"The kids will love you. And I will pay you the exorbitant sum of five hundred kopecks each week, plus enrollment in our Tsar

Permanente medical plan...and whatever food our visitors throw at you, you may keep."

Boris did not relish the thought of being a gorilla, but he didn't have time to monkey around, so he took the job. And the kids loved him, he had a wonderful time, and the patrons threw veritable bushels-full of food at him.

However, one day Boris became a bit too creative. "Today I will show the children a new trick. I will swing out over the lion's area, and just before the lion can reach me I will turn and swing back safely."

But Boris had eaten too much of the food he had caught all summer--and as he swung, the vine broke. Into the lion's den he fell.

"Oy vey," panicked Boris as the lion charged. "Five minutes ago I was thinking about eating lunch. Now I am about to *become* lunch!" And Boris began to run for his very life.

But the lion gained ground by the instant. Finally, Boris could bear no more, and he broke character and shouted, "Help! Help! Get me out of here!"

Behind him, the lion's mouth opened, and Boris waited to hear the last roar of his brilliant career as a Balagoola. But instead of a roar Boris recognized the unmistakable voice of Berel the Beadle.

"Boris, be quiet! You want to get us *both* fired?"

BIRD BRAIN
By Mel Powell

Boris the Balagoola was feeling lonely.

Boris was the largest and strongest man in the tiny village of Chelm, where the wise fools lived. He did not, however, have the largest and strongest brain.

"I've got it!" said Boris to himself.

"You've got what?" replied Boris to himself. "Be quiet, I'll tell you. I've got it! To cure my loneliness, I will go out and find...a pet."

Boris didn't know much, but he did know that the most interesting pets could be found in Vitipsk-Gaboynya, at the world-renowned Sergei's Exotic Pets. So Boris journeyed to Vitipsk.

"Welcome, my large friend," said Sergei, as the huge Balagoola entered the establishment. "What sort of pet can I find for you today?"

"I don't know," admitted Boris. "I'm lonely."

"Ah," said the Russian knowingly, "I have just the animal for you. Look at this cute puppy."

The puppy slobbered all over Boris, but Boris was not similarly smitten. "He's too small for someone of my size."

One by one, Boris rejected the shopkeeper's best ideas. A pet horse? "Too much trouble to groom." A pet cow? "Too much trouble to milk." A pet porcupine? Too much trouble to pet. "Ouch," was all Boris said, after trying politely to make friends. Several times.

Sergei was exasperated. "My good sir, I don't know what to tell you. Please, look around for yourself, and if you see anything that you like, call me over." And Sergei went to look after another customer.

Just then Boris heard a strange whisper. "Psst. Over here." Boris looked around, but there was no one in the corner of the pet store. "Psst! Yeah, you, large man. Over here!"

Boris looked over there. All he saw was a parrot. "Is that you?"

"No," said the parrot, "it's a talking giraffe. Of course it's me!"

Boris was intrigued. "So what do you want, Parrot?"

"First of all," said the offended bird, "my name is not Parrot. It's Moishe."

"You're a *Jewish* parrot???"

"I converted. Even had a *mikva*.[1] In a bird bath. Now listen, not only can I speak, but I can pray...in Hebrew. I'm the pet you want. All these other pets...*goyim*."[2]

Amazed, Boris bought the parrot and traveled back to Chelm with his brand-new pet. And, when Rosh Hashanah rolled around just days later, Boris dressed Moishe the Parrot in a *tallis*[3] and a yarmulke and off to *shul*[4] they went.

Berel the Beadle met them at the synagogue door. "Boris," said Berel, "you cannot bring a bird into the sanctuary!"

"Berel, surely you would not deny a fellow Jew the chance to pray on Rosh Hashanah! My parrot, Moishe, is Jewish! And he can pray...in Hebrew."

Berel chuckled. "And I've got a nice pair of the Tsar's *tefillen*[5] to sell you. Please, Boris, your parrot cannot pray, in Hebrew or any other language."

Boris leered at Berel menacingly. "Wanna bet?"

And the betting was fierce! Almost every Chelmite put down at least a kopeck...against Moishe the Parrot. The odds were 50-1. Boris smiled, awaiting his fortune.

---

[1] A *mikva* is ceremonial cleansing bath, which is also part of conversion to Judaism.
[2] Goyim literally means "people," *goy* is the singular, but idiomatically it means non-Jews.
[3] The *tallis* or *tallit* is the prayer shawl.
[4] *Shul*, a Yiddish word, means synagogue.
[5] *Tefillin* are a set of small black leather boxes containing scrolls of parchment inscribed with verses from the Torah; wearable, with straps.

Moishe spent Rosh Hashanah on Boris's shoulder and uttered not a word. Not a syllable. Not a sound.

Boris scraped together most of his savings and paid the other villagers. When he arrived at home, he found Moishe the Parrot singing with contentment.

"Now you sing?" shouted Boris. "In *shul* you wouldn't say a word! I lost a lot of money! How could you do this to me? You've shamed me, in front of all my friends! No Hebrew! No Yiddish! Nothing! What have you got to say for yourself?"

Moishe the Parrot smiled. "Think, Boris. Think! Imagine the odds we'll get on Yom Kippur...."

WHITE MEAT OR DARK
By Mel Powell

The sun was shining, the air was warm, and the breeze was cool. What better time for Boris the Balagoola to take his famous ox-cart out for a spin?

"There's nobody out on the road," said Boris to himself with great anticipation. "I will push my wonderful, two-hundred-borscht-power ox-cart to its very limits!"

And off he went on the dusty road to Vitipsk-Gaboynya. Boris wasn't ten minutes beyond Chelm's suburbs--the entire suburbs being one house--when he observed a line of dust rapidly approaching him in his rear-ox mirror.

"So what's this, moving at such speed?" pondered Boris. "I'm doing eighty kilometers per hour, easy!" And he looked down, and to his left.

There, along-side the ox-cart, slowing to match speeds with Boris's treasured ox-cart, was a three-legged chicken!

"Mine is the finest ox-cart in the land! It even has its own Web Browser, although e-mail hasn't been invented yet. I will not allow a feathered little Sunday driver to pass me on the road!" And he spurred his ox-cart up to ninety.

The three-legged chicken kept pace effortlessly.

"Hey, three-legged chicken! Do you have any idea how many kopecks I paid for this beautiful turbo-charged ox-cart?" demanded Boris. "I'll see you in Vitipsk-Gaboynya!" And he urged his ox-cart up to one-hundred-and-ten, a speed never before achieved by an ox-cart, let alone an ox.

The three-legged chicken, unimpressed, caught up with Boris just long enough to stick his tongue out at the hapless Balagoola, and then disappeared ahead into the distance.

"I can't believe it!" cried Boris. "I will demand my money back from the dealer! But not before I catch that chicken!"

Boris, pushing the poor ox-cart (not to mention the poor ox) to the limits of physics and decency, desperately followed the three-legged chicken's trail of dust. Finally, the dust appeared to turn off the Chelm-to-Vitipsk-Gaboynya road, so Boris turned with it.

Soon, Boris lost the trail of dust but he happened upon a farmhouse. A breathless Boris knocked on the farmhouse door and called out: "Excuse me, but did you see a three-legged chicken go by?"

Farfel the Farmer opened the door and invited the Balagoola into his kitchen for a cold drink of water. "No, sir, I did not; but I should tell you that I raise three-legged chickens myself."

"You? You are responsible for that obnoxious chicken, that foul fowl? I hate that chicken! It left my wonderful ox-cart, once the holder of several speed records, in the dust."

"A fate which you also suffered," noted Farfel, as his kitchen quickly became covered with the same dust.

"But why?" cried the exasperated Boris, still furious over having been passed on the road. "Why would you raise these rapid three-legged chickens?"

"Simple," explained Farfel. "You see, when I eat chicken, I like a drumstick. My wife, she also likes a drumstick. If you were to stay for dinner, and you also liked a drumstick, what could I do? Now I can have three drumsticks, and everybody is happy!"

Suddenly, Boris's keen marketing mind saw visions of rubles and royalties, if only he could form a partnership with Farfel to sell speedy three-legged chickens. Brilliant!

"So..." asked Boris slyly, "...and how do these three-legged chickens taste?"

Farfel sighed. "I don't know! I've never caught one!"

WHITE MEAT OR DARK? (THANKSGIVING EDITION)
By Mel Powell

[One fine year, this story was chosen to be read at a November service but, with the American Thanksgiving holiday, the record-setting chicken was sidelined for a turkey. The stories are not identical, but close; can you find the differences--other than the choice of fowl? We include it here despite the Chicken version because you might someday want to read it in America in November, too, and who are we to choose your meal?]

The sun was shining, the air was warm, and the breeze was cool. What better time for Boris the Balagoola to take his famous ox-cart out for a spin?

"There's nobody out on the road," said Boris to himself with great anticipation. "I will push my wonderful, two-hundred-borscht-power ox-cart to its very limits!"

And off he went on the dusty road to Vitipsk-Gaboynya. Boris wasn't ten minutes beyond Chelm's suburbs--the entire suburbs being one house--when he observed a line of dust rapidly approaching him in his rear-ox mirror.

"So what's this, moving at such speed?" pondered Boris. "I'm doing eighty kilometers per hour, easy!" And he looked down, and to his left.

There, along-side the ox-cart, slowing to match speeds with Boris's treasured ox-cart, was a three-legged turkey!

"Mine is the finest ox-cart in the land! It even has its own Web Browser, although e-mail hasn't been invented yet. I will not allow a feathered little Sunday driver to pass me on the road!" And he spurred his ox-cart up to ninety.

The three-legged turkey kept pace effortlessly.

"Hey, three-legged turkey! Do you have any idea how many kopecks I paid for this beautiful turbo-charged ox-cart?" demanded Boris. "I'll see you in Vitipsk-Gaboynya!" And he urged his ox-cart up to one-hundred-and-ten, a speed never before achieved by an ox-cart, let alone an ox.

The three-legged turkey, unimpressed, caught up with Boris just long enough to stick his tongue out at the hapless Balagoola, and then disappeared ahead into the distance.

"I can't believe it!" cried Boris. "I will demand my money back from the dealer! But not before I catch that turkey!"

Boris, pushing the poor ox-cart (not to mention the poor ox) to the limits of physics and decency, desperately followed the three-legged turkey's trail of dust. Finally, the dust appeared to turn off the Chelm-to-Vitipsk-Gaboynya road, so Boris turned with it.

Soon, Boris lost the trail of dust; but he happened upon a farmhouse. A breathless Boris knocked on the farmhouse door and called out: "Excuse me, but did you see a three-legged turkey go by?"

Farfel the Farmer opened the door and invited the Balagoola into his kitchen for a cold drink of water. "No, sir, I did not; but I should tell you that I raise three-legged turkeys myself."

"You? You are responsible for that obnoxious turkey, that gruesome gobbler, that foul fowl? I hate that turkey! It left my wonderful ox-cart, once the holder of several speed records, in the dust."

"A fate which you also suffered," noted Farfel, as his kitchen quickly became covered with the same dust.

"But why?" cried the exasperated Boris, still furious over having been passed on the road. "Why would you raise these rapid three-legged turkeys?"

"Simple," explained Farfel. "You see, when I eat turkey, I like a drumstick. My wife, she also likes a drumstick. If you were to stay for dinner, and you also liked a drumstick, what could I do? Now I can have three drumsticks, and everybody is happy!"

Suddenly, Boris's keen marketing mind saw visions of rubles and royalties, if only he could form a partnership with Farfel to sell speedy three-legged turkeys. Brilliant!

"So..." asked Boris slyly, "...and how do these three-legged turkeys taste?"

Farfel sighed. "I don't know! I've never caught one!"

THE BALLAD OF BORIS THE KID
by Mel Powell
based on "White Meat or Dark?"

[No one remembers...not even the author...what inspired the reimagining of the three-legged fowl story as a rhyming ballad. But here it is.]

A gathering of fools one day
In Chelm, village of the Wise,
In Council chambers, on the morn'
Heard Rivka with a big surprise,

"You von't believe," the Baker said,
"Vhat news I have for you!"
And Rivka paused, dramatically...
The Beadle said, "So, nu?"[6]

"Good Berel," Rivka grated forth,
"It's Balagoola strong."
"Oy vey!" said Schneider, Tailor he;
"Pray tell us what is wrong?"

Don't ever think, dear listener,
That things are smooth in Chelm.
Just hear the tale of woe and pain
That Rivka then did tell 'em:

---

[6] *Nu* is a Yiddish word with lots of uses. As in formal greeting, it's your "What's up? Or *"Que pasa?"* As an interjection during a conversation, it can suggest "See what I mean?" but also "seriously, you think *that* is an important issue?" Or, here, it stands for "tell me already." Very useful, *nu*?

No one in the tiny village
Suffered from such *tsouris*[7]
As did the Huge-est Of Them All:
The man we know as Boris.

A Balagoola, strong and dumb,
But with a heart of gold,
Boris set out for a ride,
Away his ox-cart rolled.

"*Halavai*,"[8] his big voice boomed,
"It's just as I had planned.
"Mine ox-cart is, without a doubt,
"The finest in the land!"

It had an ox, a shower,
And a television set,
Plus a CD player
(which was not invented yet).

Out on the road to old Vitipsk
A cloud of dust grew nearer
And Boris was amazed when he
Looked in his rear-ox mirror.

The Balagoola held his course,
The road bumpy and jerky,
When catching up to Boris was a
Strange three-legged turkey!

If you say the turkey is
American, they'll shush ya'
For Chelmites say turkeys are
Indigenous to Russia.

---

[7] *Tsouris* means "trouble."
[8] *Halavai* translates loosely as "Thank Goodness" or even "Hooray!"

And this one, with his little legs--
That numbered one-two-three--
Picked up the pace, caught up and
Winked at Boris with great glee.

"We will not suffer insult so!
"Not ox and not his master!"
And Boris yelled and pushed and made
His ox go even faster.

So Boris drove his ox-cart just
As fast as it could go,
The turkey hustled forth again
And gave Boris a show.

The finest ox-cart in the land
Cost Boris all his moola
But easily the turkey passed
The hapless Balagoola.

"Now I'm angry, and verklempt
"And track him down I must!
"I will forever follow
"That *mishuga*[9] trail of dust."

The trail ran out beside a shack,
Which made our Boris howl.
"A little farmhouse, way out here?
"For this I chased that fowl?"

The Balagaoola beat his fist
Upon the farmhouse door
Until the farmer came outside
So Boris knocked no more.

---

[9] Crazy!

"My name is Farfel, and I haven't
"Anything to offer.
"I am so poor that I have not
"A kopeck in my coffer."

"Do not worry," Boris said,
"But give me your reply:
"Did an ugly three-legs bird
"Come through and run right by?"

Farfel laughed and it was clear
The question didn't faze him,
"No, good sir, but I admit,
"Those turkeys? Well, I raise 'em."

"You see," said Farfel, "I'll explain
"And swear it's not for kicks.
"I raise three-legged turkeys
"Just because I love drumsticks."

Suddenly the Balagoola
Rolled his eyes right up,
A headache like this Boris needed
Like a *luchen kup*.[10]

But Boris's small, simple mind
Strained 'til it wasn't funny,
For drumsticks sold in Minsk and Pinsk
Could make a lot of money!

Boris said, "About this speedy
"Turkey I have chased?
"You must, please, tell right away
"Just how these drumsticks taste!"

---

[10] *Luchen kup*...the "ch" like cleaning your throat...means "hole in the head." Same idiom as in English.

The farmer smiled, or maybe sighed,
At Boris, in the sun,
"I'd really like to tell you, but
"I never have caught one…"

THE HORSE'S TALE

By Charles M. Powell

[Spoiler alert! Jewish readers, please start reading the story! For our non-Jewish friends, you should know that a "shiksa" is (as a part-endearing, part-not term) a non-Jewish woman.]

"Did you hear about Tevye?" asked Berel the Beadle.

"So what about Tevye?" inquired Rivka the Baker.

"He had a death in the family. His very old horse died."

When the reaction from the other villagers was underwhelming, Berel was angry. "If you weren't such dummies, you'd realize that a horse is part of the family any time...but don't you also realize what the loss of his horse means to our Tevye? He's the town milkman, am I right?"

"Right," said Rivka.

"How's he gonna work? Did you ever see a milkman without a horse?"

No one had.

"Believe me," said the Beadle. "This is a real tragedy. Tevye has been awake every night since the poor beast died. He cries and he wails. It could break your heart."

Boris the Balagoola joined the discussion. "In my case, it's breaking more than my heart; it's also breaking my eardrums. Tevye lives near me and his crying is keeping us all awake."

It developed that others were having similar problems. Shloime the Student couldn't study because of the noise; Pinchuk the Painter was so unnerved by the wailing that he forgot to place his dropcloth. When was the last time you saw lavender borscht?

"I suggest," said Berel the Beadle, "that we present this problem to our Rabbi."

The Rabbi of Chelm, the wisest in all of Russia, assured them that he would resolve the problem, and, early the next morning, he visited the grieving Tevye.

"Come with me, my good friend, we shall go for a walk," said the Rabbi.

Ten miles later, huffing and puffing, they found themselves at the country estate of the great Tsar, specifically at the stables of the king. When Tevye realized where he was, he started to run. "Flee for your life, Rabbi," cried the Milkman. "If they find Jews in this place we're dead."

The wise Rabbi laughed. "Come back, Tevye, I know for a fact that the Tsar is out hunting for the day. Let us go to the stables and pick you out a fine new horse."

"Steal a horse?" asked the Milkman.

"I'm a Rabbi," said the Rabbi. "Rabbis don't steal. Rabbis help souls find their best life…even a horse. Which horse would you like?"

"The white one looks wonderful, but are you sure that this is alright?"

"Sure I'm sure," said the Rabbi. "Take the white horse for your own, treat it like family as you did your previous horse of blessed memory, go home to Chelm, and stop grieving."

"But what will become of you Rabbi?"

"Not to worry," said the old man. "I'll wait here and explain it to the Tsar."

After the confused but happier Tevye departed, the Rabbi entered the now empty stall and proceeded to wrap himself in a saddle and leather stirrups. Believe me, *tefillin*[11] like that, you never saw.

Shortly thereafter, the Tsar returned with his soldiers. Seeing his white horse missing, he ran to the stall. To his surprise, there was the

---

[11] *Tefillin* are a set of small black leather boxes containing scrolls of parchment inscribed with verses from the Torah; wearable, with straps.

old Rabbi, sitting in quiet dignity, wrapped in saddle and stirrups. "Who are you?" screamed the Tsar, "and where is my white horse?"

The old Rabbi smiled, "Forgive me, your Tsar-ness, but the story is complicated. Many years ago, as a young Rabbi, I committed the transgression of courting a Gentile girl. God was so upset with me that he turned me into a white horse. Just this morning, my debt to the Lord was up, and here I am, an old Rabbi in the Tsar's stable. I trust at least the white horse has served you well."

The Tsar was perplexed…but had to admit that the white horse had done well. So he simply chased the Rabbi off of his property, and the old man laughed all the way home to Chelm.

Six months passed. Tevye the Milkman was once again the happiest man in Chelm. And the horse was happy, too, and treated like family. Tevye sang and danced all day as he sold his products on the main street of the village, until the day that the Tsar arrived unannounced.

"Oy vey!" wailed the Milkman. "He's changed his mind about the white horse. He wants him back and he'll kill me. Oy vey zmir!"

The Tsar rode right up to Tevye. He ignored the quaking milkman, turned to the horse and laughed. "A-ha, Rabbi" he said. "That's what you get for dating *shiksas* again!"

A BRIGHT FUTURE

By Mel Powell based on a story by Charles M. Powell

The High Holy Days had gone well in the little village of Chelm, where the wise fools lived. In fact, they were better than ever. Standing outside the Great Synagogue of Chelm for a breath of fresh air before *Neilah*,[12] Berel the Beadle shared his thoughts with Mendel the Messenger.

"So far, so good…no, Mendel?"

"Yes, Ber-- Yes, Ber-- right, old friend. The Rabbi has been positively inspir-- positively inspir-- brilliant."

"And," Berel continued, "Chava the *Chazzan*[13] has been amazing. What a voice!"

"No ques-- no ques-- bingo!" agreed Mendel, as the two returned to their seats for *Neilah*, the final service of the holiest day of the year.

Chava began to chant. She exuded confidence. She enunciated every word…every syllable, she emoted with fervor. She even harmonized with herself.

Then, suddenly, she squeaked.

Chava opened her mouth to try again. Not a sound.

The wise Rabbi seized control. "Don't worry, good Chelmites. Give us just a moment, and we'll continue. Meanwhile, feel free to pray among yourselves."

The Rabbi huddled in a corner of the *bima*[14] with Chava, Mendel, and Berel. After a few moments, the Messenger left the huddle and faced the congregation.

---

[12] *Neilah* is the name of the final service during Yom Kippur, just before sundown ends the holy day.
[13] *Chazzan* is the Hebrew word for the cantor, or singer of the prayers.
[14] The *bima* is the stage from which the service is conducted; many synagogues have a central area and not a raised stage, but the concept is that this is the focal point of the service.

"Hear ye-- hear ye-- listen up. Chava the *Chaz*--Chava the *Chaz*-- the singer has asked me to apologize to you. She has performed so won-- so won-- she has been terrific! But she cannot contin--not contin-- *Bupkis*.[15] No voice."

The Rabbi stepped forward. "But, dear congregants, we must finish the *Neilah* service. Can anyone among us sing? Please, Chelmites, someone come forward."

Nobody moved.

"Please, my congregants! Somebody must be able to join me on the *bima* and serve as cantor for this final hour!"

Still nobody moved, until Boris the Balagoola spoke quietly to the short, bearded man next to him and then stood slowly.

Berel was aghast. "Boris? You? You can sing?"

"Pshaw!" said the Huge One. "I am the strongest man in the village. I can carry an ox. I can carry a small house. The only thing I cannot carry is a tune. However..." And he gestured to the small bearded man, who rose slowly.

But it was no man! It was Boris's trusty dog, Fidowitz, wearing a yarmulke and a flea *tallis*[16] and wagging his *tsitsis*![17] Fidowitz always accompanied Boris to services and he was always quiet and respectful and on his best behavior...often better than Boris.

"Unheard of!" gasped the Rabbi, as the congregation burst into an incredulous babble.

"Have you a choice, dear Rabbi?" asked Boris solemnly. "Give him a chance."

So the Rabbi, with resigned reluctance, did. And what a performance! Could that dog *daven*! [18] Could that pooch pray! Could

---

[15] *Bupkis* is Yiddish for nada. Zippo. Nothing.
[16] The *tallis* or *tallit* is the prayer shawl.
[17] *Tsitsis* are the fringes at the ends of the prayer shawl.
[18] To *daven* is to pray, but this carries the feel of verbal and even physical rhythm, albeit standing in place.

that schnauzer shuckle! Fidowitz finished the *Neilah* service with flying *pais*.[19]

As the congregation left the Great Synagogue, each member shook the dog's paw.

The Rabbi, *kvelling*,[20] pulled Boris aside. "Boris, ca-nine-ahora[21] what a canine! If I didn't see it, if I didn't hear it, I would never have believed that a dog could pray the way your dog prayed. His Hebrew was perfect. His tone, his pitch, his soul. You must send him to the finest music schools to study. My dear Boris, your dog must become a cantor!"

Boris shook his head sadly. "You talk to him, Rabbi. He wants to be a doctor!"

---

[19] *Pais* (PAY-iss) are loose, long sideburns often sported by orthodox men and boys.
[20] To *kvell* is to feel and exude happiness and pride.
[21] *Kinnahora* is the verbal equivalent of "knock on wood," fending off "the evil eye" of superstition. No extra charge for the "canine" pun.

DUCK SOUP
OR
THE LEGEND OF FARFEL THE FARMER

By Mel Powell

[This story is based on an old joke. Another re-telling of the old joke, with a different twist to it, can be found by searching for a video from "The Tonight Show" (with Johnny Carson) with guest Buddy Hackett telling the joke his way. You'll see why we didn't tell it his way here, but we can't recommend the video enough. Comedy gold.]

Everyone knows that the tiny village of Chelm was populated by the wisest fools in all the land. Some said they were the wisest fools in the whole world.

But the wisest fools in all the land were plagued for all eternity with a bad reputation, for it was always the "fools" part, and not the "wisest" part, that was emphasized.

City folk looked down on them.

And one day this proved to be a major mistake, thanks to a simple man who lived well on the outskirts of Chelm. Let us relive the legend of Farfel the Farmer.

Farfel, it seems, was sitting in his modest home when he heard a thump on the roof above him. This was no ordinary thump. It wasn't the whump that Farfel heard when his wife Fagel dropped a pile of laundry onto the floor. It wasn't the klunk that Farfel heard when their tiny baby pushed her wooden doll out of the crib. And it certainly wasn't the horrendous racket that Farfel usually heard when his son, Kalman the Klutz, knocked over the furniture.

No, it was a thump. Farfel rose to investigate.

Outside, Farfel witnessed an unusual sight. Climbing over the fence into Farfel's yard was a Russian city slicker, dressed from head to toe in the gaudiest city slicker outfit ever seen in Chelm. Beyond the fence sat a fancy-schmancy horse carriage, where a driver waited patiently.

"What, pray tell, do you think you're doing?" asked Farfel.

The city slicker pulled himself to his full five-foot-four and responded. "Well, sir, do you see that duck over there, lying on your front yard? I saw that duck collide with a hawk and fall from the sky. The duck fell with a thump onto your roof, rolled down to the ground, and there it is. Because I saw it fall...it is mine. I am here to claim my dinner--that duck."

Having now figured out the cause of the thump, Farfel put his great Chelm intellect to good use. "Sir," he said, "I must respectfully beg to differ. You see, it is my house, as you acknowledge. It is my roof. It is my front yard. Therefore," said Farfel with impeccable logic, "it is my duck."

"Nonsense!" said the city slicker, actually using a word unfit for mixed company but quite common in the city. And the argument quickly deteriorated.

Finally, Farfel elected to concede a point. "It's useless for us to continue this way. Perhaps, sir, it is your duck. I will grant you this possibility, but you are here in the country, and we must settle this dispute the country way.

"Fair enough," answered the wealthy city dweller warily. "What is this 'country way?'"

Farfel explained, "It's like this: First we take stale bread, leftover from the sabbath meal five days ago. It is bread that not even our village beggars would deign to eat. This is our first course."

"Stale bread?" asked the hunter. "No big deal!"

"Then," continued Farfel, "we take the worst cut of the leftovers of the chicken dinner we ate on that very same sabbath five days ago. It is the driest, stringiest, worst-tasting chicken in the history of history. Even the family cat turns up his nose at the mere sight of this chicken, and one does not ever anger the family cat."

"Old, bad-tasting chicken?" said the city fellow, completely in the dark as to where this would lead.

"The worst," said Farfel. "And that's not all! Have you ever tasted the horseradish that we serve on Passover? Ours is so strong that, last year, one of our villagers truly believed that, except for one small problem, he had just invented rocket fuel."

"What's a rocket?" asked the city slicker.

"That was the problem. Hasn't been invented yet. But anyway...next we eat five spoonfuls of this killer horseradish, alone, unaided by any other tasty morsels or water. Horseradish. Straight down the hatch."

Now the city man began to shake, just a little. "And what happens next?"

"'We stuff ourselves to the gills with the sumptuous meal I have just described to you, and then, we polish the whole thing off with a bowl of semi-liquid borscht, very interesting borscht, too, from the famous borscht-yards in Vitipsk-Gaboynya. Vintage year, 5604." [22]

"5604?" asked the man happily. "That was an excellent year!"

"Not so much for borscht," said Farfel. "Now, that's the country way of resolving our dispute as to who gets the duck. Whichever of us is left standing after this horrible country meal gets to keep the bird. Deal?"

The arrogant city slicker was not one to back down from a challenge. Besides, he really wanted that duck now. It was a strange point of pride. "It's a deal," he said.

"Great," said Farfel. "You go first."

"What?"

"Yes," said Farfel, explaining, "that's the country way. We insist on our visitors being served first. It's only polite."

---

[22] Corresponds to 1844 on the calendar we're used to; the exact number doesn't matter, the point is that this is a year on the Jewish Calendar.

Farfel disappeared into his house, returning a few moments later with a table, a chair, and the largest collection of hideous leftovers ever seen.

And so this visitor from the big city took a seat, and he choked down what was, without a doubt, the worst meal of his life.

Slowly, ever so slowly, he stood up from the table, wavered for a moment or two, and began to stagger forward, his stomach grumbling beyond all reason. To his horror, the man realized that he could no longer see his shiny new shoes.

Clutching his aching stomach, shaking his head to try to rid himself of the awful cacophony of after-tastes, the hunter staggered his way to Farfel and, with no small amount of pain in his voice, said, "Now it's your turn to eat this abominable combination or horrible cuisine!"

Farfel smiled. "You can keep the duck."

BUSINESS AND COMMERCE

1. Pushy, Pushy
2. Business Sense
3. Citius, Altius, Kvetchius
4. Fency-Schmency
5. Commerce
6. Taking In A Partner
7. Poetic Justice
8. Why Is This Salesman Different From All Other Salesmen?
9. The Bialy Seller

Capitalism wasn't invented in Chelm, but perhaps in some ways it was perfected. One way or another, you gotta make an honest kopeck.

See also "There's No Business Like Chelm Business" in the Charity and Fundraising chapter for another take on business or commerce.)

PUSHY, PUSHY

By Charles M. Powell

The time? Then.

The Place? Chelm.

The winter? Don't ask. So much snow and rain and mud that everything came to a stop. The slow train from Minsk stopped running entirely, although it took the Chelmites three months to discover the difference.

The shops were empty--totally devoid of any goods and supplies. The townspeople were, to say the least, grumpy and short-tempered. "Love Thy Neighbor" never works during a cold and wet winter.

So imagine the surprise when it was discovered that the haberdashery had an enormous sign in the window, saying "SALE...SALE...Half off Everything in the Shop. Half off Belts...Half off Boots...SALE!"

By morning, the line reached from the haberdashers, past the synagogue, up the hill to the granary, and around the back of the dairy.

Dozens of Wise Fools, all waiting for the shop to open.

And at the front of the line, cranky and complaining? Boris the Balagoola, of course. "This sale couldn't wait until spring? No wonder they almost give away new boots. It's to replace your ruined old boots from standing in the snow up to your *pupik*[1] already!"

From the back of the line, almost a mile away, came a stir. A small figure, a tired, thin, harried, fragile man, was pushing his way slowly through the crowd. An elbow here, a strategic knee there.

After a considerable struggle--"...excuse me...pardon me...sorry, Miss...whoops..."--and considerable cursing from the line of people--"Who does he think...have you ever?...get your hand off my...in my life I never"--finally, finally he was at the front of the line...

---

[1] The *pupik* is the bellybutton. Or navel, for you medical folks.

...where Boris the Balagoola promptly picked the tiny older man up and sent him flying back to the end of the line.

Again, the pushing and yelling and elbowing and...don't ask. Again, the fragile old man worked his way to the front of the line.

Boris the Balagoola became apoplectic...he also became red in the face...a lot!

"I do not believe that you have, once again, presented yourself for a one-way flight to the end of this line! In all my life, I have never met a more obnoxious person, such *chutzpah*![2] Forget the insult to me personally, as first on this line, waiting six hours now for admittance. Think of the many men, the women, some of them with child, whom you have shoved, jostled, pushed out of the way to get--illegally--to the front of this line. Surely, you will agree with me that a person like that, who tries to cut into the front of the line, deserves a thorough thrashing?"

The fragile old man shook his head. "I certainly agree with you, Balagoola. However, if you throw me to the end of the line one more time...I will simply refuse to open my shop!"

---

[2] We're sure you know that *chutzpah* means "a lotta nerve," but we'll still tell you here, out of, you know, *chutzpah*.

BUSINESS SENSE

By Mel Powell

(from a story by Frank Gillman)

"Progress!" boomed Boris the Balagoola at the meeting of the Wise Council in the tiny village of Chelm, home of the wisest Fools in history.

"Progress, shmogress," disagreed Rivka the Baker. "So they're going to build a new train station just outside of Chelm."

"That's not the exciting part," said Boris. "The exciting part is the deal made by our good friend Kalman the Karpenter! What a genius!" And who better than Boris could determine "genius?"

Boris explained:

Andrei the Agent was the corrupt Russian representative of the mighty Tsar. Some said that, instead of a hat, Andrei wore a price tag. The profession "agent" had been invented for Andrei, the first person ever who, without doing a thing to earn it, skimmed a percentage off the top of everything.

In fact, inspired by stories of Andrei, Tevye the Milkman had recently invented skim milk.

"Welcome," intoned Andrei officiously at the official gathering. "As you know, you three carpenters are here to bid for the right to build a new train station, which the Tsar wishes to have just outside of Chelm. I will now hear your bids."

Byakin the Builder spoke first. "I am just a simple man. My needs are small. I will build the new train station for His Highness the Tsar for the sum of six thousand rubles."

"Six thousand rubles!" exclaimed Andrei. "And how do you justify that bid?"

"Easy," said the Russian, "It will cost me two thousand rubles for materials. It will cost me two thousand rubles for hiring laborers. And, as I am a businessman, I will make a profit of a mere two thousand rubles."

"Very well, you may be seated. Next?"

Felice the Frenchwoman rose. "I am zee most famous ar-shee-tect in all of La France. I have built zee finest train stations in all zee world! For your worthy Tsar, I vill build a train station of better *qualitée*, one more pleasing to zee eye, than zis foolish Cossack simpleton. It vill cost your Tsar a mere twelve zousand rubles!"

"Twelve zousand--I mean thousand--rubles!" gasped Andrei the Agent. "Why, that's twice what Byakin will charge. How would you dare charge my Tsar so much?"

"*Simplement*," explained the Frenchwoman. "Four zousand rubles for materials, of better *qualitée*, so zat zis train station does not fall apart and you spend more later anyway to repair it. Four zousand rubles to bring in zee finest craftsmen and women in zee business-- not mere laborers, *n'est pas*, but skilled artists! And, as I am world-renowned, I vill take my standard profit of four zousand. Voila! Twelve zousand rubles, and not a French *franc* less!"

Felice sat with a flourish.

"And you?" asked Andrei the Agent of the third man.

Kalman the Karpenter, the kraftsman of Chelm, stood and faced the Tsar's representative. He had done his homework. He knew everything about train stations. He knew everything about labor and material costs. And, most importantly, he knew everything about Andrei the Agent.

Kalman whipped out his pocket calculator, which hadn't been invented yet, and announced simply, "Eighteen thousand rubles."

"Eighteen!" sputtered Andrei, "Eighteen thousand rubles? Are you crazy?"

Kalman walked up to Andrei and lowered his voice. "Eighteen thousand rubles, Mr. Agent. Here's the deal. Six thousand for you, six thousand for me, and six thousand we pay the Cossack to build it!"

CITIUS, ALTIUS, KVETCHIUS [3]

By Mel Powell based on a story by Charles M. Powell

"They've canceled the whole thing!" exclaimed Berel the Beadle.

"What? Why?" asked Boris the Balagoola.

Berel explained, "You heard about those people who were trying, after all these centuries, to bring back the Olympic Games? They gave up."

"Because so many sports have not yet been invented?" wondered Rivka the Baker.

"No," said Berel, "It's because no one has yet invented television."

This was a shame, and no one was unhappier than Boris the Balagoola, who stormed out of the meeting of the Council of Elders, almost in tears.

You see, the tiny village of Chelm, where the wise fools lived, had sent a petition to Athens, Greece, seeking to be chosen as the tiny *Olympic* Village of Chelm. While the influx of tourists and athletes, not to mention sponsors, would boost the economy of Chelm, still there was the matter of the money they would need just to prepare to host the Games.

Berel explained to the Council why Boris was so upset. "Simple! Salesmanship! Thanks to Boris the Balagoola, we had raised all of the funds we would need to host the Olympics!"

"Boris did this? Boris...the Balagoola, that Boris?" said Schneider the Tailor.

"Really!" said Berel. "Every Sunday, the good Balagoola left our little Jewish village and headed off to the Great Square of Kiev, right in front of the Great Church. There, he set up a table on the far side of

---

[3] To *kvetch* is to complain; a *kvetch*, as a noun, is a complainer. Here, though, it's just a play on the word.

the square, with religious medals, rosary beads, autographed pictures of the Pope, the whole schmeer.

"Now, here is where the salesmanship comes in. Boris always wore his filthiest clothes and made sure not to bathe. As the Russians, on their way to church, passed his stand and looked at his wares, Boris cursed them in Yiddish and gave them the evil eye.

"Across the square, right in front of the church, stood a well-dressed young man, handsome, blond, looking like a typical Ukrainian villager if ever there was one, also with a table full of religious goods. He said good morning to the people, wished them a good week, and hoped that all their prayers would be answered. And do I have to tell you how well his merchandise sold?"

"And this," wondered Rivka, "by Boris, is salesmanship?"

"Let me finish!" complained Berel. "It turned out that one of the Russians was especially wealthy, and also especially angry with the dirty, smelly, rude Balagoola. Every Sunday this well-to-do man gave Boris a lecture on why he remained poor and unsuccessful by pointing to the polite young blond man, with his flourishing business across the square. But, in reply, every Sunday Boris spit at his feet and cursed him up and down. With a look of haughty self-righteousness, the Russian calmly crossed the square and bought a dozen different items from the friendly young man, encouraging others to do the same."

"So where, already, is the salesmanship?" wondered Schneider.

"Simple!" said Berel. "Finally, when all the people had entered the church and the square was very quiet, Boris walked across to the church and approached the younger man. He raised himself to his full menacing self, glared down at the fellow, and smiled, saying, 'Nu,[4] Moishe...they're going to tell us how to make a kopeck?'"

---

[4] *Nu* is a Yiddish word with lots of uses. As in formal greeting, it's your "What's up? Or *"Que pasa?"* As an interjection during a conversation, as used here, it can stand for "See what I mean?" but also "seriously, you think *that* is an important issue?" Very useful, *nu*?

FENCY SHMENCY

By Charles M. Powell

(from a story by Bret Shefter)

[Spoiler alert! Jewish readers may want to skip this note and start reading the story. Everyone else needs to know that to "schlep" is (for our purposes at the moment) to haul a heavy load from one place to another, like schlepping a heavy suitcase to the car after a train ride.]

Who goes to St. Petersburg, except on business? Certainly not anyone from Chelm, where the wise fools all lived. As Berel the Beadle would say, "St. Petersburg is for the fency-shmency."

But, as fate would have it, Boris the Balagoola found himself in Russia's capital city, delivering the census for the village of Chelm.

"How many people you got this year in Chelm?" asked the official.

"Two hundred eighty-three," answered the Balagoola.

"How many you had last year?"

"Two hundred eighty-three."

"Wait a minute," said the official. "Nobody got married; nobody had babies; nobody died?"

"Nobody died," said the Balagoola, "but also nobody new will admit that they live in Chelm."

The official nodded his head. "That makes census to me."

Somehow, the Tsar's official accepted the report quickly, and Boris found himself in St. Petersburg with spare time before his return train.

He decided to go to a shop and buy some gifts for his friends in Chelm. After asking some questions, he arrived at the fanciest shop in St. Petersburg...Romanoff's.

The Balagoola presented himself at the food counter and asked the salesman for a pound of lox. The salesman almost died.

"Lox?" he cried. "Lox? Sir, may I remind you that this is Romanoff's of St. Petersburg, the Tsar's favorite shop. We simply do not carry 'lox.' We carry Scotch Salmon."

The Balagoola laughed, "Coulda fooled me. It looks like lox, smells like lox, and surely tastes like lox. Whatever it is, give me please a pound."

After looking around for another moment or two, Boris continued. "I think," he said to the salesman, "I'll buy some dishes for the little woman."

"Dishes?" cried the offended salesman. "Sir, permit me to remind you that this is Romanoff's of St. Petersburg, the Tsar's favorite shop. We do not carry 'dishes.' We carry bone china."

"How do you like that," laughed the Balagoola. "By me, it looks just like dishes. How about I buy some pants for myself?"

The salesman nearly fainted. "Pants!" he yelled. "Pants? My good man...once again. this is Romanoff's of St. Petersburg, the Tsar's favorite shop. We would never consider carrying 'pants.' What we carry, sir, is trousers."

The Balagoola was perplexed. "You put them on like pants? They got pockets on the sides and buttons, you'll pardon the expression, down the front?"

"Of course," said the salesman.

"O.K.," said Boris, "I'll take a pair of trousers instead of the pants."

The Romanoff salesman wrapped all of the gifts and brought them to the Balagoola. "Just one minute," said Boris. "Now I'm supposed to get all of this back to Chelm on the train? You could maybe deliver it for me?"

"Sir," sneered the salesman, for the final time, I must remind you that this is Romanoff's of St. Petersburg, the Tsar's favorite shop. Romanoff's, my good man, simply does not *schlep*!"

COMMERCE
By Charles M. Powell

What is it, do you think, that makes the world go 'round? Some people will tell you that it's love; others will say that it's friendship or family. For the Wise Fools of Chelm, the answer was simple: Commerce makes the world go 'round. Permit me to give you a "for instance."

"What have you got there?" asked Rivka the Baker.

Boris the Balagoola smiled slyly. "Oh, it's nothing. Only a case of sardines."

"A case of sardines?" replied the Baker. "It's not every day that our Balagoola shows up with sardines. The truth, Boris; what's so special about these sardines?"

"There's really nothing special about these. It's just that they come from the North Sea. It seems, I am told, that they made a left turn at St. Petersburg and that's how they ended up in the North Sea."

"Aha," cried Rivka. "Look how cagey and sly is our Balagoola. These sardines must have come already from the Tsar. Admit it, Boris."

The Balagoola laughed. "Sure, I'll admit it. If you got a Tsar and he's married to a Tsarina you'll always end up with Tsardines."

"Never mind the jokes. How much you want for the case?"

"Would three rubles be too much?"

"It's a deal!" proclaimed the happy Baker.

No sooner did an equally happy Boris the Balagoola leave her bakery, then Rivka *schlepped* [5] the case of sardines down the street of the village to Schneider the Tailor.

---

[5] *Schlep* can mean lug something burdensome as it does here, or can also mean just to go a long way, usually in traffic or through the woods or uphill both ways.

"So who needs sardines?" said Schneider. "I'm a tailor. I need thread. I need pins. I need needles. Why a case of sardines?"

"Because," said Rivka proudly, "These particular fruits of 'La Mer' happen to be from the personal collection of the Tsar. They happen to have travelled all the way to the North Sea. And they probably spent their summers in the Aegean getting already a suntan."

"Sold," said the Tailor, "for seven rubles!"

Schneider was also no dummy. He sold it to Kalman the Karpenter for ten rubles, who in turn flipped it over to Tevye the Milkman for twelve rubles and six kopecks. And so it went that week throughout Chelm. It was finally purchased with much expectation by the Great Rabbi for twenty-one--count them, twenty-one--rubles, on the firm belief that these Sardines were:

One: Adopted and raised by the Tsar himself.

Two: World travelers, with enough mileage credits to travel, second class but at no cost, all the way to America.

Three: packed in a special oil blessed by the chief Rabbis of both Minsk and Vitipsk-Gaboynya.

And four: packed with each eye lovingly closed. Who wants to open up a can of sardines and find one of them staring at you?

The Rabbi finally opened a can and ate one of the twenty-one-ruble sardines. He almost died. He complained, let me tell you, bitterly to the Chelmite who sold it to him, who complained equally bitterly to the next one, and so on until Rivka the Baker called Boris the Balagoola to lodge a formal protest.

"Wait a minute," yelled the poor Balagoola, "someone ate the sardines? They weren't for eating! They were only for buying and selling!"

TAKING IN A PARTNER
By Charles M. Powell

[This is a uniquely New York-ish joke. But the entity that is the subject of the punchline is the oldest of its kind and it still exists, so...we include it.]

Schneider the Tailor took upon himself a bride. Mazel Tov, yes? Well...Mazel Tov, yes and no. Smart she was. Pretty she was. A small dowry she brought with her. But...Selma the Seamstress also brought with her an attitude. Oy, could that woman *noodge*.[6]

Now Schneider was a very good and successful tailor. His name, after all, meant "tailor." But Selma was not satisfied.

"I didn't marry you that you should be only a humble tailor all your life. A tailor is merely a tailor."

Schneider was insulted. He said to his bride, "So what, little flower, would you prefer your Schneider to become?"

"I would prefer you to own your own dress business. This way you would be a somebody."

Now Schneider, who already believed that he was a somebody, still wanted to please his little herring. So he saved his money, using even his wife's small dowry, and opened his own dress shop. He called it "Schneider Dresses." Nobody came, nobody dressed. It went bankrupt.

Still, Selma, his little *kreplach*,[7] kept *noodging*. Six months later, Schneider opened his second dress shop. It, too, failed. In fact, over the next few years, six times Schneider's Dresses went, you should pardon the expression, belly up.

---

[6] *Noodge* means to pester or harass.
[7] A *kreplach* is a dumpling, and the word can be used (but is rarely used!) as a term of endearment.

So it was that one night, in the Great Synagogue of Chelm, there was our beleaguered tailor, praying to his God for counsel. "Tell me, God, what am I doing wrong? I'm a good Jew. I'm a good person. All that I want to do is please my little stuffed cabbage. What shall I do?"

Suddenly, the *shul*[8] got very quiet: then it began to shake. The voice of the Lord was heard, speaking to the poor tailor.

"Schneider...take in a partner!"

"A partner, Lord? Who would be partners with me...a six-time loser in business?"

"I will be your partner."

"Hmmm. The 'Schneider and God Dress Shop.' I like it!"

"Close," said the Lord. "The shop should be called 'God and Schneider.' It is written that you should keep one half of the profits; my half shall be given to your Synagogue to help the poor. Agreed?" asked the Lord.

"You bet," answered Schneider.

So he begged and borrowed, raised enough money to buy a modest new dress shop, and put a big sign over the door: "God and Schneider." It was a hit. We're talking here a hit-hit. Soon Schneider opened a branch in Chelm's suburbs. Then one in Minsk, one in Pinsk, and, of course, one in Vitipsk-Gaboynya. The rubles were rolling in. The Great Synagogue became so wealthy that it even lowered its dues. That, already, is wealthy.

Schneider's wife Selma had a cousin in the New World who wrote to suggest a branch of the "God and Schneider Dress Shop" to be opened in the lower East Side of New York. They found a smart location on the corner of Essex Street and Delancey. Up went the store and the now-familiar sign. "God and Schneider." Nobody came, soon this location went out of business. Schneider was shaken. The cousin, crossing Delancey, found another location. Again it failed.

---

[8] *Shul*, a Yiddish word, means synagogue.

Back to Synagogue went the former "just-a-tailor," now a major business person. "God, what are we doing wrong? Our formula only works here in Chelm and nearby? What should we do, your holiness?"

Again the s*hul* got quiet. Again the shaking. Then God spoke: "I'll tell you, Schneider, what we're doing wrong. In the New World we need a new name for our store...a modern name...a more American name."

"O.K., Lord, I get it. So if not 'God and Schneider,' what do we call it in New York?"

"Easy," explained God. "In New York, we call it 'Lord and Taylor!'"

POETIC JUSTICE

By Charles M. Powell

(from a story by Myron Winick)

[This story, while intended as humor, is nonetheless more poignant than the rest, recognizing as it does the centuries of discrimination often faced by the Jewish people worldwide.]

Everybody knows that poets don't make money, right? Of course, right! And everybody knows that Boris was a Balagoola and not a poet, right? Again, of course, right! But he never gave up. What lacked in style and syntax, he made up for with enthusiasm and diligence. A poet, however, he was not.

Still, when the Tsar announced a national poetry competition, guess who submitted the first entry? Right again--Boris the Balagoola.

What was his poem? Exactly what you would expect from the Poet Laureate of Chelm. The poem read:

> Roses are reddish
> Violets are bluish.
> If not for the Tsar
> We all would be Jewish.

Now, great poetry this certainly was not. But somehow it touched the Tsar. They were saying, in those days, that the Tsar was indeed "touched." How else can you explain that Boris the Balagoola of Chelm won First Prize--the grand and shocking sum of one million rubles? Unbelievable, right? Of course, right.

How to spend the money? After much deliberation, Boris and the good Mrs. Balagoola decided to invest in a large house. This way they could live with their children, goats, cows, chickens, and grandparents--all in one place.

A member of the Wise Council of Elders discovered a castle for sale not far from Chelm. Off went the Balagoolas to investigate.

A castle it surely was. Actually, a castle-and-a-half. There was a moat; there was a drawbridge; there was a wine-cellar; and there was a lord of the manor...who asked haughtily, "May I help you?" in a tone that suggested little interest in helping.

"We are here, Your Manorship, to buy from you this castle."

"I'm obliged to tell you that my asking price is seven hundred thousand rubles."

"No problem!" said the Balagoola. "You want it in all cash or cash and some chickens?"

The lord of the manor was astonished "It doesn't matter. It's probably out of the question because you would have to move in tomorrow."

"Can do, Lordness," said Boris.

The owner was forced to face the real situation. "Since nothing seems to dissuade you, sir, you should be aware that I could never sell this magnificent castle to someone of the Hebrew persuasion. Nothing personal, you understand."

That sort of answer would crush--or at least anger--a normal person, but Boris the Balagoola was not your normal person. While often quick to anger, he also had a certain tendency to be surprisingly shrewd. He was a poet; he was from Chelm, where the wise fools live; and he was suddenly rich.

He and his wife walked across the road and purchased the facing property for only five hundred thousand rubles, and then for merely one hundred thousand rubles they proceeded to build an exact duplicate of the castle that they were denied. Stone for stone, brick by brick. And when the castle was finished, they invited their next-door neighbor, the lord of the still-unsold manor, over to see it.

"I can't believe this," he said. "This castle is an exact duplicate of mine. Same gate, same moat; the same wine in the same wine cellar."

"Yes," said the Balagoola, "and it cost me one hundred thousand rubles less than to meet your asking price, with even better crafts-person-ship. And what's more, my castle is already worth twice what your castle is worth!"

"How can that be, Mr. Balagoola? If the castles are identical, how can yours be twice as valuable?"

"Easy," said Boris. "Unlike you, I don't live across from a Jew!"

WHY IS THIS SALESMAN DIFFERENT FROM ALL OTHER SALESMEN?

By Charles M. Powell

[The title of the story, for our non-Jewish friends, is a play on the opening line of the "Four Questions" from the Passover holiday. "Why is this night different from all other nights," what do we do differently on Passover? One of those things is: no leavened bread; we eat matzah.]

You did know that the famous Manischewitz Wine and Matzah Company originally came from Chelm? Of course you knew. And the President of that famous company was Mendel Manischewitz, a beloved man in the community of Wise Fools.

The story is told that one day, shortly before Passover, who should present himself to the company President but Karkoff, the Salesman. The very one. The man famous throughout Russia for selling a refrigerator to a Siberian; the man who sold the Tsar a year's subscription to The Communist Daily Worker; in short, let me tell you, the best of the best.

"Have I got for you an idea," said Karkoff. "A once-in-a-lifetime. A grand slam, even though baseball hasn't been invented yet. My best ever."

"Calm yourself, Karkoff," said Manischewitz. 'What idea do you have that would possibly be of interest to my company?"

"O.K., but make sure you're sitting down. Suppose…just suppose…that I could get the Church in Rome to make a little change in one of their most important prayers?"

"What has that got to do with the Manischewitz Wine and Matzah Company?"

"Aha! I thought you'd never ask. Suppose…just suppose…that the prayer was changed from: 'Give us this day our daily bread' to--and here's the good part--'Give us this day our daily Manischewitz Matzah.' What would that be worth to your company, Mr. Mendel Manischewitz?"

The company President was astounded...almost in awe of this outrageous idea. "The Vatican would consider it?"

"Who knows?" laughed the salesman. "That's what you got a Karkoff for. How much money would you be willing to spend to accomplish this?"

The President thought about it. He added numbers. He subtracted numbers. He coughed. He made faces. He broke out in a cold sweat. He began to shake. Finally, he smiled. "Manischewitz would be willing to spend in the neighborhood of one hundred million rubles if you could somehow bring this about."

"I like your neighborhood," said Karkoff. "And for your salesman to be able to move into that neighborhood?"

"You may count on one million rubles and a lifetime supply of my *chrain*." [9]

"A deal," said the salesman, and he caught the first train for Minsk, with a transfer at Vitipsk-Gaboynya, to Warsaw, then to Budapest, to Zagreb, by boat to Italy, and by a miracle that only great salesmen can hope for...to a private meeting with the Pope in Rome.

Karkoff began his audience in this manner: "You got maybe, your Popeness, some special project that the Church wishes to finance? Perhaps a poor fellow from Russia can be of assistance."

"As a matter of fact, Mr. Karkoff, we are trying to raise funding for schools for the starving children of India. What do you have in mind?"

Karkoff was pleased. "We like helping children. I represent interests prepared to give you fifty million rubles, with only a simple request. We ask that you change the wording of one prayer. 'Give us

---

[9] *Chrain* is horseradish. The rocket-fuel kind, not the mild, cute kind.

this day our daily bread,' should please be 'Give us this day our daily Manischewitz Matzah.' Is this possible, Your Holiness?"

The Pope turned purple. "It is not possible: it is not probable; it borders on blasphemy; in short, it is absurd and I am personally insulted that you waste my time with such rubbish!"

"My humble apologies, your important-ness. I do not mean to offend. However, would seventy-five million Rubles sound less absurd--while also feeding more children?"

The Pope stormed out of his chambers and called an emergency session of the College of Cardinals. They gathered from all over the world. The Holy Father addressed them:

"My brothers...I have good news and I have bad news. The good news is that we can begin, finally, building our schools for the starving children of India."

"And the bad news?"

"The bad news is that the Wonder Bread account has to go!"

THE BIALY SELLER [10]

By Charles M. Powell

(with Bud Rosenthal & Mel Powell)

A fellow named Velvil lived in Vilna with his Chelm-born wife Lena. Sadly, Velvil passed away in a terrible accident, falling out of the window of their basement apartment. So Lena, a cousin of Rivka the Baker of Chelm, moved back to the town of her birth and joined the bakery to make ends meet.

Now it came to pass that Lena had a brilliant idea for increasing the bakery's profits--necessary to pay for her own wages. She had a pushcart built by Rivka's friend Kalman the Karpenter, and upon it she placed a sign with the prices for the cart's items. The sign read:

Hot Bialys: 2 kopecks
Cold Bialys: 2 and a half kopecks
     (I gotta blow on them, they should be cold)
Hot Tea in a glass: 2 kopecks
Hot Tea in a Clean glass: 3 kopecks
Hot Tea in a Clean glass with Raspberry Jam: negotiable
Credit Cards Accepted--Vitipsk Visa or Master-Tsar

Now it came to pass that the gentle Rabbi of Chelm, aware of Lena's precarious finances, chanced to see Lena's cart. He stopped to read the sign and smiled at the woman. He reached into his coin purse and paid the woman two kopecks but did not take a Hot Bialy. Instead, he smiled once more and continued on his way.

Strange, you say? Remember, we're in Chelm. Strange, but an act of charitable kindness.

---

[10] A bialy is similar to a bagel; round, but instead of a hole all the way through, it has a depressed middle that is filled with onions or poppy seeds or both.

Every morning for over a year the same thing happened. The Rabbi would walk by, smile at Lena, pay his two kopecks, not take a Hot Bialy, and proceed on his way.

One morning, Lena spoke to the Rabbi. "Listen, Mister Rabbi…"

The Rabbi smiled at her. "I suppose you're wondering why each morning I give you two kopecks, but I never take a Hot Bialy?"

The woman smiled back. "Frankly, that's your business. I just wanted to tell you that the Hot Bialys are now three kopecks!"

CHARITY AND FUNDRAISING

1. The New Vink
2. There's No Business Like Chelm Business
3. The Cholera of Money
4. A New Kiddush Cup
5. Tales Of The South Pacific
6. Rich Or Poor Is Not Important (As Long As You Have Money)
7. The Sole Of Charity

Money makes the world go 'round. Jews have been known for being charitable throughout centuries, despite the false aspersions cast on them. That said, there are always the cheapskates, but they stand out as against type (which sometimes is what makes them funny).

At the same time, it takes kopecks to run a place of worship, too.

(See also "Let It Ride" in the Gambling and Games chapter for a reference to charity with a bit of a different take.)

THE NEW VINK

By Charles M. Powell

"I suppose you're wondering why I called you all here today?" It was Berel the Beadle of the village of Chelm addressing the wealthiest residents of the town of fools. They were gathered in Berel's house.

"The reason that you're here is because our Synagogue needs a new vink.

"A new vhat?" inquired Boris the Balagoola.

"A vink, a vink…like the vink on a boid," replied the Beadle. "A new vink will give us more classrooms for the children; a place to store prayer books; more seats for our members. We got to have a new vink."

"Good idea, Berel," said Rivka the Baker. "From where you going to get the money?"

"Funny you asked. The money will come on this very day. It is my intention of going around the room and getting your pledges. Remember, what you don't give the Synagogue will go for taxes to the Tsar."

"Some choice," said Doovid the Doctor. "Alright already. I pledge thirty-two Rubles and four kopecks."

"Well done," said the Beadle. "Who's next?"

And so they went around the room: wincing, pleading, whining...but nevertheless contributing money for the new wing. Finally, Berel came to Schwartzbart the *Shmata*-maker,[1] the richest man in Chelm.

"So Schwartzbart? What do we put you down for?"

"Pass me by," replied the *Shmata*-person.

A hush fell over the room.

---

[1] A *shmata* is a garment, a dress, nothing too fancy.

Berel was flabbergasted. "I'd like to thank everyone in the room who contributed so handsomely for the new vink, except the one cheapskate who could afford it the most, who gave the least, and I think he should give an explanation of."

Schwartzbart rose to his full four feet seven inches.

"An explanation you want, an explanation you'll get. Everyone here knows that I'm a multi-multi wealthy person. Everyone knows that I hire more people in my dress business than the whole Russian government employs. Everyone knows about Schwartzbart only the good things. But does anyone know the troubles what I got? This, you don't know.

"Let me give you a for instance. For instance, my mother, God bless her, is 97 years old. She's got a Nartz condition, the worst in the whole world."

"You'll pardon me, but what's a Nartz?" asked the Balagoola.

"A Nartz, a Nartz...we all got one...you know, it beats, with a left wentricle, a right wentricle...with a Nartz like that, she could sneeze once, I could lose her. But that's not my only trouble.

"Let me tell you about my twin brother. He's almost my own age even, but he suffers from the worst case of Arter-itus whatever was. His fingers are so crippled he's been wearing loafers since he's three...he couldn't tie even a shoelace. And that's not all. I got nephews, nieces, never went to school, I should even know what kind of work they're out of.

"In my family I got sickness, I got poverty, I got unemployment.

"I don't help them, I should help you?"

THERE'S NO BUSINESS LIKE CHELM BUSINESS
By Charles M. Powell

"How we gonna raise some money for Chelm?" asked Berel the Beadle.

"What do you say to some Bingo?" inquired Schneider the Tailor.

Boris the Balagoola had an idea. "How about we sell High Holy Day tickets to the Goyim?"

"Terrific," scoffed the Rabbi. "Then they can sell us Christmas trees."

Rivka the Baker came up with an idea that finally made some sense.

"What if," she said, "we do a cooperative fundraiser?"

"What is it a 'cooperative fundraiser?'" asked the Balagoola.

"Well," she continued, "I could bake challah, the Balagoola could lend us his ox-cart. Shloime the Student and Schneider the Tailor could do the hauling. We'll sell the challahs, cover my expenses, and any money we make, we give to the Chelm treasury."

Everybody thought the idea was perfectly perfect, so the project was begun. Rivka baked all day and all night. You never saw so many challahs. If you made a straight line with all the bread that Rivka baked, you'd get all the way to Vitipsk-Gaboynya.

Out went the cart from village to village. They sold like hotcakes. People bought loaves and loaves.

At the end of the month there was a meeting of the Wise Council of Elders. They were all smiling. The Rabbi asked Rivka, "So how many challahs you sold?"

"Eight hundred and seventy-three, Rabbi." An ovation went up from the Wise Council.

"Fantastic! So how much money you got in the treasury?"

Rivka blushed. "Nothing, Rabbi."

"Nothing? Not a ruble even? You sold eight hundred and seventy-three challahs at a small markup, covered your expenses, and made not even a kopeck?"

"What can I tell you, Rabbi? I checked my books, I checked my inventory, I got only my expenses back…as for profit, not a kopeck."

Boris the Balagoola spoke up. "So tell me, how much it costs you to bake a challah?"

"It's easy to figure," said the Baker. "For the flour, eight kopecks. For the yeast and the leavening, six kopecks. For seeds, another two. For special Shabbos water, add three kopecks. Grand total, nineteen kopecks."

"All right," said the Rabbi, "and what do you sell the challah for?"

"You think maybe I'm a dummy? I don't want we should lose money on this fundraiser. I sell the challah for nineteen kopecks a loaf."

"Make it for nineteen, sell it for nineteen; sounds all right to me, we don't lose money" said Berel the Beadle. "Where did we go wrong?"

The Wise Council argued and debated and finally was able to come up with a way to save the day. The honor of announcing the wise decision was given to Boris the Balagoola.

He said that starting tomorrow, they would borrow a larger ox-cart.

THE CHOLERA OF MONEY

By Mel Powell

(from a story by Bud Rosenthal)

To say that Chelm was poor was like saying that Rivka the Baker had *tsouris*.[2] Boy, did Rivka have *tsouris*. Her *tsouris* had *tsouris*. And Chelm couldn't be poorer.

At a meeting of the Wise Council of Elders in the village of the Wise Fools, Rivka, serving in the honorary capacity of Village Treasurer, reported thusly:

"Last night some Cossack thieves broke into the village treasury!"

Gasps of outrage went up from the other Chelmites. "How much did we lose?" asked Boris the Balagoola.

"Lose?" said Rivka. "We're so poor that they took one look around, felt pity, and donated five kopecks."

Berel the Beadle rose. "Despite our poverty, education has always been a priority in Chelm. Thanks to our fine school, Shloime the Student now attends the *yeshiva*[3] and, even in competition with the finest students in all the land, still manages to eke out his usual barely-passing grades!"

The Council politely applauded a blushing Shloime.

"But now," continued Berel, "there are too many students in Chelm's one school. As times change, so must we. We must build a second school!"

Mendel the Messenger's voice rose above the resulting babble of voices, "But Berel, we can't affor-- can't affor-- how we gonna pay for it?"

Berel shrugged, "I don't know, Mendel. Kalman the Karpenter and Boris the Balagoola have kindly donated their services to help build,

---

[2] *Tsouris* means "trouble."
[3] A *yeshiva* is a school for Jewish study.

but we must find a way to pay for the building materials and the schoolbooks!"

After a heated debate, it was decided that desperate times require desperate measures. No one in ten years had approached mean old Mottel the Miser for a donation, not since Tevye the Milkman had made the attempt, and it had taken Boris three hours to pull the empty milk can off of poor Tevye's head.

But now the Council voted to send Shloime the Student, Chelm's finest example of academia, and the good Rabbi, Chelm's finest example of piety, to beg Mottel for the money.

"A donation! You must be kidding!" snarled Mottel.

"N-no, sir," stammered an intimidated Shloime. "Surely you value education."

The miser considered. "I'll tell you what. I'll gladly build the finest new school in the land for you, if you give in to my simple conditions."

"You are very kind," said the Rabbi. "Let us listen."

The miser chuckled. "All right. You want me to build the school, first thing is you gotta name it after me."

"I think that can be arranged," smiled the Rabbi, and Shloime nodded his agreement.

"Second, I'm tired of all this religion," said Mottel, certain that by the end of this meeting he would have committed nary a ruble to this school project. "I mean no offense, Rabbi, you're a good man. Oh, religion has its place, but not in a daily school. I don't care what you teach in your school, but I will not allow the students to wear *tsitsis*."[4]

"Hmm," pondered the Rabbi, "very well, I will agree to your demand."

"But, Rabbi--" protested Shloime.

---

[4] *Tsitsis* are the fringes at the ends of the prayer shawl.

"I'm not finished," said Mottel, taken aback at how easily the Rabbi had agreed. "The students may not wear *taliesim* either! No prayer shawls!"

The Rabbi considered. "You got it." Shloime was nearly apoplectic.

"There's more," said Mottel, suddenly becoming desperate. "The students will not, under any circumstances, be permitted to wear yarmulkes!"

"That's a tough one," said the Rabbi, "...but I think it can be arranged." Shloime was tearing at his *pais*,[5] but the Rabbi merely smiled serenely.

Amazed, Mottel rose and offered his hand to the Rabbi, "I'm shocked that you've agreed to my conditions...but now that you have, a deal's a deal. Just send me the bills."

The Rabbi thanked Mottel profusely, took the ashen Shloime's arm, and led him out of Mottel's mansion. As soon as they were out of the miser's earshot, Shloime exploded. "Rabbi, how? How could you agree to that? The students may not wear *tsitsis*? Or *taliesim*? Or, good heavens, yarmulkes? How could you, our Rabbi, agree to his conditions?"

"Simple, dear Shloime. Relax! Mottel's name will be on the building...and he has just agreed to build Chelm's first school...for girls!"

---

[5] *Pais* (PAY-iss) are loose, long sideburns often sported by orthodox men and boys.

A NEW *KIDDUSH* CUP [6]

By Charles Powell

(from an idea by Danny Dayton)

Fundraising is never easy. For an example of what we mean, let us once again visit the little village of Chelm to see how our friends there were able to approach the issue. And, as is so often the case, the process began with Berel, the Beadle of the Great Synagogue of Chelm.

It was at a meeting of the Wise Council of Elders. Berel happened to mention that the Synagogue was in need of a new *Kiddush* cup. The present one was in very poor shape. "That's bad," said one of the Elders. "Why don't we purchase a new one?"

"That's good," said Berel, "and for this we have the funds. But if we have a new *Kiddush* cup, it will make the old pointer, the *yad*,[7] look poor by comparison."

"That's bad," said Boris the Balagoola. "We should immediately obtain a new pointer."

"That's good," said Berel. "We still have enough money. But let me say that using a brand-new pointer on our beautiful old Torah is not very wise."

"That's bad," said Rivka the Baker. "It is apparent that we must invest in a new Torah, and we should do so at once."

"That's good," they agreed almost as one.

Berel was not happy, however. "It will look bad," he said. "The beautiful new Torah, but in our decrepit old ark."

---

[6] The *kiddush* is the blessing for the wine.

[7] The *yad* or pointer is, quite literally, a tiny hand with index finger pointed, at the end of a stick, held by the person who recites from the torah. One does not touch the scroll parchment itself…carefully, this is what the reader uses to keep his (and in more modern times her) place while chanting or reciting.

Shloime the Student piped up. "Easy! We commission a new ark, made of the best wood. I'm sure Kalman the Karpenter will do a fine job."

"I'll even give a discount," said the pleased Karpenter.

"That's good," beamed the Beadle. "Now I am happy!"

"I am not," boomed Boris the Balagoola. "I find it impossible to imagine a new ark, a new Torah, a new pointer and a new *Kiddush* cup--all upon our creaky, old *bima*! [8] It is simply wrong!"

"That's bad," said Berel. "Boris is right. We need a new *bima*."

"An honor to serve," said Kalman. "But more work, less discount..."

"I've got a better idea," said Rivka the Baker. "I propose that we consider moving to a brand-new Synagogue. One with a new *bima* to house our new ark, our new Torah, our new pointer, and our new *Kiddush* cup."

And that is how the wise fools of Chelm found themselves, after a two-year fundraising effort of epic proportions, in a new Synagogue when the one they had was perfectly fine.

But they finally replaced that old *Kiddush* cup.

---

[8] The *bima* is the stage from which the service is conducted; many synagogues have a central area and not a raised stage, but the concept is that this is the focal point of the service.

TALES OF THE SOUTH PACIFIC
By Charles M. Powell

Did you ever take a cruise? Once in your life you should take a cruise.

So restful. So calm. So refreshing. Unless you come from Chelm, where the fools all lived. It seems that three elders from the Wise Council took a cruise to the South Pacific. To be perfectly honest, they had set out for Minsk and they ran into this travel agent...but that's another story.

Suffice it to say that they found themselves aboard the S.S. Mein Kind,[9] sailing somewhere between Bialystock and Sumatra.

They tried shuffleboard, but every time they tried to shuffle, they got bored. They tried the casino, but as Boris the Balagoola pointed out, "If I want to gamble, I thumb my nose at the Tsar's Guards."

Still, the cruise was going well until the boat hit a goldberg near Guam. Maybe I didn't get it right. Maybe it was a greenberg. What's the difference? Goldberg, greenberg, iceberg...one of them. Anyway, they were washed upon the beach of a barren and deserted island.

Schneider the Tailor started to cry. "*Vey iz mir*! How we gonna get out of here?"

Berel the Beadle let out a wail, "Mein goodness gracious, I never saw such an empty island! Not a tree for shade; not a cave for warmth. We got, *Boychiks*,[10] *ganz tsouris*."[11]

Boris the Balagoola just laughed.

---

[9] Should probably explain this one for the Yiddish-unfamiliar. In Yiddish, the sentence *"Ess, ess, mein kind"* is a loving exhortation after putting the plate on the table to "Eat, eat, my child."

[10] *Boychik* is a term of endearment for a young male, in this context a general "fellas" or "folks."

[11] *Tsouris* means "trouble" and *ganz* means a lotta trouble.

The other two looked at him like he was crazy. "You got maybe a bump on the head when the boat sank? What's so funny?"

Boris laughed again. "Not to worry," he said. "They'll find us."

"How are they going to find us?" argued Schneider. "Who visits this part of the world?"

Boris calmed his friends. "Let me tell you why we're not in any trouble. I give it three days, tops. You see, three years ago, they called me from the Great Synagogue of Chelm, the fundraising committee. Would I make a pledge? We argued, we debated, I cried poverty, they cried poverty, what can I tell you. When it was over, I pledged twenty rubles to the Temple out of the goodness of mine heart."

Schneider the Tailor was exasperated. "So how does this help to get us off the island?"

Undaunted, the Balagoola continued. "Last year, they came to me from the synagogue again and asked me I should double my pledge. 'What, are you crazy?' I told them. 'You want, from a stone, blood?' But to make a long story not as long, they got me up to forty rubles."

Berel the Beadle went berserk. "Surely there's a point to this ridiculous story. What, may we ask yet again, does it have to do with getting us off this island?"

"Anyway, continued Boris, "the day before we took this trip, once again they got to me from the Temple. They begged. I pleaded. They threatened. I yelled. They won. I pledged one hundred Rubles.

"Let me tell you…for that kind of money, believe me, they'll find us!"

RICH OR POOR IS NOT IMPORTANT
(AS LONG AS YOU HAVE MONEY)

By Charles M. Powell

The Wise Council of Chelm, home to the wise fools, had assembled to discuss economic crisis. Berel the Beadle was summing up the situation.

"In my life, I never saw anything like it. People out of work; prices going up; taxes choking us. We gotta do something or Chelm is going to sink into the Volga."

"The Volga?" asked Shloime the Student. "The Volga is on the other side of Russia."

"See how bad it is?" said Berel.

Rivka the Baker complained, "Things are so bad that I'll have to pull my son, Shtoomie, out of school."

"That's the good news," replied the Rabbi, knowing Shtoomie's lack of scholarly discipline.

"What are we gonna do?" asked Schneider the Tailor. "How we gonna turn around the economy and save Chelm?"

Boris the Balagoola hit upon the idea. Did I say "hit upon it?" What he did was annihilate it. He mangled it; he smashed it; he pulled it and he pushed it and what came out was pure genius--at least for Chelm.

"So tell us the idea already," begged Rivka.

"It's so simple, I don't know why I didn't think of it before. Let me ask the Wise Council a couple of questions first. Number one, what does Chelm need more than anything else?"

"Money," they all agreed.

"Good," said the Balagoola.

"Not good," said Shloime. "We ain't got none."

"Question number two," continued the Balagoola. "Who is the richest Jew in all the world?"

"Easy," the Rabbi. "The Baron Rothschild of Paris, France."

"You guessed it, Rabbi."

"I guessed what?" wondered the Rabbi.

"My idea is to go to Paris, visit Rothschild, and convince him to move to Chelm."

"Brilliant!" said Rivka.

"Inspired!" said Schneider.

"A miracle solution!" said Tevye the Milkman.

"Crazy," said the Rabbi.

Whether it was crazy or brilliant hardly mattered. It was an idea worth pursuing, voted the Council, and they dispatched Boris the Balagoola to Paris.

Now, Boris in cultured Paris was a strange situation indeed. But some way, somehow, the Balagoola arranged an audience with Rothschild.

"My good Baron," he began, "I am here as a humble representative of the village of Chelm. Our town is poor but pious. Our lives are hard but rewarding. Our people are simple but dull. Grace us, O Baron, by coming to live in our humble village."

The Baron looked in wonder at this fool. "Do you expect me to leave Paris, and my castle and my hired servants, and my cooks and butlers and coachmen and valets and banks and everything else, to depart with you to the village of Chelm to live out my days? Why would I do that?"

Boris the Balagoola smiled "You could bring all those workers… but the real reason? Because we can offer you eternal life. If you move to Chelm, you will live forever."

The Baron, for whom all other things were possible, stopped, confronted by his own mortality. "If," he asked, "I move to Chelm, I will live forever?"

"You got it, Baron," said the Balagoola.

"How can you guarantee me this?" inquired Rothschild.

"That's the simplest part," said Boris. "In the history of our village, in all these years, not one--I repeat, not one--wealthy man has ever died in Chelm!"

THE SOLE OF CHARITY
By Charles M. Powell

The discussion at the Wise Council or the Eiders centered--this particular night--on charity. More specifically, on who was the most charitable of the wise fools or the village or Chelm.

"By me there's no question," said Berel the Beadle. "By me, I nominate Rivka the Baker. Think about all the bread she gives away to the homeless of Chelm."

"Hold it just ein minute," thundered Boris the Balagoola. "There are no homeless people in Chelm."

"I know, I know," said the Beadle, "but that's not Rivka's fault!"

It was Shloime the Student's turn: "My vote goes to Mendel the Messenger. He's always helping people, running errands, alerting our villagers of danger...what a nice man!"

The Balagoola laughed. "Nice, yes. Helpful, no question about. But we're talking here charity...with a capital 'cha.' We need another candidate."

Yenta the Matchmaker asked for the floor. "I nominate Shepsil the Shoemaker and I have a true story that will prove my case."

Again, the Balagoola laughed. "Shepsil the Shoemaker the most charitable person in Chelm? This I gotta hear."

"So I'll tell you," said the Matchmaker. "You know, of course, that Shepsil not only mends all of Chelm's boots, but he's so good that people from all over the other villages come to him. Which is how the good Bishop of Bialystock had his priestly slippers fixed by our Shepsil."

Boris was amazed. "The Catholic Bishop of Bialystock?"

"Who then," asked Berel the Beadle, "the Galitziana Bishop? Of course the Catholic Bishop!"

Yenta continued. "The Bishop was very pleased with the Shoemaker's work and asked how much he owed Shepsil. Now here, my friends, is the charitable part. Shepsil said that he never takes money from a Clergyman."

"I knew I should have gone to Rabbinical School," muttered the Balagoola.

"Well, the Bishop was so pleased," continued Yenta, "that he sent Shepsil a gift of fifty Rosary beads. Shepsil couldn't use them, but it was the thought that counted, and the good review he gave to his flock surely helped."

"What happened next?" asked Berel.

"Then the Pastor of the Presbyterian Church of Pinsk had his best boots soled and heeled. Shepsil the Shoemaker also told him that he wouldn't take any money from a man of the Clergy. The Pastor was so pleased, he also gave a good report to his congregants, and sent Shepsil fifty of his best Presbyterian Prayer books. Again, it was the thought that counted," said the Matchmaker.

"So then what happened," said the impatient Balagoola.

"So then," said Yenta, "who should come to Shepsil but Rabinovitch, the Righteous Rabbi of Ratislava. And by him, the same thing happened. Shepsil, the charitable Shoemaker of Chelm, refused to accept even a kopeck."

The Balagoola was finally impressed. "That's pretty good," he said. "I see where this is going. So what did the Rabbi send to Shepsil?"

Yenta the Matchmaker smiled. "What else would a good Rabbi send? He sent the Shoemaker fifty other Rabbis!"

DEATH

1. The Proper Send-Off
2. Gas
3. Sometimes It Doesn't Pay To Be A Nice Person
4. A Husband Like This Doesn't Grow Under A Tree
5. Heaven McChicken
6. The New Look
7. A Purgatory Story
8. The Cereal Killers
9. The V.I.P.
10. A Helping Hand

Part of what makes Jewish humor special is finding humor in almost anything. And Judaism has a long history of both fighting through, but also laughing through, the tears. If we lost our sense of humor we would surely lose our minds.

Some things are not appropriate for jokes...but there are aspects of death, and heaven, and other places that are worthy of exploration.

THE PROPER SEND-OFF
By Charles M. Powell

"He died," said Berel the Beadle.

"Who died?" asked Rivka the Baker.

"Farfallin the Pharmacist, that's who died."

Boris the Balagoola laughed. "You mean Farfallin is far-fallin'?"

"What are you laughing?" snapped the Beadle. "A Human being just passed away and you find that funny? I'm surprised at you."

The Balagoola looked ashamed. Rivka came to his defense.

"If the truth be known," said the Baker-person, "not one single member of our village of Chelm liked Farfallin. He was so unpleasant that when people needed a pharmacist, they would go all the way to Minsk so they shouldn't have to deal with this terrible person."

"Enough," said the Beadle. "The man just died. We should remember only worthwhile things about him."

Now, in the village of Chelm, where the wise fools all lived, the process of thinking of something worthwhile took considerable time and effort. To tell you the absolute truth, the very process of "thinking" in Chelm took considerable time and effort.

Nevertheless, the Great Synagogue of Chelm was filled to capacity that evening as the Rabbi held a special and very beautiful service in honor of Farfallin, the fallen Pharmacist. As the service was about to end, the Rabbi made a request from the pulpit.

"I am aware that Farfallin was not overly loved in our community. Problems he had with his neighbors. Problems he caused with most people who knew him. Still, he was one of us and that entitles him to a proper send-off. As is our custom in Chelm, I am asking that at least one member of our congregation say something nice about the deceased prior to his burial. Who wishes to speak first?"

The silence was deafening.

The Rabbi tried again. "Listen, my friends. You don't have to tell me what kind of man Farfallin was. We all know that his wife divorced him after only six minutes of marriage. We are all familiar with his tight-fisted, frugal--all right, I'll say it--cheap ways. Who in Chelm wasn't personally insulted by this cranky, conniving, uncaring man? Still, I say, we must find one person who has something nice to say about him."

Embarrassed, the congregation lowered their collective heads. And, still, not a single voice was raised to honor Farfallin.

"That's it!" roared the Rabbi. "We will sit here until *Tisha b'Av*[1] if we have to, but somebody in this temple of love and understanding will find it in his or her heart to say something worthwhile about our departed Pharmacist!"

Finally, finally...a hand slowly rose in the rear of the Great Synagogue. The hand belonged to Boris the Balagoola.

The Rabbi, greatly relieved, called on the Balagoola, "Boris, thank you. You have something nice to say about the deceased?"

"I have, Rabbi."

"Well done, Boris. What is the single best thing you can tell us about Farfallin?"

The Balagoola shrugged. "His brother was worse!"

---

[1] *Tisha b'Av* literally means ninth (day) of the month of Av on the Hebrew calendar. It is a solemn day on the calendar, when disasters have happened...think "9/11" nowadays. But as used here and in similar contexts it somewhat means "twelfth of never," or "We'll sit here forever!"

GAS

By Charles M. Powell

(from a story by Woody Allen)

There are certain illnesses that seem exclusive to the Jewish people.

Aggravation is one. *Shpilkes*[2] is another. But the single-most Jewish ailment in the history of our people is Gas. Passed down from father to son, mother to daughter, Gas remains a permanent fixture of our culture and our heritage.

Even as far back as Chelm, where the wise fools all lived, Gas surfaced, as it were.

Boris the Balagoola awakened one morning with the worst chest pains in all of Russia. It was apparent to the poor Balagoola that his heart was attacking him and his time was up.

Mrs. Balagoola scoffed, "All you got is Gas."

"But suppose," whined Boris, "it isn't Gas. Suppose it's the real thing, heaven forbid. Shouldn't I see a doctor?"

"You want to run up a bill of maybe twenty rubles just to find out you got Gas? OK by me," said the Missus. "By me, you got three choices. You could go to Minsk Memorial, you could go to the Pinsk Pavilion, or you can go to Cedars of Leningrad. "

Any of those seemed like a *schlep*.[3] "I think I'll ask my friend Fenchik the Furrier for advice," said Boris.

The Balagoola discovered his friend crying and moaning. "Mine God," cried Fenchik. "I think I'm having a heart attack. Such pains I never had in my whole life. Look, since we're both suffering from the

---

[2] *Shpilkes* is anxiety, apprehension, impatience; of any combination of two of those. Or all three. Like having *shpilkes* about writing this footnote.

[3] *Schlep* can mean lug something burdensome ("I gotta *schlep* this heavy backpack across campus?") or, as in this context here, to go a long way, usually in traffic or through the woods or uphill both ways.

same thing, how about I'll go to the hospital, and whatever they tell me I got, you'll know you got. This way, it only costs us one bill instead of two."

So Fenchik went and the Balagoola waited for him...and waited for him. Late that night, unable to contain himself any longer, Boris took his Gas back to the Furrier's house. "So where's Fenchik?" asked the Balagoola.

The Farmer's wife sobbed, "Don't ask."

"Whaddaya mean, don't ask? I'm asking, I'm asking."

"I'm sorry to tell you that your ex-friend and my late husband passed away today."

The Balagoola went crazy. "Oh my God, I was right...it wasn't Gas. I'm still having a heart attack! Quick, don't Just stand there crying, get me to a hospital!"

Boris was hospitalized for three days. He was probed, bled, stuck, pinched, knipped, knapped, and sent home with a bill for fifty rubles and told, of course, that he had...Gas.

On the way home he passed his late friend's house. Boris went to pay a *shiva*[4] call. "Tell me, you should be so kind, did poor Fenchik suffer before he died?"

"No," cried the unhappy widow, "All he had was Gas! But on the way home from the hospital he got run over by an ox-cart!"

---

[4] After a passing, the family observes a one-week period of mourning, "sitting *shiva*," and visitors call to bring comfort and support, as well as nourishment so the grieving family shouldn't have to deal with getting food for themselves right now.

SOMETIMES IT DOESN'T PAY TO BE A NICE PERSON

By Charles M. Powell

(from a story by Danny Dayton)

Gitlitz had made it big since leaving Chelm, where the wise fools all lived. He had invested wisely; he had bought the right real estate; he had speculated prudently and accurately. Yes, Gitlitz had done very well since leaving Chelm.

So the little village of Chelm was the last thing on his mind when his telephone rang that day. The telephone was new to Gitlitz, having been invented just for this story.

"Hello, is this Gitlitz, who used to live in Chelm?"

"Yes," said the millionaire, "to whom I got the pleasure?"

"My name is Boris the Balagoola, and I am this year Mayor of the village."

"Congratulations," replied Gitlitz. "How can I be of service to you?"

"Well," said the Balagoola "an old man named Shpilkas just passed away here in Chelm. He was very poor, extremely destitute, there's simply no money with which to give him a proper burial. Our good Rabbi remembered that you might be distantly related and perhaps you could help us bury the old man."

Many miles away, listening on his newly invented telephone, Gitlitz started to cry. "Do I remember Shpilkas? Who could forget Shpilkas? He was my favorite cousin. Every Chanukah, as poor as he was, he used to send me something. One year it would be a handmade *dreidel*,[5] another time it would be a few kopecks. He was poor and uneducated, but to me, he was a *mensch*."[6]

---

[5] A *dreidel* is the little spinning toy top, a tradition of the Chanukah holiday.
[6] A good person; it is a high compliment to call someone a *mensch*.

By this time Boris the Balagoola was also crying. "Oy, a *mensch* like that we should give a proper send-off."

"Exactly, Mr. Mayor Balagoola," said the rich man. "For me, thanks God, money is no object. So here is what I want you to do: Firstly, purchase the most impressive headstone."

"Stone," repeated the Balagoola.

"…and a coffin of the finest pine."

"Pine," said the Balagoola.

"Lastly, secure one of the finest plots in the cemetery."

"Plots," said the Balagoola.

"Then I want you to be sure that people come to the burial services. Spend whatever it takes to put out the finest spread of food to comfort the people when they come to mourn for our Shpilkas."

"Shpilkas," said Boris.

"I want a string ensemble and a choir of cantors. I want a proclamation from the Tsar and a street named after Shpilkas."

"Shpilkas," repeated the Balagoola, adding, "Street."

"Flowers everywhere. And also I want he should be buried in a fine tuxedo."

"Tuxedo, buried," confirmed the Balagoola.

"Can you do all of this, Balagoola? I will pay all costs and even make a handsome donation to the village coffers."

"Coffers" coughed Boris. "Of coff-- of course. We will do it all and send you the bill," said the Balagoola, "and we are most grateful."

And it was indeed done. It is still said that this was the finest, most meaningful funeral ever experienced in Chelm. People, flowers, music, mourning, it was first class all the way.

Gitlitz received and promptly paid a bill of three hundred rubles, ten kopecks. Everything returned to normal…for about a month.

Then Gitlitz received still another bill of forty-seven kopecks from Chelm. The bill was marked "additional funeral expenses." Without question he paid it.

However, every month, for the next six months, Gitlitz continued to get a charge of forty-seven kopecks per month. Finally, he got angry. Not having a newly invented fax-machine, he used his old telephone and called Boris the Balagoola.

"Listen Mr. Balagoola. I asked for first class, I got first class. I paid for everything to bury my dear cousin Shpilkas. The plot, the stone, the music, the choir, the flowers--everything. But why do I continue to receive a monthly bill of forty-seven kopecks?"

By now, Boris was upset, "Listen, Mr. Gitlitz. What you asked for you got. Every single request met, every detail honored. But, after all, you have to pay for the rental of Shpilkas's tuxedo!"

A HUSBAND LIKE THIS DOESN'T GROW ON TREES
By Charles M. Powell

The bad news was that Schwartzbard died. You know Schwartzbard, the citizen of Chelm, where the wise fools all lived?

The good news was that he and his wife Devorah had had a wonderful, full life together for fifty-three years. His devotion to his bride was well-known throughout the village and, in turn, his loving wife worshipped him.

It is said that they never had an argument in all those years. Well…except for the time that Devorah ran up that enormous bill at the St. Petersburg Tiffany's. And maybe one other time when she told him she was going to buy a dozen eggs and came home with a dozen eggs…from Fabergé. Still, theirs was an idyllic marriage.

So, was it any wonder that Devorah was beside herself with grief as poor Schwartzbard lay in his coffin being prepared for his final rest? She asked all the friends and relatives to please leave her alone for a few minutes with her dear deceased, which was promptly done.

Alone, she approached Schwartzbard and smiled at him sadly.

"Oy, Schwartzbard, were you a husband. Were you a loving partner. So thoughtful, so caring. My every wish…my every need.

"And when I go to buy you a cemetery plot, they tell me you already left twenty-five rubles, paid in advance, so I shouldn't have to worry myself.

"And when I go to pick out the best coffin in the village, they tell me that you already left fifty rubles, I shouldn't have the burden.

"And they also tell me that you left one hundred rubles for a stone. What a husband…you thought of everything. One Hundred Rubles for a stone!

"So tell me, dear Schwartzbard," and she held her hefty new ruby ring over the coffin, "what do you think of the stone?"

HEAVEN McCHICKEN

By Charles M. Powell

(from a story by Arthur Hamilton)

[Every once in a while a story was crafted with a break of the "fourth wall" set up as taking directly to the reader/listener. There are bits and pieces in other stories here; this one is a more overt example.]

I think that we could probably blame it on a bad piece of goose liver. I mean, Boris the Balagoola had a stomach like iron, but a bad piece of liver is a bad piece of liver.

At any rate, the poor Balagoola had a dream--OK, not so much dream, he had an Olympic nightmare. World class. Gold medal.

Now, in Chelm, where the Wise Fools all lived, a nightmare was something not to be ignored. Who knows what it meant? Who knows what it could lead to? Maybe it's best that we relate to you the dream as it happened, and you decide what it means. OK by you? OK.

Boris the Balagoola dreamed that he had died and had gone to heaven. Never mind saying to me, "There's no way that could happen." We're talking here *nightmare*.

Ask me who should meet the Balagoola at the entrance to Heaven? Who else? The Chairman of the Board...the boss of bosses...Numero Uno...the Big "G."

"Welcome," He said, "You must be tired from your trip. How about a chicken sandwich?"

Now Boris the Balagoola was wiped out. I mean, here was God...and he's whipping up a chicken sandwich for a simple, ignorant fellow from Chelm...I gotta tell you...that's why He's The Big Kahuna...no, The Biggest Kahuna...and we're not.

So the Balagoola sat down at the Captain's Table and the Big Boss brought him white meat chicken on Pumpernickel, hold the mayo. It was--do I have to tell you?--heaven!

Later in Boris's dream, God took him around, showed him what a terrific place it was. The beach; the ski slopes; the game room; the three swimming pools, one heated, one with cold water, and one empty, in case you don't swim.

Came time for dinner. God brought the Balagoola a platter with a glass dome covering it. Under the dome was a chicken sandwich.

For breakfast the next morning, God brought Boris another chicken sandwich.

"God Almighty," cried the Balagoola.

"Yes, my son?" asked the Lord.

"Tell me something, your worshipfulness. If this menu is for the *good* guys, what are they serving downstairs?"

"Beats me," replied the Holy of Holies. "The other guy never answers my texts. Why don't I give you a 24-hour pass and you check it out and come back and tell me?"

"Good idea," said Boris, "but can I do that?"

"Hey," said God, "It's your nightmare."

So Boris the Balagoola, with fear in his heart, arrived in the land of the "H" word. He resisted all temptations: the beautiful women; the racetrack; the singles bars...he went straight, instead, to the Dining Hall. There, in Hell, he had the meal of his afterlife: quiche, caviar, beef Wellington, potato *knish*[7] soufflé, Baked Alaska (and in Hell they know how to bake), brandy, espresso--and that was just breakfast.

He returned to the Lord to give his report. "I gotta tell you, Chief, they got down there a good thing going for them. In your whole life...forever, as I hear it...you never had food so good. How come, here where the *good* people go...here where we get our eternal reward...here we got chicken sandwiches, hold the mayo. Down there they got--don't ask? How come?"

---

[7] A *knish* is a baked, or sometimes deep fried, covering of dough with a filling... sometimes mean, very commonly mashed potato.

God sighed a deep and lordly sigh. "I tell you, Balagoola...you're the only one here in your nightmare. Do you know how tough it is to cook just for two?"

THE NEW LOOK
By Charles M. Powell

"What are we gonna do about Schwartzbard?"

"So what's to do? The man won't leave his house; he won't talk to his friends; in short, he's a mess."

It was an informal gathering of the Council of Chelm, where the wise fools all lived. Berel the Beadle was leading a lively discussion concerning Schwartzbard the Shoemaker, a good man who had become a widower two years previously but who was still deep in mourning.

"We gotta get him out of his house already. It's not good, the man should mourn so long."

"So, how are we gonna do it?" inquired Rivka the Baker.

"Only one way," replied Boris the Balagoola. "We ask the Rabbi to pay a visit."

So the beloved Rabbi of Chelm spent a whole day with Schwartzbard.

"My good shoemaker," he said, "you must change your every habit. I suggest you exercise and lose some weight, buy new clothes, maybe even get your nose fixed. You should even purchase a new ox-cart, one that is faster and handsomer. Live a little, Schwartzbard, like the Missus (*aleha hasholom*)[8] would want. How many more years do any of us have left?"

Now the Rabbi was much revered in Chelm and his advice was not to be ignored.

So Schwartzbard began a new life. First he had his nose fixed. Then he lost sixty pounds of excess Schwartzbard. New clothes came next. He became the talk of Chelm. But the crowning touch was his

---

[8] *Aleha hasholom* is the idiomatic "rest in peace." "May her memory be for a blessing" is a commonly used English phrase. (*Alav hashalom* for a male.)

new ox-cart. It was gorgeous! White-wall wheels; sparkling spokes; it went from zero to six kilometers per hour in only 47 minutes; in short, a classic.

And for his maiden ride, Schwartzbard invited the entire village to witness his emergence from mourning. They all watched as the "new" Schwartzbard strapped himself in, said "giddy-yap" to his new oxen, and on the first high-speed turn was promptly thrown across the town square.

Did you ever hear a story like that? Neither did Schwartzbard, who awoke in heaven in the presence of his maker.

Schwartzbard was outraged. "What are you doing, God? What kind of business is this? For two years I'm so sad and in mourning that if you took me then, I would have been the happiest dead Jew in Chelm. But now? I change! I change my clothes; I slim down; I get a sporty new ox-cart; even the new nose! I'm finally out of mourning, and now you take me? What kind of business is this?'

God, it is said, looked ashamed. "I apologize," said the Lord. "But frankly, Schwartzbard, I didn't recognize you."

A PURGATORY STORY

By Charles M. Powell

You heard the story of what happened when the Tsar died? You didn't heard? So I'll tell you. And I'll tell you, also, what it had to do with Chelm, the village of the Wise Fools.

So, as the saying goes, the Tsar kicked the Samovar. After a formal State funeral they buried him in St. Petersburg.

The Jews were so happy you would think they won the lottery.

And the Tsar appeared at the gates of Purgatory to be rewarded with his eternal punishment. The man in charge was Gimpel the Gatekeeper, a distant ancestor of Chelm's own Mendel the Messenger.

"Welcome to-- welco-- greetings!" said the Gatekeeper. "As we say down here, 'How the Hec-- How the Hec-- how's by you?'"

"I was the Tsar and I demand to be accorded treatment befitting my Royal personage," said the King.

"Royal Per-- Royal-- a blueblood? No question about, you'll get the best what we got."

The Tsar listed his preferences: "You should be so kind...I require a five-bedroom facility. There must be a special kitchen for a personal chef, and, of course, a stable for my horses."

"A stab-- a stab-- an equestrian compound? You gotta be kidding, your Tsar-ness."

"Kidding, my good Gatekeeper? I assure you that I do not intend to spend the rest of eternity living below my Royal standards. After all, a Tsar is a Tsar."

"Was a Tsar," reminded Gimpel, in true purgatory fashion, taking the situation by the horns. "Unfortunately for both of us, you are here to be punish--punish-- disciplined. But, because you were a Tsar, we are prepared to offer you a choice of Hells. First, there is the regu-- the regu-- the standard Hell. Or, if you prefer, we can offer you Chelm Hell."

Suddenly, The Tsar was worried. "What, may I ask, is the difference between the two?"

Gimpel explained: "Well, in regular Hell they strip you naked every morning and whi--whi-- smack you around for two hours. Then they hang you by your heels for an hour and pipe in music played by the worst musicians we got…while under your upside-down head is a pile of logs, which they light up and burn you all day."

"And what is Chelm Hell?"

The gatekeeper laughed. "It's about the same exact thing, but sometimes they can't remember where they put the whip....they can't light the fire…"

THE CEREAL KILLERS
By Charles M. Powell

Ruchel and Reuben Rabinovich had a wonderful marriage. They had a wonderful home, a wonderful family, a wonderful circle of friends...and a wonderful funeral.

They passed away together on the night of the first Seder in Chelm, where the wise fools all lived. Always calorie and cholesterol conscious, they ate cautiously, lots of fruit, lots of vegetables, lot of oat bran.

But they had thrown all caution--and the Kowalski Health Diet--to the wind on Passover. Together they had consumed five hard-boiled eggs dipped in pure salt water; an entire chopped liver mold in the form of The Great Synagogue of Chelm; four bowls of chicken soup, each with seven Kryptonian matzo balls; gefilte fish with high octane *chrain*;[9] one and three-quarters complete chickens: and enough pickled herring to feed an army. Then there was a little dessert and a couple glasses tea. You think maybe it was the tea that killed them?

Anyway, they both woke up in the hereafter and were met by Huvel the Host.

"Why are you called a host?" inquired Reuben.

"Well," said Huvel, "you know the Boss is called the Lord of Hosts? I'm one of the Hosts."

"So what do you do, Mister Host?"

"I take you around, I introduce you to your neighbors. I'm like a regular Welcome Wagon. Let me show you your Condo."

"Our Condo?" said Ruchel. "In Chelm we only rented."

"That's why they call this place Heaven," said the host. "And the best part is...if you ever want to sell your Condo, God has to buy it back!"

---

[9] Horseradish. The rocket-fuel kind, not the mild, cute kind.

It turned out that they got a palatial suite overlooking both the sea and the mountains, central heating and air-conditioning, three parking spaces, a wet bar...and free memberships in the "24-Hour You Should Exercise More Already" gym.

Ruchel was overwhelmed. "This already is living," she said. "A place like this you could die for!"

The Host wasn't finished yet, "And wait until you see the restaurant. Anything you want, they got. You name it, you get it."

"It's paradise," said Ruchel.

"Exactly," replied Huvel.

Reuben started to cry.

The host consoled him. "I know, it must be overwhelming to see such perfection and know that it's yours for eternity."

"That's not it," sobbed Reuben, "It's my wife...this is why I cry! If it wasn't for her *mishugena*[10] oat bran, we'd have been here enjoying all this twenty years ago!"

---

[10] Crazy, ridiculous.

The V.I.P.
By Charles M. Powell

It was at a meeting of the Wise Council of Elders that Berel the Beadle started to laugh. It began with a giggle, because Boris the Balagoola was addressing the Council and Berel didn't want to appear to be rude. Soon, the giggle had no place to go but out.

"Not polite," said the Rabbi. "The man here is talking. What's so funny?"

"I apologize to the Wise Council, but I just remembered a terrible dream I had the other night."

Rivka the Baker was shocked. "How terrible could it be, the way you're laughing? So tell us, already, about this nightmare that's so funny. Who was in this dream?"

Berel recovered enough to point to the Rabbi and to the Balagoola.

"What is this already, twenty questions?" demanded the Rabbi. "Tell us what was so terrible."

Berel finally calmed down. "In my dream, it seems that our great Rabbi and Boris the Balagaoola passed away on the same day and both ended up before their Maker, blessed be He."

"So what's so funny?" asked Rivka.

"What's so funny," said Berel, "is that God welcomed our beloved Rabbi into his kingdom, thanked him for his loving and learned work on earth, and escorted him to his permanent eternal Condo. A lovely little room, good books, a seventeen-inch television, icebox, view of the golf course…nice. You know what I mean? Nice."

The Rabbi of Chelm smiled broadly. "Even though it was only a dream, Berel, it's nice to know the good Lord takes care of His own."

Berel the Beadle started to laugh again, "Wait until you hear what happened with Boris the Balagoola."

"So tell us already."

"In my dream, it happens that God asks Boris who he is and Boris confesses that he's just the Balagoola of Chelm."

Schneider the Tailor laughed. "And God kicks him out, right?"

"Au Contraire," giggled the Beadle. "God takes our Boris by the greasy arm and escorts him to his new quarters. And you wouldn't believe...in your life...what can I tell you? A three- bedroom suite...a jacuzzi...a full-color flat-screen with surround-sound...a super stereo. What can I tell you? Heaven. Plain and simple! Heaven."

"Wait a minute," said the Rabbi of Chelm. "Why should the Balagoola be so rewarded in his afterlife?"

Berel laughed, "Funny you say that, Rabbi. In my dream you said the same exact thing."

"And what was God's answer?" inquired the Rabbi.

The Beadle explained. "In my dream, God said, 'up here we get a lot of Rabbis. How often do we get a Balagoola?'"

A HELPING HAND
By Charles M. Powell

You think you know rain? You think you know floods? Compared to Chelm, you know kid stuff. In Chelm they once had so much rain that Kalman the Karpenter stared to build an ark. That, already, is rain.

So hard did it rain that the banks of the Chelm River overflowed and fifteen feet of water flooded into the center of the village. The villagers scattered and helped each other to safety...all except Pincus the Pious. Pincus calmly put on a rain-*tallis*[11] and his *tefillin*[12] and quietly went up onto the roof of his home.

As the waters kept rising, the townspeople feared that Pincus would drown, but he just sat there praying. Schneider the Tailor, fleeing for higher ground, yelled up at him, "Get down already, Pincus! With all this rain and flooding, who do you think you are, a piddler on the roof?"

Pincus the Pious smiled. "Not to worry, Schneider. All my life I've prayed to God. You think He's going to turn his back on me now?"

But the people were still worried, Berel the Beadle somehow found a rowboat and got to Pincus's home. "Jump down, Pincus! The water's rising and I've come to save you."

"You? You've come to save me? That's what I've got God for," said Pincus earnestly. "Believe me, He will provide."

A little while later two strong-bodied students swam over, pushing a raft. "It's your last chance, Mr. Pincus," called up Leah the Teenager. "Soon the water will be over your house! Please jump down and we'll save you!"

---

[11] The *tallis* or *tallit* is the prayer shawl. (There's no such thing as a "rain-*tallis*...")
[12] *Tefillin* are a set of small black leather boxes containing scrolls of parchment inscribed with verses from the Torah; wearable, with straps.

Again Pincus the Pious smiled. "What's the matter with you two? Have you no faith? I say again--not to worry. God will take care of me."

Soon thereafter, a rescue squad from the next village arrived with a much larger boat, and still Pincus politely rebuffed them.

The waters continued to rise…and Pincus woke up in Heaven. He opened his eyes…and there was God, ready to greet him. "Welcome, good Pincus. Of course you have earned eternal life here in Heaven."

But now Pincus was angry. "Welcome? That's all you got for me? Sixty-seven years I put my faith in you. I studied day and night. I prayed day and night. This is my reward? To drown in a silly flood, with no help from you? Not a finger lifted, nothing?"

God was perplexed. "Now wait just one minute, Pincus. What do you *want* from me? I sent a raft and two boats!"

ETHNIC DIFFERENCES

1. Torah, Torah, Torah
2. Mama Lushen ("Mother Tongue")
3. Boris The Balagoola, Phone Home!
4. Matzah-Matta-U?
5. No Starch

Diversity is a strength. Some people do things and say things in different ways from the way other people do. This chapter celebrates some of the differences that make Jews, and the Jews of Chelm, unique...as is everyone.

(See also "The Horse's Tale" in the Animals chapter; "Citius, Altius, Kvetchius" in the Commerce chapter; "I Got The Horse Right Here" in the Gambling and Games chapter; "Tink Before You Talk" in the Jewish Holidays chapter; and "The Witness" in the Legal Troubles chapter; and "The Day Chelm Stood Still" in the Health and Aging chapter; for a little more of ethnic and linguistic fun.)

TORAH, TORAH, TORAH!

By Mel Powell (updating a Charles M. Powell story)

In Chelm, the tiny village where the wise fools all lived, the news spread like wildfire--or at least like a flickering candle--as Mendel the Messenger made his rounds.

"Hear ye-- hear ye-- listen up! Boris the Balagoo-- the Balagoo-- the big guy has been invited to attend the Counc-- the Counc-- he's going to Vitipsk-Gaboynya for the Balagoola Convention!"

"Exciting news!" said Rivka the Baker. "For the first time, Boris has been chosen as one of the top Balagoolas in the land!"

The problem, dear listener, was simple. Vitipsk-Gaboynya was known as a veritable bastion of learned scholars of the Torah. Everyone there, from the exalted rabbi to the lowly beggar, could quote from the Five Books of Moses as readily as calling the sky blue. Chelm, on the other hand, was known as a veritable bastion of... well...as what it was, the place where the wise fools all lived.

Boris paid a visit to the rabbi of Chelm. "It's not that I'm ashamed of my hometown," he boomed respectfully to the old scholar. "But I want to fit in at the Convention! Can you teach me everything I need to know, so that the learned citizens of Vitipsk-Gaboynya won't know I'm from Chelm? And don't just give me any of that stand-on-one-foot do-unto-others nonsense. I want the whole schmeer."

Of course, the rabbi agreed--as this was the first time Boris the Balagoola had shown any interest in the Torah beyond the fact that he could lift it tenderly over his head with only his muscular little pinkie. Day and night, for weeks before the convention--except, of course, for Shabbat--the rabbi worked tirelessly with the Balagoola. Boris had no doubt that he was ready, and to the cheers of the citizens of Chelm he proudly rode his top-of-the-line ox-cart--all cleaned up and with a fresh coat of wax, even for the ox--out of Chelm.

Upon arrival in Vitipsk-Gaboynya, Boris went to the business district and decided to sample the local cuisine. He marched right up to the clerk. "Can you help me, sir?"

The clerk smiled. "Gladly, welcomed visitor, and I shall be fully honest with you, for as the Good Book says, 'You shall do no wrong in judgment, in measures of length or weight or quantity.' Leviticus."

"Wonderful! I am most grateful. First, I'd like a loaf of bread, please, for as the Good Book says, 'When I cease your supply of bread, ten women shall bake your bread in one oven, and shall deliver your bread by weight; and you shall eat, and not be satisfied.' Also Leviticus."

The clerk blinked once. "But as the good book says in Deuteronomy, 'Man does not live by bread alone.'"

"You're right! May I also please have a small amount of your finest wine, for as the Good Book says in Genesis, 'After our father Avram rescued his nephew Lot, the High Priest gifted him with bread and wine.' And don't worry; my ox is the designated driver."

The clerk smiled. "'His eyes shall be red with wine, and his teeth white with milk.' Genesis."

"No milk, but thank you so much," replied Boris. "And, finally, I would like to sample one of your freshest whitefish, please, for as the Good Book says--in Numbers-- 'we remember the fish we ate in Egypt.'"

The clerk was impressed. "'The word is very near you; it is in your mouth and in your heart.' Deuteronomy. By the way, sir, might you be here for the Balagoola Convention? From Chelm, perhaps?"

Boris was amazed. "How could you tell? Day and night I studied with the learned Rabbi! I have no doubt, none at all, that my references to the Good Book have been completely accurate! Did I not quote appropriately about the loaf of bread?"

"You did, sir," said the clerk respectfully.

Boris drove on. "Did I not quote correctly about the wine?"

"You did, sir," said the friendly clerk again.

"And did I not cite the perfect passage for the fish?"

"You did, sir."

"Then how, pray tell, did you know I'm from Chelm?"

The clerk smiled kindly. "Because, good sir...this is a hardware store."

MAMA-LUSHEN [1]

By Charles M. Powell

[This story is not set in Chelm but finds its way into the compilation as a taste of the ethnic and linguistic differences we celebrate.]

Yiddish is such an expressive language There is a word for almost everything. Some Yiddish words have no parallels in other languages.

Some are not even literally translatable, but we don't need to *know* what they mean in order to *understand* what they mean. But once in a while the Yiddish word for something eludes us.

Which brings to mind the story of two friends who were discussing Yiddish. Both agreed that it is picturesque as well as dramatic. One recalled Damon Runyon once remarking that Yiddish is the only language in the world with middle elements with which to express middle emotions...this, probably, because Yiddish is a mixture of many languages.

One of the friends, Irving, remarked that there was one word that puzzled him. "I can't seem to find out how to say 'disappointed' in Yiddish. Do you know what the word is?" His friend, Seymour, couldn't think of it but decided to call his mother, who was the reigning *maven*[2] on the language.

Seymour dialed his mother's number and said to her, in Yiddish, "Mama, suppose I phoned you on Wednesday and told you I was coming for dinner on Friday night. As you always do, you'd start cooking on Wednesday everything I like. You'd make gefilte fish, matzah ball soup, roast chicken, potato kugel, carrot *tzimmes*,[3] and two kinds of strudel. On Friday, you would have the table all set and, just before I was supposed to arrive, I'd phone you and say I was sorry,

---

[1] *Mama-Lushen* means mother tongue; first language.
[2] A *maven* is an expert.
[3] *Tzimmes* is a stew.

Mama, but something came up and I can't come for supper. What would you be?"

Mama sighed into the phone. "Disappointed!"

BORIS THE BALAGOOLA, PHONE HOME!

By Charles M. Powell

[Spoiler alert! Jewish readers may want to skip this note and start reading the story. Everyone else needs to know that a "goy" is just the Hebrew name for "person," and "goyim" is the plural form. But in common usage, the goyim are the non-Jews.]

Have extra-terrestrials visited Earth? No one knows for sure…as far as we know. But the Wise Fools of Chelm know. Where else but Chelm would an E.T. visit?

"I would like special permission," said Boris the Balagoola, "to bring an E.T. before the Wise Council of Elders."

"An E.T.", asked Rivka the Baker. "What's an E.T.?"

"I know," said Schneider the Tailor. "It's an Extra *Tallis*." [4]

"No, it's not," said Tevye the Milkman. "It's Electric *Tsitsis*." [5]

"What are you talking," said Berel the Beadle, "electricity hasn't been invented yet."

"Let me explain," said the Balagoola. "I was walking in the woods this morning and I came upon this very strange-looking creature. When it talked to me in Yiddish, let me tell you, I almost died."

"What did it sound like?" asked the Rabbi.

"A little like a Galitz-eeyana," [6] replied Boris. "But I would like to bring it here so we can all question him."

This was promptly agreed to and the E.T. was ushered before the Council. For a few minutes they all just stared at him. Finally, Rivka spoke up.

---

[4] The *tallis* or *tallit* is the prayer shawl.
[5] *Tsitsis* are the fringes at the ends of the prayer shawl.
[6] Galitzia is a region in the general area.

"You're sure built funny," she said. "How can you see without any eyes?"

The E.T. responded, "You will notice an antenna at the front of my head. This antenna affords me perfect vision in a 360-degree range."

"Not bad," said the Balagoola. "But without a nose, how can you smell?"

"My civilization has developed a scientific process whereby we call smell through our skin. This solved the problem of a stuffy nose."

"Ain't that something!" said Rivka. "But we hear you talking to us and we don't see any lips. How do you do that?"

"I am able to accomplish this through highly-developed brain waves. I am able to communicate to you in your language directly from my brain."

"That's terrific," said the Balagoola, "but I see that you're wearing a little kippah, a little skull cap, on the top of your head. What, may I ask, is that in your civilization?"

"That is a body temperature control device. It regulates my body heat so that I may live in any environment."

"That's a cute little skull cap," said the Rabbi. "Does everyone on your planet wear one of them?"

"Not the Goyim!"

MATZAH-MATTA-U?

By Mel Powell

(from a story by Bud Rosenthal)

[Spoiler alert! Jewish readers may want to skip this note and start reading the story. Everyone else needs to know that part of the Passover (Pesach in Hebrew) ritual is to ask the "Four Questions," after which we learn the history of the holiday. The questions are opened with the general query, "Why is this night different from all other nights?" Then, the four sub-questions...on all other nights, we...but on this night specifically instead we..." You don't need a full lesson in Passover (although it never hurts!), but you need to know this much. Oh, and one more thing. The Hebrew words "Ma nishtana ha-laila ha-zeh" mean "Why is this night different? You'll figure it out. Now go...enjoy.]

Everyone knows that Shloime the Student now attends the Vitipsk-Gaboynya *yeshiva*.[7] But few know the true story of how Shloime almost became the first person ever from the little village of Chelm, where the wise fools live, to be a member of the Tsar's Royal Guards.

At the time, it was a hot topic of discussion at a meeting of the Wise Council.

"He's being what?" asked Rivka the Baker gratingly.

"He's being recrui-- being recrui-- they want him to attend their school," said Mendel the Messenger. "But why?"

"Simple," explained Berel the Beadle, "Shloime has a special talent. In our village of special talents, his talent is really special."

"What--the sour pickle thing?" asked Rivka

---

[7] A *yeshiva* is a school for Jewish study.

"Precisely," said Berel. "We all know that Shloime invented the first edible self-defense slingshot. He took two sour pickles. Then he took a noodle. So if you're about to be arrested by the Cossacks for possession of an illegal weapon, even if it's just for self-defense, you just eat the evidence."

"Brillia-- brillia-- what a great idea that was!" crowed Mendel.

"Yes, quite," agreed Berel. "And his projectiles! Mostly *kreplach*[8] and day-old bread. Plus, at *Pesach*, one of the most destructive weapons in the world: Rivka's matzah balls! One of those could take out a small house."

"Why, thank you," blushed Rivka.

"Don't forget his accuracy," chimed in Boris the Balagoola. "He once knocked the hat off of Tevye the Milkman, on his moving wagon, without mussing even a hair on Tevye's head!"

"And for this," noted Berel, "he has been recruited by the Tsar's Royal Guard Academy."

At that very moment, across town, Shloime was with a representative from that very Royal Academy. The official clanked noisily down from his horse and lifted the mask on his metal helmet. "As the person," bragged the Cossack, "who spent three weeks last year at the head of the Tsar's round table, I am authorized to recruit you. So, you want to go to Knight School?"

"No," responded Shloime, "I can't concentrate at such a late hour."

"No, no, not night school…knight school," he pronounced more carefully, "k-night with a keh-nuh."

"Oh. But how could a *nebbish*[9] like me be a Royal Guard Knight?"

"You have been selected because of your unique talent with long-range weapons," said the Cossack. "Do you think you can pass an entrance exam?"

---

[8] A *kreplach* is a dumpling.
[9] A *nebbish* is an ineffectual, timid fellow. Not terrible when self-deprecating as here; less nice about someone else!

"Maybe," worried Shloime. "So far I've been accepted at Chelm University and passed their entrance exam. I found the entrance, so I'm in."

"Well," threatened the Cossack, "the Tsar does not take 'no' for an answer! You will come to the Royal Guard Academy for Knights, and you will bring your famous slingshot!"

So Shloime packed a bag with a large supply of matzah balls and other stale tidbits and headed for the Academy in Kiev. He worried all the way there, was he strong enough to be a knight? And was he brave enough? After all, Kiev was no place for a chicken.

At the Academy, the sword-bearing cadets were amazed. Before they could get close enough to Shloime in the practice drills, the sword-less student would hit them resoundingly in their metal helmets with stale *kreplach*. Most of the cadets spent their time trying to answer the ringing in their ears.

But, despite his skills, Shloime just didn't fit in with the big, strong recruits. This was never more apparent than during the first cadet review, when the Tsar and Tsarina--their-royal-selves--inspected the knights-to-be.

The Tsar was bored, but the Tsarina was quite the perfectionist as she moved down the line. "Tuck in that chain-mail! Straighten that helmet! Tighten that chin strap! Shine that sword! Close your face-plate or go get a not-yet-invented breath mint!"

The Tsarina was tough.

Then she came to Shloime. Chelm's student stood half a head shorter than the other cadets. He wore no chain-mail garment. He carried no sword--just two pickles and a noodle, with a bag of stale matzah balls and *kreplach* tied around his waist. The only indication that he was a Royal Guard recruit was the chin strap attached to his chain-mail yarmulke. He looked and acted nothing like a knight.

The Tsarina looked at little Shloime in wonderment. Then, baffled, she turned to the Tsar, "Darling! Tell me: *Ma nishtana ha-laila ha-zeh mi-kol ha laylot?*"

NO STARCH

By Mel Powell

(from a story by Bud Rosenthal)

[For our non-Jewish readers...a "tallis" (or "tallit" depending on the Hebrew dialect) is the traditional prayer shawl, generally worn around the shoulders behind the neck. These are worn traditionally by the men. At each end, hanging down the sides when worn, are "tsitsis," the lovingly-tied string fringes. Remember them.]

It had taken years of nagging, but Selma the Seamstress had finally convinced her husband, Schneider the Tailor, to take part in the Chelm tradition of Spring Cleaning. Unfortunately, there was also another tradition in the tiny village where the Wise Fools lived: they didn't own much, but they kept everything.

Imagine the wonder and surprise when Schneider, digging through the attic, came upon an ornate cloth bag.

"What is it?" asked Selma. "Is it something we should get rid of because if it is I want you should get rid of it and not keep it and clutter up the house with it and--"

Selma was famous for talking for days on end without so much as a breath, Schneider, on the other hand, was famous for tuning her out. And so he did.

Then he opened the bag--and was stunned into even more silence than usual when in Selma's presence. Then, suddenly, he rushed out of the house, found his friend Mendel the Messenger, and dragged him back to his attic, "Look! It is amazing!" exulted Schneider. "You recall when I told you about my great-great-grandfather?"

"I rememb-- I rememb--yes, you told me about him," answered Mendel.

"Well this...this marvel...this is his *tallis*! This prayer shawl is over one hundred years old! Feel the silky texture! Such workmanship! Observe the intricacy of the fringes--and this was even before the invention of *tsitsis* implants! Look at it, dear friend!"

Mendel examined it. "Looks wonder-- looks wonder-- doesn't look a day over sixty-five. But a bit dus-- a bit dus-- gotta get it cleaned."

Schneider agreed. The Tailor was an expert on fabrics, but he did not possess the delicate equipment needed to launder this *tallis* correctly, so he set out in search of an establishment that could do the cleaning for him.

First he tried Chelm's own cleaners, operated by Shmuel the Shcrubber. Shmuel was a kind man, but he had inhaled too many soap bubbles in his time.

"What is this?" asked Shmuel.

"My great-great-grandfather's prayer shawl."

"And he couldn't bring it in himself?"

"My dear Shmuel, he's been gone tor over seventy years."

"Let me know if you find him."

By then, Schneider had decided it might be best to take his *tallis* elsewhere. Searching high and low for someone who would launder this delicate prayer shawl, with its beautiful fringes and fine embroidery, carefully, he at last left it in the care of a Russian cleaner in Kiev, a man who was renowned for once having been given the task of cleaning the Tsar's finest robe during a state visit.

Much later, Mendel saw Schneider hustling out of Chelm on his ox-cart. "What's the hurr-- what's the hurr-- where you going so fast?" asked Mendel.

"Six weeks!" called Schneider over his shoulder. "It took six weeks, but the cleaner in Kiev has finished cleaning my great-great-grandfather's *tallis*!"

Schneider burst into the Kiev cleaners. The Russian recognized him and brought out the prayer shawl, neatly folded in its bag. "My good sir," intoned the shopkeeper, "what a lovely garment, it was an honor to clean it for you and your dear departed grandfather in his memory. That will be six hundred kopecks."

"Six hund--" Schneider nearly choked on the huge price. "Are you trying to take me to the cleaners?? Six hundred kopecks to launder a simple prayer shawl?"

"Of course, The labor cost was astronomical!"

"Labor cost? For cleaning a prayer shawl?"

"Absolutely," confirmed the Russian. "Do you have any idea how long it took us to untie all those little knots?"

FOOD

1. You Are What You Eat
2. It's All In The Presentation
3. Picky, Picky, Picky
4. Throw Another Log In The Air Conditioner

From kosher laws to dining establishment behavior, food is central to Jewish life. Why should Chelm be different?

In fact, now might be a time to remind everyone of two old Jewish jokes.

First: for crossword puzzle enthusiasts, what's a nine-letter word spoken by a Jewish grandmother that means "I love you?" Answer: "Eateateat!"

Second: with the exception of Yom Kippur (when Jews fast from sundown to sundown and then typically "break" the fast with a sledgehammer), what three sentences combine to describe every Jewish holiday?

1. They tried to kill us.
2. We won.
3. Let's eat!

(No holidays were harmed in the making of this chapter, though.)

(See also "White Meat or Dark" and "Ballad of Boris The Kid" in the Animals chapter; "The Bialy-Shtarker, "Commerce," and "Why Is This Salesman..." in the Commerce chapter; "Heaven McChicken" in the Death chapter, "An Endangered Species" in the Legal Troubles chapter; and "The Craving" in the Health and Aging chapter; for a little more food discussion.)

YOU ARE WHAT YOU EAT

By Jane Powell

[We won't provide a treatise here on what makes kosher foods kosher. The basics are that you don't mix milk products with meat products, and both pork and shellfish are a no-no. To ensure that food fits the rules, much of it is prepared or produced under rabbinical supervision.]

While walking home from the Synagogue in Chelm, the tiny village where the Wise Fools live, the Great Rabbi saw one of his dearest friends and most devoted congregants, Pincus the Pious, a learned man who could usually--and respectfully--win any argument with his Beloved Rabbi.

The Rabbi, who always enjoyed his debates with Pincus, started to walk faster, to catch up to his friend.

Suddenly, horrified, the Rabbi saw Pincus go into Chelm's only non-kosher establishment: the Chinese restaurant.

Now the only reason that Chelm even had a Chinese restaurant was because visiting dignitaries from other villages in the Russian Pale had developed a taste for this foreign cuisine, not to mention having no idea how kosher meals work at all.

The Great Rabbi was shocked. He couldn't believe what he was seeing. Standing at the door, he observed Pincus sit down at a table, talk with a waiter, and gesture at a menu.

A short time later the waiter reappeared, carrying a platter of mu shu *kreplach*,[1] gefilte catfish, won ton in lobster sauce, shrimp *latkes*,[2]

---

[1] A *kreplach* is a dumpling. And none of these dishes is real…but you knew that.
[2] A *latke* is a potato pancake, usually served with sour cream or apple sauce, a tradition of Chanukah but good any time of year.

and other *treif*[3] foods that the Great Rabbi could not even bear to think about.

As Pincus the Pious picked up his chopsticks to select his first mouthful, the Rabbi could wait no longer. He burst into the restaurant and reproached his friend.

"Pincus, what are you doing? I saw you walk into this forbidden non-kosher restaurant. I watched you order this non-kosher food. And now you are about to eat this food in violation of everything we are taught about our dietary laws and with an apparent enjoyment that does not befit your pious reputation!"

Pincus, never at a loss for words, replied, "My dear Rabbi, you said you saw me enter this restaurant?"

The Rabbi nodded. "Yes, Pincus. I saw that."

Pincus continued, "And you saw me order this food?"

"Yes, Pincus," lectured the rabbi, "I saw that, too!"

"And you saw the waiter bring me this food?"

"Yes, Pincus, all of that, with my own eyes!"

"And, finally, dear Rabbi, you saw me starting to eat all of these delicacies?"

Sadly now, the Great Rabbi nodded. "Yes, Pincus, that I also saw. And that I had to prevent. Pincus--a pious man like you--what were you thinking?"

Pincus smiled. "Rabbi, I knew you were behind me on the street and I saw you at the window after I sat down. With all due respect, I don't see the problem here. As you said yourself, the entire time I have been under rabbinical supervision!"

---

[3] *Treif* means non-kosher, but you surely figured that out, too.

IT'S ALL IN THE PRESENTATION
By Charles M. Powell

The Rabbi of Chelm had a problem. Now Chelm, as you know, was the village where the Wise Fools all lived. Its Rabbi was one of the wisest and brightest of all. But the Rabbi was a learner and a searcher. There were things--even forbidden things--that he felt obliged to experience. Among the greatest of these things was the absolutely verboten experience of tasting pork.

How, said the Rabbi to himself, can I warn my people of evils if I have not myself experienced the evil? Some are beyond the pale. But what, he asked, is so terrible about pork?

The Rabbi of Chelm, a pious man, began a dialogue with his God.

"So what happens," he asked God, "if I taste pork just once?"

"What are you, *mishuga*?"[4] replied God.

"But God...I mean it only as an experiment," said the Rabbi.

"You want to experiment," said God, "get a chemistry set."

"I've got to try it once," said the Rabbi.

"So try it once," said God. "You want I should validate your parking for the privilege? Go already!"

A one-time tasting of pork is no small *gedilla*.[5] One does not merely walk into the equivalent of a diner and order a ham-and-cheese sandwich. So the Rabbi of Chelm did his research--his due diligence, as it were. What he learned was that a mere 200 kilometers from Chelm there existed a Restaurant of Restaurants, an Inn of Inns. In addition to being a resort for the wealthy, its dining room had a special dish: Roast, you should pardon the expression, Suckling Pig, presented on a sterling silver platter, an apple in its mouth, mint sprigs around, and a ribbon on its tail.

---

[4] Crazy!
[5] A *gedilla* is a big deal, as in momentous event, not business transaction.

So the Rabbi, purely as an experiment, mind you, made himself a reservation. He convinced his congregation that he needed a weekend off to rest and renew himself. And off he went, the 200 kilometers to his wonderful resort--where none of his fellow villagers would see him taste pork.

He checked in, he was given a magnificent room, and he soon showed his face in the restaurant.

The Captain, not to be confused with a lover of Jews, brought the Rabbi a slivovitz on the rocks. "What would you like for dinner, Mister Rabbi?" he inquired.

"I will have your specialty, please," replied the learned man.

"If you will permit me to put in my two kopeck's worth," said the Captain, "we are famous for our Brisket...or our flanken...or even our broosteckle."

"Thank you," said the Rabbi, "but I prefer the specialty of the house."

The Captain smiled. "But Mister Rabbi, the specialty is Roast Suckling Pig, served on Sterling Silver, with an apple in its mouth, mint sprigs and a red ribbon upon its tail. You, a rabbi, understand this, yes?"

"Of course," said the Rabbi.

Settling back to enjoy the experience, the Rabbi was amazed to see the last thing he expected--when one of his congregants, Berel the Beadle, walked into the dining room.

"So this is where you decided to come for rest," said the Beadle. "Not a bad place."

A congregant, about to see him eat pork? But the Rabbi, who could think on his feet with the best, was not the least bit perplexed. He turned to Berel and said: "You have no idea, my dear Beadle, how wonderful this place really is. Earlier today, I arrived and was given a magnificent room, with a real fireplace and a bed made of the finest goose feathers. In my room there was brandy and fine books.

"I discovered three swimming pools on the premises. One, a cold pool, one heated; and one empty--just in case I didn't swim. Everything, I mean everything about this place is presented so well."

At that moment, the Captain brought the Roast Suckling Pig, in the grand tradition--Roast Suckling Pig, served on sterling silver, with an apple in its mouth.

Berel the Beadle almost fainted. "Pork, dear Rabbi?!?"

The Rabbi smiled. "See what I mean," he said. "For dinner tonight I ordered a baked apple. And see how well they present it!"

PICKY, PICKY, PICKY
By Mel Powell

Particular is Particular, you know what I mean? Some people are so picky, so choosy…

Chelm, where the Wise Fools all live, is a tiny, poor village in Western Russia. A "Boris's Big *Boychik*,"[6] you won't find. A "Cossack's Fried Chicken"…forget about it. Maybe, if you're lucky, a "Jake in the Box."

So, it shouldn't surprise you that there was only one restaurant in all of Chelm. But this restaurant, poor though it was, came up with new tastes almost every day. They were the first to serve a giant portion of fish, called the Big Mack-erel. They were the first to provide a ten-person special, kosher beef, called the Filet *Minyan*.[7] And then one day their master cook, Shepsil the Chef, invented a strange meal of a disk of dough, melted cheese, tomato sauce, and sometimes strange ingredients on top, which for no reason anyone in Chelm understood, he called…Pizza.

So ask me who should walk into the restaurant one afternoon? A middle-aged *Farbisiner*[8] from Fahrshimilt, a farming facility five furlongs from Fartig's Furriers.

The waiter came over. "You want you should order lunch?"

"Absotively! But first, let me introduce myself," said the stranger, "I am 'Particular Pincus.' In a minute, you will know why I am called by this admittedly odd name. I've heard about your brand-new dish called Pizza. I would like to order a Pizza."

---

[6] *Boychik* is a term of endearment for a young male, but you probably figured that out.
[7] A *minyan* is a gathering of ten Jews, old-school-traditionally males only, a minimum attendance for certain prayers. Pronounced MIN-yan…not mi-GNON like the steak, but you get the gag.
[8] A *farbisiner* is a sourpuss.

The waiter shrugged--a time-honored tradition among waiters. His reply: "What's so particular?"

"Glad you asked," continued Pincus. "If you want I should ever come back to this establishment, I must insist that the dough used in my pizza be wheat harvested during the month of *Adar*." [9]

"You got," yawned the waiter.

"Hold on just ein momento," cried Pincus, "You think that's all? That's not all. The cheese...it must come from the milk of a Litvak[10] cow, no other kind. The tomato sauce must be thick enough that a wooden spoon can stand up in it...but only for six minutes, not a second longer."

"Cheese, Litvak; tomato sauce, wooden spoon, is that all?" ho-hummed the waiter.

"Not so fast," cautioned Particular Pincus. "Let's talk toppings, I want you should give me pepperoni. But not just any pepperoni, since of course we cannot mix a meat product with the cheese. So I insist on pepperoni...made from soy."

"Soy?" asked the waiter.

"Soy!" said Pincus.

"Out of soybeans from Minsk or soybeans from Vitipsk-Gaboynya?" asked the waiter.

"I'm impressed," said Pincus, "But from Vitipsk-Gaboynya, of course."

"Of course," said the waiter. "Anything else?"

"Just one more thing. A sprinkling of garlic. But not just any garlic, it must be garlic grown on the north side of the farm, not the south. Doesn't matter which farm. I'll give you that one small break."

"North side. Right," said the waiter.

---

[9] *Adar* is a month on the Jewish calendar, around March.
[10] *Litvaks* are Lithuanian Jews of this era.

"Now," said Particular Pincus, "you'll read that back so I know you've got my order down to the letter?"

"Of course, sir," said the waiter. "Pizza. Dough from wheat harvested in the month of Adar, cheese from a Litvak cow, tomato sauce of a particular thickness, soy pepperoni, northern-grown garlic."

Pincus smiled. "Thank you. Good luck."

The waiter smiled. "No, thank you, sir."

He turned toward the kitchen, caught the eye of Shepsil the Chef, and yelled: "Shepsil! Give me a number four!"

THROW ANOTHER LOG IN THE AIR CONDITIONER
By Charles M. Powell

It was maybe the worst winter in the history of Chelm. You know Chelm, where the wise fools all lived? Anyway, the cold came down from Siberia, the snow was up to their *pupiks*[11] and, in general, the villagers were a wee bit on the cranky side.

Which brings us to the one restaurant in Chelm, the Kosher Kasbah. What a place! The decor was from Morocco...the waiters were from Galitzia...the owner was from Greece...the chef was from Poland...and the food was from hunger.

It was Saturday night and the Kasbah was jammed, Chelmites were waiting two hours in the snow for a table. Praying and resting on the Sabbath had created a huge collective appetite, so the restaurant was packed with hungry, cranky people, grumbling into their borscht, yelling at the waiters, and generally being socially unpleasant.

Boris the Balagoola called the waiter over. "Mister Waiter-Person...in this sad excuse for a dining establishment, it is cold like a tundra."

"Like a what?" asked the poor waiter.

"A tundra, a tundra," snapped the Balagoola. "It's like a Russian Steppe with ice on it."

"We don't have that," said the waiter. "We only have vodka."

"Listen, idiot," stormed Boris, "It's very, very cold in this place. Is there any way you could turn up the heater or something, I shouldn't freeze off my *latkes*?"[12]

"Right away, sir," and off went the waiter.

---

[11] The *pupik* is the bellybutton. Or navel, for you medical folks.
[12] A *latke* is a potato pancake, usually served with sour cream or apple sauce, a tradition of Chanukah but good any time of year. Here it's just used as a metaphor, but you knew that.

It didn't take twenty minutes and the Balagoola was bellowing once again. "Waiter, what are you doing, trying to melt us? Too much heat, too much, already. Turn down the heater before my borscht curdles and my pirogen start to fry."

"Right away, sir," said the waiter, and scampered away.

Well, my friends, this went on for half the night. "Turn up the heater…turn down the heater…too cold…too hot…" It was fright night for the poor waiter.

In a corner table, Rivka the Baker called the waiter over, "I must commend you for how you are dealing with my obnoxious friend Balagoola. It's unbelievable what he's putting you through…up with the heater, down with the heater. How do you endure it?"

"That's all right, Madam Baker, I don't mind," smiled the waiter. "Our restaurant doesn't have a heater."

GAMBLING AND GAMES

1. I Got The Horse Right Here
2. Let It Ride
3. Without A Paddle
4. When Chelm Freezes Over

Of note here in the first story is not the gambling itself, but the unique relationship Jews have with their deity. Here that relationship is imputed to everyone…if you feel the need to argue with the almighty, argue!

The second story is merely about perspective.

And the third and fourth bring sports to Chelm.

(See also "Bird Brain" in the Animals chapter for a little more wagering.)

I GOT THE HORSE RIGHT HERE
OR
THE SERMON ON THE MOUNT

By Charles M. Powell

[Spoiler alert! Jewish readers, please start reading the story! For our non-Jewish friends, you might not be fully aware that the little object Jewish men wear atop their heads for prayers (or always, for the most observant and orthodox) is called a "kipah" (kee-PAH) in Hebrew most better known in English usage as a yarmulke, the Yiddish word. Although somehow you will rarely if ever hear the "R" pronounced. Read on!]

His name was Gimpel the Gambler and he lived in Chelm, the village where the wise fools all lived. He was one of the few non-Jews in the village, in fact.

But Gimpel, while not Jewish, still fit in quite nicely with the Wise Fools; he was the worst gambler known to the region, and he was down to his last few kopecks. Depressed, he went to his church in the next village over, to have a little chat with the God of us all.

"God," cried Gimpel, "what are you doing to me?"

"You called, my son?" sayeth the Lord.

"You bet," said Gimpel.

"No, *you* bet," reply-eth God.

"That's my problem," continued the Gambler. "All my life I've been a good person. I give to everything, provided I got it. I go to church--you'll pardon the expression--religiously. I got one bad habit, the gambling, but all these years, I gotta figure that by now you owe me."

"I owe you?" thundered the Lord. "I created you!"

"You'll pardon my impertinence, your Holyship, but did I ask you to? And who's to blame for my gambling? Begging your worship, but if you created me then you are responsible for my faults!"

A long pause ensued. Finally, the Lord cleared his throat.

"An interesting point you raise," sayeth the Holy One. "Alright, my son, I have decided: the Lord owes you one favor. What is your pleasure?"

"My pleasure," cried Gimpel, "has nothing to do with this discussion. As far as a favor...is it possible to have an all-winning day at the Vitipsk-Gaboynya Racetrack just once, O King of Kings?"

"What then?" spake the Lord. "On this day next week you will win each race upon which you wager. You must remember, however, that you are to bet only on the horse whose name refers to a hat."

"A hat?" queried the Gambler.

"And only a hat," replied the Lord. "But after this one day of complete success, you may never gamble again."

Gimpel knew that he had to make a killing. This was his last chance, so he sold everything he owned to raise cash. He sold his cart to Tevye the Milkman for twelve Rubles. He sold his library of book--one book--to Shloime the Student for six kopecks. To Boris the Balagoola went his copper samovar.

The fateful day arrived and Gimpel was ready. In the first race, sure enough, there was a horse named Bella's Bonnet. Gimpel wagered conservatively, testing the word of God. The horse won by ten lengths.

In the next race, Gimpel saw a horse named Copsin's Cap. Gimpel bet all he had--and won. All day long, the gambler could do no wrong.

He was rolling in rubles. On the last race of the day he bet it all, using the same system. The horses ran, the crowd cheered...and Gimpel lost.

"How can this be?" screamed the Gambler, "God, you promised!"

So, once again, the Lord spoke to Gimpel. "I promised what I promised, my son, I am a God of my word. What was the name of the losing horse you bet on?"

"I followed your advice to the letter, your Bigness," cried the Gambler. "In the final race, I bet on Chernobyl Chateau."

The Lord again cleared his throats. "My son, a chateau is a house. Chapeaux means hat."

Gimpel started to cry.

The Lord asked him if he remembered the name of the horse that won.

"It was a Japanese horse, I think, Lord."

"A Japanese horse, Gimpel? What was its name?"

"Its name?" cried the Gambler. "Its name was 'Yamaka.'"

LET IT RIDE

By Mel Powell

The tiny village of Chelm, where the wise fools lived, was really poor. How poor was it? It was so poor that a thief once broke into the town treasury, took one look, and donated five kopecks.

"Don't think we're the only ones who are poor," said Rivka the Baker. "You heard?"

"Heard what?" thundered Boris the Balagoola.

"Just to make some money, they opened a casino!"

"Who did?" inquired Schneider the Tailor.

Explained Rivka, "A tribe of Indians from America has come to the Pale. Someday the Americans will figure out that these people are not from India, but for now…"

"Can we do this, too?"

"No, my good Tailor, we cannot open a casino. Only they are permitted by the Tsar to run this casino."

The Council of Elders sent Boris and Rivka to investigate, and-- two hours of back-seat driving from Rivka later--Boris pulled his ox-cart up to the Indians' Casino. They were greeted at the door by a friendly fellow. "Welcome to our casino."

"Welcome to the Pale!" replied Rivka politely.

"Thank you. It is nice to see such a friendly Pale face. Allow me to introduce myself. My name is Flowing From River."

"My name," boomed the Balagoola, "is Boris, and this is *Kvetching* From *Tsouris*."[1] Rivka rolled her eyes and told the greeter her real name.

And they entered the casino to look around. They decided to separate, promising to meet in an hour.

---

[1] *Kvetching* is complaining and *tsouris* is trouble.

Later, outside for some fresh air, Boris found Gimpel the Gambler rocking back and forth in great discomfort next to a small wooden shack. Just then a Cossack pushed his way past, put a kopeck into a slot, and opened the door and entered the tiny shack.

"These Americans!" complained Gimpel. "You got maybe a kopeck I can borrow for when this Cossack is done?"

"What's this?" asked the confused Balagoola.

"The Americans have invented the first Pay Outhouse. But I've lost all my money at the games, and now I can't afford to get into the outhouse!"

"You gotta pay to use the outhouse?" thundered Boris. But, however large and stupid, Boris had a heart of gold. He gave the poor fellow a kopeck and went to look for Rivka.

The door to the outhouse opened and, nodding pleasantly, the Cossack held the door open for Gimpel. Amazed at his good fortune of not having to pay, the Gambler entered the outhouse, still in possession of Boris's single kopeck.

Which Gimpel, when he returned to the casino, bet on his lucky number: seven. Suddenly he had two kopecks. He let it ride. Two became four, four became eight, and, before three hours of incredible Luck had passed, Gimpel the Gambler had become the richest man in the Pale!

Back in Chelm, Rivka reported to the Council, "It's not such a wonderful idea, this casino. Some fellow cleaned them out already."

The Council dropped the idea and the matter was forgotten.

Until one week later when Rivka the Baker rushed over to the Balagoola, "Did you hear? Turns out that the man who got rich is the one you gave the kopeck to...and he wants to reward his benefactor!"

"A reward!" boomed Boris with glee. Thanking Rivka, he ran to his ox-cart and headed for the home of the rich man he had helped.

"Greetings," said Gimpel, "but who are you?"

"You don't remember me? I'm here for my reward!"

"A reward for what? What have you ever done for me?"

"Now listen here," said Boris, raising himself with menace to his full I.Q. "I gave you one kopeck, and from that kopeck you made a fortune, and now you say you want to reward the man who made it all possible. That's me!"

The Gambler laughed. "What are you talking? It's not you. I want to thank the Cossack who held the outhouse door open!"

WITHOUT A PADDLE

By Charles M. Powell and Mel Powell

Shloime the Student had a fortunate experience when he was selected to be Chelm's first Exchange Student. As often happens in the village of wise fools, the Council of Elders was unclear on the concept, and Shloime was exchanged for a cow and two chickens.

But, during the month he spent in Kiev, Shloime learned a few things.

"I heard about a boat race," he breathlessly told the Council of Elders on his return to Chelm. "A school puts seven people into a canoe, and you row as fast as you can, and so does the school on the other side of town, and you see who wins. We could do this!"

And with that the Council of Elders agreed that the Chelm *yeshiva*[2] should compete, and the Council sent Mendel the Messenger to Vitipsk-Gaboynya to challenge the Russian university.

On the day of the race, Shloime and six fellow students from Chelm arrived in Vitebsk, put their boat in the water, took their positions…and the race was on.

The Vitipsk-Gaboynya University boat won the five-minute race by twenty minutes.

Humbled, Shloime returned to Chelm to report to the Council of Elders, then went to see the Rabbi, hoping for consolation.

"Be proud," consoled the Rabbi, "it was your first attempt. The Chelm *yeshiva* will do better next time. Tell me, Shloime, you are a student. Did you learn any lessons, you and your six teammates in the boat?"

"Of course, Rabbi," said Shloime. "And what we've decided to do next time is to do what the Vitipsk-Gaboynya team did, the opposite of our method. In their boat, *six* people rowed and only *one* yelled!"

---

[2] A *yeshiva* is a school for Jewish study.

WHEN CHELM FREEZES OVER
By Mel Powell

[A note of context. This story was written in the early summer of 1993, shortly after the Los Angeles Kings of the National Hockey League had reached the championship final for the first time in franchise history but lost the Stanley Cup to the Montreal Canadiens. It was written for Shofar synagogue is Los Angeles, and the author was rather well known to be a lifelong fan of the Kings. The story should speak for itself except for one over-the-top inside moment--you'll figure it out--being written around a fairly old joke; but offering up this context couldn't hurt. The author also must add that his beloved Kings went on to win the Stanley Cup in 2012 and again in 2014.]

Berel the Beadle banged his ceremonial gavel, "I hereby call to order this special meeting of the Wise Council of Elders."

Now, a special meeting was not exactly unheard of, but it was rare indeed. When one of the Wise Fools of the tiny village of Chelm requested a special meeting, it meant that something important was about to happen.

Rivka the Baker rose. "Thank you, Berel, for agreeing to my request for this meeting. I hereby place in nomination, for an honor bestowed upon few, the name of Shloime the Student to be inducted into the repository of our greatest inventions, the Chelm Chall of Fame!"

The chaos that followed could only be described in one word, "hubbub," a word which had led years earlier to the induction of Berel the Beadle into the Chelm Chall of Fame. Berel's *bubbe*[3] often babbled. This bothered Berel. Whenever Berel the Beadle's *bubbe* babbled, Berel blurted, "Huh, *bubbe*?" Hence the invention of the word "hubbub."

---

[3] *Bubbe* (BUH-bee) is a Yiddish nickname for a grandmother.

The Chelm Chall of Fame was devoted to all of the greatest inventions of Chelm. Boris the Balagoola, for example, was a Chall-of-Famer for his invention of the ox-phone. The phone didn't work, but who's gonna tell that to Boris--you?

Rivka had been inducted for her invention of the world's hottest *chrain*[4]--so hot that, as legend had it, the *chrain* was once turned down even by a starving sheep. This led to the naming of the entire region known as The Ewe-*chrain*.

Berel banged the gavel again to quell the continuing chaos, "Shloime, as is customary you will please describe the invention for which Rivka offers you this great honor."

"It would be my privilege, Please, let us adjourn to the shores of Lake Latke."

Mendel the Messenger was flabbergasted, "You mean outsi-- outsi-- in this weather?"

"Rivka defended her nominee. "Yes, Mendel, this is the worst cold snap we have ever had. Who ever heard of Chelm freezing over in the middle of June? But trust me; it's worth the trip. Once you've seen the invention, you'll know why Shloime deserves to be inducted into the Chelm Chall of Fame."

Grumbling, the Council members bundled up and trudged out to the frozen lake, There, Shloime explained his new game. "This morning, Rivka and I were carrying some food across the lake to Yenta the Matchmaker, Rivka unfortunately slipped on the ice, and a single *knaidlach*[5] fell out of her bag and slid across the frozen surface. I reached out with one of Rivka's rolling pins for the now-frozen *knaidlach* but all I did was k-nock it back to Rivka. Then she k-nocked it back to me, and I k-nocked it back to her, and so on. We both realized that this was fun! I call my new game K-nock *Knaidlach*."

"So," prompted Schneider the Tailor, "tell us some more about this k-nockey shtick."

---

[4] *Chrain* is horseradish. The rocket-fuel kind, not the mild, cute kind.
[5] A *kneidlach* is a dumpling.

"Tell, shmell," boomed Boris, "Let's play!"

"OK," agreed an enthusiastic Shloime. "We start the game by having two people go to the frozen *knaidlach*, which I have put in the middle of the lake, and face each other. One of them will then make off with the *knaidlach*. I call this a face off."

"I volunteer!" shouted Boris.

"Good!" said Shloime. "Go take a face off."

The Balagoola rose menacingly, "Whose face?"

Berel called for order, "For safety's sake, perhaps we should suspend that rule. So what else happens, Shloime?"

The student continued, "We also have punishments for certain bad behavior."

"Such as?" wondered Schneider.

"This morning," noted an embarrassed Shloime, "I was forced to give Rivka the Baker our new game's first penalty. I made her sit on that large, flat rock. She was sentenced to two minutes for nagging."

"It was a bad call!" argued Rivka.

"That should be four minutes," retorted Boris, still bitter over losing the chance to take a face off.

"Wait a minute!" announced Shloime. "I have just this moment invented a new rule."

"So what's this rule?" asked Rivka.

"I don't know how to use this yet," Shloime explained, "but remember when Kalman the Karpenter tripped over his own fishing pole and fell off the side of the pier? We can call the rule 'off side.'"

"Is there a penalty for that?" asked Rivka.

"That depends on how far off the side you fall."

Just then Boris noticed a flash of metal, "Say, Schneider, what's that nice silver chalice of hot tea you're holding?"

"It's just a mug I bought for my cousin Stanley in North America. But it was so nice that I decided to keep it."

"Oh," ruminated Boris, "So you're drinking from Stanley's Cup."

"Well…almost."

*** ***

And that was how the residents of the tiny village of Chelm spent a cold but enjoyable morning, playing the new game of K-nock *Knaidlach* on frozen Lake Latke.

Later that day, two important things happened, First, the unseasonable cold snap suddenly ended, and a hot summer sun came out and melted the ice.

And second, that evening, Shloime the Student was, by unanimous vote of the Wise Council of Elders, inducted into the Chelm Chall of Fame far the invention of his brilliant even newer game…water polo.

HEALTH AND AGING

1. I'm All Ears
2. What's His Name's Memory Course
3. The Tooth And Nothing But The Tooth
4. The Day Chelm Stood Still
5. The Craving
6. The Miracle of Birth
7. Forgive Me

We get older. Things happen. We're not saying we're complaining, it beats the alternative, but…what was, was.

(See also "The Witness" in the Legal Troubles chapter and "Marital Bliss" in the "Marriage/Divorce" chapter for other takes on aging.)

I'M ALL EARS
By Mel Powell

Got a problem? Need to talk it out with a sympathetic ear? There was no one in the tiny village of Chelm, where the wise fools lived, better suited to handle such problems than kindly old Lipkis the Listener.

When Tevye the Milkman's cow went dry for two weeks, Tevye sought out Lipkis, and Lipkis listened. When Rivka the Baker's yeast went flat, she sought out Lipkis, and Lipkis listened. Even when Mendel the Messenger got the hiccups, compounding an already-serious communication problem, Mendel sought out Lipkis, and Lipkis, against all odds, listened. And everyone always felt better! What a *mensch*[1] was Lipkis!

Mind you, no one's problem was ever solved. But kindly old Lipkis always listened. The villagers were so appreciative that they even pooled their money and gave him two chickens, the best seat at the Great Synagogue, and the first wristwatch in Chelm.

Then Lipkis himself developed a problem, and he sought out Rivka for advice. "Rivka, the tables are turned, and I need your help!"

"Anything, old friend," said Rivka. "Here, have a cookie."

"Thank you. It's like this. My good wife Zelda has suddenly developed a terrible hearing problem, and I don't know what to do. She refuses to admit that she has a problem!"

"That's no problem," promised the Baker, and she proposed a plan. Excited, Lipkis the Listener decided to try it.

Lipkis went home and, leaving Zelda busily preparing dinner in the kitchen, he went to the bedroom at the back of the house, "Zelda, my darling," he hollered at the top of his lungs, "what's for dinner?" Lipkis waited but heard no reply at all.

---

[1] A good person; it is a high compliment to call someone a *mensch*.

The Listener then walked to the bedroom door, and bellowed again, "Zelda, my darling, what's for dinner?"

Nothing.

Finally, sure that now he could prove to Zelda that she had a hearing problem, Lipkis walked to the kitchen door, and shouted for the third time, "Zelda, my darling, what's for dinner?"

Angrily, Zelda spun away from the stove, and shouted back,

"Pot roast, Lipkis! For the third time already, pot roast, you *shmendrick*![2] And for the fifth time, *you* have the hearing problem!"

Mendel spread the word of this crisis. The entire concerned village sought to help Lipkis the Listener with his hearing loss, so the Wise Council of Fools was quickly convened.

"I have a solution!" announced Berel the Beadle. "My second cousin's sister-in-law's brother's barber from Kiev has heard of a new invention--a hearing aid device!"

Immediately, Boris and his speedy ox-cart were dispatched to bring back this invention. And, sure enough, the hearing aid device seemed to do the trick!

One day, a few weeks later, Lipkis was out walking when he came upon Schneider the Tailor. Schneider had been away at a cross-stitch convention, and so he had not heard of the Listener's troubles. "Lipkis, what's that sticking out of your ear?" The Tailor was quickly brought up to date with the fact of the new invention. Lipkis had learned that this type of device was being manufactured by different businesses and explained this, too.

"So," said Schneider after Lipkis finished his story, "this new hearing aid device works?"

"Wonders!" raved Lipkis.

"Tell me about it!"

---

[2] This is like saying 'You turkey!" in English. Not really mean, but not nice, and insulting to an actual turkey.

"Let me tell you!" began Lipkis. "I can hear everything! This hearing aid is so wonderful, that if I were in my house, and a mosquito, wearing the softest of slippers, were to land on the window of the house of Mendel the Messenger, who as you know lives on the other side of town, while my wife Zelda was talking to me--and boy can she talk--during a thunderstorm, no less, I could hear every one of the mosquito's tiny feet land on that window! I got mine from the best of the manufacturers!"

"Amazing device!" agreed Schneider. "What kind is it?"

Lipkis looked at his wristwatch. "Two-thirty."

WHAT'S-HIS-NAME'S MEMORY COURSE

By Mel Powell

(from a story by Lew Horn)

The town crier of Chelm, the village where the Wise Fools lived, was having memory problems.

Although Mendel the Messenger's father, the beloved Mordecai the Messenger (now Emeritus) had memory problems, Mendel's condition wasn't related or hereditary. Mendel had slipped on the winter ice and had bumped his head. And now he had…what was it? Oh, yes…memory problems.

He forgot to announce baby namings and weddings and bar mitzvahs. At times, he forgot his friends' names. At times, he forgot his own name. He tried his best, but he just couldn't remember.

"So, Mendel," bothered Rivka the Baker one day. "Did you remember to deliver my message to Sasha the Supplier from Siberia?"

"Of cour-- of cour-- certainly!" answered Mendel. "You wanted to buy six bagels and a bouq-- a bouq-- a bunch of flowers."

"What? Mendel, I said I needed to make six hundred bagels, and that I needed five sacks of flour…for the Purim *Hamantashen*![3] You're lucky I'm not, you'll pardon the expression, Haman!"

"Oh, yeah? Well, you're lucky that I'm not King Ahashu-- King Ahashu--" [4]

"Gesundheit," Rivka retorted.

---

[3] Haman was the bad guy in the story of this holiday…go back to the story for the name of the holiday…and *Hamantashen* are the traditional triangular cookies that represent Haman's signature three-cornered hat.

[4] The King in the *Purim* holiday story was Ahashueras (in Hebrew, Ahashverosh)…the point is the funny-sounding name, not his biography. But the heroine, Jewish Queen Esther, did marry him and save the day in other ways.

Such was the sad state of affairs in Chelm. One day, uncertain that Mendel would ever recover his memory without seeking help, Mendel's wife couldn't stand it anymore.

"Mendel," she said, "it is time for you to see a doctor!"

"No way-- no way-- forget about it! I hate doct-- hate doct-- medical practitioners."

"Well, how about trying that new fellow who has moved here from his tiny village in Burma? He says his new invention, holistic medicine, can cure anything!"

"I don't wann-- I don't wann-- oh, OK, I'll try it."

Off Mendel went to his appointment with the Burmese healer who had just set up shop in Chelm. "Greetings and salutations, my dear Mr. Messenger. It is so wonderful to welcome you into my humble establishment."

Mendel held up one finger. "Now listen he-- listen he-- just wait a minute. I won't take any dru-- any dru-- any medication!"

"No, no, good sir, I don't use artificial medication. Here I use only completely natural plants and herbs and flowers."

"Oh, that's goo-- that's goo-- that's much better."

"I understand from your good wife that you have memory problems. Is that correct?"

Mendel was indignant. "I beg your-- I beg your-- what are you talking about?"

"Ah, it is much worse than I thought! However, I have a solution for your problem," promised the smiling Burmese gentleman. "Take these only-natural capsules, one capsule twice each day, get plenty of rest, and your memory will return. Don't worry, I will write it all down for you. And don't forget where you put this piece of paper."

Mendel the Messenger took the small bottle of capsules and the note, He thanked the holistic doctor politely for his time and went home, not believing for a minute that a flower could cure his memory.

After all, what did the cauliflower do for him yesterday? Or was it the day before…

But these capsules seemed to be working! Mendel's memory made a dramatic recovery at last.

One day Mendel's old friend Boris the Balagoola stopped by to pay a visit. Mendel's wife quickly went to the kitchen to make some tea while the two men sat down for a chat.

"Mendel!" crowed Boris, clapping the Messenger on the back, perhaps a bit too hard. "It is so good to see you back to normal."

"It's good to see-- good to see-- I'm glad you're here, Boris."

"So tell me, Mendel, what do you call those miracle capsules that you got from this Burmese fellow?"

"Oh, that's easy. It's, um-- it's, um--. Oy! Listen, Boris, what do you call-- do you call--what's the name of the plant with the long stem that's got thor-- got thor-- that's got those pointy things on the sides, and on top has the peta-- has the peta-- has the red flower at the end?"

"You mean a rose?"

"Rose! A-ha! Precise-- Precise-- bingo!" And Mendel shouted into the kitchen, "*Rose*! What do you call those memory capsules?"

THE TOOTH AND NOTHING BUT THE TOOTH
By Charles M. Powell

"So, ask me how my tooth feels," said Boris the Balagoola.

"So how does your tooth feel?" inquired Berel the Beadle.

"Don't ask!" replied the Balagoola.

Boris was the largest man in Chelm, where the wise fools all lived. Now it stands to reason that the largest man would have the largest teeth. If you agree with my premise, you must also agree that when a man like that develops a toothache, then--oy vey, it's got to be some kind of toothache.

"So why don't you go see a dentist?" asked Rivka the Baker.

"When was the last time you saw a dentist in Chelm? Maybe once," said the Balagoola, "when the Rabbi invited his dentist cousin from Minsk to visit. That was two years ago, and--my luck--I didn't have a toothache when he was here."

The Rabbi interjected. "He doesn't have time come back to Chelm anyway. Apparently the teeth are terrible in Minsk."

"All this talk isn't helping my toothache any," complained the Balagoola.

"So if the rabbi's dentist cousin won't come here, why don't you go to the dentist?" asked Shloime the Student.

"I should make a trek like that to Minsk?" said Boris. "I don't even know if he's a good dentist."

The Rabbi had a suggestion. "Of course he is! When my cousin was here, he fixed a toothache for Tevye the Milkman. Why don't you ask him how good a dentist my cousin is?"

The Balagoola, his face swollen and his mouth throbbing, paid a visit to Tevye.

"What kind of a dentist was the fellow from Minsk?" said Tevye. "I can only answer that by relating what happened to me just last week at Schneider the Tailor's."

"Wait one minute," growled the Balagoola. "The dentist was here two years ago. Who cares what happened to you last week?"

"Be quiet and listen to me," replied the Milkman. "Two years ago the dentist worked on my tooth. Last week--"

"Again last week. Who cares from last week?"

"Last week," continued Tevye, "I was at Schneider the Tailor's getting my best coat pressed for Passover. I bent over to watch the Tailor press the coat. Unfortunately, my beard got caught in the press and under the iron. The pain--do I have to tell you--was excruciating."

Boris the Balagoola exploded. "What does this have to do with the dentist and my toothache?"

"Simple," said Tevye. "With the pain from my beard...it was the first time in two years that my tooth didn't hurt!"

THE DAY CHELM STOOD STILL

By Mel Powell based on a story by Charles M. Powell

"Rabbi, do you think there's intelligent life in outer space?" asked Rivka the Baker as she and Chelm's spiritual leader enjoyed a pleasant walk beneath the stars in the village where the wise fools lived.

At that moment, Boris the Balagoola joined them, "I have a dilemma of historic proportions, Rabbi! I can't decide what to name my new female ox. What do you think of 'Oksana?'"

The Rabbi smiled, and whispered to the Baker, "My dear Rivka, I'm not so certain there's intelligent life down here..."

Suddenly a stranger stepped out of the shadows. "I believe," he said in an unrecognizable accent, "that I can answer that question for you."

Rivka peered into the darkness at the man, but he was hidden in the shadows. Needless to say, he was as unrecognizable as his accent, "How could you answer such a question? Are you from the University of Vitipsk-Gaboynya?" wondered Rivka politely.

The man stepped out of the shadows and into the moonlight--and he was no "man!" He had three eyes! He had three arms, too! And huge ears, shaped like bagels!

Boris announced authoritatively, "He's not from Vitipsk!"

"No, my good Balagoola, I am not," said the smiling creature. "I have large ears, and three eyes and three arms, but the rest of me is identical to a Human male."

Boris looked askance. "You mean...?"

"Everything," the creature replied, "As for my name...well, it is unpronounceable, even to Humans like you, who can actually say the word CH-anukah without lapsing into a coughing fit. But you may call me...um...Schpock."

"As you wish, my good Schpock," said the Rabbi warmly, reaching to shake one of the creature's three hands. "How can we help you?"

"I have traveled far to visit your world, Rabbi. I am now stranded here, as my space-shuckle was damaged when I landed."

"A space-shuckle? Maybe I can fix it for you," suggested Boris.

"I doubt it, sir, but you are most kind to offer," said Schpock, winking at the Rabbi and Rivka simultaneously with two of his three eyes. "I have lived among many of the peoples of Earth and studied their ways. I have finally determined that I want to live out my days on your planet as a Jew."

"How wonderful!" beamed the Rabbi. "We will welcome you with open arms. No offense."

"None taken," assured the alien, shrugging all three shoulders.

"We must formally convert you to our faith, then," gushed Rivka. "First thing you gotta do to be really Jewish is you gotta learn to answer a question with a question. Can you do that?"

"Why would you do that?" replied the alien.

"Perfect!" said the Baker.

"Mr. Schpock," the Rabbi continued, "conversion to Judaism is quite an enterprise. First and foremost, you must commit yourself to our *Talmud*.[5] Study and learn! And a rabbi must then verify your understanding of our laws."

"No problem, Rabbi. I have brain capacity like Boris, here, has muscles."

"Then you must be a pretty smart guy!" crowed the Balagoola.

"Tell him about the *mikva*," urged Rivka.

The Rabbi continued "If you wish to convert, you must go to a *mikva*--it's a ceremonial bath--for ritual prayers and cleansing."

"Sounds good," said the extra-terrestrial.

Boris added his two kopecks' worth, "Ask us about the *bris*!"

---

[5] The *Talmud* is the entire body of Jewish law, but as an adjective here it means learned in the ways of Jewish law and tradition.

"What is a *bris*?" asked the alien Schpock.

"Don't ask!" said Boris.

But the Rabbi explained that all males seeking to convert must first have a circumcision. The creature raised an eyebrow, then another one, then the third one...so the rabbi tactfully described the process.

Schpock was sherioushly shaken. He turned even greener. He fixed all three of his eyes on the Balagoola's two and implored, "Be honest, Mr. Boris. Did your circumcision hurt?"

Boris smiled, "Let me tell you, Mr. Alien Star Person Schpock. After I had my circumcision, I didn't walk and talk for a year and a half!"

THE CRAVING
By Charles M. Powell

The story we are about to tell you is true. Only the facts have been altered, so as not to insult anyone living, dead, or somewhere in-between.

It was in the village of Chelm, where the wise fools all lived.

Farfel and his wife Fagel, 87 he, 86 she, lived in the retirement community. Separate little homes, one big dining room for everyone. Plus shuffleboard, which hadn't been invented yet.

It was a terrible night. Rain, snow, wind...who remembers? But terrible? No question.

Late in the evening, Fagel, sitting on the sofa of their little two-room apartment, whacked Farfel on the arm with her book. Farfel closed his book and inquired, "Vhat you vant?"

"I got a craving," she said.

"You got a vhat?"

"A craving, an 'ankering, I got to have a banana split."

"Vonderful!" sobbed Farfel. "So you'll take two aspirins and you'll call me in the morning and we'll order for you a banana split."

"I gotta have now...it's a yen."

Farfel knew when the battle was lost. "Okey, dokey, pussycat. It's 20 below zero; snow coming down like Siberia; give me already your order for this would you believe banana split, and I'll go to the kitchen behind the dining hall and get it for you."

Fagel smiled, "You're a very good husband, Farfel. You want to write down the order?"

"Hold it, hot-shot. You're the one with hardening of the brain around the arteries. I'm not the person with memory problems. You tell me, I'll bring."

Fagel collected her thoughts. Calmly, she placed her order. "Bring me two slices bananas. I don't want no one-and-seven-eighths. On top, I need three scoops ice-scream. The left scoop has to be Rocky Road. On the right, give me Cherry-cheesecake."

"And the middle scoop?"

"Ah...that's the tricky part. In the middle, I want it should be 'oney vanilla. Not plain vanilla--'oney vanilla. You heard me?"

"I heard you, I'm sitting right here."

"You sure you don't wanna write down?"

"You're the one what's senile. I don't gotta write down."

"Okay. Then on top of that, I want hot fudge. But not Hershey's-- gotta be Fox's U-bet. I know they got both in that kitchen. Gotta be Fox's U-bet. You heard?"

"I heard."

"Okay, on top of that, pineapple glaze...then whipped cream, and a full maraschino cherry. You heard me? I don't want no half cherries."

"I heard you."

"Last chance--you want maybe a pencil?"

"Enough with the 'write it down,' I got this," huffed Farfel. And with that, dear reader, this 87-year-old man put on boots, a poncho, a horse blanket...don't ask...and out into the snow he ventured, all the way to the dining room and the retirement community kitchen.

And it was slow going. Two hours later he returned...bedraggled, shivering, soaked to his *tsitsis*[6]...and onto their little table he triumphantly placed a paper bag.

Fagel, with shaking hands, opened the package lovingly brought by her husband.

The bag held three onion bagels.

---

[6] *Tsitsis* are the fringes at the ends of the prayer shawl, but we don't mean it literally here.

She looked at Farfel. She looked at the bagels.

"Look who's got hardening of the brains? I told you to write down!"

"What's the matter?" demanded Farfel. "I brought you exactly what you ordered."

"You're *mishuga*.[7] This is not what I asked for. You forgot the cream cheese!"

---

[7] Crazy!

THE MIRACLE OF BIRTH

By Mel Powell

(from a story by Bud Rosenthal)

The tiny village of Chelm, where the wise fools lived, was famous for a number of reasons, but most famous perhaps for its veritable encyclopedia of brilliant inventions.

Inventions were the topic of an unusual meeting of the Wise Council of Elders, so unusual that even the Rabbi attended.

"There has never been an invention like this one!" declared Berel the Beadle, as he led the Council down the streets of Chelm.

"It's hard to believe," noted the Rabbi, "that any invention can be as amazing as your ox phone, Boris!"

"It's even harder to believe," said Boris the Balagoola, "that any invention can be as amazing as Lipkis the Listener's Hearing Aid Device! *Nu*,[8] Lipkis?"

"What?" asked Lipkis.

"Never mind," said Boris.

"So now the Council is on the way to the home of Golda the Grandmother," continued Berel, "to see the fruits of this new invention. Rivka, since you know Golda best, why don't you explain it to us?"

"Certainly, my dear Berel. It's a pill, my fellow Council Members. A pill made up of local herbs, a little bit of matzah meal, and a whole lot of luck."

"And what does this pill do?" wondered the Rabbi.

---

[8] *Nu* is a Yiddish word with lots of uses. As in formal greeting, it's your "What's up? Or *"Que pasa?"* As an interjection during a conversation, it can mean "See what I mean?" but also "seriously, you think *that* is an important issue?" Or, here, it stands for "isn't that right?" Very useful, *nu*?

"You take a woman of a certain age, and you give her one pill a day for three weeks. This pill has made it possible for Golda, at the age of eighty-four, to get pregnant and have a happy, healthy daughter!"

"Golda's previous child was born fifty years ago!" said Boris in amazement. "She's got a new one?"

"Bingo!" said Rivka. "Remember, Sarah had Isaac at the age of ninety! So it's another great miracle."

"Was it artificial insemination?" asked Boris.

"No," explained Rivka, "it was Fischel Insemination, Fischel the Fishmonger made a donation!"

"It's a *shanda*![9] Shameful!" complained the Rabbi. "Not one kopeck to the synagogue, but for this he donates!"

Berel had time for one last question as the Council arrived at the door of Golda's house. "How did Golda, at the tender age of eighty-four, actually give birth?"

"Very carefully," answered Rivka, as she knocked on the door.

"Hello!" said Golda. "Please, come in."

And she sat them all down and served tea and honey. After twenty minutes, Berel finally asked politely, "So, dear Golda, can we see your baby?"

"Not just yet," said Golda, and she went into the kitchen and fetched her famous prune Danish, which she served all around.

"These are terrific," said Boris. "But when can we see meet the baby?"

"Soon, soon," promised Golda. "First, how about a game of mah jongg?" So as not to be rude, the Council reluctantly agreed.

Finally, Rivka could bear it no more. "Golda, we've been friends for so long...a long time. Are you stalling? Why don't you want us to see the baby?"

---

[9] *Shanda* means "a shame" and can also mean a controversy, in context, which is does a little here.

158

At last, Golda broke down. "Of course I want you to see the baby. She's a wonderful baby, and she never, ever cries! I just wish she *would* cry so I can remember where I put her!"

FORGIVE ME!

By Charles M. Powell

The High Holidays were fast approaching and the little village of Chelm, where the wise fools lived, was bustling with activity. At the regular meeting of the Wise Council of Elders, an ancient and revered custom was taking place; a custom as holy as any practiced in this village of fools.

Tradition had it that just before the High Holy Days all Chelmites would gather and "confess" to each other their wrongdoings of the previous year. Having unburdened themselves of their sins, the wise fools could then enter the Holy Days free of guilt and pure of soul.

With the full village assembled, the Rabbi spoke first: "Humbly," he cried, "I beg forgiveness of you all. I am only a simple man trying to be your spiritual leader and I fear that I may never solve all of your problems and fill all of your needs. May I have your forgiveness, please?"

"You got it, Rabbi," said Boris the Balagoola.

Shepsil the Blacksmith rose. "Seeing the Balagoola reminds me of a terrible sin that I committed this past year. Boris brought me his horse to shoe. God forgive me, I only changed the two rear shoes, but charged him for all four. Will you ever forgive me?"

The Balagoola smiled. "Since my horse only goes uphill most of the time anyway, it's no problem. You're forgiven."

"Thank you, my dear friend," said the blacksmith.

"You're welcome," replied Boris, "but you still owe me two shoes."

"While I'm confessing," said the smith, "I also did the same thing to Tevye the Milkman. I hope he'll forgive me, too."

"Who am I to forgive you?" said the Milkman. "When I paid you milk for the shoes I skimmed off the cream. We're even. Our sins are cancelled."

The Rabbi smiled ruefully. "Let's hope God thinks it works that way."

Rivka the Baker was next. "I would like to ask forgiveness of Birnbaum the Butcher. All year long I come into his shop and I frankly admit that I was impossible. I was so picky it must have driven him crazy--not to mention eating out his heart, his liver, and all those other things that only butchers know about. Will you forgive me, Birnbaum?"

"No problem," said the butcher. "Besides, I had my thumb on the scale every time, so you paid more."

"That's unforgivable," said Rivka.

The last person to unburden himself was Moishe the Elder. Moishe was the oldest man in Chelm, having survived ninety-two winters and three demanding wives. A widower for thirty-seven years, Moishe, his old bones aching, rose to address the villagers. in a quivering voice, he said, "I wish to confess to you all about Zeesel, the mailman's daughter, and myself."

Rivka laughed. "What's to tell, Moishe? You're 92 and she's 19."

The old man continued. "You all know how lonely I've been all these years. Without a woman in the house the days are long and the nights are cold. So, if you'll all forgive me, I wish to confess to seeing Zeesel."

Berel the Beadle suppressed a laugh. "Tell us, Moishe. How often do you see the young woman…the very, very young woman?"

"Well," said the Elder, "I walked her to the *mikva*[10] last night and today we went on a picnic together. Tonight we're planning a candlelit dinner…which stands to reason, as the light bulb has not yet been invented…and then tomorrow we plan to get up early and go to the old age home to visit my grandson."

---

[10] A *mikva* is ceremonial cleansing bath.

The Rabbi was perplexed. "You're an unmarried man. Zeesel is also single. Despite the obvious difference in age, you're both entitled. Tell me, Moishe. Why are you confessing to us?"

The old man smiled. "Confessing to you? I'm confessing to everyone!"

HUMAN FOIBLES AND QUIRKS

1. I Dream of Bupkis
2. Dances With Dunces
3. What, Me Worry?
4. Luck Be A *Latke* Tonight
5. Tobacco Road
6. Roses Are Red
7. Nice Material
8. Secondary Education
9. Still Going
10. Never An End To Learning
11. Who Brought The Pickles?
12. A Bridge Too Far

Nobody's perfect. Everybody's got something that makes him or her unique, different, exasperating, glorious...and not necessarily fitting into another category or chapter!

(Almost every other story could have reserved a place in this chapter, so no references this time!)

"I DREAM OF *BUPKIS*" [1]

By Mel Powell

Boris the Balagoola was undeniably a charter member of the wise fools of Chelm. Big, yes. Likeable, yes. Smart? Not even close.

As an example--now just one example, mind you--the following once happened in the village.

"My good man," asked a visitor to Chelm, "I am doing some research about education in this land. May I ask you one riddle?"

"Go ahead," agreed Boris.

"If you are your father's son but not your brother, who are you?"

Boris pondered. "I'll get back to you."

Boris was at least smart enough to know when to ask for help, so he did. He happened upon Shloime the Student and assumed that the student would be far enough along in his studies to be able to assist.

"Shloime," said Boris, "I need the answer to this riddle: if you are your father's son but not your brother, who are you?"

Shloime rolled his eyes. "Simple, dear Boris. I'm me."

"Ahh!" exclaimed Boris knowingly. "Now I understand."

Boris returned to the visitor. "I have the answer. Ask me again."

"Very well. If you are your father's son but not your brother, who are you?"

"Simple, dear sir. I'm Shloime the Student!"

So you see, Boris the Balagoola was far from a genius. The only thing lower than his I.Q. was the temperature in Siberia.

And this is the very same Boris who stumbled one day over a strange looking little lamp in an alley. "What's this? A lantern? And so tarnished!" And he took out a cloth and rubbed it vigorously.

---

[1] *Bupkis* is Yiddish for nada. Zippo. Nothing.

Need we tell you what happened next?

"Thank you! Oh, thank you!" exclaimed the Genie. "You have released me from centuries trapped in this lamp! Please, sir, ask me for anything--I will gladly grant you one wish, whatever you desire. You wish is my command!"

Boris pondered. "A wish?"

"Anything."

"Anything?"

"Anything!"

Now Boris was stupid, but he had a heart as big as his bala-goolish muscles. He reached into his pocket and pulled out a map.

"You see this area of Russia, Mr. Genie? So many *pogroms*![2] So much needless suffering. My wish, Mr. Genie, is that you put an end, once and for all, to all the pogroms here, in this land, on this map."

Now it was the Genie's turn to consider. "Sir, let me see that map. While I am grateful to you for my freedom, I am also a bit out of practice. Forgive me, but could you perhaps think of something a bit easier for me to handle than an end to all pogroms?"

Boris was disappointed, but he switched to his second choice. "In that case, your Genie-ship, I'll make it easy. My wish is to be the wisest man in all the land, so that when anyone comes up to me, I know the answer to everything!"

The Genie mulled this over, scratched his chin, considered some more, and then looked at Boris and politely asked: "May I please see that map again?"

---

[2] Merriam-Webster defines a "*pogrom*" (puh-GRUM) as "an organized massacre of helpless people." If you've ever seen "Fiddler on the Roof," although no one is murdered, you surely recall the scene when the bad Russians come into town and, for no reason, cause a lot of destruction.

DANCES WITH DUNCES
By Charles M. Powell

Remember the American Old West, when men were men and women were not enough of? Remember? This was before Kevin Costner even.

And remember the Wells Fargo stagecoach? Not the one from the commercials we got sick of. We're talking here the real McCoy. Four horses, a weather-beaten old driver, and a guy to ride shotgun.

As with most things, it turns out that "riding shotgun" was invented in Chelm, the tiny village where the wise fools lived...interesting, because shotguns hadn't been invented yet.

Still, the Tsar's army often caused trouble for the villagers, so when tensions were high, Tevye the Milkman always brought someone with him on his milk runs...to ride Bow and Arrow. Those had been invented.

On this day, the task fell to Pincus the Peddler, for the first time. Pincus was having a slow day of peddling, so he agreed to serve as Tevye's ox-cart companion for the tidy sum of twelve kopecks for the day.

Tevye loaded the milk, politely soothed his trusty ox, handed Pincus the bow and a quiver of arrows, and off they went for the day's deliveries around the region.

Just outside of town, Tevye reminded Pincus what his job entailed. "Now, partner for the day, your job is to look up the road as far as you can and tell me if you see any of the Tsar's guards."

"That's it? That's all what I gotta do? No problem."

An hour into the journey Tevye asked, "Ya see any Russian soldiers?"

"Not a one," replied Pincus.

"How about now?" Tevye asked an hour later.

"I see a dot in the distance, but who knows what it is. Could be a yak…or even a Cadill-yak…I'll keep looking."

Ten minutes later, an anxious Tevye asked again.

"Well," said the Peddler, "the dot's only about this big," and he held his fingers an inch apart, "and It looks like it could be one of the Tsar's guards, but I'm not sure yet."

"Keep looking!"

Twenty minutes later there was no doubt. Pincus poked Tevye, held his fingers four inches apart, and said, "Now he's this big. I can see he's wearing the uniform of the Tsar's army. He also looks very angry, like he's got a bunion or maybe he's constipated."

"So," said Tevye, "take the bow and arrow and shoot him before he can arrest us for being Jews or call for reinforcements!"

Pincus was shocked. "I couldn't do that. He looks angry, but also like a really nice guy."

"I'm telling you," said the Milkman, "I also try to be a nice guy but you gotta get him before he gets us!"

"Please," cried Pincus, "don't ask me to do that."

"Why not?" asked Tevye.

"Because," said Pincus, holding his fingers an inch apart, "I know him since he was this big!"

WHAT, ME WORRY?
By Charles M. Powell

Mendel the Messenger announced it from the Chelm Town Square: "Emergency meet-- Emergency meet-- we're all getting together tomorrow! Attendance is manda-- is manda-- you better be there!"

Needless to say, the entire village of Wise Fools showed up.

"So what's the big deal?" asked Rivka the Baker.

"Must be about the Tsar," replied Schneider the Tailor.

"Can't be the Tsar," said Boris the Balagoola. "He's already in his Winter Palace, snug like a schlub in a rug."

"Rug? The Tsar wears a hairpiece?" asked Berel the Beadle.

Mendel the Messenger picked up on it. "The Tsar wears a tou-- wears a tou-- wears a wig?"

The Rabbi of Chelm banged the gavel and called the Wise Fools to order. "The reason," he said, "that it was necessary to call an emergency meeting has to do with the many problems that beset our village. These problems are causing stress and anxiety."

"You mean like the high unemployment rate?" asked Rivka.

"Exactly," said the Rabbi.

"Or the poor attendance at Shabbat Services?" said Schneider.

"Exactly," said the Rabbi.

"Or the terrible shape that our roads are in?" said the Balagoola. "Even our potholes have potholes."

"Exactly," said the Rabbi.

"And how about the roof on the Great Syn...the Great Syn...the *Shul*?"[3] asked Mendel. "It lea-- it lea-- the water dri-- such a flood!"

---

[3] *Shul*, a Yiddish word, means synagogue.

"Exactly," said the Rabbi.

Rivka asked the next question: "So, you got any ideas, Rabbi?"

"Exactly...excuse me...I do indeed," replied the Rabbi, "but I will need your permission to act on my idea."

"What do you wanna do?" asked Boris.

"I wish," said the Rabbi, "to propose that the village of Chelm hire a Worrier."

"Excuse me?" inquired the Baker, "What is it a Worrier?"

"Also," said the Balagoola, "is this a Home Worrier or a Road Worrier?"

"Oh, they can worry anywhere," the Rabbi explained. "A Worrier is someone who is paid to take your problems and worry for you. If you have a toothache, you go to a Dentist. If you need butter, you go to Tevye the Milkman. Chelm and its poor people have many worries. I suggest we hire a professional Worrier.

"Think about it," continued the Rabbi. "We have a problem with the economy? Let the Worrier worry about it. The roads are bad? Give the problem to the Worrier."

Berel the Beadle was not convinced. "How much it costs us to hire this Worrier?"

"One hundred rubles a week," answered the Rabbi.

"What? Excuse me, Rabbi, but are we crazy?" exploded Berel. "We got two kopecks in the Treasury. How we gonna pay this Worrier without money?"

The Rabbi smiled. "Let *him* worry about it!"

LUCK BE A *LATKE* TONIGHT [4]

By Charles M. Powell

Throughout the ages, the calendar date Friday the 13th has struck fear in the hearts of people.

Where did the custom begin? Why, in the little village of Chelm, where the wise fools lived, of course. It all began when Berel the Beadle knocked on the door of the Great Synagogue. Now, the village of Chelm was certainly full of fools, but it was also full of very poor people. Although the Synagogue was in dire need of kopecks for much-needed repairs, money was never available. So, when Berel knocked, the response was immediate: the door of the Great Synagogue fell down.

An emergency meeting of the Wise Council of Elders was called. The answer, according to Schneider the Tailor, was that Chelm was unlucky that day. After all, the door hadn't fallen on any other day.

Rivka the Baker compounded the problem. Reuben the Roofer had been repairing her bakery roof. When Rivka entered her shop, she walked under his ladder. Reuben, the ladder, and the bakery roof all fell down at the same time. "Unlucky," agreed the Wise Council.

Boris the Balagoola also had an unfortunate situation develop this day. While driving his cart on a back road his horse was frightened by a black cat crossing his path. Boris was thrown and the load of potatoes that he was hauling was ground into vodka. The cat lapped up the vodka, became cantankerous and punched the Balagoola in the nose. [In the cat's defense, there is nothing scary or unlucky about black cats. Cantankerous, yes.]

Berel the Beadle was perplexed. "Why should all of these things happen to us on this one day? Something must be wrong with the day."

---

[4] A *latke* is a potato pancake, usually served with sour cream or apple sauce, a tradition of Chanukah but good any time of year. No significance here, though; it's just a play on the song from "Guys and Dolls."

The Wise Council voted unanimously that Friday the 13th would forevermore be listed as an official day of bad luck.

Shloime the Student delved into the religious books to find an explanation. "If," he explained, "you were to add up the Ten Commandments and the five books of Moses, and then subtract the four questions from Passover, it would add up to 13, thus explaining the bad luck."

Berel reminded Shloime that the calculations added up to eleven.

"See what I mean?" said the student. "More bad luck!"

The Rabbi, quietly listening to the discussion, could contain himself no longer. "First of all, my friends, today is Tuesday, not Friday. Secondly, it's the 21st of the month, not the 13th. The only bad luck that I am aware of is that I have the…fortune…of living here in Chelm."

So you see, there is really no need to fear Friday the 13th.

You might be just as unlucky on Tuesday the 21st.

TOBACCO ROAD
By Mel Powell

[A note: we don't encourage tobacco use or smoking...but the story remains!]

"I heard the most amazing story at the convention!" reported Berel the Beadle to the Wise Council of Fools of the tiny village of Chelm, where the wise fools lived.

"So tell us already," demanded Boris the Balagoola.

"As you know, I have just returned from the annual gathering of every *shamus*[5] of every synagogue in the region. It is the Association of Sha-mi. "

"You mean *'shamuses?'*" corrected Shloime the Student.

"You join your group, I'll join mine!" retorted Berel. "Anyway, I heard the most amazing story from Shepsil, the *shamus* of Congregation B'nai Vitipsk-Gaboynya, about Perchik, the man who almost got the *shamus* job instead of him."

And he shared Perchik's story:

Perchik walked home, depressed. Once again, he had applied for a job and, once again, he had been politely rejected. "So what happened this time?" asked his wife, Esther.

"Same as always!" said Perchik. "The job requires reading--not even writing, just reading--and I cannot read! So they wouldn't hire me as the *shamus* of B'nai Vitipsk-Gaboynya. The job is available because the former *shamus* went to America to become a screenwriter."

"You'll get another job," said Esther encouragingly.

---

[5] You learned in the book's introduction that a "beadle" is the person responsible for the set-up of the synagogue, not quite maintenance, just being sure everything is in place and ready. *Shamus* (SHAH-muss) is the Hebrew word that that person.

"No, I don't think so," said Perchik. "I'm through looking. You see, my dear, on the way home I noticed something. It's five blocks from our home to the synagogue, and there is not a single tobacco shop between here and there! I will make a job for myself, by opening my own tobacco shop!"

And so he did, opening Perchik's Pipes of the Pale.[6] He sold pipes, and tobacco, and even the Tsar's Tsigars. And all of his products came with the Surgeon General's warning, which stated: "Well, they're no worse than a *pogrom*." [7]

It was on a sunny day some ten years later that Shepsil the Shamus, from B'nai Vitipsk-Gaboynya, entered the original Perchik's Pipes. "Good day, Shepsil," said Perchik.

"Good day, Reb Perchik!" said Shepsil respectfully, for after ten years, Perchik was renowned all over the Pale. Perchik's Pipes had become a franchise, and dozens of Perchik's Pipes stores were doing terrific business, Perchik himself was worth several million rubles.

"I wonder," continued Shepsil, "how you came to such a fortune?"

"Simple!" said Perchik. "I buy a pipe for one ruble, I sell it for three rubles. That's a three-percent profit already!"

"Brilliant!" agreed Shepsil.

"And you see, I have been blessed. I have achieved all of this success even though I cannot read!"

"Millions of rubles," said Shepsil, surprised, "and you cannot read! My goodness, Reb Perchik, just think where you'd be today if you could read!"

---

[6] You also learned *this* one in the introduction, but we'll remind you: The Pale was the Western area of the Russian Empire where the Jews were permitted to live, and these were their villages.

[7] Merriam-Webster defines a "*pogrom*" (puh-GRUM) as "an organized massacre of helpless people." If you've ever seen "Fiddler on the Roof," although no one is murdered, you surely recall the scene when the bad Russians come into town and, for no reason, cause a lot of destruction.

Perchik thought about it. "You're right, Shepsil. If I could read, today I'd be the *shamus* of Temple B'nai Vitipsk-Gaboynya!"

ROSES ARE RED

By Charles M. Powell

In the little town of Chelm, February is the favorite month, and certainly not because of the weather. It snows quite heavily and it's very cold in the part of the world know as The Pale.

So why is February such a favorite? The answer is simple, but only if you live in Chelm, with the wise fools. It's because they celebrate Walinchyne's Day.

What a lovely custom! Chelmites exchange Walinchyne cards. Shy people are able to express their devotion anonymously to their loved ones. Gifts are exchanged, fun is had by all.

And how, you may ask, did this charming annual event come about? No one truly knows.

But there was a poet many years ago in Chelm whose name happened to be Walinchyne. He was madly in love with Tsipkah, the Rabbi's daughter. Walinchyne used to write love poems to her, poems such as:

If pretty Tsipkah were only mine,
You'd see a happy Walinchyne.

Or this one:

Manischewitz is my favorite wine,
But Tsipkah I love - Signed Walinchyne!

Poor Tsipkah was bombarded with love poems every day, sometimes every hour, always politely, a note at the door. (Although Walinchyne was unfailingly polite and unquestionably harmless, this almost led to the invention of the first hashtag.)

Finally, she could stand the annoyance no longer. Walinchyne was called to the Rabbi's house and ordered to stop already with the poems.

He begged the Rabbi. He pleaded with Tsipkah. With his typical compassion, the Great Rabbi--and his kind daughter--relented and agreed to allow Walinchyne one day a year to submit his poetry to Tsipkah. And the Rabbi randomly chose February 14th as that day.

Now, other young men also sought the hand of the Rabbi's daughter. Most were Russians, for Tsipkah was of surpassing beauty and great intelligence…and her intelligence and strength intimidated the young Chelm men to near paralysis. When the day in February came, poems were flying into or across Chelm.

Tsipkah had a choice to make and she chose…from among all suitors…the poet Walinchyne. He had won the day with his beautiful and sincere poem of love:

Roses are Red-ish,
Violets are Blue-ish.
I'm poor and I'm ugly,
But at least I am Jewish.

And so, that is why, in Chelm, February is the favorite month of the year. Happy Walinchyne's Day.

NICE MATERIAL
By Mel Powell

Of course you've heard--and who hasn't heard?--of Nikita the Nobleman?

Maybe you know him as Nikita the Very Rich, or even Nikita the Very Powerful. Perhaps you know him by his own favorite name, Nikita the Very Wise. You may even have heard his critics call him Nikita the Nosher, but that's another matter…quite a bit of matter, for Nikita was not a small person.

So wise was Nikita that on occasion even the great Tsar himself would call on Nikita for counsel. So great was Nikita's reputation tor giving good advice that even the people in the tiny village of Chelm had heard of him. But they weren't impressed, for if there was one commodity of which Chelm had a surplus, it was good advice.

"Well, how very nice," exclaimed Nikita one fine day in his imposing home in St. Petersburg. "The Tsar so appreciates the advice I gave him last week that he has sent me this bolt of positively exquisite cloth."

Nikita sent for his chief fashion adviser, for even the greatest advisers are wise enough to seek advice, and an hour later the advisor arrived. "What beautiful cloth," said Piotr Cardin. "Your brilliantness, you simply must have a new suit made from this, that is its best use. But only the finest tailor in all the land shall be allowed to touch this cloth, lest it be ruined forever."

Nikita agreed, and off he went to meet the Tsar's Chief Tailor, Mikhail of Minsk. Mikhail knew of Nikita's huge reputation (and girth) and had even heard of the fine cloth. Mikhail measured Nikita from head to toe and from stem to stern.

"So?" demanded Nikita. "When will my suit be ready?"

Mikhail of Minsk cleared his throat in embarrassment, "Um, I'm very sorry, Your Smart-ness, but there is just not enough cloth here to fit your…how shall I say it…your importance."

"Then I will find another tailor!" bellowed Nikita, no less determined to have a new suit made out of this cloth. But Prokofiev of Pinsk was equally flummoxed by the cloth-to-subject ratio, and even the vastly talented Vitali of Vitipsk-Gaboynya could not find enough material in the bolt of cloth to suit Nikita's suit.

Again Nikita hit the road. And again Nikita did not get a new suit. All he got was hopelessly lost. Coming upon a small village, Nikita leaned out of his elegant horse-cart and asked, "What village is this?"

"Chelm," answered Rivka the Baker. "You were expecting maybe Paris? What do you want?"

"I am looking for the finest tailor in the world. You could not possibly help me."

"Pshaw," advised Rivka disdainfully. "You are in luck." And she took him directly to the shop of Schneider the Tailor.

"What can I do for you?" asked Schneider politely.

"I am Nikita," postured the ample adviser, "Nikita the Very Rich and Very Important! Make me a suit, and I shall pay you handsomely. I am frightfully wealthy. You may call the Tsar and check."

"I will take a check only if you have two forms of photo I.D. Since none of checks, photographs, or even I.D., has been invented yet, I'll take cash."

Then Schneider looked at the fine cloth, and eyed Nikita carefully. "Come back tomorrow at three o'clock. Your suit will be ready."

"You don't want to measure," asked the confused.

"I just did," Schneider assured him. "See you tomorrow, three o'clock."

The astounded Nikita went home, and could barely wait to return to the shop the next day. At precisely three o'clock he squeezed his ampleness through the door to collect his suit. And there it was! Hanging right in the middle of the shop was the most beautiful suit he had ever seen. He tried it on…and it was a perfect fit, too.

"Tell me," raved Nikita, "I must know. How were you able to make a suit for me when the finest tailors in the land told me there was not enough cloth to fit me?"

"Of course I have heard of your reputation. Throughout the land you may be a very big and important man. But this is Chelm. And in Chelm…you're not such a big k-nocker. It was easy."

Nikita, a bit insulted, nevertheless paid for his suit, reached for his clothes, and started to leave.

But before he reached the door, Schneider called after him. "By the way…you could use maybe this extra pair of pants, too?"

SECONDARY EDUCATION
By Charles M. Powell

Every once in a while, the Council of Elders of the village of Chelm, where the wise fools lived, would meet to argue, to cajole, to debate, to compromise, to learn...about controversies of major importance.

And sometimes less major.

We begin with Berel the Beadle. "How many, do you think, are there SECONDS in a year?"

Rivka the Baker: "Seconds? What are you talking seconds? Who cares and who knows? For this we have to have a meeting of the Council? Better I should be home making bagels!"

Schneider the Tailor was curious just the same. "A good question. How many seconds are there in a year?"

Boris the Balagoola asked, "Which year?"

Mendel the Messenger demanded, "What diff-- What diff-- Whaddaya mean, one year is the same as every other!"

"Oh, yeah," challenged the Balagoola. "How about a Leap Year? An extra day, more hours, and, of course, more seconds! So I ask you again, Mr. Beadle, which year?"

Berel the Beadle started to laugh. He knew--he had always known--that any question or any subject was likely to start a verbal brawl in Chelm.

"Let's say, for the sake of this august discussion, a regular year, no leaping."

"August discussion?" inquired Rivka, "What about October discussion? Or November? I love November, the leaves turn red and fall off the trees."

Shloime the Student interrupted, "Turn red and fall off the trees? Sounds like the Bolsheviks!"

Berel the Beadle returned to the issue. "Again, I ask you…how many seconds in a year?"

Boris the Balagoola spoke up: "I know. It's easy to figure out. Any idiot could figure it out."

At this point the Rabbi decided to wax eloquently. "By me, the answer to this question is that the difference between God and Man is the following. Man made the ox-cart, and said, 'this is sensational.' God made a tree and said 'this is beautiful.' Then man made a candlestick, and said 'this is excellent.' And God made a kitty-cat and said, 'this is better.' And the wheels fell off the ox-cart but the tree continued to grow. The candle in the candlestick eventually burned out, but the kitty-cat continued to delight, and to control its Humans. And that is the difference between Man and God."

After ten minutes, when the Council finally figured out that the Rabbi was not helping, Rivka the Baker scratched her head. "So how many seconds are there in a year?"

Boris the Balagoola had the answer. "This is not confusing! There are exactly twelve seconds in a year!"

"Hold-- hold-- Just ein minute, Balagoola," said Mendel. "The whole world knows that there are sixty seconds in just in a single minute. How you got twel-- twel-- only a dozen seconds in a whole year?"

Boris the Balagoola knew a pigeon when he saw one. "I'm willing to bet ten, count them, ten rubles, that I can prove that my answer is correct."

The Messenger was elated. "Oh, boy, oh boy, I finally got the Balag-- the Balag-- Mr. Boris! I offer to double that wager! Twenty rubles says there are more than twelve seconds in a year!"

The Balagoola laughed, "There are only twelve, and I will now prove it to you. There is the second of January; the second of February; the second of March…"

STILL GOING

By Mel Powell

(from a story by Bud Rosenthal)

The sky was blue and still is. Two plus two equaled four and still does. And Selma the Seamstress was talking.

In fact, that was what caused all the trouble in the village where the wise fools lived.

So, it was with great sadness that the Chelm courtroom fell silent as Mendel the Messenger, taking his turn in the rotation as Judge of the Chelm Court, called the next case.

"Hear ye-- hear ye-- listen up. I need some backgr-- backgr-- gimme some facts."

Rivka the Baker stood. "Once, I was accused of being the town loudmouth. Now nobody listens to me anymore! Selma the Seamstress never shuts up. All morning long, she talks. Then she eats lunch. Then she talks all afternoon, eats dinner, and talks until bedtime. I am told," Rivka continued, "that she even talks in her sleep."

"It's true," admitted Selma's husband Schneider the Tailor from the back of the courtroom.

Judge Mendel solemnly inquired, "What about the other defen-- defen-- what about her?"

Rivka, with some envy, pointed at the other defendant. "Nobody--not even Selma--can talk as much as Louise the Lip."

Mendel considered this, "Tell me about Lou--Lou-- tell me about the Lip."

Rivka did not hesitate. "We villagers all know that Louise the Lip is Selma's best friend. She is also the town gossip. However, I must admit, at least she comes by her information honestly. Louise is the Editor-in-Chief of Chelm's only daily newspaper, 'This Week in Chelm.' And," continued Rivka, "legend tells us that Louise the Lip and Selma the Seamstress once had three different conversations going simultaneously."

Thus informed, Mendel was ready to begin. "Thank you, Rivka." He banged his gavel and called the case. "The peo-- the peo-- Chelm versus Selma and Louise. Who's the first wit-- the first wit-- who saw what happened?"

Shloime the Student cane forward. "I did, Your Robed-ness. It was awful."

Selma and Louise, who sat at the defense table, ignoring the trial and sharing the latest village news in hushed tones, had hired the best lawyer they could find, Abraham the Advocate. He stood. "Objection, Your Honor. The use of the term 'awful' is conclusory, not to mention vague, ambiguous, inadmissible, inflammatory, and several other things which I shall not state aloud in mixed company such as this."

Mendel banged his gavel. "Objection overru-- overru-- I have no idea what you're talking about so forget it. Contin-- contin-- go ahead, Shloime."

"I observed Selma and Louise in a moving ox-cart on the main road in Chelm."

"What was their rate of spee-- rate of spee-- how fast were they going?"

"The ox-cart was doing about seven, but their mouths were doing about twenty-six each," opined Shloime.

"Well, who was dri-- was dri-- who had the reins?"

"That's just it, Your Gavel-ship. Neither of them! They were too busy talking. The ox-cart went out of control and forced another driver off the road into a ditch."

"Was anybody hur--hur-- any damage?"

"Nobody was hurt," replied Shloime, "but poor Tevye had to wait almost three hours for help because no one has yet invented a spare tire."

"Thank you, Shloime. You may step d-- step d-- you're excused."

Mendel looked down at the defendants, who were still talking between themselves. "Selma and Louise, has cith-- cith-- you got anything to say?"

This question, as phrased, was a mistake of epic proportions.

Six days later, Court was reconvened, after the two women wound down enough for Judge Mendel again to be heard. Neither had moved, nor had either noticed that the courtroom had been empty since six days earlier. Fortunately they'd brought their own snacks.

With great poise, Mendel once again took the bench.

"Selma the Seamstress and Louise the Lip, I find you guilty of criminal neglige-- neglige-- you shoulda looked where you were going. I sentence each of you to ninety day-- ninety day--three months in the Chelm jail."

The women, still talking about topics totally unrelated to their impending prison term, were led away.

Three months later, amid great fanfare, the news-starved citizens of Chelm gathered at the main entrance to the jailhouse. A great celebration and feast was provided by Kaplan the Katerer, and the entire village waited with great anticipation.

The gate opened.

Nobody appeared.

The next morning, the villagers gathered again. "Perhaps we miscounted," suggested Rivka. "Schneider, did you visit your wife in prison?"

"Definitely not," admitted Schneider. "Believe me, I have kept track of every day my beloved wife Selma has been incarcerated and kept away from me, her loving husband. (But boy have I enjoyed the quiet.)"

Day Two dragged by. So did Day Three. By Day Four, the villagers, still gathering by the gate, were becoming concerned, both with the whereabouts of the missing Selma and Louise and the realization that, for four entire days, nobody had had anything better to do than wait outside of a prison.

But on Day Four, finally, at long last, the women appeared.

They were silent. It took a moment to recognize them without their voices.

"So?" asked Rivka, "You've been locked up for three full months, no freedom, lousy jail food. What took you four extra days to leave your cell?"

Selma shrugged. "We wanted to finish the conversation."

NEVER AN END TO LEARNING

By Charles M. Powell

(based on a Sholom Aleichem tale)

[Character note. Even Berel the Beadle, a wise "fool," is smarter than this. But he was used for this old, old parable, so here we are.]

"There is never an end to learning," said Berel the Beadle. "They say that in Vilna there is much to learn, so I am going there to learn!"

When the Chelmites heard this, they thought: "Nonsense. Others come to learn from our wise villagers but we have nothing to learn from anyone. We know all there is to know."

Said Berel, "For a wise man, there is never an end to learning. I shall go to Vilna and see what I shall see."

When he reached Vilna, he asked: "Who is your wisest citizen?" Everyone recommended the Mayor of Vilna.

When he found the Mayor of Vilna, he said: "I hear that you are a wise and learned man. I have come to learn. May I have a lesson, please?"

Asked the Mayor of Vilna: "Who is my father's son, my mother's son, and is not my brother?"

The Wise Man of Chelm thought and thought. Finally, he gave answers, many answers. "Your cousin. Your aunt. Your niece. Your nephew. Your sister."

The Mayor of Vilna shook his head in turn. "No. No. No. No. No."

Berel admitted sadly, "I cannot guess further. I don't know."

"It is…I." patiently said the Mayor of Vilna, "Yes, I."

"Ah!" said Berel. "How wise! How clever! How smart!"

He could scarcely wait to get back to his own town and there tell the people what he had learned.

When he returned to Chelm, Berel did not waste a minute before he assembled the people in the town square, where he asked the same question as the Mayor of Vilna. "Who is my father's son, my mother's son, and is not my brother?"

The people of Chelm made guess after guess but, of course, all their guesses were incorrect. Berel the Beadle would just smile and say a kind and polite "no," knowing how he would soon teach his friends and fellow villagers this valuable lesson.

And so it went on, hour after hour. Finally, as the sun began to set, the people of Chelm gave up…and insisted on learning the answer.

"Simple," said Berel. "Who is my father's son, my mother's son, and is not my brother? The answer is: the Mayor of Vilna!"

WHO BROUGHT THE PICKLES?

By Charles M. Powell

The weather in Chelm is not such a picnic, so many of the Council of Elders were against the idea of a picnic for the entire village where the wise fools lived.

"It'll rain," said Schneider the Tailor.

"It'll snow," said Rivka the Baker.

"Our children will run around and get lost for hours," said Kalman the Karpenter.

The last argument convinced them all to do it.

So, on a breezy day in June, the village of Chelm held a picnic. And what a picnic.

Hundreds of people showed up, each with a lunch basket. Berel the Beadle jokingly asked who had brought the ants for the picnic. Feival piped up that his aunt was there from Finsk, as well as a cousin, twice removed, from Vilna.

The games were unbelievable. The three-legged race was a high point until Shloime the Student fell and sprained all three of his legs. The horseshoe contest had its problems as well. Boris the Balagoola, threw the closest horseshoe, but he neglected to detach the horse. This slowed up the game considerably, not to mention annoying the horse.

Next came Pin the Tail on the Ox. Everything went well until someone actually pinned the tail on the ox. The ox promptly pinned the pinner to the barn door and demanded an apology, thus ending that game.

And what is a picnic without baking and cooking contests? Rivka the Baker won the cooking contest. Her finished product, a calf's-foot gelatin, had hardened for three months. After collecting the blue ribbon for her delicacy, she was kind enough to donate her culinary wonder to the men for later use that afternoon as a soccer ball. How could the poor Rabbi know, when he kicked out the first ball to begin the match, that he would sprain his toe?

Schneider the Tailor surprised everyone by defeating that very same Rivka in the *Ruggelach*[8] Bake-Off. Berel the Beadle was the official judge, and he awarded the blue ribbon in this event to the Tailor before he discovered the tape measure in one of Schneider's *ruggelach*.

Still, with the songs and the food and the camaraderie of real friends, the day was a beautiful one for all of Chelm.

Later, exhausted, the Council of Elders passed a resolution that a good time was had by all. The resolution passed four to three. It was a wonderful day. But let me tell you...it was no picnic!

---

[8] *Ruggelach* is a small filled pastry.

A BRIDGE TOO FAR

By Charles M. Powell

[Among older...or perhaps all...Jewish people, there's a three-word English phrase that carries a depth of emotion unparalleled by any other English phrase. We'll leave it at that. Don't cheat and skip to the end.]

"We got already troubles," said Rivka the Baker. "The whole bridge game is *farfalen*."[9]

The game of Bridge was relatively new to Chelm, but Rivka had organized a regular group of four players--all equally confused--whose card games were already legendary in the village. Their weekly Bridge matches were known as "The" Game and all of Chelm picked sides and cheered for their favorite players.

But it was all in danger of collapsing. One of the women, Shifra, the wife of Shepsil the Shtarker, had moved, with her husband, to Minsk. That left three women, and everyone knows, even in Chelm, that you need four for Bridge.

"So who we gonna get?" asked Yenta the Matchmaker.

"How about Relya, the roofer's wife?"

"No good," thundered the wife of Boris the Balagoola. "When Relya drinks tea, she slurps. Who could play Bridge with someone slurping?"

"OK, then how about Molly, the *Mohel's*[10] sister?"

"No good by me," said one of the ladies. "She's a whiner."

"That's odd," said Rivka, "Except four cups at Passover, I never saw her touch even a drop."

---

[9] *Farfalen* is Yiddish for hopeless or doomed.
[10] A *mohel*, pronounced "moil" rhymes with "toil," is the specialized rabbi who performs the ritual circumcision of the male baby.

"Not wine...*whine*! She *kvetches*[11] all the time! She's plain and simple not my glass tea."

All day and all night they dissected Chelm, looking for a perfect fourth. Finally, they agreed upon Becky the Balaboosta.[12]

They met with her and asked if she would like to join "The" game.

"Would I like to join 'The' game? What an honor, what a privilege. Of course, I would like to join 'The' game."

"Then you gotta follow the rules."

"Anything, anything. What are the rules?"

Rivka looked Becky right in the eye. "We are not allowed to talk about our grandchildren. We all got...and once that starts, goodbye Bridge game."

"No problem," said the Balaboosta. "I've only got the one daughter, Tzibulla, and she isn't in any rush, may a bunion grow on her toe."

So the game was back on and all was well once again in Chelm...for about a year.

One day in the middle of a hot game, Becky the Balaboosta announced that she could not play Bridge the following week.

"Is everything all right, honey?" asked Rivka the Baker.

"Thanks God, yes," said Becky. "It's just that my daughter Tzibulla will be delivering my first...you know what...and I'm going to Vitipsk to be with her."

"Mazel Tov," they all wished her and away she went.

The three ladies met to discuss the situation while the Balaboosta was gone.

---

[11] To *kvetch* is to complain; a *kvetch*, as a noun, is a complainer.
[12] *Balaboosta* is an archaic Yiddish term for "perfect housewife and mother." But let's face the reality that the word sounds like an English term that crunches two words together, the second of which is "buster," and we'll leave you to your own interpretation of the deeper meaning.

"It's her *first* grandchild, we got to let her say something."

"But we got rules!"

"Suppose, for one time, we waive the rules?"

"Impossible," said Rivka.

"Tell me why?" asked one of the ladies.

"Tradition!" said Rivka.

At any rate, Becky the Balaboosta returned to Chelm a grandmother. Her daughter, Tzibulla, had given birth to a beautiful nine-pound bouncing baby. No one knew if it was a boy or a girl because it hadn't stopped bouncing yet.

The game started. Becky was busting, but she abided by the rules.

Finally, Rivka spoke up. "Listen, Balaboosta, I know we got rules but since this is your *first* grandchild, we passed a waiver. We voted that you can talk about it--but only in three words. Can you do it in three words?"

"Of course," said the Balaboosta.

"Let's hear, already."

Becky steadied herself. Tears came to her eyes as she thought of her grandchild. In three words she said it all: she said it for every loving grandparent in the whole world.

"In your *life*..."

JEWISH HOLIDAYS

1. The Holiday Spirit
2. How Many Chelmites Does It Take To Change A Lightbulb?
3. Tink Before You Talk
4. Brain Food
5. Hide And Seek
6. Chelm: The Horseradish Capital Of The World
7. The Passover Salesman
8. Bottoms Up
9. He Did It Again

There are lots and lots of Jewish holidays. No need for a full treatise on all of them, but for this chapter there are two you need to know about. They are holidays steeped more in Jewish history than religion.

Chanukah (or Hanukah or any of the similar spellings) is, as Adam Sandler explains, the festival of lights. Short version: the Jews were conquered and the bad guys made a mess of the Temple. The Jews didn't like that, rebelled, and kicked out the bad guys. They needed to clean up the temple by working 24/7, but the bad guys had left behind only enough oil for the lamps to burn for one night. And, as with many things related to Chelm, electricity hadn't been invented yet. The oil kept the lamps going for eight full nights...a miracle...and the Temple was ready for visitors. To commemorate the miracle, Jews light the nine-candle *menorah* to celebrate the holiday, one the first night, two the second; eight in all, the ninth candle being the "helper," lighting all the rest.

Passover (*Pesach* in Hebrew) is the holiday that commemorates the Jews' exodus (get it?) from slavery in the land of Egypt. Again the Jews decided they'd had enough of the bad stuff and Moses (with his brother Aaron) went to the Egyptian leader, the Pharaoh, and said "we're outta here." Unsurprisingly, the Pharaoh said "not so fast." So Aaron and Moses said, look, we're not going to start a fight here, just let us go be free...or else we're gonna hit up your people and your lands with some plagues. Ten such plagues ensued and finally the Pharaoh not only released them but offered to drive them to the airport (which hadn't been invented yet). OK, no airport...after the miracle of the parting of the Red Sea got them out of Egypt, they walked through the Sinai Desert for 40 years (no GPS yet, either), eventually coming to The Holy Land. They had to leave so quickly that their bread didn't have time to bake and rise...hence the unleavened matzah we eat for the holiday at the "*seder*," the celebration.

Let's get going!

(See also "Does a Bear *Kvetch* in the Woods" (Passover) and "Fore! (He's A Jolly Good Fellow)" (Yom Kippur, the Jewish day of atonement) in the Synagogue/Tradition chapter and "Matzah Matta-U" (Passover) in the Ethnic Differences chapter additional references to Jewish holidays.)

THE HOLIDAY SPIRIT

By Charles M. Powell

[And while we won't present a treatise on all of the various Jewish holidays, the opening story for this chapter will tickle our Jewish readers...and also give our non-Jewish friends just a touch of explanation of several of the other major holidays.]

"I love our holidays," said Berel the Beadle. "There's always something festive and special about a Jewish holiday."

Now Berel made this rather innocent statement in front of Chelm's Wise Council of Elders--a statement he would soon regret.

And it came as no surprise that Schneider the Tailor bellowed, "Holidays? I'll tell you the best of all the Jewish holidays has to be Passover. What a joy! All the children shaking noisemakers every time they hear Haman's name. *Hamantashen*![1] The reading of the *Megillah*.[2] Passover is beautiful!"

Berel could not believe his ears. "Schneider, my dear friend, you're confused. That's not Passover you described; it's *Purim*."

Rivka the Baker laughed, "My favorite holiday has always been *Shavuos*.[3] What a wonderful time! The Torahs are taken out into the streets. The *shofar* is sounded. Your name will be inscribed in the good book, but only if Elijah comes. *Shavuos* is a wonderful time."

---

[1] Haman was the bad guy in the story of this holiday...go back to the story for the name of the holiday...and *Hamantashen* are the traditional triangular cookies that represent Haman's signature three-cornered hat.

[2] The *Megillah* is the story of this holiday, or the book that contains the story.

[3] <u>*Shavuous*</u> (or *shavuot*) translates to "weeks." It is the Spring festival holiday.

Berel almost fainted. "*Shavuos* is a wonderful time, Rivka, but you just described Rosh Hashanah,[4] *Pesach*,[5] and *Simchat Torah*."[6]

Fortunately, it was Shloime the Student who finally brought some sense and order to the discussion. "I can't believe what I am hearing today. How can you possibly get those Holidays all mixed up? If you want to talk holidays, permit me to submit to you an explanation of Chanukah, my favorite time, because it contains a most significant moment."

"Thank God," said Berel the Beadle. "Tell us."

"Judah the Maccabee who recaptured the great Temple. He and his men set about driving out the pagan idols and purifying the defiled sanctuary. Having once again sanctified our most holy place, Judah looked to kindle a flame of consecration. He was able to find only a tiny amount of proper oil to light, but, miraculously, this oil burned for eight days and eight nights. It was truly a miracle, my friends. And it all took place on what has become Chanukah. "

Schneider raised his hand, "But tell us, Shloime, what is that most significant moment that you mentioned?"

Shloime smiled. "That is my favorite part of Chanukah. You see, when Judah finished praying in the clean Temple, with the oil burning for eight days and nights, he went outside on the steps of the great Temple and looked down. Now, if he could see his shadow…"[7]

---

[4] Rosh Hashanah, literally "head [of] the year," the Jewish New Year, is when your name is metaphorically inscribed into the book of life for the coming good year.

[5] *Pesach* is the Hebrew name of Passover, when traditionally the prophet Elijah visits.

[6] *Simchat Torah* – a *simcha* is a blessing or happy occasion – is the holiday celebrating the giving of the Torah to the Jews, and the Torah is taken from the Ark and lovingly paraded.

[7] You knew this, but we're thorough. Shloime had it correct…right up to the shadow…

HOW MANY CHELMITES DOES IT TAKE TO CHANGE A LIGHTBULB?

By Mel Powell based on a story by Charles M. Powell

How many Chelmites does it take to change a lightbulb?

How many, you ask? None, of course, since lightbulbs hadn't been invented yet in the tiny village of Chelm, where the wise fools lived. Now, Chanukah in Chelm, on the other hand, did have its rich tradition of *menorahs*[8] and *dreidels*.[9] And they also had *latkes*[10] so heavy that three years ago Boris the Balagoola had built a specially designed fork to lift them--so no lightbulbs, but they had invented the first fork-lift.

But the one tradition unique to Chelm was the annual celebration of fibbing.

Yes, fibbing. Every year, Chelm held a "Lying Contest." It was scheduled for the second night of Chanukah--but was always held on the fourth night, because the organizers who advertised the second night were lying. And the rules were as simple as the contestants: the fib must be about Chanukah, and it must be believable.

So who was the champion? For seven years in a row, the famous Farber the Pharmacist, better known as Farber the Fibber. And this year was no different, as once again he took home the gold medal and had it bronzed. Here was his tale:

Three unfortunate *gonefs*[11] decided to steal rubles from the Tsar's treasury. They were, of course, caught in the act and sentenced to twenty years in jail.

But the Tsar was in one of his rare good moods. None of the three thieves had a long "rap parchment"--in fact, none had ever previously committed a crime. So the Tsar commuted their sentence to just five

---

[8] The *menorah* is the ceremonial candelabra.
[9] A *dreidel* is the little spinning toy top, a tradition of the holiday.
[10] A *latke* is a potato pancake, usually served with sour cream or apple sauce, a tradition of Chanukah but good any time of year.
[11] A *gonef* is, for want of a better loose translation, a bonehead.

years each, and even permitted each of the three to choose one favorite thing to take with him to jail.

The first thief, Label the Lover from Lithuania, chose his wife. She agreed to be locked up with him, and away they went to their cell.

The second thief, Hendel the *Handeler*[12] from Pinsk, requested a telephone--which had just been invented, thank goodness--to be installed in his cell, and the Tsar complied and signed him up with AT&T: All Talk & *Tsouris*.[13]

Finally, the third unfortunate thief, Pincus the Pious from Chelm, made his choice. "You should please incarcerate me with a single Chanukah *menorah* and a five-year supply of Chanukah candles."

Needless to say, his request caused a stir within Tsar tscircles. Pincus was asked to explain his strange selection.

"First of all, I am, despite my transgression, a pious and God-worshipping man. I am ashamed of my crime, so choosing a religious item is, for me, an act of contrition. Also, Chanukah is a joyous holiday, and that will cheer me. I will look forward to each of my five Chanukahs when I can once again light up my cell and my life with great anticipation."

A deal was a deal, and the Tsar complied, and a *menorah* and a five-year supply of candles was locked up with Pincus the Pious of Chelm.

Five years passed, and the Tsar ordered the three rehabilitated criminals released.

Label the Lithuanian Lover was now the father of four beautiful Litvaks. He and his wife had used their jail time well and were blessed with a lovely Litvak family.

Hendel the Handeler had used his telephone wisely. Over five years he had bought, he had sold, and he had made a small fortune. He left prison a very wealthy man.

---

[12] A *handeler*, which also comes in the verb form "to *handel*," is a bargainer.
[13] *Tsouris* means "trouble."

And what of Pincus the Pious, from the tiny village of Chelm? His cell door was unlocked, and he stepped out into the sunshine for the first time in five years, a free man.

He looked at his jailers, and politely asked: "Would anyone here happen to have a match?"

TINK BEFORE YOU TALK

(A Passover Parable)

By Charles M. Powell

[While this is not a traditional Chelm story, having no connection to our favorite little village, it nonetheless merits inclusion as the quintessential tale of Jews understanding the power of Passover and its goodies, and non-Jews not so much...until now.]

The telephone rang in Israel.

"Teitlebaum's Tel Aviv Tink Tank, Teitlebaum talking. To whom I got the pleasure?"

"Tink tank?" asked an unmistakably American-accented voice.

"Tink Tank. T-Haitch-I-N-K, Tink. We tink of everything. You got a problem, we got a solution. If the solution don't vork, you don't pay, and we tink again."

"Tank you--excuse me, thank you," said the caller. "I am Brigadier General Thomas, and I am speaking to you from the Pentagon in Washington. You may be our last hope."

"Now you're talking," said Teitlebaum. "So what's the problem?"

The General carefully explained how the United States was trailing other powers in the development of a supersonic fighter plane. "The problem," said the General, "is that when our planes get up to 3,000 miles per hour, the wings snap off. We've tried everything. Nothing works."

"You ain't tried everytink yet, buddy. You ain't tried us. You'll give me a call on Tuesday, or maybe Toisday, and we'll have for you a solution."

The General laughed. "Tuesday? Or even Tois--Thursday? I'll have you know that the government has been working on this problem for years. The best minds from M.I.T., Cal Tech--even the Germans' best engineers can't solve the problem of the wings breaking off."

"Not to worry. You'll call Tuesday. If it don't work, you don't pay."

The General reported to the Chief of Staff, who reported to the Secretary of Defense, who reported to the President, who reported to the re-election campaign's top donors--and they all laughed. What *chutzpah*[14] these Israelis had!

But on Tuesday, bright and early, they all gathered in the Pentagon and placed the call.

"Teitlebaum's Tel Aviv Tink Tank, Teitlebaum talking. To whom I got the pleasure?"

"It's General Thomas and our top people on the line. We don't suppose you've got a solution yet?"

"Today's your lucky day Brigadoon General. Of course we got for you the answer. First you take an airplane, Then, you need a knoll punch."

"A what?" asked the General.

"A knoll punch. Something you can punch a knoll with."

"Oh, you mean a hole punch. Yes, I'm sure we can find one."

"Good," said Teitlebaum. "You punch a knoll every six inches where the wings meet the plane. That'll do it."

The Pentagon exploded with outrage. "The problem, Teitlebaum, is one of stress! Drilling holes at the point of stress can only make it worse!"

"You got a better idea?"

"Well...no."

---

[14] We're sure you know that *chutzpah* means "a lotta nerve," but we'll still tell you, out of, you know, *chutzpah*.

"You got remote control, so if the idea don't vork, no one gets hurt?"

"Yes."

"So you'll try. If it vorks, send money. If not, not."

And with that the U.S. Government, with no other options or ideas, drilled holes, six inches apart, on both wings of its best and fastest fighter plane. Up into the sky it flew, remote-piloted from the ground with a Human-sized mannequin to get the weight and balance just right, a thousand miles per hour, two thousand, twenty-nine hundred. Now the big test--would the plane make three thousand without the wings snapping off?

The phone rang in Israel.

"Teitlebaum's Tel Aviv Tink Tank, Teitlebaum talking. To whom I got the pleasure?"

"It worked, Teitlebaum! It worked! How did you know? The best engineers in the world couldn't figure it out, but you did! Payment is on the way. How did you do it, Teitlebaum?"

"Well, your Generalship, it was easy--if you happen to be Jewish. You see, we Jews have a similar problem on one of our sacred holidays, Passover. We eat this cardboard that we call Matzah. It comes in sheets, with perforations. Did you *ever* try to break a piece of matzah at the perforations?"

BRAIN FOOD

By Mel Powell

(based loosely on a story from Chaim Topol's "To Life!")

Igor The Cossack happened one day to pass through the tiny village of Chelm, where the wise fools lived. He ran into Mendel the Messenger.

"Excuse me," said Igor, "but perhaps you could answer a question that has intrigued me for quite some time."

"Certainl-- certainl-- what do you want to know?" asked Mendel.

"Simple," said the Russian. "What is it that makes Jews so smart?"

Mendel smiled. "It's the appetit-- the appetiz-- it's the gefilte fish."

"What in the world is gefilte fish?"

Mendel indicated Rivka's bakery, just half a block away. "Foll-- Foll-- walk this way."

Mendel escorted Igor into Rivka's humble establishment. Only true Chelmites knew that Rivka the Baker was famous not only for her breads and sweets, but also for her incredible gefilte fish.

After Mendel made the introductions, Igor spoke to the Baker. "Your messenger, here, tells me that it is gefilte fish that makes Jews so smart. What is gefilte fish?"

"Simple!" explained Rivka. "It's minced carp mixed with bread, onions, and hard-boiled eggs--which are then made into fish cakes, which you boil."

"Really," said Igor. "I want to become smarter, just like the Jews. May I try some of this gefilte fish?"

"Of course!" Rivka served up a portion, "That'll be five kopecks, please."

Igor wrinkled his face, thinking five kopecks sounded quite expensive for this small plate of strange fish. But what price intelligence? Igor paid. He found that he didn't much care for the taste of intelligence, either, but he persevered, wishing to improve himself. Then he bid Rivka and Mendel a good evening, tipped his fur hat, and left.

The following week, the Cossack passed through Chelm again where he calmly paid five kopecks and calmly ate his portion of gefilte fish--actually learning to like it. Well, if not, then at least tolerate it.

And this went on for six more weeks. But in the sixth week, Igor returned, agitated. He had obviously come to a ponderous decision.

"My dear Baker, are you not cheating me by charging me five kopecks? Do you expect me to believe that a little piece of over-priced gefilte fish could actually make me clever?"

"Ah, now you see how it works," replied Rivka. "You're getting smarter already!"

HIDE AND SEEK

By Mel Powell

(from an idea by Barbara Ruskin)

The word "*afikomen*" is Greek for "dessert." And so it is widely believed that the custom of hiding the *afikomen*[15] at *Pesach*[16] began among Jews at the height of the Greek empire. Right?

Wrong.

As with most of the world's finest creations, the custom of hiding the *afikomen* was invented by the good citizens of the tiny village of Chelm, where the wise fools lived.

How, you may ask? I'll tell you.

The people of Chelm had gathered for their seder. As was traditional, the seder was frequently interrupted by spirited discussions of relevant issues. And, as was also traditional, "four cups of wine" was a suggestion...but not a limitation. So the spirited discussions frequently got out of hand.

"What are you talking?" boomed Boris the Balagoola. "You call into question if Rivka prepared the matzah legally?"

"That's not what I'm saying," said Schneider the Tailor. "I'm just asking for an explanation of the rules!"

Rivka the Baker stood up. "You think maybe someone should consider asking *me*?"

"Yes!" agreed Boris, grabbing the middle matzah and handing it to Rivka. "Let's hear it from the matzah *maven*!"[17]

Rivka began. "The rules about the care and feeding of your *Pesach* matzah are very strict! For instance, the matzah must be prepared,

---

[15] The *afikomen* is a part of the ceremonial Passover matzah that is hidden during the ceremony and then sought later by the children.
[16] *Pesach* is the Hebrew name of Passover.
[17] A *maven* is an expert.

using only flour and water, in just eighteen minutes!" The good Rabbi nodded agreement.

"Eighteen minutes? That's it?" asked Schneider the Tailor.

"Yes," answered Rivka, "and do you know why? OK, I'll tell you. That's how long it takes to walk a Roman mile."

Again the Rabbi nodded, but the room exploded in argument. A few voices were heard above the din. "A mile? What...the matzah's gotta run a marathon?" wondered Berel the Beadle.

Frieda the Feminist demanded, "And why isn't it called an afi-ko-person?"

"How *long* it takes to walk it? What if the baker has a limp? What if the Roman walking the original mile had a limp?" asked Shloime the Student.

"So what do the Romans know about matzah?" huffed Boris.

Rivka held her hands up for silence. "You want to argue, or you want to learn something? Eighteen minutes it is, and that's that." Rivka went on to explain about how the flour must be monitored by rabbinical authorities to make sure it never comes into contact with water before the actual baking begins. Even the grain itself must be watched over, from harvest to oven. Smiling, the rabbi nodded.

"And then," said Rivka, "there are the other rules."

"Oy vey," said the rabbi, but nobody heard....

"Other rules?" rumbled Boris.

"Other rules! The perforations in the matzah must be exact. So exact that not even the strongest balagoola can break the matzah at the perforations!"

Boris tried it. And, of course, the perforations and the split of the matzah were not even in the same time zone. Needless to say, time zones hadn't been invented yet.

"And," continued Rivka, "there are rules about the texture!"

"You're kidding," said Schneider.

"Not at all," said Rivka. "The surface of the matzah must be bumpy, to remind us of the rough desert, where we wandered for forty years...and eighteen minutes. Here, test the texture for yourself."

And with that she handed half of the middle matzah to old Bakalchuk the Blind Man, who took it and slowly ran his fingers over the surface. "Who *writes* this garbage?" he asked.

And that, needless to say, created another hubbub. Boris wanted to know what the matzah said. Schneider wanted to know if it could be read from start to finish in only eighteen minutes. Boris wanted to eat already. Finally, Rivka could bear no more.

"That does it! You want to question my careful, loving preparation of the matzah! Fine! You don't *deserve* to partake of my *afikomen*! You want it? You gotta find it!"

So she grabbed the *afikomen*, stormed out of the room, hid the *afikomen*, and a tradition was born.

And that, dear listener, is how the good people of Chelm, where the wise fools live, invented the hiding of the *afikomen*. There's just one problem. They still haven't found it...and Rivka forgot where she hid it.

CHELM: THE HORSERADISH CAPITAL OF THE WORLD
OR
BEI MIR BIST DU CHRAIN [18]

By Charles M. Powell

The village of Chelm--where the Wise Fools all lived--actually had a principal export. It was the world's foremost supplier of *chrain*, that vicious arid delicious horseradish, a staple of the Passover Seder.

A special meeting of the Wise Council of Elders was called prior to the holiday to debate the issue.

"So how hot we gonna make it this year?" asked Schneider the Tailor.

"As hot as it takes," replied Berel the Beadle.

Boris the Balagoola explained: "What we got here is a full range of hot. We can make choking, sputtering wheezing hot, or we can make it hand cooling off your mouth, but no choking, hot. In between we got may levels: eye-watering, nose-twitching, foot-stomping, air-gasping, and the simple but always effective 'passing out.'"

Shloime the Student discussed the public service that Chelm offered with its horseradish. "First of all, with our *chrain*, sick people don't need penicillin. Also, it's wonderful for the Sinai. Clears them right up."

It was time for the Rabbi to restore some sense. "The decision we make here could affect Jews all over the world. So, how hot is hot?"

The Rabbi began fielding the swelling tide of questions--and answers--from the floor...and even the ones coming from the Chelmites.

---

[18] *Bei Mir Bistu Shoen* is a Yiddish song (the title means "To Me, You Are Beautiful") popularized with English lyrics in the 1930 by the Andrews Sisters. *Chrain* is horseradish, as you'll learn in the story in a moment, and this secondary title for the story is just a play on the words.

"Why do they call it 'horse' radish?"

"Because to eat it you gotta be strong like a horse."

"Where did the word '*chrain*' come from?"

"From the bird…the Whooping *chrain*."

"Why is the color red?"

"After you eat some, did you ever look at your face?"

"Isn't some horseradish white?"

"Sure it is, but that's a horse of a different color."

"So where does the red actually come from?"

"Beets."

"Makes sense. Nobody beats our *chrain*. So why do you cry when you eat it?"

"Because it hurts too much to laugh."

"Who invented horseradish?"

"The famous American author Ichabod *Chrain*."[19]

The discussion went on well into the night, with the Rabbi finally concluding: "My friends, after all is said and done, what is the best wine that goes with the hottest horseradish?

"Easy," said Boris the Balagoola, whining: "Quick, pass me the seltzer!"

---

[19] Ichabod Crane, but you knew that.

THE PASSOVER SALESMAN
By Charles M. Powell

[A quick reminder: when the Jews were given permission by the Pharoah to quit being slaves and leave for the Holy Land, they got out fast. The pharaoh went back on his word and a little while later sent his army to haul the Jews back. The story's miracle is that the waters of the Red Sea parted and the Jews ran across the dry sea bed to safety...and when the Pharaoh's army followed them in, the waters flooded back and the Jews had escaped.]

Schwartzbard was having trouble finding a job in Chelm. The economy was bad, the taxes were high, the pogroms were active, Jews were being attacked in their villages--in short, a typical year in Chelm, where the wise fools all lived.

Passover was fast approaching and Schwartzbard had a great idea. He presented himself to Avram the Artist, who owned the only art gallery in the village.

"Today is your lucky day, Mr. Artist. I am Schwartzbard, the world's greatest salesman, and, if you will permit me, I will prove to you that I can sell anything, anytime, anywhere...how about?"

"Thank you anyways, mister salesman, but I've already sold all my paintings. It's Passover season, which seems to be a good time for me, despite the economy."

Schwartzbard was not a great salesman for nothing. "O.K., Avram, how about I sell for you a painting you haven't even painted yet? What if I took an empty canvas, brand new, never touched by a paint brush...put it in a nice frame...hung it in your empty gallery...and got somebody in this village of wise fools to actually buy it? What if?"

The artist laughed. "That would certainly prove to me that you're the best salesman in all of Russia. In addition to a commission of ten percent, I would be delighted to offer you permanent employment, but only if you really make a sale."

Thus challenged, Schwartzbard went to work. After hanging the elegantly framed--but totally empty--canvas in a place of honor on the empty gallery wall, the salesman put a sign in the window. The sign read:

AVRAM THE ARTIST'S BEST PASSOVER PAINTING EVER

SPECIALLY PRICED--BUT ONLY FOR ART LOVERS

The sign did it. There was an enormous line at the door. First in was Rivka the Baker. "Listen, mister; forget the Avram Passover Picture. How much you asking for a small Chagall?"

Schwartzbard scratched his head. "For you, only one hundred rubles."

"That's ridiculous," said the Baker. "Over in Vitipsk-Gaboynya they sell a small Chagall for only seventy-five rubles, but they've run out of them."

"Big deal," said the salesman, "when I run out of them I also charge only seventy-five rubles!"

Next in the door was Boris the Balagoola. "I read your sign and I'd like to see the Passover painting."

"Not so fast, friend," answered Schwartzbard. "We only show the Avram to discriminating art collectors."

The Balagoola thought for a minute. "No question I'm a serious collector. Paintings I got. The real question is whether I'm discriminating enough, I hate the Tsar's Cossacks and I admit to discriminating against Galitzianas. Does that count?"

"Close enough," cried the salesman, recognizing a pigeon when he saw one. He took Boris the Balagoola up to the empty canvas.

"Well, what dya' think, mister collector? Is this not a beauty? Look at the power, the emotion, the impact of Passover itself. The expression of freedom that the holiday truly represents, the wonderful simplicity. The truth...what dya' think?"

The Balagoola was confused. "If this is a Passover painting, where are the Israelites fleeing from their Egyptian oppressors?"

The salesman smiled, "Good question. Obviously, you know your history as well as your art. The Israelites have already fled."

"So where's the Egyptian oppressors?"

"I'm really impressed with you," said the salesman. "The Egyptians are on their way and haven't as yet arrived at the exact moment that the great Avram has captured on canvas."

"OK," said the Balagoola, "if you can answer this one, I'll buy the Avram. Where's the Red Sea?"

"This is the Red Sea," said Schwartzbard.

Boris squinted to get a better look at the empty canvas "So if this is the Red Sea, where's the water?"

Schwartzbard smiled. "Where's the water? It already parted!"

BOTTOMS UP
by Charles M. Powell

One of God's most interesting inventions is the matzah.

Why, you may ask? I'll tell you. Think of all the wonderful things that you can do with the ordinary, everyday matzah.

You can use it as a Frisbee--pity the one who has to catch it.

You can use it as cardboard for your shirts.

Matzahs make great surf boards…briefly.

They make terrific greeting cards...if you write very carefully.

It can be delicious as wallpaper.

Very interesting, indeed, is the matzah.

So why was there such a fight over it at the annual Chelm Second Night Seder? It seems that Boris the Balagoola and Berel the Beadle almost came to blows over the question of the buttered matzah.

The Balagoola insisted that matzah, if buttered on one side and then dropped on the floor, would *always* land butter side up.

Berel said that was ridiculous. They argued for hours, until Rivka the Baker solved the problem by suggesting that the experiment actually be attempted.

Schneider the Tailor produced the matzah. Berel buttered it. With the entire Wise Council of the Elders looking on, Boris the Balagoola held the matzah up high and flipped it up in the air and it dropped onto the floor. It fell butter side down and stained the rug.

"See," said Berel the Beadle, "I told you so."

The Balagoola was unperturbed. "Is it my fault you buttered the matzah on the wrong side?"

HE DID IT AGAIN?

By Mel Powell based on a story by Charles M. Powell

[Remember that Yom Kippur…key-PORE if you pronounce it as intended in Hebrew, but more commonly just spoken as KIPP-er…is the holiest day of the Jewish year, the Day of Atonement, when we apologize for our misdeeds of the previous year and promise to be better. And we fast, from sundown to sundown, for this holiday… food is a no-no.}

Berel the Beadle laughed. "He did it again!"

"Who did what again?" asked Rivka the Baker.

"I refer, of course, to Kalman the Karpenter, who pulled off another of his classic capers."

"Was it like the pranks he perpetrated on *Pesach*[20] and *Purim*[21]?"

"Worse," said the Beadle. "Also it was worse than his shameful *shanda*[22] on *Shavuos*.[23]"

"Good heavens!" said Rivka. "So tell me already."

"It was a kipper caper."

"A kipper caper? When did it happen?"

"On Yom Kippur."

Rivka couldn't believe it. "You mean to tell me that Kalman the Karpenter carried a kipper to the congregation on Yom Kippur?"

"Correct."

---

[20] *Pesach* is the Hebrew name of Passover.
[21] *Purim* is the very festive holiday celebrating Queen Esther's saving the Jews of ancient Shushan.
[22] *Shanda* means "a shame" and can also mean a controversy, in context, which is does a little here.
[23] Shavuous (or *shavuot*) translates to "weeks." It is the spring festival holiday.

"And who uncovered the caper?"

"Cantor Cohen. That was the capper."

Rivka coughed. "Catastrophic! Cantor Cohen cornered Kalman the Karpenter carrying a kipper on Yom Kippur?"

"Also a *kreplach*,"[24] continued Berel. "In a concealed crate. The Cantor caught Kalman right after *Kol Nidre*."[25]

Rivka smiled. "*Kinnahora!*[26] Cantor Cohen can be congratulated for his courage in cancelling the clever caper. I take it the case is closed."

Berel nodded but sighed. "I shudder to think about Chanukah in Chelm!"

---

[24] A *kreplach* is a dumpling.
[25] *Kol Nidre* is the centerpiece musical prayer on the holiest night. It means "all vows."
[26] *Kinnahora* is the verbal equivalent of "knock on wood," fending off "the evil eye" of superstition.

LEGAL TROUBLES

1. Horse Sense
2. The Ox-cidental Tourist
3. An Endangered Species
4. We Have, Your Honor
5. The Witness

Disputes happen. Laws are broken, or at least bent to the limits of credulity. Sometimes it goes all the way to Court. In the village of wise fools, justice is often a concept unto itself.

(You can find some legal issues in "Sometimes It Doesn't Pay to be a Nice Person" in the Death chapter; "Still Going" in the Human Foibles and Quirks chapter; and "How Many Chelmites Does It Take to Change a Lightbulb?" in the Jewish Holidays chapter.)

HORSE SENSE

By Charles M. Powell

Why a Wise Council of Elders? The answer is simple: Why not?

It was the duty of the Wise Council to arbitrate, compromise, legislate, and generally keep the village of Chelm peaceful and harmonious. And, since the wisest fools in this famous village of wise fools served on the Wise Council, how could it not work?

So, when the Council was called into emergency session, the entire town turned out to watch justice dispensed. The issue on this particular day concerned Boris the Balagoola and Tevye the Milkman, or rather, it concerned their horses.

Boris the Balagoola spoke first: "We keep, my ex-friend Tevye and I, our horses in the same stable. The problem is that neither one of us remembers who owns which horse. When I get to the stables in the morning I discover that Tevye, the idiot, has left with his milk cart and *my* horse. Now, learned Council, if this happened once or twice, or even several times, I would understand it. But it happens all the time and frankly, my horse is better than his horse."

Tevye looked at it slightly differently. "Boy! A story like that I never heard. The problem has developed because Boris the Balagoola has a head like an onion. He barely remembers his wife's name, never mind which horse is his. He calls my horse by his horse's name; he washes his horse and dries mine…he's a total idiot and I would ask the Wise Council once and for all to help us distinguish between the horses so that I have mine and he has his."

"A major problem," said Rivka the Baker.

"This, already, is a tough one," said Schneider the Tailor.

"Perhaps we should ask the horses to come testify?" asked Berel the Beadle.

But instead the Wise Council put their collective heads together and came up with a solution. "Tomorrow morning," announced Berel the Beadle, "you will place a red ribbon around Tevye's horse's ears.

This way you will both know that it is the Milkman's horse with the ribbon and the problem will be solved."

A good solution, no? Well thought out, no? Fool-proof, no?

No.

Because one week later the two men were back before the Council, still confused as to who owned which horse.

"All right," said Shloime the Student, "Tomorrow morning you will put a blue blanket on the horse belonging to Boris the Balagoola. Then you will know once and for all: red ribbon is Tevye's horse; blue blanket is the Balagoola's."

Brilliant, yes? Simple, yes? You think they were still confused?

Yes.

So once more they stood before the Wise Council for advice. This time the Great Rabbi of Chelm was forced to jump in. "This problem has gotten entirely out of hoof--er, hand," he said. "We have more important things to discuss and this has taken too much of our time. The Council will hand down a temporary solution, one that will do for the time being until we have more time to think this through properly."

The villagers leaned forward in anticipation of the learned Rabbi's solution.

"Because it is so difficult to tell the horses apart, starting tomorrow Boris will own the black horse and Tevye will own the white horse. Council dismissed."

THE OX-IDENTAL TOURIST
By Mel Powell

It had been a bad week in the Pale, the region that included the tiny village of Chelm, where the wise fools lived. Although Chelm had been spared, there had been a *pogrom*[1] in Pinsk, where the Cossacks had taken over and forced the Jews to learn the Macarena, which thank God hadn't been invented yet.

Boris the Balagoola had good friends in Pinsk, and he complained to the Mighty One of their plight. "Lord, who rules over us all with wisdom, will this madness ever cease? Please, give me a sign that there will be peace!"

And sure enough, a voice boomed down from the Heavens.

"Boris. Don't wait for a sign."

So it hadn't been such a good week for Boris, either. His top-of-the-line, state-of-the-art ox-cart had to go in the shop for maintenance. Not only was the cart out of commission, but it was also a vacation day off for Boris's trusty Ox. These days of rest were a new requirement, now that the local farm animals had unionized and formed the AFL-CI-EIEIO.

Off went Boris to Herschel's Rent-an-Ox and, next door, to Kopeck Rent-a-Cart, and he was back in business for the day.

While Boris was riding around, taking care of business, he was busy plotting revenge against the Cossacks and not watching the road quite well enough. Suddenly, on a winding and foggy road, there was a terrible crash!

When the dust settled, Boris's rented ox-cart was a pile of rubble, the kind of rubble that would cost many rubles to repair.

---

[1] Merriam-Webster defines a "*pogrom*" (puh-GRUM) as "an organized massacre of helpless people." If you've ever seen "Fiddler on the Roof," although no one is murdered, you surely recall the scene when the bad Russians come into town and, for no reason, cause a lot of destruction.

And the other ox-cart involved in this ox-on collision was also shmushed beyond recognition. Only the oxen were left standing, politely exchanging insurance information. A passer-by ran to summon help from the local constable.

Boris crawled out of the wreckage. Amazingly, he was unhurt! He watched, with the compassion that only one with such a huge heart can show, as the other driver appeared from beneath his own mangled cart.

"Are you hurt?" asked Boris.

"I don't think so," said the young Russian.

Then Boris peered closer. "Say, you look just like the Cossack who led the *pogrom* in Pinsk the other day! You fit the description precisely!"

"And what of it, large Jewish man?" challenged the Cossack.

But, in that very moment, Boris had a change of heart. "Good sir," he said, "don't you think that this is a sign? Our very survival--that both of us should leave the scene of this horrible crash unscathed?"

"A sign?" asked the Cossack.

"Yes, a sign!" said Boris. "A sign that our two peoples are meant to live together in peace and harmony!"

And, strangely, the Cossack's face brightened. "You know, you're right! That a Russian and a Jew could collide so violently, however accidentally, yet remain unhurt...surely that is a sign! We will live in peace at last!"

"Exactly," said Boris. He reached his hand back into the wreckage of the ox-cart and found the only object that had also survived the crash unscathed. "We must drink a toast to our friendship, with this fine new bottle of kosher wine! You first, be my guest!" He broke the seal, unscrewed the cap, and handed the bottle to the Cossack.

"You are correct again, my Jewish comrade!" said the Cossack. "To peace and brotherhood!" And he took a mighty swig of the wine and returned the bottle to Boris.

Boris solemnly screwed the cap back on and put down the bottle.

The Cossack looked at him, already flushed and seeming light-headed but still smiling. "My new friend, you're not going to drink, too?"

"No," said Boris. "I think I'll just wait for the constable to arrive...."

AN ENDANGERED SPECIES
By Charles M. Powell

It was Mendel the Messenger, walking down the main street of Chelm, the village of wise fools, calling the citizens to a special meeting of the Council of the Elders.

"Hear Ye-- Hear Ye-- listen up. Your presence is reque-- reque-- come to the Town Hall tonight. The police apprehe-- they apprehe-- Berel the Beadle got busted and is on trial. Show up just after dinn-- after dinn-- after dessert."

The village was buzzing. Their good Beadle had been arrested? Impossible! Such a pious man, such a *mensch*.[2] It had to be a mistake.

The Town Hall was packed. Presiding was the Rabbi. The charges were read.

"You are charged, Mr. Beadle, for a crime so heinous, so uncaring, so outrageous, that it hurts me to relate it even."

"My God," cried Rivka the Baker. "What did he do?"

Boris the Balagoola chimed in: "If he clobbered his rude, noisy neighbor--the *mamser*[3] had it coming!"

The Rabbi called for order. "You were arrested deep in the forest having just killed--and found in the process of eating--a very rare Whooping Crane bird."

The villagers were stunned.

The Balagoola spoke up: "Whooping Crane? My youngest daughter had that last winter."

"That's whooping cough, you dolt," replied Rivka.

"What am I, a doctor?" grumbled the Balagoola.

---

[2] A good person; it is a high compliment to call someone a *mensch*.
[3] A *mamser* is effectively the opposite of a *mensch*. Leave it at that, please; the more literal definition is ruder.

The Rabbi continued with the trial: "As we all know, this bird is listed by the Tsar as an endangered species and must be protected. I simply cannot understand how you, such a good man, could do this terrible thing. You must be punished and most severely."

The poor Beadle looked crestfallen, "My dear Rabbi...surely you know me well enough to know that there had to be mitigating circumstances involved."

In the audience Tevye the Milkman raised his hand. "Tell me, Rabbi, this 'mitigating' idea, isn't that when the birds fly south for the winter to Miami Beach?"

"No," boomed the Balagoola, "Mitigating is the headache I had last night."

"Oy," sighed the Rabbi.

"You got also a headache?" asked Boris.

Returning to the trial, the Rabbi asked Berel the Beadle to explain himself.

"Well, Rabbi, you know that I am not a man of violence. I don't believe in hunting. I am a gentle man, a pious man, a student. I went into the forest to commune with nature."

"Ha, I thought so," yelled the Balagoola. "Commune with nature...he's a Communist!"

"Go on, Berel," sighed the Rabbi.

"Well, your Rabbi-ship," continued the Beadle, "I got lost, totally lost. For a full week I wandered the forest looking for a way out. I was starving to death. Only my faith in God kept me alive. And then I came upon this beautiful Whooping Crane. Its leg had been broken and it was in obvious pain. I said to myself, 'Berel, it's you or the bird!' I had to put him out of his pain, plus I was starving. I don't know what you would have done, Rabbi, but to save my life and to spare the bird's further suffering, I said a *brocha*,[4] and, sobbing, dispatched this

---

[4] A *brocha* is a blessing or simple prayer. Remember, that ch sound is like clearing your throat.

227

wonderful bird. I would never harm an animal without desperate need, let alone an endangered animal. It took me two hours to light a fire and I was arrested--saved, really--by the Tsar's police."

The crowd was aghast.

"Clearly," said the rabbi, these are mitigating circumstances. Human life is dearer to the Lord than even the life of a rare, endangered bird--and to add to your argument, the bird was suffering. This case is dismissed, and you are free to go. But, before you go, dear Beadle, answer for me a question. You may be the only person in the world to have tasted an endangered Whooping Crane. How would you describe the taste?"

Berel scratched his head. "I don't know Rabbi. Maybe a cross between a Condor and a Bald Eagle?"

"WE HAVE, YOUR HONOR"

By Charles M. Powell

(from a story by Myrtle Atlas)

For weeks, the jury was locked in serious deliberations. Now in the village of Chelm, where the wise fools all lived, serious deliberations are very serious. Finally, the Judge had decided that enough was enough, or, as she so aptly put it: "*Genug*!"[5]

So the jury was summoned to the courtroom and the foreman, Boris the Balagoola, was asked if they had arrived at a verdict.

"We have, your judgeship," replied the Balagoola.

"After six weeks, would you be kind enough to share this news with us, my dear foreman?"

"Absolutely," answered Boris, "but first we got couple of things we jurors feel we should say. We would like first to compliment the District Attorney. In my life I never saw such an open-and-shut case. His organization, the presentation of the facts--brilliant. What a job! Chelm is very lucky to have him as its prosecutor."

The Judge interrupted. "That's very nice. So, Mister Foreman, may we assume that the jury has reached a decision of 'Guilty?'"

"Not so fast, your Highship," replied the Balagoola. "I would like to address myself to the lawyer for the defense. Did you do some kind of job! Not a dry eye on this jury, let me tell you. If I'm in trouble, no question whatsoever, you're my lawyer."

Again, the Judge spoke up. "So the verdict is 'not guilty?'"

But the Balagoola pressed on. "And you, your Honor! Can you run a trial? No nonsense, no monkey business...a landmark case. I'm honored--we're all honored, we should be in your courthouse."

"Thank you, Mister Foreman, but--without appearing to be impatient--may I have the temerity to ask of you a simple question, to

---

[5] *Genug* means "enough already," but you surely figured that out.

end this trial. I ask you, FOR THE FINAL TIME, have you reached a verdict?"

"We have, your Honor."

"And that verdict is?" pursued the Judge.

"We have unanimously decided that, since the prosecutor is so brilliant, and the defense so wonderful, and you, your Judgeship, so terrific--that who are we to interfere? It's OK by us, YOU three decide!"

THE WITNESS
By Charles M. Powell

Accidents happen. I mean, even in the safest village, accidents happen. And Chelm was certainly not the safest village. The town of wise fools--made up of hot-tempered and brilliantly illogical people--was a breeding ground of accidents so it was no surprise when Berel the Beadle reported the latest.

"Oy," he said.

"Oy, what?" asked Schneider the Tailor.

"Oy vey zmir," cried the Beadle.

"This one sounds bad," said Shloime the Student.

"Oy gevalt," continued Berel.

Rivka the Baker was upset. "Listen, if you're going to complain about your children again, I'm leaving!"

"Worse," said Berel.

"What could be worse than your children?" inquired Schneider.

"An accident is worse. There was an accident at the corner of *Daam* and *Tzfardeyah*,[6] Boris the Balagoola's cart and Tevye the Milkman's cart...what a collision. Ask me," said the Beadle, "about the damage."

"So what was the damage?" asked the Baker.

"Don't ask," said Berel. "Fortunately, there was a witness: old Mrs. Goldfarb, who as we know owns the poultry store."

As was the custom in old Russia, the Tsar assigned a District Judge to hear the case so as to assess proper damages. Of course, both Boris the Balagoola and Tevye the Milkman blamed the other for the

---

[6] The inside gag here is that *dahm* (water turning to blood) and *tzfardeyah* (infestation of frogs) are the first two of the Ten Plagues, from Passover, visited upon the Pharaoh by Moses and God to get the Pharaoh to free the Jewish slaves. Hence the joke of the street names.

accident. It became apparent that the old woman's testimony would be critical.

With the old woman in the witness box, Boris's attorney went first and treated her very gently because of her advanced years. "Could you please tell the Court your name?" he asked.

"Bessie Goldfarb," she replied.

"And would you be kind enough to tell us your age?"

The old woman sighed. "*Kinnahora*,[7] eighty-tree."

The attorney hesitated. "Mrs. Goldfarb," he said. "You will notice the clerk in the corner. He writes down every single word that you say. Every word, every phrase. And what he writes down becomes a legal document. Please, I beg of you, do not add any extra words to your answer. Let me, then, ask of you again: what is your age, Mrs. Goldfarb?"

Mrs. Goldfarb smiled, "*Kinnahora*, eighty-tree."

The Judge laughed and called the State's attorney to the bench. "Counsel," he said, "I think I can be of assistance to you. I'm Jewish and I understand the problem. If you allow me to ask the question, perhaps we can get the proper response."

"Be my guest," replied the lawyer.

So the Judge leaned down and smiled at the old woman in the witness box. "Tell us, Mrs. Goldfarb...*Kinnahora*, how old are you?"

And she answered, "Eighty-tree!"

---

[7] *Kinnahora* is the verbal equivalent of "knock on wood," fending off "the evil eye" of superstition.

MARRIAGE/DIVORCE

1. Yenta and the Perfect Match
2. Divorce, Chelm Style
3. Putt Seriously, Folks
4. I Do
5. Marital Bliss
6. The Marriage of Mendel

There may not be a safe way to tell a joke about telling jokes about marriage...staring one, living in one, ending one...so we'll just go to the stories.

(See also "The Craving" and "What's-His-Name's Memory Course" in the Health and Aging chapter and "What I Did On My Summer Vacation" in the Vacations chapter for more references to marriage and its quirks and long-term wonders.)

YENTA AND THE PERFECT MATCH
By Charles M. Powell

A visit from Yenta the Matchmaker always set off a chain reaction of events, and such was the case when she visited the home of Fufchik the Butcher. Now, in Chelm, where the Wise Fools lived, it was known that Fufchik was by far the wealthiest man in the village. It was also known that Fufchik's eldest son, Yankel, was of marrying age and that his father had not yet approved of any of the local girls for his son.

The sight, then, of Yenta descending upon the Fufchik house set up the following chain reaction:

"Oy," said Mrs. Fufchik. "She'll ask only for a glass of tea and end up eating me out of house and home."

"Oy," said Yankel the bachelor. "She'll try to push another bargain on Papa and I'll end up married to someone who smells like a cow, clucks like a chicken, and eats like a horse."

"Oy," said Fufchik the Butcher. "Another scheme, another 'perfect match' that isn't, another fruitless evening."

"Oy, oy, oy," said Yenta, sitting down heavily to her glass of tea. "It grieves me that such a boy, a scholar yet, from such a family should not have a bride. It's a crime against the whole town of Chelm. But this time, without question, I have solved the problem, I have the match of matches. In the history of matches this match will be recorded."

"Oy," said the family Fufchik.

"We are all agreed," said Yenta, "that Yankel is a very special, very unique, very wise young man."

"Oy," said Yankel, the very wise young man.

"For such a boy," continued the Matchmaker, "there is only one match that could possibly make sense. My match of matches is Yankel with no one else but…the daughter of the Tsar!"

"Ridiculous!" thundered Fufchik. "For one thing, the girl--may her parents stay far from Chelm--isn't even Jewish!"

"For such a boy, who wouldn't willingly convert?" Yenta smiled knowingly.

"So even if she converts--and who wants her to?--why would she be interested in a match with our Yankel?"

Yenta stood tall, every inch of her four feet eleven inches indignant.

"From a father I'm hearing this? Do you have any idea what a prize your son is? Forget the fact that he is seemingly tall and relatively handsome. Did he not win the coveted *'Shofar* Award' for not dropping a Torah once all year? Does he not have his own library even, of scholarly books, even though I know both books are out being rebound? Does he not have the finest ear for music in Chelm, witnessed by the time Berel the Beadle blew his nose in Temple and Yankel, mistaking the noise for a *shofar*,[1] yelled, "*Tekiyah*!?" [2]

A hush fell over the house. All eyes turned to Fufchik. He stroked his beard. He walked around the room. He looked at his son. A tear came to his eye. Finally, he said, "All right, I'm not against it."

"I'm not against it either," said Yankel with a slight air of resignation. "I'll do it for my people and for Chelm."

"All right," added Mrs. Fufchik, "I'm not against it also. I guess I'm not really losing a son; I'm gaining a palace-in-law."

Standing up, Fufchik the Butcher, on behalf of his family, proudly proclaimed to Yenta: "So be it! We are in unanimous agreement. It's a match."

"Thank God," sighed Yenta wearily. "At least now half my job is done!"

---

[1] Now you need to know that the *shofar* (sho-FAR) is the ram's horn, ceremonially blown like a trumpet, most notably at the Rosh Hashanah (New Year) and Yom Kippur (Day of Atonement) services. Also Shofar was the name of the Los Angeles-area synagogue where most of these stories were read aloud over the years, but that's an aside.

[2] *Tekiyah* is one of the "calls" of the *shofar*, this one a single tone...the most common in the ritual.

DIVORCE, CHELM STYLE
By Mel Powell

No married couple in Chelm, the tiny village where the wise fools lived, seemed happier than Schneider the Tailor and Selma the Seamstress. A nice home, a good business for each of them, two wonderful grown children.

The telephone had not yet been invented. Long-distance calling was provided by the Friends and *Mishpucha*[3] Plan, with an intricate system of ox-carts, carrier pigeons, and a lot of shouting. But, dear listener, somehow in Chelm they had access to telephones. Just go with it.

And so Schneider the Tailor picked up the phone in Chelm and placed a call to his son, Mottel, in a little town called Anatevka. "Mottel," said Schneider sadly, "you're my oldest child, and there's something I must tell you. I'm divorcing Mama."

Mottel was shocked, "But Papa, you can't just decide to divorce Mama after all these years of blissful marriage! What happened?"

Schneider sighed. "It's too painful for me to talk about it. I only called because you're my son, and I thought you should know. Please, call your sister and tell her. It will spare me the pain."

"But where's Mama?" asked Mottel. "May I please talk to her?"

"No, I haven't told her yet. Believe me, this hasn't been easy. I've agonized over it for several days, and I've finally come to a decision, I have an appointment with Avram the Attorney the day after tomorrow."

"Papa," begged Mottel, "please, don't do anything rash! I'm going to take the first train to Chelm. Promise me that you won't do anything until I get there."

Schneider considered. "Well, all right. You're my son, my only son, so I promise. Next week is Passover. I'll hold off seeing the lawyer until

---

[3] *Mishpucha* means "family."

after the Seder. Call your sister in Vitipsk-Gaboynya and break the news to her. I just can't bear to talk about it anymore." He sighed heavily and hung up the phone.

Minutes later, the phone rang in Chelm. It was Dora, Schneider and Selma's other child. "Papa," said Dora, "I just heard from Mottel! Please, let us talk to you first!"

"What for?" asked Schneider. "We're going to get a divorce!"

"Papa," implored Dora, "I will catch the next train to Chelm. My brother and I will both be there soon. Promise me that you won't do anything until we get there."

Schneider pondered. "Well, all right. You're my only daughter, so I promise." He sighed heavily and hung up the phone.

Schneider turned to Selma. "It worked, my darling. This year they're both coming for Passover. Now, how are we going to get them to come here for Rosh Hashanah?"

PUTT SERIOUSLY, FOLKS
by Jane Powell

Boris the Balagoola, the biggest and strongest man in the tiny village of Chelm, where the wise fools lived, had the biggest body and the biggest heart in the Pale.

So who had the biggest place in his big heart? It was Becky, of course, his devoted wife. But her devotion was nothing compared to his. He had dedicated his very life to her comfort--even though his fellow Chelmites couldn't understand why.

"What a *noodge*!"[4] critiqued Rivka the Baker.

"Who are you to-- who are you to-- you should talk!" said Mendel the Messenger.

Schneider the Tailor needled, "All she does is sit around all day and let Boris provide for her. The only time she leaves the house is to play her beloved golf!" Golf, mind you, had been invented in Scotland, and had only recently reached the Pale...on four or five bounces. The Tailor found the game offensive, as it was played in its original form by men who weren't wearing anything under their *tsitsis*. [5]

Suffice it to say that no one in Chelm quite understood the Balagoola's great devotion to his wife.

Like most Chelmites, Boris was poor, but he saved every extra kopeck to lavish gifts on his dear Becky.

A beautiful house, a goose-down-feather bed, precious paintings, sparkling jewelry, and her favorite: a set of expensive, top-of-the-line golf clubs.

Becky sat Boris down one day for a serious conversation: "Tell me, Balagoola: what would you do if I died?"

---

[4] *Noodge* means to pester and harass...or the person who does the pestering and harassing, as here.
[5] *Tsitsis* are the fringes at the ends of the prayer shawl, but that's not really the joke here, now is it?

"What?" said Boris.

"We've been married a long time. Sure, sometimes we fight and I go visit my mother in Vitipsk-Gaboynya--"

"And sometimes," muttered Boris, "your mother visits here and then we *really* fight."

"Don't interrupt," scowled Becky. "You always treat me well. You buy me wonderful things, even when I don't need them. Such as last year, when you bought me the cemetery plot, which I haven't used yet. But you meant well, and--"

"It's because you're my wife, Becky, and--"

"I said don't interrupt me," barked Becky. "I'm not finished. You'll listen?"

It was not a request.

"OK, Becky," said the Balagoola. Boris's size and strength intimidated everyone...but Becky.

"So," demanded Becky, "If I die, I want you should get married again."

Boris was shocked. "Becky! How can you say such a thing? No one could ever compare to you, dear Becky."

"I insist," insisted Becky. "You'd be lonely, and I want you should be happy, so promise me that you'll get married again!" With great reluctance, the Balagoola gave his word.

"Good," said Becky. "Now, I want also that you and your new wife should live in this house."

"In this house--our house? I could never do such a thing!"

"Once again, dear husband, I insist," insisted Becky once again. "It took you years to pay off this house. You love this house, and you should live in it and be well even after I'm gone."

Again, reluctantly, the Balagoola gave his word.

Becky demanded, "You will also allow the new wife you find someday, after I'm gone, to have the paintings and even my fine jewelry. This new wife of yours should enjoy such beautiful things."

Boris protested mightily, but to no avail.

"And our goose-dawn-feather bed...you will sleep in it with the new wife."

"Becky, please!" begged the distraught Balagoola. "How can you say such things? I cannot sleep in our bed with some other wife!"

"Boris, I insist," Becky insisted again. "It took you years to make your comfortable spot in the bed. I want you should get a good night's sleep, even after I'm gone."

With great reluctance, the Balagoola promised.

"And, finally," said Becky, "I want you should give my most prized possession to her. I want you should give her my favorite golf clubs."

"No," roared Boris. "Absolutely not!"

"What are you--*meshuga*? [6] You'll live in our house, enjoy our paintings and my jewelry, even sleep in our bed--but you won't give her my golf clubs? Why won't you give the new wife my golf clubs?"

"Because," explained Boris, "she's left-handed!"

---

[6] Crazy!

"I DO"

By Mel Powell

[Spoiler alert! Jewish readers, please start reading the story! For our non-Jewish friends, you should know that nachas *means good tidings, good news, good things coming to pass that are cause for heart-bursting celebration.]*

"You can't be serious!" cried Rivka the Baker.

"No, it's true," insisted Selma the Seamstress.

"Your cousin's husband had three daughters from America?"

"No, my dear Rivka, my cousin from America's daughter had three husbands."

Rivka remained confused. "So your American husband's three daughters had a cousin?"

Selma persisted. "No, no, I have an American cousin, she has an American daughter, and her daughter had three husbands."

"Ohhhhh!" At last Rivka understood.

Now Selma's cousins were legendary in Chelm. It was believed among the wise fools of the tiny village that wherever you went, around the world, you were always within earshot of one of Selma's cousins. Her family tree was a veritable forest.

"You see, Rivka, my cousin's daughter first married a wealthy and successful young accountant. A nice Jewish boy."

"So what happened?" asked Rivka.

"Numbers, Rivka! The poor man was obsessed with numbers. He counted each noodle in his chicken soup. He counted each tsitz in his *tsitsis*.[7] He even counted God."

---

[7] *Tsitsis* are the fringes at the ends of the prayer shawl.

"God? How could he count God? There's one God!"

"So he counted to one."

"Amazing!" cried Rivka. "And she left him?"

"That's right, Rivka, and she got a divorce."

Rivka wondered: "Did she forget to get a *Gett*?" [8]

"No, the *Gett*, she got."

"So she got a *Gett*."

"You bet. They were in debt. He was a lousy accountant," explained Selma.

"What next?" asked Rivka.

"Next," said Selma, "she married a wealthy and successful young doctor. A veterinarian. Another nice Jewish boy."

"And what happened?" asked Rivka.

Selma shook her head sadly. "It seems this young doctor was always working. Day and night, night and day, all he cared about? His animals. And never went to synagogue. He cared more about rabies than Rabbis!"

"Amazing!" cried Rivka. "So she left him?"

"That's right, Rivka, and again she got a divorce."

"Another *Gett*? From this vet with the pets?"

"A matching set! What a duet! Then," continued Selma, "she married a wealthy and successful young lawyer. A third nice Jewish boy."

"And what happened to this poor unfortunate girl with this rich lawyer?" asked Rivka.

"This one was in trouble from the get-go. He wanted to know everything about everything!"

---

[8] A *gett* is a ceremonial divorce under very old Jewish law.

"Such as?"

"He wanted to know if the *ketubah*[9] would stand up in court. He wanted to know if he would be held liable should anyone slip and fall while dancing at the reception. He wanted to know if God recognized the laws of community property. The Rabbi fielded all questions with infinite patience. But then, this lawyer insisted on knowing exactly why he was supposed to break the glass at the end of the ceremony."

"And did the Rabbi give him the answer?" asked Rivka,

"Indeed," responded Selma. "The exasperated Rabbi explained to the groom that he had to break a glass just before he became a husband because it would be the last time he would ever put his foot down on anything." [10]

"How true," said Rivka. "And what happened?"

"Again, a divorce," answered Selma sadly. "The poor girl."

"Did she get a *Gett*?"

"No, not yet. But she will; don't fret, no sweat!"

Rivka took a deep breath, "You are telling me that your American cousin had one poor daughter who, in her tumultuous and unstable young life, married and divorced a rich accountant, a rich doctor, and a rich lawyer?"

"Precisely," said Selma.

There were tears in Rivka's eyes. "From one daughter, such *nachas*!"

---

[9] The *ketubah* is the formal Jewish marriage contract, ornate and often displayed in the home.

[10] Non-Jewish friends: that's not the reason. But it is a very old Jewish quip. (The real reason: to serve as a reminder to the marrying couple that there will be bad times--things break--along with the good, and to get through the obstacles together as a team.)

MARITAL BLISS
By Mel Powell

Mendel the Messenger burst into the meeting of the Wise Council of Elders of the tiny village of Chelm--late.

"I apolo-- I apolo-- I'm very sorry," gasped Mendel as he tried to catch his breath.

"Not to worry, good Mendel," said Berel, who held that evening's ceremonial gavel. "But is everything all right?"

"I appre-- I appre-- thanks for asking. But it was because of my grandfather and his forgetf-- his forgetf-- his memory problem. Last Tue-- last Tue-- last week he turned eighty-four years old!"

"*Kinnahora*!" [11] cheered the entire council in unison.

Rivka the Baker chimed in. "What's with your grandfather? I haven't seen forgetful old Mordecai the Messenger Emeritus for weeks, ever since he married young Hilda the Heartbreaker."

Now Boris the Balagoola was interested. "How did I miss this news? The beautiful twenty-three-year-old Hilda, who never went on more than one date with any young man in the village, is now married--and to the eighty-four-year-old retired Messenger Emeritus--*kinnahora*--who started Mendel in the family business?"

"It's true," said Shloime the Student sadly. "Even I went out on a date with her once. Just once. Last Purim, to the Carnival. She broke my heart, too."

Berel restored order, "Mendel, so tell us already--what's with your grandfather?"

Mendel explained. "I was on my way over he-- over he-- to the meeting, when I came upon my grand-- my grand-- Mordecai, in the park."

---

[11] *Kinnahora* is the verbal equivalent of "knock on wood," fending off "the evil eye" of superstition.

"What was he doing in the park?" asked Rivka.

"He was sitting on the bench cry-- cry-- sobbing up a storm."

"How come?" asked the concerned Balagoola.

"He said 'Hello, Grandson. How are you fee-- how are you fee-- sit down.' So I did.

"'I'm so happy! Listen, Mendel, although I will always miss your late Grandmother--may she rest in pea--in pea--*aleha hasholom*, [12] I have found a new mate! Hilda is won-- Hilda is won-- what a woman!"

"Then why are you cry-- are you cry-- so what's the matter?" I asked him.

"'Hilda is wonderful in the kitch-- in the kitch-- like a gourmet chef! And my memory is awf-- is awf-- I can't remember a thing, but her memory is perfect, and she makes sure I never mis-- never mis-- that I take my medicine on time. And she's also terrific in the bedr-- the bedr--'"

"'I'll take your word for it, Grandfather,' I told him quickly," said Mendel.

"So," boomed Boris, "tell us already, Mendel, why was he crying?"

"I asked him again! 'Grandfather, if she's so perf-- so perf-- amazing, why are you sitting here in the park, crying?'

"'Because, grandson...I forgot where I live!'"

---

[12] *Aleha hasholom* is the idiomatic "rest in peace." "May her memory be for a blessing" is a commonly used English phrase. (*Alav hashalom* for a male.)

THE MARRIAGE OF MENDEL
By Charles M. Powell

Boris the Balagoola was ecstatic. "Mazel tov, Mendel. Finally, finally."

Rivka the Baker added her two kopecks' worth tearfully: "I'm so happy for you, I could cry like a baby."

Mendel the Messenger blushed. "Thank y-- thank y-- I appreciate your good wishes. Next wee-- wee-- in a few days we'll have a party, I'll bring her."

Schneider the Tailor laughed. "After all these years, finally you found the girl of your dreams. Mazel tov!"

"Tell us," inquired the Balagoola, "that despite the fact that everyone in Chelm introduced you to every single girl, why were you always so picky?"

Mendel scratched his head. "There was always something wro-- wro--a flaw. If the gir--gir-- woman cooked like my Mama, she would look like my Papa."

Rivka sneered. "That's *your* story. By me, you never got married because you're the cheapest man in Chelm. What girl would marry you?"

"Not tr--not tr--you made that up," protested Mendel. "My first girlfriend broke up with me because of illness."

"Yeah," said the Balagoola. "She got *sick* of how cheap you are."

Mendel the Messenger went on the attack. "Au con-- au con-- again not true," he said. "It was I who left my second love…for religious reasons."

Rivka shook her head. "The girl told me that the religious reason was that he worshiped money."

Boris the Balagoola chimed back in, "And what about Chana from Minsk? She you wouldn't marry because you said she had a speech impediment. You of all people."

Mendel was outraged. "Now wait a-- wait a-- just ein minootin here. She did have a speech impediment. Another fell--fell--another man would ask her out and she couldn't say 'no.'"

A *Kiddush*[13] was offered and everyone calmed down. "Tell me, Mendel," said Rivka the Baker. "Who introduced you to your bride-to-be?"

"Nobody," said the Messenger. "We just happened to meet. I'm not blam-- not blam-- this one's nobody's fault!"

And so it went; and so they were in love; and so they were married.

The bride showed no signs of nagging. The groom showed no signs of being terminally cheap...or nagging.

One morning, the new Mrs. The Messenger giggled to Mendel over breakfast.

"My Mendel," she tittered. "Last night I had the most wonderful dream. I dreamed that you had purchased for me the finest sable fur coat in all of Russia. It cost six hundred rubles, I dreamed--more than you earn in ten years--but you bought it for me anyway. And how happy you made me; and how beautiful I looked. Wasn't that a wonderful dream, Mendel?"

Mendel remembered the criticism of the Chelmites. He remembered the charges of frugality. He searched for just the right words, just the proper response. And God was with him that morning.

Mendel smiled at his bride. 'What a wonderful dream that was, my darl-- my darl-- my wife. From this morning forth, in all your *dreams*, you should wear it in good health!"

---

[13] The *kiddush* is the blessing for the wine.

POLITICS

1. Un-Conventional Wisdom
2. The Great Chelm Convention
3. Happy Days Are Here Again

Politics, elections, governance, leadership…isn't that always the purview of the "wisest" fools, who don't quite understand that they're fools?

UN-CONVENTIONAL WISDOM
By Mel Powell

Chaos reigned on the floor of the annual Chelm Mayoral Convention.

Oh, it wasn't the bitter debate about the platform, because shortly after it collapsed, Kalman the Karpenter fixed it.

It wasn't even the confusion around the campaign's environ-mental debate, where the only thing that got recycled was the rhetoric.

No, it was the bitter infighting.

It started with a stirring speech by Schneider the Tailor. "If elected, gentle citizens," intoned Schneider, "I promise to bring about change in our little village!"

"What are you saying, Schneider?" asked Shloime the Student. "If it's broke, you'll fix it?"

"No," said the Tailor, "but if it's torn, I'll mend it!"

A wave of support greeted the next candidate, the ever-popular Boris the Balagoola, with campaign signs springing up everywhere--"Join the Chorus--Vote for Boris!"--"Boola Boola, Balagoola!" [1]

Boris appealed to the delegates. "I am the only candidate qualified to keep out the Cossacks…by building a huge wall at the village limits!"

Rivka retorted, "Boris…Cossacks have ladders."

---

[1] "Boola Boola" is an old-style catch phrase connected to Yale University. As it happens, the author attended Yale, and this was known to most of the congregation in the Los Angeles area when this story was ready at the end of a service. As it happens, so, too, did the talented actor (Bret Shefter) who read the story aloud that evening. After reading this line…and while the congregation chuckled and groaned, Bret gave the author a look that could have withered an ivy-covered stone wall. In defiance…the author leaves this reference in the story. Boola Boola!

Berel the Beadle swore he didn't know anything about anything and yielded the floor without speaking.

Finally, the outgoing Mayor, Rivka the Baker, rose. "My friends, good citizens, gentle candidates, let me ask you but one question. Why do you want this *mishugena*[2] job? Headaches, nothing but headaches. Listen to what Berel, my predecessor, did for me, on my first day in office.

"He left three sealed-with-wax letters for me, and told me, 'Rivka, open the first letter when you face your first crisis as Mayor. When you suffer your second crisis, open the second letter. When all else is lost, when things look really bleak, only then should you open the third letter.'"

"And did it help?" asked Boris.

"It was perfect," answered Rivka. "Remember when I ordered the re-painting of the temple seats the night before a service, but in the horrible humidity the paint didn't dry?"

Schneider chuckled. "When the choir stood up, their robes didn't. What a sight! Of course we remember! What did the first letter say?"

Rivka quoted: "'Blame it on the last Mayor!' I did, and you forgave me. Then I suffered my second crisis, when I gave a disastrous speech to a troop of the Tsar's horse soldiers. This, as we all remember, led to the first-ever strike of the Rider's Guild."

"And the second letter?" asked Boris.

Rivka explained: "That one said: 'Tell them that your programs are not yet in place!' So I did, and you gave me another chance. But then we reached the crisis that brings us here today. Our fragile economy is suffering the worst recession since Berel's hairline."

And she held up a sealed-with-wax envelope.

---

[2] Crazy!

The candidates exchanged nervous glances. It was Boris who, with fear and apprehension, demanded: "*Nu* [3]-- open it already! What does the third letter say?"

Rivka opened it, and read aloud: "'Start preparing three letters!'"

---

[3] *Nu* is a Yiddish word with lots of uses. As in formal greeting, it's your "What's up? Or *"Que pasa?"* As an interjection during a conversation, it can mean "See what I mean?" but also "seriously, you think *that* is an important issue?" Or, here, it stands for "get on with it!" Very useful, *nu*?

THE GREAT CHELM CONVENTION

By Charles M. Powell

[This is another of the handful of stories that do not involve the regular cast of characters, with just a cameo by our friend Berel the Beadle.]

One might believe that the institution of political conventions began here in America. Not so! It began many years ago, in the little town of Chelm, when the Wise Council of Elders called a convention to choose a new President for their Great Synagogue.

Perchik, the outgoing President, had served for many years, and served well, if not wisely. He had been elected President because it was his ox-cart that was needed to transport students, books, wedding parties, and all such important things. Besides, his home had a large oak table around which the Synagogue Elders could meet and argue and debate and fight and compromise and eventually come up with the wrong decision on everything.

For example, it was under Perchik's administration that membership increased to 112 Jews, even though there were only 67 chairs in the Synagogue. This, it was wisely reasoned, would inspire a good turnout in the event of plague. Unfortunately (some said, on this issue), Chelm was never touched by plague. Often, at services, standees would faint, but it seemed always to be from boredom during an especially long sermon and never from plague.

Then, Perchik once led the battle to establish a Singles group for the Great Synagogue. When it developed that many more women than men attended, it was the wise President who decreed that the Singles group was open only to married couples, thus assuring an equal number of men and women.

It was no simple task to replace such a President. A convention was finally called to make the selection. Much time and many glasses of tea were consumed, and the choice narrowed to two wise elders:

Fafalin and Chulnik. Both men had impressive credentials. Each had served on the Wise Council of Elders. Each had proved himself a first-class fool, a key qualification.

The battle lines were drawn between the two men. Chulnik's name was placed in nomination by Berel the Beadle. Berel reminded the Council that Chulnik had sponsored the rule setting all Chelm clocks back 20 minutes, thus assuring a prompt starting time for late starting Shabbat Services. There was much support for a man so wise.

The name of Fafalin was placed in nomination by Laybel the Locksmith. Fafalin was famous for solving the *Oneg Shabbat*[4] problem. It seemed that the tables, laden with cakes and tea and schnapps, were impossible to get at, as the congregants would cluster around them. The solution--which escaped all but was obvious to Fafalin--was to hold services in the *Oneg Shabbat* room, and the *Oneg Shabbat* in the Sanctuary, because everyone could get to the *bima*.[5]

And so the balloting began. Chulnik took an early lead. Then Fafalin forged ahead. Then Chulnik. Again Fafalin. The proceedings went well into the night with no winner.

Finally, to break the deadlock, both candidates put on their coats and boots and went for a walk to discuss the situation.

Alone, away from the din and heated emotions of the convention, Chulnik laughed and said, "To tell you the truth, Fafalin, I have no great desire to be President of this or any other Synagogue, I have no head for figures; I've never liked the Cantor, and worse, I don't even have an ox cart."

Fafalin was amazed. "'You mean you went this far and don't even want the job? Why?"

"If the truth be known," sighed Chulnik, "my wife really felt--"

---

[4] *Oneg Shabbat* is a social time, usually with snacks, after a service.
[5] The *bima* is the stage from which the service is conducted; many synagogues have a central area and not a raised stage, but the concept is that this is the focal point of the service.

"Go no further, my wife also felt," said Fafalin. "Besides, I don't even have an oak table."

The solution was obvious at least to the Wise Fools of Chelm. Arm-in-arm, the two candidates returned to the convention hall and announced that, because one did not own a cart and the other had no oak table, serving as President would be unheard of for either of them.

The convention was thrown into chaos. Finally, a secret ballot was taken. Except for a single vote, the convention triumphantly drafted Perchik, the outgoing President.

There was only one dissenting vote. It was cast by Perchik, the incoming President.

HAPPY DAYS ARE HERE AGAIN

By Charles M. Powell

(with Lew Horn)

"The best thing about Chelm," said Berel the Beadle, "is our democratic process. When we hold elections, we hold elections."

"What's the big deal about electing a new Mayor?" said Schneider the Taylor. "Four or five of our citizens run for office, we hold primaries, we hold elections, and we get a new Mayor!"

Berel smiled. "Democracy, democracy. In Moscow they got a Tsar. In Warsaw, they got a King. Who gets to vote? Who ever heard of an election? Only in Chelm do we go through all of the democratic steps to find the best person for each office."

Shloime the Student laughed. "You call this year's candidates the best? You'll excuse me, but a good Mayor we won't get. A herring could do a better job!"

Kalman the Karpenter started listing the candidates. "First, there's the incumbent, Mottel the Mayor. He doesn't campaign. He sits in his rose garden and watches the value of the kopeck drop."

Rivka the Baker weighed in. "How about the one who promises things no one has even asked for yet? He owes so many favors, he won't have time to be Mayor, he'll be too busy writing thank-you notes."

Berel interrupted. "Remember what he said when Tevye asked him about the new farm bill?"

"Who could forget?" said Kalman. "He said, 'If we owe it, we should pay it!'"

"I think," said Boris the Balagoola, "that it's always best to elect a rich man to office. You don't worry he has to steal from you."

"Or maybe a poor man," said Rivka. "He is not used to spending a lot of money, so the budget is safe."

Schneider the Tailor laughed. "You want to cut costs, elect Morris the *Mohel*." [6]

Well, dear listener, what can I tell you about the election? The chaos! The craziness! All to elect the Mayor of the tiny village of Chelm.

And when election day came, guess who voted? Nobody! What am embarrassment. What a scandal. Even the candidates didn't vote--for themselves. And that year, everything ran like clockwork.

In fact, it was such a success in Chelm that the next year they didn't elect a mayor in Minsk, Pinsk, or Vitipsk-Gaboynya, either!

---

[6] A *mohel*, pronounced "moil" rhymes with "toil," is the specialized rabbi who performs the ritual circumcision of the male baby.

SHOW BUSINESS

1. All The World's A Stage
2. Right On Cue
3. Everybody's A Critic
4. Speak The Speech
5. You're Gonna Love It

    Also: Funny Business *
       (found at the end of the stories, "A Final Tale")

There's no business like it.

And who better to bring unique skills and talents to the profession...or their unique take on those who ply the trade...than the wise fools?

ALL THE WORLD'S A STAGE

By Mel Powell updating a Charles M. Powell version
of a Roger Caras story

Avram the Actor--chief Thespian of the little village of Chelm, were the wise fools all lived--hadn't worked in years.

Well, he hadn't worked as an actor in years. He had worked as a waiter in the Chelm Cafe, but he was fired tor approaching every table with the question: "To order...or not to order?"

Before that, had a gig as an assistant to the assistant messenger, but he quit because he didn't like the billing. Currently he was employed as the dialect coach in the Chelm *cheder*.[1]

But Avram was an optimist. Every day he contacted his agent, seeking a gig. And every day the secretary gave the same answer: call back tomorrow.

Then, one morning, Avram's phone--which hadn't been invented yet--rang. It was the agent himself! Amazing. Unheard of.

"Avram, sweetheart, have I got a job for you. A play. A sure-fire hit. You get featured billing. The play opens in Vitipsk-Gaboynya, bound for Minsk and a premiere in Pinsk. But you have to be there for tonight's performance, ready to go on. The actor who had the part is out of the show. Someone told him to break a leg--and he did."

Avram was caught between excited and upset. "A featured part? Bound for Pinsk? But how big a part? Do I have any creative control? I was a headliner! I did Shakespeare, I did de Balzac, I did Sholom Aleichem!"

The agent waited for the actor to wind down. "Avram, baby, it's one line. But it's a critical line. And, besides the billing, you get a one-year contract."

Avram was outraged. "Just one line?"

---

[1] A *cheder* is an elementary school, including basics of the Hebrew language.

Even through the phone, Avram could see his agent dismiss the concern with a wave of his fifteen-percent hand. "Avram, pussycat, read my lips. Take...The...Part. You won't get another chance if you turn this one down. Today, nobody remembers you're still alive. I barely remember you're still alive....Look, this is your big second chance. The play revolves around this line. And you have to learn it and be in Vitipsk-Gaboynya by curtain time tonight."

Avram thought it over. For less than a fraction of a portion of an instant he thought it over. "I'll take the part. I'll do it. But this is far beneath my talents. What's the line?"

The agent quoted it carefully: "Hark, is that a cannon I hear?"

"What kind of line is that? What is this play, anyway?"

"Listen, don't worry. It's a period piece. Just get there. Period. You'll be sewn into your costume and put into your makeup as soon as you arrive. You're the same size as the last actor. That's why you got...um...that's one of the reasons you got the part. Just worry about your line. It's all arranged. Do what I tell you and be sure that you know your line."

Avram was insulted. "I'll know my line already. How do I get there?"

The agent explained. "Boris the Balagoola is pulling up to your door right now. I just spoke to him on his ox-phone, because I knew you'd say yes. He'll drive you to the theater in Vitipsk-Gaboynya. Once you get there, they'll take care of you. Now, let me hear the line."

"Hark, is that a cannon I hear?"

"Perfect! Break a leg! Metaphorically, not like the other guy."

Now Avram, while angry--even though he was glad to be going on stage again--was, after all, a professional. So, as he rode with Boris, he rehearsed his line. All the way from Chelm to Vitipsk-Gaboynya. Over and over. Boris, a stranger to theatrical productions, handled Avram's incessant rehearsals well enough. The ox, however, wanted to punch him.

"Hark, is that a *cannon* I hear?"

"Hark, is *that* a cannon I hear?"

"Hark, is that a cannon *I* hear?"

"Hark, is that a cannon I *hear*?"

No question, Avram knew the line cold. (So did the ox.)

As the doorman at the stage entrance in Vitipsk-Gaboynya admitted Avram, he said to the actor, "OK, new actor, let me hear your line."

Avram, annoyed, nonetheless obliged him. "Hark, is that a cannon I hear?"

The wardrobe master, sewing Avram into the costume, said, "Let me hear your line."

"Hark, is that a cannon I hear?"

The makeup artist went to work. "Say the line, please. But keep your mouth still, I'm working here."

"Mrk, mm at a cm-mm I mmph?"

"Very good."

Finally ready, Avram waited in the wings. The stage manager approached, pocket-watch in hand, whispering, "OK, actor, say the line."

Avram could bear no more. He snapped, "I know my line already!"

The stage manager backed down not even an inch. "My orders are to hear it anyway. Listen, actor, all of our jobs depend on you. The play depends on you. Your career depends on you. Say your line!"

Avram, fuming and completely out of patience, said, emphatically, "I know my line!"

The stage manager became frantic. "Just say it! One more time! Say it! You've got only ten seconds before you go on!"

"OK, OK. Hark--"

But it was too late, time was up, and the stage manager pushed Avram out onto the stage. The stage was pitch dark, the theater jam-packed and stone silent. This was Avram's big moment.

Suddenly, a deafening blast of cannons sounded!

Avram ducked. "What the heck was that?!?"

RIGHT ON CUE
By Charles M. Powell

"Oh, boy," said Boris the Balagoola, "the Yiddish Theatre is coming to town."

Once a year, the touring company of actors found its way to Chelm, its purpose to entertain the wise fools of the village before moving on to greener pastures and brighter audiences.

The Theatre troupe always hired three or four local people to fill out their cast, and so they were meeting with Berel the Beadle that very day.

Devorah the Director was talking: "First, we will need three young girls for our schoolroom scene. Can you find them for us, good Beadle?"

"No problem," said Berel. "I'll get Rubella, the Rabbi's middle daughter; plus Boris the Balagoola's younger sister; and then Yenta the Matchmaker. She's not so young but she could use the exposure. Who else do you need?"

"The only other casting is for the role of the Messenger. It's a small part but it's crucial," said Devorah.

"No problem," said the Beadle. "I got for you the perfect choice. A man who's done this very part many times."

"Terrific," said the director. "Who've you got in mind?"

Berel smiled. "Who else but the best? I'll do the part myself, no problem."

"You did it before?"

"Many times."

"Wonderful. Rehearsals are at ten in the morning."

"Count me out. Rehearsals I don't need."

"But you'll need a costume..."

"No problem," said Berel. "I got my own."

"And you know your cue?"

"Listen, Miss Director Person, you're new to the traveling troupe, but I've played this role for years. I can do this part with my eyes closed. I'll be there, and believe me, I know my cue."

Thus assured, the play was set for the following week in the Social Hall of the Great Synagogue of Chelm.

Need I tell you the turn-out that night? Anybody who was anybody was there. Schneider the Tailor, Rivka the Baker, Tevye the Milkman, everybody. Even Mendel the Messenger, who annually refused the role of Messenger in the play, not wanting to be type-cast. The play was the highlight of the social season. Tickets were selling for six kopecks and it was rumored that Kalman the Karpenter had built the entire set in exchange for only two tickets.

Needless to say, it was Standing Room Only as the play began. The actors were superb and Berel, watching from the wings, was sure that he had never seen a better performance. The audience was laughing; the audience was crying; let me tell you, it was a magical evening.

Berel the acting Messenger was awaiting his cue to go onstage. Avram the Actor was in the midst of his longest soliloquy. As it drew to an end, Avram said, "Hark, I think I hear the messenger approaching?" He looked toward Berel in the wings.

Berel looked back at him. The stage manager ran up to the Beadle. "That's your cue," he said. "Get on stage."

"Not yet," said Berel. "I know when my cue comes."

On stage, the actors were in a frenzy. Avram repeated, "Hark, I'm *sure* that I hear the messenger coming."

In the wings, Berel moved not a muscle. "Get out there," begged the stage manager.

"Not until I hear my cue," insisted the Beadle. "I've done this part for years and, believe me, I know my own cue."

Onstage, the actors were berserk. Finally, Avram the Actor could stand the wait no longer. Losing full control, he bellowed: "Will someone get that idiot, that nincompoop, the *mishugena*[2] messenger out here immediately?"

"A-ha," said Berel, "THAT'S my cue!"

---

[2] Crazy, ridiculous!

"EVERYBODY'S A CRITIC"

By Mel Powell

(from a story by Mel Present)

"Papa! Good news!" said the happy Dora the Daughter as she burst into the family home in Chelm.

"So, what's this news?" asked Perchik, the papa.

"I'm getting married!"

Now this, indeed, was news. Papa Perchik had not received a visit from Yente the Matchmaker. And getting married in Chelm without Yente's input was almost as unusual as holding a conversation in Chelm without Yente's input.

"All right," said Perchik cautiously, not wanting to overreact to his daughter's news until, like any other wise fool of Chelm, he had more information to misinterpret. "Who is the husband-to-be?"

The love-struck Dora cooed, "I'm going to marry Arturo! Arturo the Actor!"

Papa scratched his suddenly troubled head. "Who, pray tell, is Arturo the Actor? I know of Chelm's own Aharon the Actor,[3] but I don't know any 'Arturo.'"

"They're the same person, Papa. Aharon changed his name to Arturo to play more ethnic roles."

Perchik rolled his eyes. "Well, whatever the name, under no circumstances will I give my blessing for my only daughter to marry the lowest-of the low, an actor!"

"But, Papa--"

"Don't you 'but papa' me, young lady. What a life you have if you marry an actor! An uncertain future! Long hours waiting for the results

---

[3] An inside joke, as our long-time friend and member of the synagogue was the Israeli character actor Aharon Ipale, and as a nod to him the reference stays put. Look up his credits; you surely saw him in something.

of auditions! Endless late nights wondering when he'll get home from his job…waiting tables! I will not allow you to marry an actor!"

"Now, Papa, it could be worse," explained the heartsick Dora. "I could marry a doctor and never see him because he was on call all the time."

"But he'd be rich," said Papa.

"And, Papa," argued Dora, "it could be worse yet. I could marry a lawyer."

"But he'd be rich! And at least a horrible lawyer is consistent, unlike your hyphenate husband-to-be, part-actor, part-waiter, and he probably always wanted to direct, anyway."

The daughter decided to fight dirty. "Yes, Papa. But I could marry Boris the Balagoola's son."

Perchik paused. "OK, so I'll consider your actor."

But in fact, as the weeks passed, no argument could move Perchik from his position of positively profound prohibition of the marriage of his only daughter to an actor.

Finally, Dora begged her father to give her intended a chance. "Papa, at least come see him in his new show. He's the leading man! You'll come see him act, and then you'll know that he'll be good for me, and provide for me, and take care of me forever."

Perchik, trying to be reasonable, could not ignore her plea so off they went to see the show.

Arturo the Actor emoted like he never had before. The audience laughed, the audience cried. What a performance!

After the show, Perchik turned to Dora and smiled, "Darling daughter, I admit that I was wrong, I apologize. I gladly give you my blessing."

"Oh, thank you, Papa!" gushed Dora. "Thank you so much! But, Papa, what made you change your mind? Why will you now allow me to marry Arturo, even though he's an actor?"

"Listen," said Perchik. "I can explain. Now that I've seen him perform, I can tell you: he's no actor!"

SPEAK THE SPEECH, I PR...PR...PRAY YOU ...

By Charles M. Powell

To be an actor on the stage is a wonderous thing. To be an actor on the stage in Chelm, where the Wise Fools all lived, was something else.

Now, Mendel the Messenger and his good wife, Tanya the Telephone Operator, had a son bitten by the acting bug. Bitten? He was consumed.

Let them tell the story; first, Mendel:

"You want to be an act-- an act-- you want to be in the theatre? What kind of craz-- what kind of craz-- *mishigas*[4] is that? You'll starve to death."

"Yea, verily fa-- fa-- Dad. I am burning with passion."

"Burning with pash--burning with pash--don't talk dirty in front of your mother! If you're so hotsy-totsy, I'll introduce you to Malka's daughter, who is known, you should pardon the expression, as "The Luscious Litvak."'

The mother, Tanya the Telephone Operator, spoke up. "Mendel, I'll not have you talking dirty in front of the kinder."

"Ki-- ki-- child? He's not a child; he's an actor. So does my son, the passion flower, want to meet Malka's daughter?"

"No, thank you, fa-- fa--Pop. My career comes first."

Well, there are not too many roles for a fledgling thespian with no experience and a touch, if you will, of a speech impediment. True to his father's prediction, the young actor was starving.

To keep himse lf going, he took a job as a singing waiter, but his rendition of "Chattanooga Choo-Choo" was a disaster.

---

[4] Madness!

Tanya, his mother, did the best she could as town telephone-person. Witness: "One ringy-dingy...two ringy-dingy...good morning. You've reached Chelm 2-7-9. Have I got for you an actor?" Or, better yet, "I'm sorry for breaking in on your party line, but do either of you need an actor? No? How about a waiter?"

Nothing was working. They tried getting the young man an agent. Even Tanya, the village telephone-person, couldn't get one to return the call. Not even the Jewish agent, William Morris. You would think that they would return at least 15 percent of their calls.

So things were not looking good when--out of the blue--the young actor called his parents with some startling news. Tanya, of course, answered the phone:

"One ringy-dingy...two ringy-dingy...'You have reached the residence of Mendel the Messenger, en famile. To whom do you wish to schmooze?...and by the by...do you know of an acting gig for my son?"

"Mama it's me, your s-- your s-- your actor."

"Hello, actor. When was the last time you ate a meal, actor?"

"Grea--grea-- wonderful news, Mama. I just got a jo-- jo-- a role on a soap opera, whatever that is. A continuing role, yet."

Mendel chimed in: "A soap opera? You don't wash? So tell me, Actor, what part are you going to play?"

"They gave me the part of a Jewish husband."

Tanya sighed. "To tell you the truth, I'm a little disappointed. I was hoping you'd get a speaking part!"

"YOU'RE GONNA LOVE IT"
By Mel Powell

"Recession? What recession? We're in no recession!" said the Mayor of Chelm while standing on the unemployment line.

Despite such protestations, it was clear that the economy was in fact receding even faster than Berel the Beadle's hairline. To support the Great Synagogue of Chelm, the Wise Council of Elders decided to hold a gala fundraising event of a scope and magnitude greater than ever before in the tiny village.

Rivka the Baker announced, "It will be a show of shows, an evening of entertainment that will make the not-yet-invented Golden Globe Award look like a Copper *Knish*!"[5]

Mendel the Messenger volunteered to select the single act that would comprise the entire gala show, and one week later he reported back to the Council, "Shloime the Stu—the Stu-- the college boy was the first to audi-- audi-- try out."

"What was his act?" asked Rivka.

"He was to discu-- discu-- talk about the political ideol-- ideol-- blather of the last seven tsars in the form of rhyming coup-- rhyming coup-- a poem."

"Did he make it into the show?"

"No. But he did manage to cure my insom-- my insom-- now I can sleep at night."

Rivka wondered "So what was the act you did choose?"

Mendel recounted the tale:

*** ***

---

[5] A *knish* is a baked, or sometimes deep fried, covering of dough with a filling… sometimes mean, very commonly mashed potato…but here it's used just an alliterative play on words.

"Excuse me," said the gentleman who appeared at the door. "Are you Mendel the Messenger? Permit me to introduce myself. I am Avram the Agent."

Many people were famous throughout the land. Avram the Agent wasn't one of them. The only thing Avram had ever done right as an agent was to calculate that ten percent of nothing amounts to less than nothing. His only solace was knowing that at least agents weren't hated quite as much as lawyers.

"Can I hel-- can I hel-- what do you want?" I asked him.

"My good Mendel--can I call you that?--it is not what you can do for me, but what I can do for you. Have I got an act for your fundraiser!"

And with that, Avram presented his act. "Observe, Mendel, sweetheart, as I place this little piano right here. And my trusty dalmatian will sit on the little piano bench here. And atop the piano…" and Avram reached into his pocket "…I place the crown jewel of my act, this tiny field mouse."

At a signal from Avram, the dalmatian began to play the piano with skill and emotion, and the mouse began to sing, and with such tones! Never before had Mendel heard such wonderful music!

"This is terrif-- this is terrif-- Wow!" I exclaimed. "You're hi-- you're hi-- you got the gig!"

"Wonderful," said Avram. "We'll take a meeting and cut a deal. We'll do lunch. My people will call your people."

*** ***

Rivka was delighted. She and Mendel advertised the fundraiser far and wide, never forgetting to mention the amazing dalmatian piano-player and the angelic voice of the singing mouse. Spirits and the needed funds were raised, and at the conclusion of the show the Wise Council Committee congratulated Mendel on a talent search well done.

But one week later, a guilt-ridden Avram located Mendel.

"My good Messenger," apologized Avram, "I come to you humbly, filled with remorse."

"What's the prob-- what's the prob-- talk to me."

"I have lied to you, good sir, perpetrating an evil deception against you and the good people of Chelm. The act--the piano-playing dalmatian-and-phenomenal-singing-mouse--was not nearly as good as it appeared to be! A cruel hoax! A fraud!"

"How com-- how com-- what are you talking?"

"Mendel, don't you understand? The act is a sham! It's a trick! There's nothing special about it. The mouse can't sing at all. He lip-synched! The dalmatian is a ventriloquist!"

SYNAGOGUE AND TRADITION

1. Fore!! (He's A Jolly Good Fellow)
2. Balagoola Island
3. Ticket, Please
4. Don't Cry For Me, Balagoola
5. Beadle-De-Dumb
6. The *Melamed*
7. Natural Selection
8. Does A Bear *Kvetch* In The Woods?
9. When You Wish Upon A Tsar
10. The Woodcutter

The center of life in a small Jewish village is the Synagogue, with its warmth, ritual, and tradition as a gathering place. And its quirks. And the quirks of those traditions. There's a lot to unpack.

(See also "A Bright Future" and "Bird Brain" in the Animals chapter; "A New Kiddush Cup" and "The New Vink" in the Charity and Fundraising chapter; and "The Rodent Less Traveled" in the Youth chapter for other visits to the Synagogue that could have reserved a place in this chapter.)

FORE!! (He's a jolly good fellow)
By Mel Powell

[A quick note: there are a couple of "inside" jokes here that pertain to the Los Angeles area congregation and its meeting place, but they fit so they might as well stay. Also, for our non-Jewish friends...and forgive us, you probably know this already...Yom Kippur is the holiest and most solemn day of the year. Jews atone for their sins of the past year and promise to do better, as God inscribes us in the "Book of Life" for another year. Yom Kippur is a day for quiet reflection, not fun and games.]

Confusion reigned in the synagogue of the tiny village of Chelm, where the wise fools lived.

"So where in the world is he?" boomed Boris the Balagoola.

"Where in the world is who?" asked Rivka the Baker.

Mendel the Messenger explained. "Our good rabbi is miss-- is miss-- isn't here yet."

Schneider the Tailor was aghast. "But it's Yom Kippur morning! And it's precisely--" and he checked his digital watch, which hadn't been invented yet-- "twenty minutes after ten o'clock! And Yom Kippur services always begin at precisely ten o'clock. More or less."

It was sad but true. Although ox-cart parking had been a nightmare, and the synagogue's shiny new air conditioning system-- which also hadn't been invented yet--had caused icicles to form on Pincus the Pious's *pais*,[1] everything had gone smoothly these High Holy Days.

Just then the rabbi rushed in, apologizing for the terrible ox-cart jam in Cold-Borscht Canyon, and promised he'd be ready in just a few minutes.

---

[1] *Pais* (PAY-iss) are loose, long sideburns often sported by orthodox men and boys.

"This has happened before, you know," said Rivka the Baker.

Shloime the Student argued. "I can't remember any such thing!"

"That's because you're too young," huffed Boris. "It was our former rabbi years ago, it was time for services, and no rabbi!"

"Where was he?" asked Shloime.

Schneider the Tailor spoke up. "No one knew where the rabbi was! Well, not exactly no one." Schneider began the story:

*** ***

On the top floor of the Executive Suite in Heaven, a harried, overworked, underpaid angel, stubble on his chin and polyester in his suit, had burst into The Big Office.

"Boss! Boss! You gotta hear this, Boss!"

"What is it, Angel 86?" intoned the Lord, peering up from behind his computer screen. (In Heaven, computers had already been invented.) "It's Yom Kippur! Can't you see I'm busy scrolling through this year's CD-ROM of Life?"

"But Boss: that's just it, Boss! It's Yom Kippur."

With infinite patience, the Holy One put down his Holy Mouse. "Tell me something I don't know," said God. "Which won't be easy, because I know everything."

*** ***

Boris the Balagoola interrupted Schneider's story. "Listen here, Mr. Tailor. You've got it all wrong. Don't even think about arguing. Let me tell it." And Boris continued the story:

*** ***

The little angel took a deep breath, then blurted out: "I was doing my random check of the world when I saw this rabbi--a rabbi, mind you--playing golf! Golf, Your Worshipfulness! He's so addicted to the game that he snuck out early--before Yom Kippur services--to get in his eighteen holes! He's at the first tee as we speak!"

At this news The Lord began to pay attention. "Golf, hmmmm. Which rabbi?"

"From the synagogue in Chelm!"

"Oy vey," said God.

"Exactly!" said Angel 86. "What do you want I should do to punish him, Boss? What do you want I should do?"

The Chief Executive Officer of All Things pondered. "All right, this calls for a severe punishment. I hate to do it, and I usually like to be lenient with rabbis, but this is too much. You get out there to that golf course and give that Rabbi a hole in one!" Then God turned his attention back to his computer screen.

The angel, flabbergasted, wings twitching in consternation, stood frozen. "Um, Boss? You OK, Boss? You want me to *punish* this golfing rabbi by giving him a hole in one? You call this punishment?"

"You question my orders?" mused The Lord calmly, without looking up. The angel gulped.

"Um, no, Sir, um, Boss." The angel hustled out of The Office and gave the Rabbi a hole in one on the first hole.

He burst back into the Boss's Office. God calmly told him to go give the rabbi *another* hole in one. The Angel sputtered and shook... but off he went to catch up with the rabbi on the fourth hole.

He burst back into the Boss's Office again.

"I did it, Boss. I don't understand it, but I did it. I gave him a second hole in one! But I gotta go on record as complaining about this outrage! Smite me down, if you must, Boss, but I gotta know why! A hole in one! For playing golf on Yom Kippur? How is this punishment???"

With infinite wisdom and patience, the Official Scorer of All Games smiled at the little angel. "Think, 86; *think*! A hole in one! Then another on the same day. On Yom Kippur! And he's a rabbi! Now...*who's he gonna tell*?"

BALAGOOLA ISLAND

By Mel Powell

[For our non-Jewish friends...but it likely applies to all religions and denominations...rivalries between and among congregations and synagogues are as old as, well, congregations and synagogues.]

You heard, of course, the story of Boris the Balagoola being stranded on a desert island.

You didn't heard?

So you'll listen and you'll heard.

Boris the Balagoola of the little town of Chelm, where the wise fools lived, went on a sabbatical from his Balagoolering. Unfortunately, his boat capsized, and Boris was stranded for five years on an island somewhere between Oy and Vey-Zmir. Fun, it wasn't.

But five years later, almost to the day, a search party from Vitipsk-Gaboynya found him, alive and well on his island.

The leader of the search party was amazed. "How did you survive, with no one to talk to?"

"Oh, I had plenty of friends. One was a volleyball, although the sport hasn't been invented yet."

"You were friends with a volleyball?"

"He was much nicer than that hollow log over there. So, before I leave, you'll permit me to show you my island?"

"Of course, Mister Balagoola. There's so much construction on this island. You did this all by yourself?"

"You see here on this island maybe the Vienna Boys Choir? Of course, I built it all myself!"

"So what's that building?"

"It's a Post Office. For five years, every morning, I came looking for a letter from home."

"And none came?"

"Just junk mail."

"And what's this building?"

"That's a *mikva*."[2]

"But there are no women on the island."

You never know," said the Balagoola.

"And these two buildings?"

"Those are Synagogues. The one on the right is my regular *shul*.[3] Every morning, clockwork, that is where I pray."

The rescuer was confused. "Why would one man, living alone on a desert island, need to build two Synagogues? It makes no sense. The Post Office, maybe. A *mikva*, unlikely. But two Temples? What do you need with a second Synagogue?"

"*That* Synagogue? *That* Synagogue I wouldn't be caught dead in!"

---

[2] A *mikva* is a ceremonial cleansing bath.
[3] *Shul*, a Yiddish word, means synagogue.

TICKET, PLEASE
by Mel Powell

It was Yom Kippur morning in Chelm, the tiny village where the wise fools lived. And, as was customary on Yom Kippur, the entire village gathered to pray in the synagogue.

But, over the years, word had spread throughout the land. Far and wide, no synagogue enjoyed the popularity of the Great Synagogue of Chelm. So popular were the services that Kalman the Karpenter had to build a second room onto the synagogue...and, a year later, they had to build an entire college campus.

It was into this chaos that Label the Latecomer rushed up to the door of the Great Synagogue. Label was infamous for his ability to procrastinate. He got around to putting up his storm windows in June. He got around to having his midnight snack at breakfast. And he got around to ordering his ticket for Yom Kippur...well, he didn't get around to it at all.

It was just his luck that Boris the Balagoola was taking his turn to greet his fellow Jews at the door.

"Ticket, please," boomed Boris.

"Ah, yes, good *yuntif*,[4] Mr. Balagoola. You see, it's like this. I must get a message to Berel the Beadle! May I please enter the synagogue?"

"Good *yuntif*, Label," greeted Boris, shaking the man's hand. "You look terrific. Have you lost weight? Ticket, please."

"Boris," pleaded Label, "I haven't got a ticket! But I must get a message to Berel! Please, you must let me in!"

Rivka the Baker wandered over to the door. "Ah, good morning, Label! So, Boris, what seems to be the trouble?"

---

[4] *Yuntif* is a slang, Yiddish-adjacent version of the Hebrew words *yom* (day) *tov* (good), so "good *yuntif*" means "good day" but is reserved for holidays or even just the sabbath.

Boris sighed. "Label doesn't have a ticket! But he says he must get a message to the good beadle!"

"Berel?" said Rivka. "He's sitting in his customary seat in the front row. But, Label, you know you must have a ticket!"

"Rivka, you must help me! It wasn't my fault! I got the news from Mendel the Messenger that the High Holy Days were approaching, but I didn't realize that they were coming so soon! I forgot to order my ticket! I must get a message to Berel the Beadle!"

Rivka and Boris huddled. Finally, Rivka turned to Label. "Dear Label, today is the Day of Atonement. It is the day when we cleanse ourselves of our sins. So...for the sin you have sinned by forgetting to buy your ticket...we absolve you, and we trust that The Almighty will do the same."

"Oh, thank you, thank you," said Label, thrilled. "As soon as I balance my checking account, I will make a nice donation!"

"We'll be lucky to see it by next *Tisha b'Av*,"[5] muttered Rivka.

Label rushed forward, took a *tallit*,[6] and took a prayer book, and reached to open the door to enter the Great Synagogue of Chelm.

As Label started through the door, Boris called after him threateningly. "Label, you may go in, even though you don't have a ticket. And you may give your message to Berel the Beadle. However..."

"Yes?" asked Label fearfully.

Boris wagged a huge finger at Label. "Don't let me catch you praying!!"

---

[5] *Tisha b'Av* literally means ninth (day) of the month of Av on the Hebrew calendar. It is a solemn day on the calendar, when disasters have happened...think "9/11" nowadays. But as used here and in similar contexts it somewhat means "twelfth of never," or "We'll sit here forever!"

[6] The *tallit* or *tallis* is the prayer shawl.

DON'T CRY FOR ME, BALAGOOLA
By Charles M. Powell

The people of Chelm, where the wise fools lived, could never hope to see the Western Wall of the ancient temple in Jerusalem. Knowing this, and being the wisest fools in the land, they proceeded to designate the Western Wall of their local Synagogue as a sur-rogate place of worship for its holy counterpart in Israel. Understand that they did this with love and piety and in no way was it meant to demean or diminish the importance of the real Wall.

No sooner than the Wise Council of Elders declared the Temple wall holy than Boris the Balagoola would spend hours praying and weeping and wailing and tearing at his clothes and pulling his hair and beating his chest and in general--let me tell you--*kvetching*[7] up a storm.

So much so, that Rivka the Baker gingerly approached him.

"Tell me something, Boris: Why you crying this way?"

"I'm crying for all the sick people."

"And the people who aren't sick?"

"Also them."

"They got doctors and nurses for sick people."

"Glad you reminded me," and the Balagoola began wailing so that God might protect the doctors and nurses.

Along came Schneider the Tailor. "Mine goodness," he said. "You're *kvetching* so much I can't even sew a hem. For whom are you praying today?"

"Today," sobbed the Balagoola, "I'm asking God to take care that the tailors shouldn't stick themselves with needles. Also that Bakers shouldn't inadvertently burn themselves on the bagels."

---

[7] To *kvetch* is to complain; a *kvetch*, as a noun, is a complainer.

"What a nice person you are," said the Baker and the Tailor.

"You're welcome," sobbed the Balagoola.

Along came Tevye the Milkman. "Maybe you got a prayer could help old cows give more milk? My cow is, you'll pardon the expression, an udder disgrace."

Rivka the Baker was incensed. "A pious man like our Balagoola shouldn't be bothered with cow prayers. On his shoulders rests the troubles of the whole world, already. Tell me, Boris. Do your prayers always work?"

"Well, I'll tell you," sighed the Balagoola. "Some days I feel like I'm talking to a wall!"

BEADLE-DE-DUMB

By Charles M. Powell

[Spoiler alert: for our non-Jewish readers, there's a wonderful Yiddish word that sounds a lot like an English word that means to push something gently...but the Yiddish word means to pester and harass...or the person who does the pestering and harassing.]

In the village of Chelm, where the fools all lived, the town brothers Berel and Shmerel couldn't have been more dissimilar.

Berel, as the good Beadle of the Synagogue, was beloved by all. He would sit in the Temple from early in the morning to late at night, praying to God and thinking good thoughts.

His brother Shmerel, on the other hand, was a no-good-nick. He drank too much; he cheated; he lied; and worse, he never stepped foot into the Great Synagogue of Chelm.

Life, however, is not always fair. Goodness is not always rewarded and evil is not always punished.

So it was that Shmerel, the bad brother, had everything his heart desired. Money, a big farm, the newest ox-cart, several cows...in short, all the comforts.

Berel, despite his goodness and piety, had little to show for his efforts. He was poor, he was destitute, he never knew where his next meal was coming from.

The unfairness of the situation was not lost on the good Beadle. Early one morning, before the regulars arrived for the morning prayers, Berel had a conversation with his God.

"Good morning, your Greatness."

"Good morning, Berel."

"It goes well with you, Lord?"

"Thank you for asking, but...oy, don't ask," said the Lord.

"I know how busy you are, Master of the Universe, but I wonder if I may ask of you a question?"

"Be my guest," answered the Lord.

"It is a well-known fact, dear Lord, that my brother Shmerel is a--how shall I say it--he's a bum. You, who sees all and knows all, must be aware of his lack of character. Why, then, King of the Universe, does he have every joy in life? Shmerel, a man who never prays to you, while I sit here every day, morning, noon, and night and I pray, and I pray..."

"The answer is simple," said the Lord. "Frankly, dear Berel... you're a *noodge*!"

THE *MELAMED*

By Charles M. Powell

(from a story by Bud Rosenthal)

You know what a *Melamed* is? Of course you know what a *Melamed* is. It's a very learned person. In the village of Chelm, where the wise fools all lived, everybody thought of himself as a *Melamed*. Now, if the truth be known--and you I can tell--from you I don't keep secrets there was really only one genuine *Melamed* in all of Chelm. You guessed it...who else? The Rabbi.

Now all Rabbis are smart...that's why they're Rabbis...but the Rabbi of Chelm was, how shall I say it...Mega-smart. You want to talk about a *Talmudic*[8] scholar? By heart he knew every comma, every interpretation, every nuance, every everything. No question about it, the Rabbi of Chelm was a *Melamed* and a half.

You would think that this truly wise man would surround himself with other wise people, but that was not the case. Who was his best friend? If you won't laugh, I'll tell you. Smile, all right, but no laugh. His best friend was...did I hear somebody laugh? His best friend was Boris the Balagoola.

What, you may ask, did they have in common? The answer is simple: Nothing. But best friends they were. The Balagoola worshipped the Rabbi. If the Rabbi had allergies, the Balagoola sneezed. If the *Melamed* felt cold, the Balagoola shivered. But the greatest service that Boris could perform for his beloved Rabbi was to drive him from town to town so that the Rabbi could dispense his learning and teachings. Every month, the Rabbi devoted one whole week visiting village after village, solving their problems, answering their questions, helping them to understand their *Talmud*. And who drove him back and forth across the Pale in his ox-cart? Boris the Balagoola.

---

[8] The *Talmud* is the entire body of Jewish law, but as an adjective here it means learned in the ways of Jewish law and tradition.

This went on for I can't tell you how many years. Always the Rabbi offered to pay his dear friend, always Boris refused. What is a friend for? But after one particular trip the Rabbi was adamant.

"Boris," he said, "this was the most difficult trip ever. The worst rain, the most mud. I tore my coat, you sewed it. My boots got wet, you loaned me yours. You waited patiently hours in the rain for me to return. Something, something you must let me do for you, Boris. Ask me anything, it's yours."

The Balagoola thought...not an easy task for him. Finally he responded. "There is one thing, Rabbi, but I'm sure it's out of the question."

"So you'll try me," said the Rabbi.

"How about, on your next trip, we change roles?"

"You mean, you'll be the Rabbi and I'll be the Balagoola?"

"Bingo," boomed the Balagoola.

How could the *Melamed* refuse? Off they went, the next month, the Rabbi driving the ox cart and the Balagoola sitting proudly in the back, dressed in the Rabbi's finest robes, looking every inch a *Melamed*.

At last they came to Vitipsk, a small village of very pious, very wise people. And were they happy to see a Rabbi. A learned man had not visited them for twenty years.

"Rabbi," they said to the Balagoola, "you'll come inside, leave your Balagoola here, and over tea, you'll please solve for us a *Talmudic* problem that has been troubling us for over twenty years."

So, with the Rabbi sitting in the rain and Boris sipping tea with honey in a warm house, they asked the *"Melamed"* for a solution.

Here was the dilemma: "The *Talmud* clearly states that the Jewish day begins at sunset of the previous night. No problem. The *Talmud* also clearly says that when there are three--exactly three--stars visible in the sky, it's officially night."

"So what's your problem?" asked Boris, the fake Rabbi.

"Our problem, Oh learned *Melamed*, is: what happens when it's cloudy and we can't see any stars? When is it nightfall?"

Boris began to laugh. "Pious men of Vitipsk. This is why you called me here? For this simple interpretation? To a learned *Melamed*, this is almost an insult. This is so easy even my Balagoola could answer it: Go ask him."

NATURAL SELECTION
By Charles M. Powell

And so it happened that when the Rabbi of the Great Synagogue of Chelm, where the wise fools lived, retired, and a search was initiated for his replacement.

A Committee had to be formed.

"This Committee," announced the President, "will be composed of five brilliant people, who will be able to recognize the perfect Rabbi when they see him. They must be able to tell immediately if he is well-versed in Torah and *Talmud*,[9] if he is committed to the existence and love of God to his very soul, whether he is a dedicated husband and family man if he is married, and if he will be completely responsive to the needs of the congregation."

"The President is right. The President is so smart," shouted various members of the congregation happily. "This is exactly what the Committee must do. But how will we find five such brilliant people to serve on this committee?"

"By picking a Committee of three wise congregants to find them. This Committee of three will search for the Committee of five. The three, therefore, must be people dedicated to the well-being of the Synagogue. They must be able to forget their own desires and only think of the desires of the congregation."

"The President is so marvelous, he is so wonderful," agreed various members of the appreciative congregation. "He knows what the Committee of three should be like to find the Committee of five, who must find the perfect Rabbi. But how will we pick this great Committee of three?" they wondered.

"To select this Committee of three," sagely answered the President, "we must form a Committee of two. Two perfect Human

---

[9] The *Talmud* is the entire body of Jewish law, but as an adjective here it means learned in the ways of Jewish law and tradition.

beings with surpassing wisdom, Judaic commitment, kindness of soul, and unwavering courage."

"How exceedingly fortunate we are to have such a magnificent President," celebrated the congregation. "But now tell us, wondrous President, please. How do we find these two members of this committee to select the three to select the five to select the perfect Rabbi?"

"Oh," smiled the President confidently. "To find these two is too important a job for just anyone. We'll wait and let the new Rabbi select them!"

DOES A BEAR *KVETCH* IN THE WOODS? [10]

By Mel Powell

[Spoiler alert: for our non-Jewish readers, know that there is a specific blessing, along the lines of "saying grace" before a meal, that Jews use before breaking bread.]

Boris the Balagoola, wrapped in a blanket, shivered as he sat before the Council of Elders in the tiny village of Chelm, where the wise fools all lived.

"Thank God for Rivka!" said Boris.

"It was nothing," said Rivka in her usual grating tone.

"No, it was that something. If you hadn't scared him off at the last minute with that horrible voice of yours, I'd be dead for sure. Thank God you came looking for me and screeched my name!"

It was earlier that afternoon when Boris the Balagoola had been rescued from a cave in the mountains at the edge of the Wild Woods of Vitipsk-Gaboynya. We know how he had been saved, but how, the Council wondered, had he come to be in a cave in the first place?

Boris told his tale of terror.

"As you know, my friends, sometimes I enjoy quiet solitude, time alone, to think and ponder."

Now Boris, large and strong, had the combined intellect of an ox-cart, a *latke*,[11] and a rock--so when he pondered, he pondered.

"I knew I wouldn't have much time left to walk, to stroll, to commune with nature, what with winter almost upon us. And what a terrible winter we are expecting!"

---

[10] To *kvetch* is to complain; a *kvetch*, as a noun, is a complainer.

[11] A *latke* is a potato pancake, usually served with sour cream or apple sauce, a tradition of Chanukah but good any time of year.

The Council all nodded knowingly. Eight years ago, after similar forecasts proved correct and the winter storms brought the most torrential rains in memory, Chelm's own Noah the Nosher had disappeared along with his wife and two of every kind of animal in town.

Boris continued, "So I decided that I would go camping in the woods before the weather changed. This made sense to me, as I am an expert camper."

This the Council politely ignored. The last time Boris had gone camping was six years ago. Last week the Tsar's mandatory volunteer bucket brigade had finally put out the campfire.

"As luck would have it, I found myself face to face with a bear! A giant bear with huge paws and teeth and fur and, if you'll pardon my saying, very bad breath. What could I do? I ran for my life.

"But the bear followed me for hours! As fast as I ran the bear ran just as fast! Still, I tried to escape, but I became lost in the woods. I zigged when I should have zagged, schlemeiled when I should have schlemazeled, and trapped myself trapped in a cave! The bear advanced towards me and tied a bib around its huge neck in preparation for a meal of Boris."

The Council was aghast. "So, what happened already?" asked Schneider the Tailor.

Boris sighed, "I have many faults, I know. But a good Jew I have always been! Understanding that these would be my last moments on this Earth, I closed my eyes and said the *Sh'ma*. [12]

"When I opened my eyes, I saw the most amazing spectacle! The bear, this hungry bear, also had its eyes closed. He was *davening*![13] Surely, a Jewish bear would never harm a good fellow Jew! I was sure that my life was saved!

---

[12] The *sh'ma* is the holiest and most basic Jewish prayer, affirming the one God.
[13] To *daven* is to pray, but this carries the feel of verbal and even physical rhythm, albeit standing in place.

"Then I leaned closer to hear the bear's quiet words…and just before Rivka's bellowing voice scared the bear into retreat, I listened to the bear's simple, sweet, humble little prayer:

"*'Ha motzi-lechem min ha-aretz…amen!'*"

WHEN YOU WISH UPON A TSAR
By Mel Powell

"Rabbi, please reconsider!" begged Berel the Beadle.

"Not to worry," said the good Rabbi, "I've always wanted to take a vacation in St. Petersburg, and that's what I will do immediately after Yom Kippur."

Boris the Balagoola chimed in. "Rabbi, didn't you hear the news of the terrifying ordeal suffered by the three leaders of the Vitipsk-Gaboynya synagogue because they decided to take such a vacation? I'm talking the rabbi, the cantor, and the president of the synagogue."

"So what was the problem?" asked the rabbi.

"They were kidnapped! Captured on the road to St. Petersburg and taken prisoner by a bunch of drunken Cossacks!"

Berel continued the tale, "A tragedy! Thank goodness they escaped late that night when the cossacks passed out from the vodka. But what they went through first was terrible!"

The rabbi sat forward, listening intently, as Mendel the Messenger went on with the story, "The cossacks told the rabb-- the rabb-- the three travelers that they were in big trou-- big troub-- were gonna be killed."

Rivka took over "But these horrible cossacks were so drunk that they wanted to be neighborly about it. They would grant the rabbi, the cantor, and the President each one wish. And only then they would kill them."

The rabbi began to wonder if he should vacation elsewhere.

Schneider the Tailor picked up the thread. "The Rabbi went first. He said, 'If this is to be my last day, I wish to give each of my sermons from the past year one more time, the *Talmudic*[14] lessons, the

---

[14] The *Talmud* is the entire body of Jewish law, but as an adjective here it means learned in the ways of Jewish law and tradition.

humanitarian issues, the personal struggles--all of the sermons, once again.' The cossacks rolled their bloodshot eyes...but a deal was a deal."

Shloime the Student jumped in, "Then they turned to the good cantor and asked him for his wish. 'My wish,' said the cantor, 'is this: if I am to die today, I want to chant one last time every melody, every harmony, every word and note of all of the wonderful music of the Jewish faith. All of it, one last time.' The cossacks even more reluctantly agreed to grant this wish, but a deal was still a deal."

Boris the Balagoola chipped in his last two kopecks' worth. "Now, mind you, this would never happen at our synagogue, but wait until you hear the last wish of the President of Temple B'nai Vitipsk-Gaboynya!

"He said, 'My wish? You want to know my wish? This is my wish. Because you are giving my rabbi the honor of delivering *all* of his sermons again, and you are giving my cantor the privilege of chanting *all* of the music again, my wish is...would you please kill me first?'"

THE WOODCUTTER
By Jane Powell

"My God!" said Berel the Beadle.

"Mine, too!" said Boris the Balagoola.

And entire Wise Council of Elders of the tiny village of Chelm, where the wise fools lived, sighed in despair, for the situation was serious indeed.

The problem was finding an experienced woodcutter because the people of Chelm were up to their *tsitsis*[15] in trees. The previous woodcutter, Wimpel, had wended his way to Warsaw and was weaving wugs...excuse me, rugs. Berel the Beadle suggested that Mendel the Messenger be dispatched through Chelm to see if he could find someone with woodcutting experience.

So Mendel set out through the streets of Chelm with his big bell--the one he always used to broadcast the news to the townspeople--and rang his bell and called again and again, "Woodcutter wan-- Woodcutter wan-- We need someone with a good axe! Anyone who can cut down a tree should go imme-- imme-- hustle to the Town Hall and report to the Wise Council!"

Soon a long line of volunteers formed in front of the Town Hall, and the Council of Elders began interviewing the applicants. After hours of questions and dozens of Chelmites, still no one could be found to wield an axe.

As the next man walked in, Berel exclaimed, "Meyer the *Mohel*![16] What are you doing here? How could a frail, 87-year-old man possibly chop down even a twig, let alone a tree?"

"Berel, my boy," answered Meyer, "don't you know that when was a young man I was the world's greatest woodcutter? It was only twenty

---

[15] *Tsitsis* are the fringes at the ends of the prayer shawl, but here it's just an "up to my eyeballs" idiomatic use of a funny-sounding word.

[16] A *mohel*, pronounced "moil" rhymes with "toil," is the specialized rabbi who performs the ritual circumcision of the male baby.

years ago that I decided I didn't want to work so hard anymore and I retired and became a *mohel*. I figured that with all my experience I could do something in the same field that would be easier. After all, cutting is cutting!"

"Impossible," said Berel. "Meyer, if you even try to lift the axe, you'll hurt yourself."

"What have you got to lose?" said Meyer, "Gimme already a test."

The Wise Council pondered for a while and decided that since they had no other volunteers, there was really nothing to lose…except, perhaps, Meyer the *Mohel's* life, in case (God forbid!) he had a heart attack from the exertion.

And so they took an axe and went into the forest. "Which trees do you want?" asked Meyer.

"Here," said Kalman the Karpenter, "try this sapling if you must try something."

With one flick of the wrist, Meyer cut down the little tree. "Now where are the trees you really want?" he asked.

"Try this medium one," said Berel, "and be careful."

Three swipes of the axe, and down went the tree.

"Not bad," said the Berel.

"Well," Said Boris, "maybe you can cut down those three big trees for next year's *sukkah*.[17] If we had the money, we would have rented the cutting equipment from Minsk. But I guess you're all we've got, Meyer."

Meyer laughed. "Equipment? You're dealing with the world's greatest woodcutter."

Meyer was asked to make the trees fall to the left, which he promptly accomplished in less time than it takes to put on a nice pair of boots.

---

[17] The *sukkah* is the temporary "shelter" build each year for the *Sukkot* (which is the plural of *sukkah*) holiday, a harvest festival.

"Fantastic!" said Berel.

"Unbelievable!" said Boris.

"In my life I never saw..." said Rivka.

"Meyer," asked Berel, "where did you learn how to do that?"

"Well," said Meyer, raising himself to his full five feet three inches, "for many years I was the chief woodcutter in the Sahara Forest."

"Sahara 'Forest?'" asked Berel. "Don't you mean the Sahara Desert?"

"Sure, NOW!"

TRANSPORTATION AND TECHNOLOGY

1. Killing Time
2. The Hitchhiker's Guide To Chelm
3. The Latest Model
4. Right On Time
5. A Kopeck For Your Thoughts
6. Frequent Schlepper Miles
7. Up, Up, and Oy Vey

One of the running gags across the stories has been inserting modern (for us) technology into the late-1800s period of Chelm.

Planes (which hadn't been invented yet), trains (which had), and automobiles (which hadn't, but that's why we have ox-carts!), among other futuristic ponderings, make for great fodder for wise fools.

KILLING TIME
By Charles M. Powell

Wrist watches were new to Chelm.

Now, we're not talking here Tiffany. We're not even talking here K-Mart. What they had, in those days, in the village of the Wise Fools of Chelm, were simple, primitive--how shall I say it--Mickey Mouse-type watches.

So why should we be surprised to hear about the old man walking down the main street of Chelm, *schlepping*[1]--you heard me?--*schlepping* the two biggest suitcases in the history of Chelm.

Now, who else should be strolling down the promenade but our good friend Boris the Balagoola. Being late for an appointment, he approached the old man and said politely, "Excuse me, sir, could you tell me, please, the time, s'il vous plaît?"

The old man sighed, put down the two heavy suitcases, and looked at his watch.

"The time is 5:04 and one quarter. The sun sets tonight at 7:59 PM. The sun rises tomorrow at 5:57 AM. Also, while we are nowhere near an ocean, I can tell you that the tide goes out at 11:15." So saying, he sighed, lifted the suitcases, and continued *schlepping* down the street.

Boris the Balagoola was amazed. "Wait just one minute," he yelled after the old man. "All that, you got from a wristwatch?"

The old man smiled and put down the heavy burden. "Also, happens to be an AM/FM crystal-set radio and it plays cassettes--if they ever get invented--of popular music."

"That's good, that's good," said the Balagoola.

---

[1] *Schlepping* can mean lugging something burdensome as it does here, or can also mean just to go a long way, usually in traffic or through the woods or uphill both ways.

"That's not all," said the old man. "You turn over the watch and guess what? On the other side is a 12-inch color television. When television studios get invented, I will be ready."

Boris went crazy. "That watch, I've gotta have! Right now...100 rubles. What do you say?"

"I'm sorry," said the old man. "My children had this watch made special for me for my 80th birthday. It's one of a kind. There's no way I could sell it to you." Once again he lifted his heavy load.

The Balagoola was undaunted. "Not even for 500 rubles?" he called after the man. "Here? On the spot? Cash on the barrel-head?"

The old man thought carefully. With that much money he could go already and join his sister in Waukegan, Illinois, U. S. of America.

"O.K., Balagoola...you got already a deal!"

Off came the one-of-a-kind watch. The Balagoola handed over the money, put on the watch, and merrily took his leave.

"Wait, come back!" cried the old man, pointing to the two heavy suitcases. "Don't forget the batteries!"

THE HITCHHIKER'S GUIDE TO CHELM

By Mel Powell

(from a story by Bud Rosenthal)

Boris the Balagoola was beside himself.

He had just come from the number one ox-cart dealer in Chelm, having slapped his rubles on the table and driven off the lot. And there he was, in his fancy new, latest model, top-of-the-line ox-cart, a covered ox-cart no less, stopped at the largest intersection in the tiny village of Chelm.

And Boris was beside himself. "Just as the dealer guaranteed, my new ox-cart is the finest there ever could be. Why, I have even a telephone in my ox-cart!" Boris was quite proud of this detail because the telephone still had not yet been invented.

"And I even have a color television set in my ox-cart!" This was even a greater miracle because at that time nobody in Chelm had yet invented even good theater.

Suddenly, Boris looked through his tinted-glass window and, lo and behold, there was a covered ox-cart identical to his. For a moment Boris believed that somehow he actually was beside himself.

"Hello, Boris!" called Rivka the Baker from the open window of her identical ox-cart.

"Hello, Rivka," replied the taken-aback Boris.

"So?" asked Rivka. "New ox-cart?"

"Yeah," replied Boris, boasting, "And mine even has a telephone! Has yours?"

Rivka wrinkled her nose disdainfully. "Pshaw! Mine ox-cart, my dear Boris, has not one, not two, but three telephones, one in the front, one in the back, and one for the ox."

Boris replied. "Oh, yeah? Mine also has three telephones. I was…just testing. But do you have a color television set?"

Rivka again wrinkled her nose, again disdainfully. "Of course I do, Boris. And mine even has cable!"

Boris didn't believe her. "So then what's your favorite cable network?"

"H.B.Y." responded Rivka.

"You mean H.B.O.," corrected Boris.

"No, my dear Balagoola, H.B.Y., the How's By You network."

Boris was deflated; it seemed that, at best, he only shared the record for having the best ox-cart in Chelm. That was when Rivka dropped her stale *kreplach*[2] into Boris's soup.

"So, Boris," said Rivka, subtly driving her melodic voice directly into the poor Balagoola's very soul, "have you got a bed in your ox-cart?"

Now Boris was truly vanquished, and without a word drove directly back to the ox-cart dealer, Cal Weintraub (and his dog Shmuel).[3] To get there, Boris had to turn around right there in the intersection. Have you ever tried to get an ox to make a U-turn in an intersection? Don't ask. A ram could make a ewe turn, but an ox?

Eventually, Boris made it back to the dealer, where the furious Balagoola took the dog Shmuel hostage until such time as the good Mr. Weintraub installed a bed in Boris's ox-cart. (Boris, despite his menacing reputation, was quite good with pets and Shmuel had wonderful playtime. Don't tell Cal Weintraub.)

Three hours later, the ox-cart was ready, and Cal Weintraub even threw in a full tank of premium super-unleaded borscht.

---

[2] A *kreplach* is a dumpling.
[3] Southern Californians will remember Cal Worthington, a car dealer with attention-grabbing television commercials, which had a catchy jingle and a different exotic animal in each one nonetheless referred to as "his dog Spot." They ran from the 60's all the way to the 90's. No one else will get it, but we're leaving the reference in as these stories were born in Southern California!

Boris said to himself, "Now I will prove to Rivka that I have at least as fine an ox-cart as she has! So much for that baker's one-ups-woman-ship!"

The Balagoola drove far and wide and fast, and finally found Rivka's ox-cart parked proudly outside of the new Minsk Mini-Mall.

Boris knocked on the tinted-glass window and waited.

After a moment, Rivka rolled down the window. "Now what do you want, Boris?"

"Rivka, now I, too, have a bed in my ox-cart--a tsar-sized bed, no less--so your ox-cart is no longer better than my ox-cart!"

Rivka was too angry even to wrinkle her nose this time. "Boris, for this you got me out of the shower?"

THE LATEST MODEL
By Mel Powell

"You heard?" asked Berel the Beadle.

"Heard what?" wondered Rivka the Baker.

"You heard how Boris destroyed the world's first ox-less ox-cart? No? OK, I'll tell you." And he did.

Boris the Balagoola loved his brand-new, state-of-the-art, top-of-the-line ox-cart. It was the best ox-cart in the village of Chelm, where the wise fools all lived. This ox-cart had telephones (including one for the ox, no less), cable TV (in color, no less), a bed (tsar-sized, no less,) and, thanks to stiff competition from Rivka the Baker, even a shower. Only the bed had even been invented yet--but Boris had it all.

And Boris was satisfied, until the price of hay rose to two kopecks a bale--with the threat that it might go as high as three! How lucky for Boris that Mendel the Messenger came by with the latest news. "Hear ye-- hear ye-- listen up. Today's advert-- today's advert-- here's a commercial. Come on down to Cal Weintraub's ox-cart dealership[4] for a test dr-- for a test dr-- try out his newest model, an ox-less ox-cart!"

"Good morning, good Mendel," boomed Boris. "I should go take a test drive at Cal Weintraub's. And I just love his dog, Shmuel. What do you think?"

"Why not?" asked Mendel. "Visit with Mr. Wein-- visit with Mr. Wein-- go see Cal."

And Boris drove straight to the dealership, where Cal Weintraub himself came out to greet him.

---

[4] In case you are reading the stories out of order in the book, we share the same explanation from the previous story: Southern Californians will remember Cal Worthington, a car dealer with attention-grabbing television commercials, which had a catchy jingle and a different exotic animal in each one nonetheless referred to as "his dog Spot." They ran from the 60's all the way to the 90's. No one else will get it, but we're leaving the reference in as these stories were born in Southern California!

"Ah, Boris the Balagoola. So nice to see you. You look terrific--have you lost weight?--and have I got a deal for you! You can go to Pinsk, you can go to Minsk, you can go to Vitipsk-Gaboynya, and I will beat any price you can find. I'm sure I have something you can afford!"

"What's a Ford?" asked Boris.

"Hasn't been invented yet. Here, take a look at this ox-less ox-cart!"

And sure enough, there was an ox-cart...but no ox!

"So how does it work?" queried the huge Balagoola.

"Simple," smiled Cal Weintraub. "It works by voice." Boris and Cal climbed onto the ox-less ox-cart. "You ready? Observe. Steer with this wheel here. And as for moving..." Cal leaned a little bit toward the front of the ox-cart, where there was a tiny drawing of an ox, and he whispered in the direction of the drawing: "*Halavai.*"[5] And the cart began to creep forward!

"You want to go faster? Speak louder. Observe. *Halavai!*" And the cart went faster. "You want to stop? Observe. *Genug!*"[6] And the cart stopped on a ruble!

"Amazing!" cried Boris. "Cal, I will take it for a test-drive, please, and if I like..."

"You'll like."

"...I'll buy!"

"You'll buy. Remember, "*halavai*" to go, "*genug*" to stop. And be careful! It's the only one of its kind ever invented!"

"I got it!" said the excited Balagoola. Cal got out, and Boris took the wheel of the ox-less ox-cart. "*Halavai!*" And it started to go.

"*Halavai halavai!*" It went faster.

---

[5] *Halavai* translates loosely as "Thank Goodness" or even "Hooray!"
[6] *Genug* means "enough already!"

"*Halavai halavai HALAVAI!*" The cart flew through the streets of Chelm and up into the hills.

"This is terrific!" exulted Boris as he and the ox-less ox-cart wound its way through the mountains, executing tight turns that could never be accomplished with an animal, much less a stubborn ox!

But the mountain road was about to run out, right on the edge of Chashka Cliff, named for the unfortunate Chashka the *Chazzan*,[7] *aleva sholom*,[8] whose final contribution to Chelm a century earlier had been the discovery of said cliff.

Boris was frozen with fear. He had forgotten the word to stop the cart! "Gesundheit!" And the cart went faster. "Gestalt!" The cliff grew closer. "Get me outta here!" The end was near! "*GENUG*!!!!" And the ox-less ox-cart screeched to a desperate, wheels-grinding, dust-flying, gut-wrenching halt--right at the edge of disaster, with the front wheels teetering over that very edge.

Boris fell off the side of the cart and sat there on the ground, gasping for breath, thankful to be alive. Wiping his sweaty brow, he whispered, "Oy, *halavai!*"

---

[7] *Chazzan* is the Hebrew word for the cantor, or singer of the prayers.
[8] *Aleva sholom* is the idiomatic "rest in peace." May her (or his) memory be for a blessing.

RIGHT ON TIME

By Mel Powell with Harriet Kottick

(inspired by the 1992 Academy-Award Winning Documentary Short Subject "Omnibus.")

Shloime the Student was terrified. What a tongue-lashing he had received yesterday from the head rabbi at the yeshiva[9] in Vitipsk-Gaboynya! If poor Shloime showed up late just one more time, he might lose his scholarship and bring shame and disgrace upon the entire village of Chelm, where the wise fools lived.

But the tardiness was never Shloime's fault! He caught an early train every morning but it was always the train's fault, somehow running late! So, as Shloime sat in his usual seat in the first car aboard the 7:19 commuter train, he prayed that, just this once, the train would arrive at Vitipsk-Gaboynya right on time.

"Tickets!" demanded the stern Russian conductor.

Shloime handed his over, asking politely, "Will the train arrive on time today at Vitipsk-Gaboynya?"

"Vitipsk-Gaboynya? This train doesn't stop at Vitipsk-Gaboynya."

"What are you saying?" gasped Shloime. "Every morning I take the 7:19 to Vitipsk-Gaboynya! In fact, this is my usual seat! How can you tell me that today the train doesn't stop at Vitipsk-Gaboynya?"

"Yesterday," intoned the conductor, "this train stopped at Vitipsk-Gaboynya. Today, it does not. The schedule changed. You can get off at the stop before or the stop after. But there's no stop at Vitipsk-Gaboynya."

Tears welled in Shloime's eyes. "Please, you don't understand! If the train doesn't stop at Vitipsk-Gaboynya, I will be late, and I will

---

[9] A *yeshiva* is a school for Jewish study.

lose my scholarship! I will bring shame and disgrace on my family, my friends, arid my entire village!"

"I'm very sorry," sympathized the conductor, sincerely distressed about Shloime's plight. "Listen, rules are rules. Tomorrow you'll take the 7:04 train, which stops at Vitipsk-Gaboynya. There's no way I can stop this train at Vitipsk-Gaboynya unless I want my own next stop to be in Siberia. But I'll tell you what I can do."

"Yes? Yes?" pleaded Shloime.

"I can't stop the train, but I can slow it down as we reach the Vitipsk-Gaboynya station. It will be dangerous--"

"My life is over anyway," interrupted Shloime. "Do go on."

"It will be dangerous," continued the conductor "but you seem fit, so perhaps it can be done. I will count down for you. When I say 'jump,' at that exact moment, you must jump from the train to the platform with your feet running just as fast as they can go. You must keep running as fast as the train is going or you will fall and break your neck in seventeen places. But then, when you slow down, you will be at the Vitipsk-Gaboynya station, right on time!"

"Oh, thank you, thank you," slobbered Shloime. "I will never forget you for this!"

And, a few minutes later, the conductor hustled Shloime to the door of the train as they approached the Vitipsk-Gaboynya station. "Ready? Three...two...one...JUMP!"

Shloime jumped. Shloime, as they say, hit the ground running, and he ran as fast as his legs would carry him. Once he almost tripped when he glanced back to thank the kind conductor one last time with a wave, but he regained his footing.

"I'm going to make it!" he cried. "I'm going to make it! I'm going to get to the yeshiva and be right on time!"

At that moment, Boris the Balagoola looked out the window of the last car of the very same train. "Say," he wondered aloud, "isn't that my young friend Shloime the Student running alongside this train?"

A huge hand reached out of the last door of the train, scooped up a shocked Shloime by the scruff of the shirt collar, and pulled him back on.

"Thank goodness!" crowed Boris. "I'm glad I caught you! Shloime, if it wasn't for me, you would've missed the train!"

A KOPECK FOR YOUR THOUGHTS
By Charles M. Powell

[Here we get a story retelling a part of Boris the Balagoola's past.]

Berel the Beadle couldn't stop laughing. Tears rolled down his face. He coughed and he wheezed and he sputtered, but he couldn't stop laughing.

"What's so funny?" asked Rivka the Baker.

Berel kept laughing.

"You got to tell us, already. We're entitled."

"All right, all right, already," laughed Berel, who pulled himself together and told the story.

"Our friend, Boris the Balagoola, decided to visit his old uncle in Minsk. Now Boris had never before taken the great Russian railroad train and the entire experience was strange and quite frightening for him.

"It was the return voyage that presented the problem. When the Balagoola entered the Minsk Railroad Station his eye caught the strangest sight he had ever seen. It was a machine."

"A machine?" asked Rivka the Baker.

"A machine," said Berel the Beadle. "But one that tells you how much you weigh and sundry other details."

"Sundry? What means sundry?" asked Schneider the Tailor.

"You'll see," said Berel.

"Well, the Balagoola was so fascinated by the machine, he put a kopeck into its slot. The machine made a funny noise and then--you won't believe this--it spoke to Boris. It said 'Your name is Boris and you are a Balagoola. You weigh two hundred twelve pounds. You are Jewish and you're waiting for the train to Chelm."

Everyone was amazed. A machine talked and it knew all those things? Unbelievable!

Berel continued. "Now the Balagoola, in addition to being amazed, was angry. He decided to challenge the machine--to fool this iron, Russian menace.

"So Boris ran out of the station and returned with his old uncle. Once again, the Balagoola put in a kopeck, but this time he put his uncle on the scale. The machine promptly reported the following: 'Your name is Finster Farfoofnick. You are Jewish and you weigh one hundred fifty-eight pounds. Your nephew, Boris the Balagoola, is waiting for his train to Chelm.'

"Well, do I have to tell you how crazy Boris got? He was obsessed with fooling the machine. This time, after thirty minutes, the Balagoola's uncle found a woman who was of mixed background and even more mixed upbringing. Again, they returned to the machine. In went the Balagoola's last kopeck. The machine came out with its answer:

"'Your name is Sophie Farshimel and you weigh one hundred thirty pounds. You are part Gypsy, part Rumanian, part Hungarian, part Ukrainian, and fifty-three years of age. You are Finster Farfoofnick's friend, and his nephew, Boris the Balagoola...just missed his train to Chelm.'"

FREQUENT *SCHLEPPER* MILES [10]

By Mel Powell

[And here we get a story about the Boris the Balagoola of "today" in Chelm.]

Boris the Balagoola had finally had enough.

"I have had enough!" he boomed.

"What's the matter, Boris?" asked Rivka the Baker. "Sit, already, so the train can get started on the way to Vitipsk-Gaboynya!"

But Boris wouldn't budge. "I am no fool," said this wise fool from the tiny village of Chelm. "Just because we are poor, it doesn't mean that we always have to sit in the back of the train to Vitipsk-Gaboynya!"

"But Bor-- but Bor-- but Balagoola," said Mendel the Messenger, "you know we can't afford a ticket in First Cla-- First Cla-- up there in front."

"Nonsense!" insisted Boris. "The three of us take this train once a week! Rivka purchases dough for her donuts, mandel for her mandelbread and rugs for her *ruggelach*;[11] you, Mendel, attend the meeting of the United Messenger Service; and I work out at the famous Goldyabinsky's Gym! We are loyal regular customers, and just once we deserve to sit in First Class!"

Both Rivka and Mendel knew that this would not be possible. But were *you* gonna make Boris sit down? Boris headed for the front of the train, where he chose a comfortable seat, proudly, in the First-Class Car.

---

[10] *Schlepping* can mean to go a long way, usually in traffic or through the woods or uphill both ways, as it does here, or can also mean lugging something burdensome.
[11] *Ruggelach* is a small filled pastry.

Needless to say--but I'll say it anyway--Boris was soon approached by a uniformed assistant to the assistant conductor.

"Excuse me, sir," said the young Russian. "It appears that you have a round-trip ticket from Chelm to Vitipsk-Gaboynya and back, but your ticket is in the coach car. This is First Class."

"You think I'm a fool?" roared Boris in his most intimidating tone. "I know this is First Class, and that is how I demand to be treated! Now, I'll have a short schnapps, a slim slivovitz, and a monster Manischewitz, if you please. And an extra bag of those honey-roasted pirogie."

The Russian was definitely intimidated, since this was his first day on the train. He sought out the assistant conductor--the only Jewish assistant conductor, thanks to the Tsar's new Affirmative Action rules--who came over to confront Boris.

"Pardon me--oy! We've got to chat about this choo-choo," said the attendant. "You've got a ticket for the coach car, and this is the First-Class Car. This train cannot depart the Chelm Station until each passenger is in the correct seat."

"Forget about it!" refused Boris. "I take this train once a week, I'm one of your best customers, and it's time I was treated like a First-Class passenger. Now, please give me a set of headphones. I don't care that onboard entertainment has not been invented yet. And don't forget that I ordered the kosher meal."

The assistant conductor was also powerless, so he summoned Cherkassy the Conductor, the great man himself! Cherkassy was the famous Russian conductor who held the record for the Trans-Siberia train races, with a winning time of just under four years.

"Tell me, Assistant: this fellow who demands First Class aboard my train…he's going to Vitipsk-Gaboynya, yes? And he's from here in Chelm, yes?" The assistant nodded. "Very well. I'll handle it."

With that, Cherkassy the Conductor walked over to Boris, leaned over, and whispered earnestly, almost apologetically, in Boris's ear.

"Really?" asked Boris, surprised. The Conductor nodded politely. "Well, then, thank you kindly," said the Balagoola, who rose and headed back to the coach car without protest.

Boris returned and stuffed his huge frame into the tiny coach seat between Rivka and Mendel. "Who knew?" said Boris in wonder.

"Who knew what?" asked Rivka.

"All this time we've been taking this train, and I never knew! The First-Class car doesn't stop in Vitipsk-Gaboynya!"

UP, UP, AND OY VAY

By Mel Powell

Even the little village of Chelm could not avoid it. Progress had come, and the Wise Council of Elders, after a four-day debate, finally admitted that progress indeed existed.

At the meeting of the Council, Berel the Beadle reported, "As you know, I have just returned from Warsaw, and there I saw the most incredible things. I saw big birds!"

Rivka the Baker laughed. "That's it? Big birds?"

"Yes! Big birds with people in them! It's a new form of progress! They call them 'airplanes.'"

So, of course, in order to keep step with the whole world, the Wise Council commissioned the construction of an airport and purchased their very own airplane. The problem then arose of who should be the pilot. Naturally, the Council volunteered a protesting Berel the Beadle, who reluctantly agreed to learn how to fly.

When Berel was ready, the rabbi's wife was asked to break a bottle of slivovitz against the plane, in order to launch it. Greatly honored, she hurled the bottle with all her might.

Now, there's good news and bad news. The good news is, they were able to save the slivovitz for a later occasion. The bad news is, they were not able to save the plane for any occasion. It fell to pieces, the bottle was taken away, and the Chelmites anxiously awaited the arrival of their second plane (by air mail).

This, time, however, the Chelmites were prepared. "Ha," laughed Berel, speaking to the Wise Council, "you think we're foolish enough to risk another bottle of slivovitz? Never! I have a better plan!" The Chelmites gathered their school children together, and they threw grapes.

After they spent a week painting over the grape-juice stains, the plane was sent on its first flight, amid great fanfare.

For this momentous inaugural Chelm-to-New York flight, they filled their new "Chelm Airways" plane with excited paying customers and took off.

Soon after they reached the ocean, Berel got on the intercom and said confidently, "Hello, Ladies and Gentlemen, I've got good news and bad news. The good news is, welcome to the flight, we're making good time. The bad news is, due to mechanical difficulties with this airplane, in precisely three minutes our plane will be brought to a safe, smooth landing…not a crash, mind you…in the middle of the ocean."

The passengers, needless to say, were horrified. But Berel, with his pilot's training and with the situation well in hand, continued. "At the count of three, everybody who can swim will please go to right side of the plane. Everybody who can't swim will take a seat on the left. Ready? One, two, three!"

You have never seen such scurrying. Within seconds, the plane was divided into swimmers and non-swimmers. Berel was delighted.

"Now," he continued, "the plane will land in the ocean smoothly in one minute and twenty-five seconds. When the plane hits the water and glides to a gentle stop, those of you on the right, who can swim, will exit the plane by the door over the right rear wing. No other doors will be opened."

The passengers anxiously awaited further word, as Berel continued, "When the plane stops, you will jump off the rear of the wing and swim precisely thirty-two strokes away. Then you will turn left and swim twelve strokes to our life rafts, where our crew will meet you. There you will find blankets, herring, sweets, and glasses of tea.

"The plane will crash--I mean land, but in the water--in forty-five seconds. Follow these instructions and you will all be fine.

"Now, for those of you on the left side of the plane, who cannot swim--thank you for flying Chelm Airways!"

TRICKERY

1. Border Crossing
2. Fahrvergnugen

Life wasn't always--or ever--easy for the Jews under the Tsar's rule.

Any opportunity to trick, deceive, or otherwise pull a fast one on the Tsar's guards or government, or the local Cossacks in general, was an opportunity worth taking.

(You'll find a little trickery in "A Horses Tale" in the Animals chapter and "The Ox-cidental Tourist" in the Legal Troubles chapter.)

THE BORDER CROSSING

By Charles M. Powell

Berel the Beadle had left Chelm, where the Wise Fools all lived, to visit his wife's family in St. Petersburg. Chelm, which was in the Pale--that gray area that was sometimes Russia and sometimes Poland--was, when the Beadle took this vacation now in the hands of Poland. This meant crossing a border, not a safe thing ever for a Jew. Still, with his worn suitcase, Berel approached the Russian border guard.

"Unpack your case, Jew, so I may see what you are trying to smuggle out of Mother Russia."

"Smuggle, your guardship? Me, Mister Cossack? I wouldn't think of it." Berel unpacked his suitcase.

"What's that?" asked the guard, pointing to a small statue of the Tsar.

"What's that? It's not a *what*; it's a *who*," replied the Beadle. "That's a statue of our Tsar."

"I know it's the Tsar, you Fool. My question is: why would you be taking a statue of the Tsar out of Russia if you are leaving here?"

"Simple," said Berel. "I have spent some wonderful time in your country and I wish forever to be reminded of my generous benefactor."

"Well," said the obviously pleased guard, "what a grand gesture. You may proceed to Poland."

Berel hurriedly repacked his case and crossed the border...only to be stopped on the other side by a Polish border guard.

"Halt, Jew, and show me what you're trying to smuggle into Poland!"

"Smuggle, your guard-ness? Me? I wouldn't think of it," said the Beadle as he once again unpacked his suitcase and revealed the statue.

"What's that?" the guard inquired.

"What's that? Excuse me, sir. It's not a *what*; it's a *who*. That's a statue of the Tsar."

"I know that, you idiot. My question is: why would you bring a statue of the hated Tsar into Poland, now that you are no longer ruled by that tyrant?"

"Simple." The Beadle smiled. "This way, now that I am free of him, each day I will look at his statue and spit on the Tsar."

The Polish guard laughed. "That's wonderful. I hadn't thought of that! I may buy a statue myself. Proceed to Chelm."

When Berel arrived in his home village, he was greeted with great joy and celebration. Boris even helped him carry the suitcase the last few streets to Berel's home, where he asked about Berel's trip while his friend unpacked.

Suddenly, out of the suitcase came the statue of the Tsar.

"Who's that?" asked Boris.

Berel the Beadle smiled and relaxed for the first time that day. "Who's that, Boris, you ask? My friend, it's not a *who*; it's a *what*. What that is...is ten kilos of gold!"

FAHRVERGNUGEN

By Charles M. Powell

In the little village of Chelm, where the Wise Fools all lived, the townspeople were always on constant alert to protect against the horrible *pogroms*.[1] These vicious acts of anti-Jewish violence were an ever-present source of concern to the poor villagers. Hence, the emergency meeting of the Wise Council of the Elders…really, of the Subcommittee on Safety and Struction.

"Hold it, hold it," boomed Boris the Balagoola. "What's 'Struction'?"

"Obvious," said Shloime the Student. "Struction is the opposite of DE-struction, which we don't want."

Boris was chagrined. "Now I see the advantage of a good education!"

Berel the Beadle called the meeting to order. "Resolved," he intoned, "that we post people to watch all roads into town and sound an alarm if the Tsar sends in his hoodlums. Resolved also that no stranger is told where the Great Synagogue of Chelm is located, we shouldn't have there any violence. Agreed?"

The Council voted unanimously, except for the Balagoola, who was still pondering "Struction." Then came the bad news, Mendel the Messenger came running into the hall.

"Oh Boy, Oh Boy….we got terr-- we got terr-- we got a disaster."

"Disaster?" said Boris. "Go tell the 'Zastor' Committee."

"It's not funn-- it's not funn-- don't laugh, the Tsar just invented a new armored cart that singlehan-- that singlehan-- that all by itself destroys synagogues."

---

[1] Merriam-Webster defines a "pogrom" (puh-GRUM) as "an organized massacre of helpless people." If you've ever seen "Fiddler on the Roof," although no one is murdered, you surely recall the scene when the bad Russians come into town and, for no reason, cause a lot of destruction.

"This is very serious," agreed Berel, "How we gonna save our synagogue? Messenger, what do they call the Tsar's new cart?"

"They call it the Fahr--the Fahr--the Fahrvergnugen." [2]

Even the strange word struck fear in the hearts of all who heard it. Worse yet, one showed up in the village square the very next morning. This is how Berel the Beadle described it: "It was terrible to look at, the Fahrvergnugen. On its left side was a Klopper, and on the right side, a Knipper. If it ever drove into a synagogue it would Klop and Knip and that would be that."

The terrifying Fahrvergnugen returned the next day, and this time the chief of the Cossacks stepped out of the cart, looked around, and chose to speak to Mendel the Messenger. "You, Jew, tell me where your house of worship is."

Mendel was panic-stricken. "We don't h-h-have one, your Soldier-Ship. Our village is too poor to have one."

"Stop it," said the Cossack. "We know you have a Temple. How do we drive there in our Fahrvergnugen?"

Mendel thought quickly--not an easy task for a Chelmite. "You make a left at the corner and go up Sk--Sk--Skinny Street. But I don't know if you'll find a synagogue there."

The Tsar's men quickly turned the Klop-and-Knipper around and found Skinny Street. "Is this Skinny Street?" demanded the Cossack menacingly to the villager they found there.

"Yes," said the unintimidated and large Boris the Balagoola. "You know why they call it 'Skinny Street?' I got arms wider than this street."

So up the street drove the Fahrvergnugen and the street was so skinny that off scraped the Kloppers. Still further up, they lost most of the Knippers.

Just then, Boris started to yell and wave at the big ox-cart. The Tsar's men figured that they would finally get proper directions to the

---

[2] There's no magic here; the Volkswagen-made car was somewhat popular when this story was first written, and it's just a funny word.

local temple, and they still had enough Knippers left on the Fahrvergnugen to do damage.

There was no way to make a U-turn. But as they backed down Skinny Street, off scraped the last Knippers, rendering the Fahrvergnugen useless to destroy anything.

Furious, they confronted the Balagoola. "Even though it's too late now, tell us why you called us back!"

Boris smiled. "I just thought you should know--I don't know where the synagogue is either!"

VACATIONS

1. There's No Place Like Home
2. What I Did On My Vacation
3. From Chelm To Jerusalem
4. What I Did On My Summer Vacation

Even Chelmites sometimes need to get away.

(See also "It's All In The Presentation" in the Food chapter, "Tales Of The South Pacific" in the Charity/Fundraising chapter, and "When You Wish Upon A Tsar" for other takes on leaving Chelm for a bit.)

THERE'S NO PLACE LIKE HOME
Charles M. Powell with a bit of Mel Powell update

[This one is a bit unusual, attached to Chelm but with only a cameo or two from any of the regular characters. That said, it has long been considered a classic by the denizens of the modern synagogues who have heard the tale.]

Relya was a world traveler. As a matter of fact, she traveled more than anyone in Chelm.

A wealthy widow with an itch to travel, Relya had been to Minsk. She had been to Pinsk. She had been, even, to Vitipsk-Gaboynya. This particular summer Relya decided to go someplace different. She chose Katmandu, Nepal.

"What are you, crazy?" asked Boris the Balagoola. "Who keeps Kosher in Katmandu?"

Rivka the Baker was worried. "I looked it up on a map. They got there the Hermiaya Mountains."

Boris said, "You mean the Himalayas."

Rivka bridled: "What are you, a sexist?"

Relya could not be talked out of it, and somehow, some way, she made it to Nepal. Checking into the Katmandu Hilton, she sought out the Concierge. "You the person who arranges the side trips?"

"Yes, I am, Madam Relya. Can I be of assistance?"

"I would like," she said, "to meet, personally, the Grand Guru."

The concierge laughed...politely. "Impossible. The Tsar was turned down. Heads of State all over the world have been refused. Even 'Sixty Minutes' was denied an interview, and they haven't even been invented yet. Besides, the Guru lives in a cave on top of the highest mountain in the HimaLAYas--or HiMALayas--whichever you prefer--and he has taken a vow of silence."

"Listen, mister, you don't understand. Money, by me, is no object. I gotta see the Guru, and I'm prepared to *noodge*[1] you forever until you work it out."

Now understand that Relya was a widow because she *noodged* her poor husband to death. When it came to *noodging*, Relya was an Olympic Gold Medalist.

For three weeks, night and day, she drove the poor concierge crazy. She showed up at his desk every hour on the hour. Somehow she got his home telephone number and called him in the middle of the night. Finally, he gave in.

"Enough, Madam Relya. It's all arranged, but I promise that you will be sorry. Here's what you must do: Tomorrow morning at dawn, a tribe of fierce headhunters will escort you through the densest jungle on earth. For a full week you will have to hack your way through impassable vegetation, with tigers and snakes on all sides of you. And never forget that your guides are vicious headhunters."

"Then I'll meet the Guru?"

"No, not yet, Madam Relya. After the jungle, you will come to a raging river that you must cross. You have exactly 3 minutes and 11 seconds to do so. Otherwise, the crocodiles will eat you...and always remember that you are being escorted by heinous headhunters."

"Then the Guru?"

"No, not yet, Madam Relya. If you have survived so far--and almost no one has--you will be at the base of the highest mountain in the HimaLAYas...or, you know...and a new guide, a convicted murderer doing penance, will now take you, hand over hand, up the side of the mountain. Your right side will receive second degree burns from the sun. Your left side will be frostbitten. Only one in 10,000 people ever survive the climb. But...if by some slim chance you make it...there will be the Guru, in his cave, surrounded by his fierce followers. Now is the most critical point in your odyssey."

"My odyssey?" wondered Relya.

---

[1] *Noodge* means to pester or harass.

"Yes. You are permitted to say only three words to the Guru. If you inadvertently utter even a fourth word, they will behead you on the spot. Although I may have underestimated the dangers, do you still wish to go on this journey?"

Relya was ecstatic. "I wouldn't miss it! This already is a vacation you could die over."

What can I tell you, dear listener? God must go out of his way to protect the poor fools of Chelm. Somehow, some way, Relya made it to the cave. Burned on one side and frostbitten on the other, more dead than alive, Relya stumbled into the cave.

She recalled her instructions. *"Remember, Madam Relya, only three words are permitted."*

Crawling forward--slowly and painfully--she looked the Guru in the eye. Taking a deep breath, Relya uttered her allotted three words. "SHELDON, COME HOME!"

WHAT I DID ON MY VACATION
By Charles M. Powell

"You saw the story in the newspaper?" asked Berel the Beadle.

"I couldn't believe it," replied Boris the Balagoola.

"Someone would be kind enough to fill me in?" begged Rivka the Baker.

"Well," said the Beadle, "there was this ad in the newspaper, the Chelm Chronicle, that offered an all-expenses-paid, luxury Chelm River cruise for only three Rubles."

"You gonna go?" asked the Baker.

"Does a bride go to a *mikva*?[2] Does a bear sleep in the woods? Does a *mohel*[3] work on tips? Of course I'm going to go."

Boris agreed. "For that kind of money, for me also it's Barn Voyage."

Early the next morning, Berel showed up at the pier on the Great Chelm River. He walked up to a well-dressed gentleman and said: "I'm here for the cruise."

"We have many cruises," replied the gentleman. "We have a tour of the Greek Islands; we have a St. Petersburg Museum visit; we have the Warsaw, Poland one-day-and-four-nights special; and, of course, the Chelm River Cruise."

Berel answered promptly. "For me, it's the 'Of-Course-The-Chelm-River Cruise.'"

"Of course," said the gentleman. "That will be three Rubles, please."

---

[2] A *mikva* is a ceremonial cleansing bath.
[3] A *mohel*, pronounced "moil" rhymes with "toil," is the specialized rabbi who performs the ritual circumcision of the male baby.

As soon as the Beadle paid his money, the gentleman promptly hit him over the head, placed the unconscious Berel on a small raft and pushed him down river.

An hour later, Boris the Balagoola also showed up at the river. "I'm here," he said, "for the Chelm River Cruise and here are my three Rubles."

The gentleman took his money, also hit him over the head, also placed him upon a raft, and also pushed the Balagoola onto the river.

Later that day, both Chelmites awoke on their rafts, which by this time had drifted far downstream. Berel, spotting Boris on his raft, yelled first.

"Ahoy, out there. Is that you, Boris?"

"Yo," yelled back the Balagoola.

"Do you know how to fish?" inquired Berel.

"It gives me a splitting haddock," said the Balagoola. "How about you?"

Berel replied: "Once in a while I fish, but just for the Halibut. Are you on the Chelm River Luxury Cruise, too?" asked the Beadle.

"Of course," replied the Balagoola.

"Tell me something," shouted Berel the Beadle, "do they serve breakfast on this cruise?"

Boris the Balagoola shrugged: "They didn't last year!"

FROM CHELM TO JERUSALEM
OR
NU, VOYAGER? [4]
By Charles M. Powell

There is a path in Jerusalem, the Holy City, that winds its way down from what is called Mount Zion and ends up at the Western Wall. The Wall, called "*Kotel*" in Hebrew, is the heart and soul of any Jew's visit.

Such was the case with Boris the Balagoola, on his pilgrimage to the Holy Land from Chelm, where the wise fools all lived. And what a trip it was.

First, a horse-cart to Pinsk. Then, a train-ride to Minsk. Then, a side-trip to Vitipsk-Gaboynya (his wife sent some *kichel*[5] to a cousin), and finally to a port city. The Holy Land was only three weeks away.

But here he was at last, Boris, the Balagoola of Chelm, in the Holy Land, in the Holy City, and of course, totally lost.

He spied an old *Chasid*,[6] sitting, facing East, and praying for all he was worth before eleven open prayer books. Gingerly, gently, Boris approached the old man. "Excuse me, *MeIamed*,[7] please answer for me a simple question from a visitor to your country. If I continue along this path, how long will it take me to reach the holy of holy Western Wall?"

The *Melamed* missed not a beat. "*Shulchain Ad Morom, V' Kadosh Shimo...*" He ignored completely the good wise fool of Chelm.

Boris was perplexed. "Excuse me, old man, A simple answer, please. If I continue along this road, how long will it take me to arrive at the Wall?"

---

[4] *Nu* is a Yiddish word with lots of uses. As in formal greeting, it's your "What's up? Or *"Que pasa?"* As an interjection during a conversation, it can mean "See what I mean?" but also "seriously, you think *that* is an important issue?" Very useful, *nu*?
[5] *Kichel* are cookies or hard cakes.
[6] A *chasid* is an Orthodox Jew, the *chasidim* (plural form) are one sect.
[7] *Melamed* is very learned person, and used as a polite term for a teacher.

The old man continued to pray: "*Mi Chimocha, B'al givurout... umain.*"

The Balagoola was now beside himself. "Hold it just 'ein' momento, old man. I am a guest in your country. Please...tell me...how long would it take me to walk to the Wall?'

Still the praying: ..."*V'Seem-cha Kaddosh...umain.*"

Furious, the Balagoola threw up his hands and continued along the path.

Twenty steps later he suddenly heard the voice of the *Melamed*. "Forty-four minutes and eleven seconds."

Boris stopped in his tracks. He doubled back and looked at the old Chasid. "You gotta be crazy. Why would you put me through all of this? My heart is pounding, my blood pressure is--forget about it--why didn't you tell me right away how long I gotta walk?"

The man looked up from his books. "First I had to see how *fast* you walked!"

WHAT I DID ON MY SUMMER VACATION
By Charles M. Powell

The formal meeting of the Wise Council of Elders had ended, and the wisest people in all of Chelm sat around gabbing. Well, not all of them were gabbing. Schneider the Tailor was asleep in the corner and Shloime the Student was talking to himself--but he always talked to himself.

The subject of the gabbing was "What I did on my summer vacation." The answers were strictly from Chelm.

Rivka the Baker reported that she had been on a trip around the world. "Enough. Next year," she announced, "I'll go someplace else!"

Boris the Balagoola talked about the bridge he had single-handedly built in the Teitelbaum Valley. Berel the Beadle said, "But there's no water in the Teitelbaum Valley."

"I know that," said the Balagoola, "but don't tell the twelve Cossacks who are fishing from the bridge today."

Berel the Beadle reported that he spent his summer vacation building three swimming pools at his home. "Three pools?" said Rivka. "Who needs three pools?"

Berel smiled. "Simple," he said. "One pool will be heated for my friends who like to swim in warm water. The second pool will be unheated for those who like cold water. The third pool will be empty."

Wondered Schneider, "But why would you need a third pool, particularly if it's empty?"

"Listen," said Berel. "I've got friends who don't like to swim!"

Shloime the Student spent his summer vacation working on his inventions. He was able to come up with a pair of self-cleaning trousers for students who hated doing their own laundry. He thought about, but discarded, an idea for an eleven-foot pole. When asked what its use would be, Shloime explained that it was for people you wouldn't touch with a ten-foot pole.

The Rabbi had asked Kalman the Karpenter to spend his summer vacation building an ark for the Synagogue. Kalman had done a superb job: the ark was completed beautifully with every nail just so and every detail absolutely perfect. The ark stood, tall and majestically, in front of the Great Synagogue...and it bore two goats, two cows, two horses, two chickens, and thirty-two rabbits.

"Not that kind of an ark," the Rabbi had bellowed. "I meant an ark for the Torahs."

"Not to worry," said the carpenter. "There's plenty of room in the ark for the Torahs. I couldn't find any koala bears anyway."

The Rabbi was disturbed at what he thought was a village-wide waste of summer vacation time. "Not one book was read," he said. "Not a single act of charity was undertaken. It's a disgrace, and you should all be ashamed."

The Wise Council agreed completely. "By the way, Rabbi," asked Rivka. "How did you spend your summer vacation?"

"Me?" said the Rabbi, "I've just returned from a pleasure trip to Minsk."

The Balagoola laughed. "What did you do in Minsk that was such a pleasure?"

The Rabbi smiled. "I visited my in-laws and dropped off the *Rebbitzen*." [8]

---

[8] *Rebbitzen* is an old term for a rabbi's wife. Before you protest, you can flip the story and have the rabbi drop off her husband instead; there's just no Yiddish term for him!

YOUTH

1. Today You Are A Man
2. The Bar Mitzvah Speech
3. The Rodent Less Traveled
4. A Talk On The Child Side
5. A Tall Tale
6. The Wise Children of Chelm
7. The Good Son

Youth is wasted on the young, but perhaps less so in Chelm. Everybody has an opinion...even the children. And the relationship between parents and children...even "grown" children...can also be ripe for humorous consumption.

(See also "The Cholera of Money" in the Charity/Fundraising Chapter "Divorce, Chelm Style" and "I Do" in the Marriage/Divorce chapter and "There's No Place Like Home" in the Vacations chapter for more references to children, adult or otherwise.)

TODAY YOU ARE A MAN

By Mel Powell based on a story by Charles M. Powell

[The bar mitzvah is the ritual ascension to adulthood for the Jewish male child, at age 13. (Generations of Jewish boys have complained bitterly...if I'm a man now, how come I still gotta do chores and have a bedtime? There's logic to the idea, but it's a losing pro-position.) In more modern times, the bat mitzvah is celebrated for the Jewish female child, but at least in America only since the 1920s or so. That feels like the distant past until you remember that, say 1922 on our calendar was the year 5682 on the Jewish calendar. At any rate, on with the celebration!]

Berel the Beadle beamed with pride. "Today," he said, "you become a man. Not until you become a parent yourself will you understand how proud I feel today. Thank you, God," he prayed, "for permitting me to live to this day so that I may see my child become a man."

"But, Papa," said the child, "I must correct you."

Now Berel the Beadle was not an easy man to correct. Chelm was the tiny village where the wise fools all lived. Frighteningly wise decisions were passed down by Chelm's Council of Elders, and the Rabbi was known throughout the Pale for his wisdom. Berel the Beadle was the center of all that was wise in the wise village of Chelm. How dare a child attempt to correct such a man!

The good Beadle narrowed his eyes and looked at his eldest offspring. "Are you saying, my child, that I am not happy that today you become a man?"

"It's not that, Papa. I know how proud you are."

"And when you are called up to the Torah to read your portion, your mother and I and your little brother will *kvell*.[1] And everyone in

---

[1] To *kvell* is to feel and exude happiness and pride.

the congregation will smile, and whisper: 'Today, the eldest child of Berel the Beadle becomes a man.'"

"Yes, Papa, but--"

"And," continued Berel, "when you chant your *Haftarah*[2]--slowly and beautifully, without a single error--and the great Rabbi looks at me and nods his head in approval, could you question then, my child, how happy I will be?"

"Of course not, Papa. But surely you must realize--"

"Realize? I realize that today you become a man in a world of opportunity! Perhaps someday you will be able to visit the Holy Land! Perhaps you will have the opportunity to study under a great teacher. And someday, in a land of opportunity such as America, a Jew will have the chance to be Vice-President...while you, of course, run for President."

"Yes, Papa. Thank you, Papa. I think, however..."

"You think, however? Just thirteen years old and you think, however? Today you become a man and *tomorrow* you may have permission to think, however. And that's the final word on the subject!"

And so, somewhat confused and very bewildered, the eldest child of Berel the Beadle, Ruchel Natalya, went to prepare for her *Bat Mitzvah*.

---

[2] The torah, of course, is the holiest Jewish text, the Five Books of Moses, or the "Old Testament." The *haftarah* is accompanying commentary and is recited or chanted by the young celebrant.

THE BAR MITZVAH SPEECH

By Charles M. Powell

(inspired by "The Real Inspector Hound")

A Bar or Bat Mitzvah in Chelm--the tiny village where the Wise Fools all live--is no small deal. It is, instead, a very big deal.

Of course, it is traditional for the Bar Mitzvah child to prepare a speech in which he thanks his parents, his grandparents, the Rabbi, and his rich uncle or aunt. But in Chelm this tradition is taken even farther. The Bar Mitzvah child ls required to present his speech, in advance, to the Council of Elders, the wisest fools in the village. The Council then has the speech examined, analyzed, and finally approved or disapproved by Kaplan the Critic.

On this particular occasion, a young man named Farfel presented his speech to Berel the Beadle, who immediately delivered it to the Council of Elders. With a week to go before the Bar Mitzvah, Kaplan the Critic received the speech.

"I wish to thank," the speech began, "my dear parents for their love and care and attentiveness...and also for the boots they handed down to me from my older brother, Shloime the Student. My grandparents, too, I thank for their help and encouragement. For the Rabbi, a special thanks for showing me how wonderful it is to be a Jew. Thank you all, and next year we should all be in Jerusalem."

"Not a bad speech," observed Berel, who had stayed for the meeting "What is your opinion?" he asked the Critic.

"Shallow! Lacks emotion! Two thumbs down! It's hopelessly lacking in structure and syntax!"

"But what do you expect from a Bar Mitzvah speech?" asked Berel.

"I'm glad you asked that, my dear Beadle" grumbled Kaplan the Critic. "Let me at once admit that this speech has élan while at the same time, avoiding éclat.

"Having said that--and I think it must be said--I am bound to ask: does this speech know where it is going? Does it declare its affiliations? There are moments--and I would not begrudge it this--when the speech...if we can call it that (and I think, on balance, we can), aligns itself uncompromisingly on the side of life. 'Je suis, ergo sum,' it seems to be saying. 'I am; therefore, I exist.'

"But is that enough? We are entitled to ask: what, in fact, is this speech concerned with? It is my belief that here we are concerned with what I refer to as the nature of identity. I think we are entitled to ask--and here one is irresistibly reminded of Rashi's cry of *'Halavai'*[3]--I think we are entitled to ask: 'Where Is God?'"

"Who?" asked Berel, befuddled.

"I say only that we are entitled to ask," answered Kaplan.

And so days went on, as Kaplan the Critic picked each phrase apart. Each sentence was parsed. Each word was dissected. Berel kept reminding the Critic that the week was passing quickly. But, still, he analyzed and orated...and pontificated...and argued with himself and the speech...and debated some more.

"In regard to this speech," said Kaplan, "to say that it is without pace, point, focus, interest, drama, wit, or originality is to say simply--"

Berel interrupted: "Is to say it isn't your glass of tea!"

"Precisely! If we examine this more closely--and I think that close examination is the least tribute this speech deserves--we will find that within the austere framework of what is seen to be, on one level, a simple Bar Mitzvah speech the writer has given us--yes, I will go so far--he has given us the Human condition."

After several more days of heated consideration, the Critic finally reached his conclusion. "It is a perfectly suitable speech for a Bar Mitzvah."

---

[3] *Halavai* translates loosely as "Thank Goodness" or even "Hooray!"

Berel the Beadle smiled. "I'm glad you approve of it," he said, "because it was given yesterday morning in the Synagogue and everyone loved it!"

THE RODENT LESS TRAVELED
OR
RAT'S ENTERTAINMENT

By Mel Powell

(from a story by Bud Rosenthal)

[Spoiler alert! Jewish readers, please start reading the story! For our non-Jewish friends, you should know about the old rueful "joke" that, too often in secular life, a connection to one's formal Judaism fades after a certain, specific ritual.]

"The problem," complained the good Rabbi, "is getting out of hand!"

Now, when the Wise Council of Fools in the tiny village of Chelm faced a problem that was getting out of hand...well, the meeting quickly got out of hand.

"How are you going to fix it?" boomed Boris the Balagoola at Berel the Beadle.

"Me? ME?" complained the Beadle. "What about you?"

"You're the *shamus*,"[4] explained Boris threateningly.

"But we must do something!" begged the Rabbi, "The chair legs have teeth marks, there are holes in the floor, and the curtain on our lovely ark is in tatters!"

The argument raged until Rivka the Baker, currently the Mayor of Chelm, smacked her rolling pin on the table. Silence quickly fell.

---

[4] You learned in the book's introduction that a "beadle" is the person responsible for the set-up of the synagogue, not quite maintenance, just being sure everything is in place and ready. *Shamus* (SHAH-muss) is the Hebrew word that that person.

"Now that's better! This is getting us nowhere! If the Rabbi says the synagogue is infested with mice, then it's up to this Council to solve the problem!"

Unfortunately, as was usually the case with the Wise Council of Fools, no one had any good ideas. Someone suggested that perhaps the mice could be chased out by old Reb Katz and they put the idea up for a vote. But the Katz idea was scratched...after it lost by a whisker.

Shloime the Student spoke up. "Dear friends, I happened recently to hear of a Cossack in Kiev who removes unwanted animals. I believe his name is Arnold the Ex-terminator."

After a discussion, it was decided not to invite to Chelm anyone with such a name...

"I have an idea!" bellowed Boris. "I know of a young Russian who might be able to help."

"Who is this person?" asked Rivka.

Boris explained: "Piotr. He's a piper from Pi-PER-nick."

"Piotr the Piper from Pipernick? Why would he want to help us?"

"He's a pauper," explained Boris. "But what a *punim*!"[5]

The rabbi rose. "I assume, dear Boris, that he is pious?"

"Precisely!" said Boris.

"You mean...?" wondered Berel.

"Yes," said Boris, "Our mouse problem can be solved by Piotr the pious pauper piper with the *punim* from Pipernick."

"Perfect!" said Rivka. "But we have so little money, will he first accept a partial payment?"

"Perhaps. But he might prefer payment in full."

Mendel the Messenger spoke up, "Pshaw! Are you say-- are you say-- do you mean to tell me...that Piotr the pious pauper piper with the punim from Pipernick will perhaps pick a paltry partial payment?"

---

[5] *Punim* means "face" but the connotation is "what a cute/good-looking person."

The Council burst into spontaneous applause. "Mendel," said Boris, "You said that without stuttering! That was wonderful!"

Mendel smiled, "Thank you-- than-- you're too kind."

Unfortunately, it was discovered that Piotr the piper from Pipernick had fled to Pennsylvania, where he now fingered a frenetic fife for the Philadelphia Philharmonic.

The Council pondered for hours, and others made suggestions, but they could come up with no solution and decided to give up.

The Rabbi did show his optimistic side, explaining, "Well, they may be mice, but they never miss a *minyan*."[6]

It was some weeks later when the good Rabbi, in his travels, happened to meet his old friend Rabbi Chertok, of the great synagogue in Minsk, The Rabbi explained his predicament to the aged scholar.

"Not to worry," said Rabbi Chertok. "The very same thing happened to us here in the Minsk synagogue!"

"What did you do?"

"Simple. I gathered all the mice into the main sanctuary and bar mitzvahed them all. I haven't seen them since!"

---

[6] A *minyan* is a gathering of ten Jews, old-school-traditionally males only, a minimum attendance for certain prayers.

A TALK ON THE CHILD SIDE

By Mel Powell

"Now this already," worried Berel the Beadle, "is getting to be a problem."

The Wise Council of Fools of the tiny village of Chelm nodded their agreement. All except Boris the Balagoola.

"Why now, all of a sudden?" he boomed. "You've been saying that for two years!"

"Because," explained Rivka the Baker imperiously, "most parents spend the first two years of their child's life trying to get them to talk. Then they spend the teenage years trying to get them to shut up already. But little Shaindel, daughter of our beloved Avraham and Dvusha, is six years old and hasn't spoken a word."

"But it wasn't a problem when little Shaindel was four?" demanded Boris.

"Of course it was a problem," noted Berel. "In Chelm, everybody's a critic. It's genetic. So at some point everyone has something to complain about, but not little Shaindel--not a word. And now that we've sent in the heavy artillery, which hasn't been invented yet, and still we've failed, now it's a problem!"

Boris nodded. "So what's this heavy arterial--arthurian--whatever you just said?"

Berel explained, "As we all know, Selma the Seamstress never shuts up. That's the bad news. The good news, of course, is that she could draw a marble statue into a conversation. Mind you, after 'hello, Selma,' the statue would never get another word in edgewise. But there would be a conversation!"

Schneider the Tailor--Selma's husband--spoke up, a privilege he rarely enjoyed at home. "Yesterday, dear citizens, my good wife Selma went to the home of Avraham and Dvusha, who are such wonderful, devoted parents, to try to draw little Shaindel into a conversation. Bear in mind, Wise Council, that Shaindel is clearly a child of above-average intelligence. She can write clearly when called upon. She understands anything you may say to her. She has shown an aptitude for mathematics. Rivka tells me that she is quite good near an oven. But she won't say a word--not even to complain!"

"So?" wondered Boris, "Did Selma get little Shaindel to talk?"

Sadly, Schneider just shook his head "no."

The very next morning, six-year-old Shaindel sat at the kitchen table. Her mother Dvusha brought her breakfast, her father Avraham kissed her on top of the head, and then Dvusha went about other morning tasks as Avraham prepared to leave for his shoemaking shop.

Moments later, little Shaindel stood up, "Dear Mother? Forgive me, but I must tell you that these scrambled eggs you have made for my breakfast are a tad bit runny. And there is just a bit too much pulp in this fresh orange juice. And, Father, I must say it is time for me to have a new pair of shoes, as these have worn almost completely out in the sole--and you, a shoemaker!"

Dvusha almost dropped the frying pan onto the floor, "My child! My lovely daughter! You spoke! At long last, you have said your first words."

"Of course, Mother," said Shaindel matter-of-factly.

"But why," wondered Avraham through tears of joy, "why have you never spoken until now?"

"Well, Father," said Shaindel, "quite frankly, up until now everything's been fine..."

A TALL TALE

By Mel Powell

(with Bud Rosenthal)

Ari the Athlete, a strapping young fellow, was the finest youth athlete in Chelm. Ari was many things. Intelligent, kind-hearted, articulate…and impossibly tall. How tall was he? So tall that his mother enrolled him in Height Watchers.

In school, on the rare occasions when Ari was daydreaming, his teacher would tell him to get his head out of the clouds…and it was almost literally accurate.

And so, as Ari the Athlete's bar mitzvah day approached, Ari faced the first crisis of his young life. Politely, he knocked on the door of Schneider the Tailor's shop.

"Ari the Athlete!" said Schneider, looking up…and up and up…at Ari. "How nice to see you, *boychik*.[7] Come in, come in. What can I do for you?"

"Reb Schneider, sir, it's almost time for my bar mitzvah. You made that beautiful suit for me last month, but now I need a nice, dressy coat to wear over it."

"Oh boy, are you lucky!" said Schneider. "Have I got a coat for you!" He rushed to the back of his shop, and returned a moment later. "Just arrived from Kashmir. Pure cashmere. It's perfect for you, like it already has your name on the label. Only 200 kopecks, but as a bar mitzvah gift I'll give it to you for half-price, only 150 kopecks."

"I'm grateful," said Ari with courtesy, looking at the coat skeptically, "but are you sure the coat will fit?"

"Ari," said Schneider, "am I Schneider the Baker? Am I Schneider the Milkman? Of course not. I am Schneider the Tailor. Trust me, the coat will fit. Here, try it on."

---

[7] *Boychik* is a term of endearment for a young male.

"It is very nice," agreed Ari. "But Reb Schneider, the right sleeve is too short. Look!"

Schneider clucked his tongue, "Ari, Ari, my *boychik*. You're going to pass up a beautiful coat like this because one sleeve is a little too short?" Schneider gently grabbed Ari and tilted him to the right. "There, now the sleeve isn't too short!"

Ari glanced down and saw the that the right sleeve was now just the right length. "But Reb Schneider, now the coat bunches up at the shoulder."

Schneider chuckled "Ari, in this coat, this beautiful coat, you will be the envy of all the boys in Chelm. And you will be the object of desire of all the girls. You're going to pass it up a bargain like this because the coat bunches up a little? Here, just lean forward a bit."

And Schneider now tilted Ari a bit forward. Sure enough, the coat no longer bunched up at the shoulder.

Ari seemed pleased, but then he noticed something. "Reb Schneider, look! Now the left side is too short."

Schneider had to agree. "But Ari, you can't pass up this beautiful cashmere coat at this price. When you walk, just shuffle along a little, leading with your left foot, like this." He demonstrated. Ari shuffled forward. The coat was no longer too short on the left side.

Convinced, Ari politely paid for the coat, thanked Schneider profusely for the generous gift of the discount, and left the shop, listing to the right, tilting forward, and shuffling with his left foot.

On the road outside the shop, Ari passed two elderly women, Sadie and Bessie, visiting from a neighboring village. They took one look at Ari the Athlete, never having seen him before, shuffling along at an impossible angle.

"Vat a *shanda*,[8] Sadie," said Bessie. "That a boy so young should be so terribly afflicted!"

---

[8] *Shanda* means "a shame" (and can also mean a bad controversy, in context, but not here).

Sadie shook her head sadly, agreeing. "But Bessie, look how nice his coat fits!"

THE WISE CHILDREN OF CHELM
By Charles M. Powell with a bit of a Mel Powell update

The tiny village of Chelm, where the wise fools lived, was home to the wisest people anywhere in the world, and no one would believe otherwise. Especially the wise fools of Chelm.

And how do you suppose they ended up with the wisest people in the world? By raising the wisest children, of course!

"There is nothing," bragged Rivka the Baker, "that our children cannot accomplish! Why, in an effort to avoid being upstaged by the children of Kiev, this year the children of Chelm have picked a perfect plan for the surprise breakout performance of their Purim play!"

"And what, pray tell, is that?" wondered Boris the Balagoola.

"They're going to do it at Chanukah!"

Brilliant, agreed the Wise Council of Elders. Especially Berel the Beadle. Berel, you see, was the proud papa of the smartest child in Chelm. How smart was he? Berel boasted: "My little Yankel is as smart as a whip! Have you heard what he told me this morning? If the King of Russia is called the 'Tsar,' and the Queen is known as the 'Tsarina,' then their children must be the 'tsardines!'"

Brilliant, surely…but how much bragging could the villagers endure?

"Not much more," said Boris threateningly at a closed-door session of the Wise Council--without Berel.

And so it was decided that Berel would present his little Yankel before the Council for a test. If Yankel was, indeed, the wisest child in Chelm, then Berel could brag until Tevye's milk cows cane home. If not, well…it was Boris who warned Berel of the "if not."

"If not, then enough already with the bragging!"

Berel agreed, and Yankel stayed up nights for a full month, studying for the test…whatever it might be. Meanwhile, the wise

Council consulted experts from Minsk to Pinsk to Vitipsk-Gaboynya for help in preparing the questions.

On the appointed day, Yankel was ushered into the Council chamber. With Berel waiting nervously outside, the test began.

First, Schneider the Tailor rose solemnly and held his fist high in the air. Yankel thought for only an instant and then raised his open hand.

Next, Boris the Balagoola held up two beefy fingers. Yankel responded immediately by raising one index finger.

Finally, Rivka the Baker held up a single piece of matzah. Yankel, without hesitation, walked to a luncheon tray and raised an egg. The Council exploded in wild applause!

Instantly, Mendel the Messenger raced from the Council chamber to broadcast the news. "Hear ye-- hear ye-- listen up! Yankel, the son of Berel, is the wises-- the wises-- boy is that boy smart!"

Later that evening, Shloime the Student returned from his studies at the *yeshiva*[9] and asked Rivka and Boris what test they had devised for Yankel and how the boy had fared.

"A most difficult test, Shloime!" said Rivka. "We spoke to Yankel in an ancient biblical sign language! First, Schneider raised his fist, signifying that a cruel dictator would one day rule the world. Little Yankel raised his open hand, telling us that Schneider was wrong, and that the combined nations and peoples of the world would band together to stop him!"

"Then," continued Boris, "I raised two fingers, like so. Yankel, instead, raised only one, like so. In the ancient sign language, I was asking, 'Are there two gods?' And Yankel showed us that there was only one. A genius!"

"And for the final question," concluded Rivka, "I held up a matzah, meaning that the world was flat. But Yankel knew better. He held up an egg. Of course, the world is round!"

---

[9] A *yeshiva* is a school for Jewish study.

Shloime agreed: Yankel was the smartest child in Chelm.

Meanwhile, Berel, at home, was beside himself with joy. "I always knew how smart you were, Yankel; but to be so acclaimed by the Council! Tell me, son, what was the difficult test they gave you?"

Little Yankel shook his head. "To tell you the truth, Papa, I think that the entire Council is *mishuga*.[10] As soon as I walked in, Schneider the Tailor shook his fist at me. I raised my hand to ward off the blow...but of course he didn't hit me. Then the Balagoola threatened to poke my eyes out with his two fingers, but I shook a finger right back at him in warning. Lastly--and, as far as I can tell, this was the only test--Rivka held up a matzah. So I held up an egg, After all, how else can you make matzah brei?"

---

[10] Crazy!

THE GOOD SON

By Mel Powell

Yenta the Matchmaker was a lucky woman indeed.

"I have everything," she boasted to her friends one morning in the tiny village of Chelm, where the wise fools lived. "A great job, helping our wonderful young people find the perfect spouse...whomever I say is perfect. Wonderful friends. Even a hobby!"

Such a hobby, well...for this she was not terribly beloved, for Yenta the Matchmaker knew everything about everyone and told everyone about everything. Her gossip was so famous that she was often interviewed in secret by the Vitipsk-Gaboynya Enquirer. But I digress.

Yenta also had three fine sons, who had grown up and left Chelm to seek their fortune in Leningrad. And one day these three young men gathered over a glass of tea to discuss the gifts they had recently given Yenta on the occasion of her birthday.

The eldest son, Yenta's first-born, Chashka, said, "I built a big house for our dear mother, the finest mansion in all of Chelm. Even the guest rooms have guest rooms."

"Pshaw," said the second son, Label, "she should sit in her house all day? I sent our mother the finest top-of-the-line, state-of-the-art ox-cart. Plush velvet seats, fifty kilometers to the gallon of ox-feed (forty in the village), a champion ox with a certificate from Anti-Stubborn School...and a highly-trained driver, no less."

Yenta's youngest, Shmuel, was not impressed. "Dear brothers, I am not impressed. I have you both beat."

"Nonsense," said Chashka.

"*Mishuga*,"[11] predicted Label.

So Shmuel explained.

---

[11] Crazy!

"You remember how Mama enjoyed reading from the Torah? But you know that her eyesight is not what it once was. So I sent Mama a remarkable parrot! It can recite the entire Torah! It took the Elders in the Great Synagogue of Minsk six years to train the parrot to read Hebrew, and the Elders in the Great Synagogue of Pinsk another six years to teach him the Torah!"

Now the older boys were listening. Shmuel went on.

"He's one of a kind, this parrot. Mama just has to name the chapter and verse, and the parrot recites it--and then interprets it. And if you give him an extra cracker, he recites the *Haftarah*[12] as well."

Chashka and Label agreed...their dear younger brother had truly bested them.

In Chelm, Yenta the Matchmaker sat down to write her thank-you notes.

"Dear Chashka," she wrote to the eldest, who had built her a new home. "Thank you for the house. It is huge, the envy of all who see it. Of course, I live in only one room, but I have to clean the entire house."

"Dear Label," she wrote to the middle son, who had sent her the transportation. "The ox-cart is wonderful. Never have I had such a smooth ride. Of course, I'm old. Where I got to go? And the driver is incredibly rude--and doesn't like it when I give directions."

"Dearest Shmuel," she wrote to the youngest, who had given her the *Talmudic*[13] parrot. "You, my baby son, my *boychik*,[14] you have the good sense to know just what your mother truly likes.

"The chicken was delicious!"

---

[12] The *haftarah* is accompanying commentary to the Torah.
[13] The *Talmud* is the entire body of Jewish law, but as an adjective here it means learned in the ways of Jewish law and tradition.
[14] *Boychik* is a term of endearment for a young male.

A FINAL TALE

This story belongs in the Show Business Category. But as you will see, having read the collection of stories and experienced, among the many, the handful that became "classics," this story needed to find itself here as the grand finale.

Thank you for taking this journey with us and with the Wise Fools of Chelm.

FUNNY BUSINESS

By Mel Powell

The townspeople of the tiny village of Chelm were thrilled that, after so many years of conflict with their neighbors, their own Shloime the Student had a houseguest, a young Russian classmate named Vladimir the Visitor.

"Vladimir," welcomed Shloime, "it is so good to see you. And you have come to Chelm at just the right moment, perhaps my favorite time of year! Today we hold Chelm's Annual Comedy Convention!"

"How wonderful!" responded a delighted Vladimir. "Would I, a humble visitor, be permitted to attend?"

"Of course!" answered the student, "Everybody is welcome, because it's funnier that way!"

"Please, Shloime, do tell me about this convention, so I will be more prepared to enjoy it completely."

"Vladimir, we laugh about everything! We have comedy cooking demonstrations. We have comedy eating contests. We have comedy musical performances. We even have comedy sports! And everything is Closed-Captioned for the Humor Impaired. But tonight's highlight, bar none, mind you, is the Great Joke-Telling Open Forum. We sit around for hours and tell our favorite jokes!"

Words cannot describe the excited anticipation with which Vladimir approached his first Chelm Comedy Convention. And he was not disappointed, as the day flew by. As evening fell, it was time for the Joke-Telling exhibition.

Shloime explained to Vladimir: "You're going to love the moderator of the Joke-Telling Forum, our chief humorist, Gloria the Giggler! Just you wait!"

Gloria, laughing as always, took the stage with her gavel, "Gentle citizens," began Gloria the Giggler--but then she burst out laughing. The Chelmites cheered wildly, interpreting this to mean, "Let the Joke-Telling Begin!"

Boris the Balagoola politely raised his hand, and Gloria the Giggler pointed with her gavel to turn the floor over to the Huge One.

Boris rose, stone-faced. He surveyed the crowd, and then announced solemnly, "Forty-two!"

And the crowd, led by Gloria the Giggler, flew into hysteria!

Vladimir looked around in amazement. He didn't get it.

Shloime, doubled over with laughter, straightened long enough to explain: "We've done this for so many years that we all know the jokes. So, to save time, we've numbered them. Forty-two is one of my favorites, about a new ox-cart for Boris himself."[1]

When Gloria the Giggler had calmed down--about fifteen minutes later--she recognized the raised hand of Rivka the Baker.

Rivka rose. "Nine-teen!" she proposed with mock drama. Gloria the Giggler needed oxygen.

Shloime, trying to catch his breath, explained, "That's about the Yom Kippur Kipper Caper! I love that one!" [2]

---

[1] "Hitchhiker's Guide to Chelm," Transportation and Technology Chapter.
[2] "Yom Kippur Kipper Caper," Jewish Holidays Chapter.

Berel the Beadle was recognized, holding the gazes of the many villagers around the room, and then…at just the right moment…announced, "FIVE!"

When Shloime the Student picked himself back up of the floor from laughing, he explained, "It's the funeral joke--his brother--his brother--!" [3] And Shloime collapsed back into laughter.

"A funeral joke?" wondered Vladimir to himself. "This is an interesting convention…"

The joke-telling went on for hours. It was rumored that Gloria the Giggler's thorough enjoyment of the evening was registered all over the world by seismographs, which hadn't been invented yet.

Finally, Vladimir inquired of Shloime: "Might I be permitted to participate?"

Eagerly, Shloime answered, "Everyone is entitled to participate, and we would be honored to have our guest do so."

"Great," said Vladimir. Give me a good one." Shloime leaned over and whispered into the Russian's ear, and Vladimir raised his hand.

Gloria the Giggler glanced gleefully into the crowd and saw the visitor's hand, "Vladimir, our honored visitor, you wish to tell a joke? How wonderful!" And she exploded in delighted laughter.

Vladimir rose, prompted by a grinning Shloime. He looked out among the villagers. "Sixty-two!"

Silence greeted the Russian visitor. Even Gloria the Giggler looked at him politely but oddly. Abashed, Vladimir sat down, and Gloria the Giggler moved on to the next joke-teller.

"Shloime, my friend, what happened? You said that number sixty-two was a good one!"

Shloime shook his head sympathetically, "My dear Vladimir, it's all in the delivery!"

---

[3] "The Proper Send-Off," in the Death Chapter.

SCRIPTS FOR YOU AND YOUR FRIENDS

One night, both of the talented actors who read the stories aloud at the end of the services happened to be present on an evening when a specific story was timely. Now, this happened often; but with this story, just once, we didn't have to choose; the story was adapted into a two-person script, and they read it, together, for the congregation. What a blast!

We learned from the fun that a small handful of other stories were easily adapted into multi-reader formats.

Just in case you enjoy that sort of thing, we include them here in the special section.

1. Balagoola Island (Synagogue/Tradition Chapter)
2. Business Sense (Business and Commerce Chapter)
3. Complete Yom Kippur Chaos (from He Did It Again, Jewish Holidays Chapter)
4. The Craving (Health and Aging Chapter)
5. Divorce, Chelm Style (Marriage and Divorce Chapter)
6. Fore! (He's a Jolly Good Fellow) (Synagogue/Tradition Chapter)
7. The Good Son (Youth Chapter)
8. The Holiday Spirit (Jewish Holidays Chapter)
9. Picky, Picky, Picky (Food Chapter)
10. The Proper Send-Off (Death Chapter)
11. Sometimes It Doesn't Pay To Be A Nice Person (from Death Chapter)
12. Ticket, Please (Synagogue/Tradition Chapter)
13. Tink Before You Talk (Jewish Holidays Chapter)
14. What I Did On My Vacation (Vacations Chapter)
15. The Woodcutter (Synagogue/Tradition Chapter)

BALAGOOLA ISLAND (Script Version)

By Mel Powell

RESCUER: Ahoy there! Yes, you, alone on that island!

BORIS: Thank goodness! You are here to rescue me?

RESCUER: Are you Boris, the Balagoola of the village of Chelm? We're the search party from Vitipsk-Gaboynya, we've been looking for a year!

BORIS: That's me. Please, let me show you around before you take me home, for which I am of course grateful.

RESCUER: Of course, Mister Balagoola. There's so much construction on this island. You did this all by yourself?

BORIS: You see here on this island maybe the Vienna Boys Choir? Of course, I built it all myself!

RESCUER: So what's that building?

BORIS: It's a Post Office. For five years, every morning, I came looking for a letter from home.

RESCUER: And none came?

BORIS: Just junk mail.

RESCUER: And what's this building here?

BORIS: That's a *mikva*.

RESCUER: A *mikva*? But there are no women on this island!

BORIS: You never know.

RESCUER: And those two buildings over there?

BORIS: Those are Synagogues. The one on the right is my regular *shul*. Every morning, clockwork, that is where I pray.

RESCUER: Why would one man, living alone on a desert island, need to build two Synagogues? It makes no sense. The Post Office, maybe. A *mikva*, unlikely. But two Temples? What do you need with a second Synagogue?

BORIS: *That* Synagogue? *That* Synagogue I wouldn't be caught dead in!

BUSINESS SENSE (Script Version)
By Mel Powell

ANDREI: Welcome. As you know, I am the famous Andrei the Agent, loyal servant of the Tsar, and I am here to accept bids from all three of you to build a new train station just outside of the tiny village of Chelm. You, Russian...you go first.

BYAKIN: I am Byakin the Builder. I am just a simple man. My needs are small. I will build the new train station for His Highness the Tsar for the sum of six thousand rubles.

ANDREI: Six thousand rubles! How do you justify that bid?

BYAKIN: Easy. It will cost me two thousand rubles for materials. It will cost me two thousand rubles for hiring laborers. And, as I am a businessman, I will make a profit of a mere two thousand rubles.

ANDREI: Very well, you may be seated. You...foreigner. You're next.

FELICE: I am Felice the Frenchwoman. I am zee most famous ar-shee-tect in all of La France. I have built zee finest train stations in all zee world! For your worthy Tsar, I vill build a train station of better qualitée, one more pleasing to zee eye, than zis foolish Cossack simpleton. It vill cost your Tsar a mere twelve zousand rubles!"

ANDREI: Twelve zousand--I mean thousand--rubles! Why, that's twice what Byakin will charge. How would you dare charge my Tsar so much?

FELICE: *Simplement.* Four zousand rubles for materials of better *qualitée*, so zat zis train station does not fall apart and you spend more later anyway to repair it. Four zousand rubles to bring in zee finest craftsmen and women in zee business--not mere laborers, *n'est pas*, but experts! And, as I am world-renowned, I vill take my standard profit of four zousand. Voila! Twelve zousand rubles, and not a French *franc* less.

ANDREI: And you, Jew? Your turn.

KALMAN: I am Kalman the Karpenter, of Chelm. May I approach and speak to you privately for a moment?

ANDREI: That is highly irregular, but…you may approach.

KALMAN: You are well known in the land. My bid is…eighteen thousand rubles!

ANDREI: Eighteen? Are you crazy? Eighteen thousand rubles, when I have bids already for only twelve thousand and six thousand?

KALMAN: Listen, Mr. Agent. I've done my homework. About the train station, and about you and your vast personal wealth while being a mere agent for the Tsar. Eighteen thousand rubles, and here's the deal. Six thousand for you, six thousand for me, and six thousand we pay the Cossack to build it!

COMPLETE YOM KIPPUR CHAOS (Script Version)

By Mel Powell

[We leave the names of the wonderful actors, our friends, in the script, as a well-deserved salute to Lew Horn and Bret Shefter.]

LEW: Can you believe it?

BRET: Can I believe what?

LEW: He did it again!

BRET: Who did what again?

LEW: Kalman the Karpenter.

BRET: Kalman the Karpenter? Continue!

LEW: Kalman carried out another of his classic capers.

BRET: Kalman cooked up Chelm controversy?

LEW: Catastrophic! It was a kipper caper.

BRET: A kipper caper? When did it occur?

LEW: On Yom Kippur. He carried a kipper into the congregation.

BRET: You mean to tell me that Kalman the Karpenter carried a kipper into the congregation on Yom Kippur?

LEW: Correct. Also a carp.

BRET: Kalman carried a carp and a kipper on Yom Kippur?

LEW: Into the congregation!

BRET: You're kidding, was it parallel to the plagues he perpetrated on *Pesach* and *Purim*?

LEW: Worse even than the shameful *shanda* on *Shavuos*!

BRET: So who uncovered Kalman's kipper caper?

LEW: Cantor Cohen. That was the capper.

BRET: In-credible! What confounded confusion! Cantor Cohen cornered Kalman the Karpenter carrying a kipper and a carp on Yom Kippur?

LEW: Also a kreplach. Cantankerous Cantor Cohen caught Kalman and confiscated the carp, the kipper, and the kreplach. Right after Kol Nidre.

BRET: Cantor Cohen can be congratulated for his courage in canceling the caper and capturing the crook! The case is closed?

LEW: Completely. And Kalman the Karpenter cannot cause any more crises.

BRET: The Council called the cops?

LEW: Correct. And the cops incarcerated Kalman in Krakow.

BRET: What a conclusion! Consider what chaos Kalman can create for the Krakow cossacks on Christmas!

LEW: And I can't wait for Chanukah in Chelm!

BRET: Kinn-a-hora!

THE CRAVING (Script Version)

By Mel Powell from CMP story

HUSBAND: Ow! Vhat for you smack me with your book? Vhat you vant?

WIFE: I got a craving.

HUSBAND: You got a vhat?

WIFE: A craving, an 'ankering, I got to have a banana split.

HUSBAND: At this hour? Vonderful! Outside we got rain, snow, wind, terrible. So you'll take two aspirins and you'll call me in the morning and we'll order for you a banana split.

WIFE: I gotta have it now. It's a yen.

HUSBAND: Okey, dokey, pussycat. It's 20 below zero; snow coming down like Siberia; I'm 87 years young; give me already your order for this would-you-believe late-night banana split, and I'll shlep to the kitchen behind the dining hall of the Chelm Retirement Village and get it for my 86-year-old vife.

WIFE: You're a very good husband. Now, you want to write down the order?

HUSBAND: Hold it, hot-shot. You're the one with hardening of the brain around the arteries. I'm not the person with memory problems. You tell me, I'll bring.

WIFE: Bring me two slices bananas. I don't want no one-and-seven-eighths. On top, I need three scoops ice cream. The left scoop has to be Rocky Road. On the right, give me Cherry-cheesecake.

HUSBAND: And the middle scoop?

WIFE: Ah…that's the tricky part. In the middle, I want it should be 'oney vanilla. Not plain vanilla--'oney vanilla. You heard me?

HUSBAND: I heard you, I'm sitting right here.

WIFE: You sure you don't wanna write down?

HUSBAND: You're the one vhat's senile. I don't gotta write down.

WIFE: Okay. Then on top of that, I want hot fudge. But not Hershey's--gotta be Fox's U-bet. I know they got both in that kitchen. Gotta be Fox's U-bet. You heard?

HUSBAND: I heard.

WIFE: Okay, on top of that, pineapple glaze...then whipped cream, and a full maraschino cherry. You heard me? I don't want no half cherries.

HUSBAND: I heard you.

WIFE: Last chance--you want maybe a pencil?

HUSBAND: Enough with the 'write it down,' I got this.

NARRATOR: Two hours later...

WIFE: Oy, you're covered in snow, what took so long?

HUSBAND: I got what you asked. Here, open the bag.

WIFE: Look who's got hardening of the brains! I told you to write down!

HUSBAND: Vhat's the matter? I brought you exactly what you ordered!

WIFE: You're meshuga! Three onion bagels, sure, but you forgot the cream cheese!

DIVORCE, CHELM STYLE (Script Version)

By Mel Powell from CMP story

MOTTEL: Hello?

SCHNEIDER: Mottel? This is your father Schneider the Tailor of Chelm.

MOTTEL: I know who you are, Papa.

SCHNEIDER: I'm not used to this just-invented telephone device yet. I am calling you because you are my oldest child, and there's something I must tell you. I'm divorcing Mama.

MOTTEL: But Papa, you can't just decide to divorce Mama after all these years of blissful marriage! What happened?

SCHNEIDER It's too painful for me to talk about it. I only called because you're my son, and I thought you should know. Please, call your sister and tell her. It will spare me the pain.

MOTTEL: But where's Mama? May I please talk to her?

SCHNEIDER: No, I haven't told her yet. Believe me, this hasn't been easy. I've agonized over it for several days, and I've finally come to a decision. I have an appointment with Avram the Attorney the day after tomorrow.

MOTTEL: Papa, please, don't do anything rash! I'm going to take the first train to Chelm. Promise me that you won't do anything until I get there.

SCHNEIDER: Well, all right. You're my son, my only son, so I promise. Next week is Passover. I'll hold off seeing the lawyer until after the Seder. Call your sister in Vitipsk-Gaboynya and break the news to her. I can't bear to talk about it anymore.

NARRATOR: Ten minutes later…

SCHNEIDER: Hello? This is Schneider the Tailor of Chelm.

DORA: Papa! Mottel just called! Please, let us talk to you first.

SCHNEIDER: Dora, my wonderful daughter, what's to talk about? We're going to get a divorce.

DORA: Please! I will catch the next train to Chelm. My brother and I will both be there soon. Promise me that you won't do anything until we get there.

SCHNEIDER: Well, all right. You're my only daughter, so I promise. See you soon. Good-bye.

(pause)

Selma! It worked, my darling wife. This year they're both coming for Passover. Now, how are we going to get them to come here for Rosh Hashanah?

FORE!! (He's a jolly good fellow) (Script Version)

By Mel Powell

ANGEL: Boss! Boss! You gotta hear this, Boss!

BOSS: What is it, Angel 86? It's Yom Kippur! Can't you see I'm busy scrolling through this year's CD-ROM of Life?

ANGEL: But Boss: that's just it, Boss, Holiest of Holies, Master of the Universe! It's Yom Kippur.

BOSS: Tell me something I don't know. Which won't be easy, because I know everything.

ANGEL: I was doing my random check of the world when I saw this rabbi--a rabbi, mind you--playing golf! Golf, Your Worshipfulness! He's so addicted to the game that he snuck out early--before Yom Kippur services--to get in his eighteen holes! He's at the first tee as we speak!

BOSS: Golf. Hmmmm. Which rabbi?

ANGEL: From the Synagogue in Chelm.

BOSS: Oy vey.

ANGEL: Exactly! What do you want I should do to punish him, Boss? What do you want I should do?

BOSS: All right, this does call for a severe punishment. I hate to do it, and I usually prefer to be lenient with rabbis, but this is too much. You get out there to that golf course, and you give that Rabbi a hole in one!

ANGEL: Um…Boss? You OK, Boss? You want me to *punish* this golfing rabbi by giving him a hole in one? You call this punishment?

BOSS: You question my orders?

ANGEL: Um…no, um, of course not, Boss! I'm on it.

(pause)

ANGEL: OK, Boss of all Bosses, I did what you said. I gave the Rabbi a hole in one. What do you want I should do now?

BOSS: Go back down there and give him another hole in one.

ANGEL: Boss? Are you-- (gulp) Um, yes, Boss! Be right back.

(pause)

ANGEL: I did it, Boss. I don't understand it, but I did it. I gave him a second hole in one! But I gotta go on record as complaining about this outrage! Smite me down if you must, Boss, but I gotta know why! A hole in one! Twice! For playing golf on Yom Kippur! How is this punishment???

BOSS: Think, Angel 86; *think*! A hole in one! Then another, on the same day. On Yom Kippur! And he's a rabbi! Now...*who's he gonna tell*?"

THE GOOD SON (Script Version)
By Mel Powell

CHASHKA: As the eldest of the three sons of our dear mother, I challenge each of you to give her a better birthday gift than I have this year. I have built for her a large house, the greatest mansion in all of Chelm. It is so luxurious that even the guest rooms have guest rooms! Surely I will be her favorite son.

LABEL: I am merely the middle child, but my birthday gift is more impressive than yours. I sent our mother the finest top-of-the-line, state-of-the-art ox-cart. Plush velvet seats, fifty kilometers to the gallon of ox-feed--forty in the village--a champion ox with a certificate from Anti-Stubborn School...and a highly-trained driver!

SHMUEL: I am the youngest, and always the favorite, and will be again. You remember how Mama enjoyed reading from the Torah? But you know that her eyesight is not what it once was. So I sent Mama a remarkable parrot! It can recite the entire Torah! It took the Elders in the Great Synagogue of Minsk six years to train the parrot to read Hebrew, and the Elders in the Great Synagogue of Pinsk another six years to teach him the Torah! Mama just names the chapter and verse, and the parrot recites it--and then interprets it. And if you give him an extra cracker, the parrot recites the Haftara as well!

CHASHKA: Mishuga, both of you. We will see who mother favors.

MAMA: Dear Chashka, my wonderful first-born. Thank you for the mansion. It is huge and beautiful, the envy of all who see it. Of course, I live in only one room, but I have to clean the entire house.

Dear Label, my kind and generous middle son. The ox-cart is wonderful. Never have I had such a smooth ride. Of course, I'm older now--where I got to go? And the driver is incredibly rude--he doesn't like it when I give directions.

Dear Shmuel, my youngest, by baby son, my boychik. You have the good sense to know just what your mother truly likes.

The chicken was delicious!

THE HOLIDAY SPIRIT (Script Version)

by Mel Powell from the CMP story

BEREL: I love our holidays! There's always something festive and special about a Jewish holiday

BORIS: Holidays? I'll tell you the best of all the Jewish holidays has to be Passover. What a joy! All the children shaking noisemakers every time they hear Haman's name. Hamantashen![1] The reading of the Megillah.[2] Passover is beautiful!

BEREL: Boris, my dear Balagoola friend, you're confused. That's not Passover you described; it's Purim.

RIVKA: My favorite holiday has always been and will continue to be Shavuos.[3] What a wonderful time! The Torahs are taken out into the streets. The Shofar is sounded. Your name will be inscribed in the good book, but only if Elijah comes. Shavuos is a wonderful time.

BEREL: Shavuos is certainly a wonderful time, Rivka, but you just described Rosh Hashanah,[4] Pesach,[5] and Simchat Torah.

SHLOIME: I can't believe what I am hearing today. How can you possibly get those Holidays all mixed up? If you want to talk holidays, permit me to submit to you an explanation of Chanukah, my favorite time, because it contains a most significant moment.

---

[1] Haman was the bad guy in the story of this holiday...go back to the story for the name of the holiday...and Hamantashen are the traditional triangular cookies that represent Haman's signature three-cornered hat.
[2] The *Megillah* is the story of this holiday, or the book that contains the story.
[3] Shavous (or *shavuot*) translates to "weeks." It is the spring festival holiday.
[4] Rosh Hashanah, literally "head [of] the year," the Jewish New Year, is when your name is metaphorically inscribed into the book of life for the coming good year.
[5] *Pesach* is the Hebrew name of Passover, when traditionally the prophet Elijah visits.

BEREL: Thank God, Shloime. Tell us.

SHLOIME: Remember, my friends, that it was Judah the Maccabee who recaptured the great Temple. He and his men set about driving out the pagan idols and purifying the defiled sanctuary.

RIVKA: Go on, Shloime.

SHLOIME: Having once again sanctified our most holy place, Judah looked to kindle a flame of consecration. He was able to find only a tiny amount of proper oil to light, but, miraculously, this oil burned for eight days and eight nights. It was truly a miracle, my friends. And it all took place on what has become Chanukah.

BORIS: But tell us, Shloime, what is that most significant moment that you mentioned?

SHLOIME: That is my favorite part of Chanukah. You see, when Judah finished praying in the clean Temple, with the oil burning for eight days and nights, he went outside on the steps of the great Temple and looked down. Now, if he could see his shadow... [6]

---

[6] You knew this, but we're thorough. Shloime had it correct...right up to the shadow...

PICKY, PICKY, PICKY (Script Version)

By Mel Powell

WAITER: Welcome to the Chelm Café, home of the famous Shepsil the Chef. You want you should order lunch?

PINCUS: Absotively! But first, let me introduce myself. I am 'Particular Pincus.' In a minute, you will know why I am called by this admittedly odd name. I've heard about your brand-new just-invented dish called Pizza. I would like to order a Pizza.

WAITER: What's so particular?

PINCUS: Glad you asked. If you want I should ever come back to this establishment, I must insist that the dough used in my pizza be wheat harvested during the month of *Adar*.

WAITER: You got.

PINCUS: Hold on just ein momento. You think that's all? That's not all. The cheese...it must come from the milk of a Litvak cow, no other kind. The tomato sauce must be thick enough that a wooden spoon can stand up in it...but only for six minutes, not a second longer.

WAITER: Cheese, Litvak; tomato sauce, wooden spoon; is that all?

PINCUS: Not so fast. Let's talk toppings, I want you should give me pepperoni. But not just any pepperoni, since of course we cannot mix a meat product with the cheese. So I insist on pepperoni...made from soy.

WAITER: Soy?

PINCUS: Soy.

WAITER: Out of soybeans from Minsk or soybeans from Vitipsk-Gaboynya?

PINCUS: I'm impressed. But from Vitipsk-Gaboynya, of course.

WAITER: Of course. Anything else?

PINCUS: Just one more thing for your Shepsil the Chef. A sprinkling of garlic. But not just any garlic, it must be garlic grown on the north side of the farm, not the south. Doesn't matter which farm. I'll give you that one small break!

WAITER: North side. Right.

PINCUS: Now, you'll read that back so I know you've got my order down to the letter?

WAITER: Of course, sir. Pizza. Dough from wheat harvested in the month of Adar, cheese from a Litvak cow, tomato sauce of a particular thickness, soy pepperoni, northern-grown garlic.

PINCUS: Thank you. Good luck.

WAITER: No, thank you, sir. [Turns:] Shepsil! Give me a Number Four!

THE PROPER SEND-OFF (Script Version)

By Mel Powell from the CMP story

RABBI: We gather today to lay to rest a citizen of our tiny village of Chelm, Farfallin the Pharmacist. As your rabbi, of course it is my duty to speak well of this man, who lived here his entire life except for his schooling in the Anatevka Apothecary Academy.

BEREL: Good luck, Rabbi!

RABBI: Be kind, Berel. But I will never lie to you, my congregation. If the truth be known, not one single member of our village of Chelm liked Farfallin. He was so unpleasant that when people needed a pharmacist, they would go all the way to Minsk so they shouldn't have to deal with this terrible person.

RIVKA: I went to Pinsk! It's farther away than Minsk, the better to get away from Farfallin!

RABBI: Rivka, we know. Farfallin was not overly loved in our community. Problems he had with his neighbors. Problems he caused with most people who knew him. Still, he was one of us, and that entitles him to a proper send-off.

YENTA: Rabbi, we are all familiar with his tight-fisted, frugal--all right, I'll say it--cheap ways. That's why his wife divorced him; after just six minutes of marriage! Five minutes after the wedding, he gave her a bill for half the reception. One minute later, divorced! And after how hard I worked to match them!

RABBI: Yes, Yenta, yes. But we have traditions here. And as is our custom in Chelm, I am asking that at least one member of our congregation say something nice about the deceased prior to his burial. Who wishes to speak first--with something nice?

(pause)

RABBI: Who in Chelm wasn't personally insulted by this cranky, conniving, uncaring man? But someone must have something nice to say!

(pause)

RABBI: That's it! We will sit here until Tisha b'Av if we have to, but somebody in this temple of love and understanding will find it in his or her heart to say something worthwhile about our departed Pharmacist!

(pause)

RABBI: Boris! Boris the Balagoola, I see you've raised your hand. Thank you. You have something nice to say about the deceased?

BORIS: I have, Rabbi.

RABBI: Well done, Boris. What is the single best thing you can tell us about Farfallin?

BORIS: His brother…was worse.

SOMETIMES IT DOESN'T PAY TO BE A NICE PERSON
(Script Version)

By MP from the CMP story

(from a story by Danny Dayton)

BORIS: Hello, is this Gitlitz, who used to live in Chelm? Now he's a millionaire?

GITLITZ: Yes, he is--I mean, I am. To whom I got the pleasure?

BORIS: My name is Boris the Balagoola, and I am, this year, Mayor of the village.

GITLITZ: Congratulations! How can I be of service to you?

BORIS: An old man named Shpilkas just passed away here in Chelm. He was very poor, extremely destitute, there's simply no money with which to give him a proper burial. Our good Rabbi remembered that you might be distantly related and perhaps you could help us bury Shpilkas.

GITLITZ: Do I remember Shpilkas? Who could forget Shpilkas? He was my favorite cousin. Every Chanukah, as poor as he was, he used to send me something. One year it would be a handmade *dreidel*,[7] another time it would be a few kopecks. He was poor and uneducated, but to me, he was a *mensch*."[8]

BORIS: Oy, a *mensch* like that we should give a proper send-off.

GITLITZ: Exactly, Mr. Mayor Balagoola. For me, thanks God, money is no object. So here is what I want you to do: Firstly, purchase the most impressive headstone.

BORIS: Stone.

GITILTZ: And a coffin of the finest pine.

BORIS: Pine.

---

[7] A *dreidel* is the little spinning toy top, a tradition of the Chanukah holiday.
[8] A good person; it is a high compliment to call someone a *mensch*.

GITITZ: Lastly, secure one of the finest plots in the cemetery.

BORIS: Plots.

GITITZ: Then I want you to be sure that people come to the burial services. Spend whatever it takes to put out the finest spread of food to comfort the people when they come to mourn for our Shpilkas.

BORIS: Shpilkas.

GITLITZ: I want a string ensemble and a choir of cantors. I want a proclamation from the Tsar and a street named after Shpilkas.

BORIS: Shpilkas Street.

GITLITZ: Flowers everywhere! And also I want he should be buried in a fine tuxedo.

BORIS: Tuxedo, buried.

GITLITZ: Can you do all of this, Balagoola? I will pay all costs and even make a handsome extra donation to the village coffers.

BORIS: Coffers. Dear Gitlitz, we will do it all, and send you the bill. We are most grateful.

NARRATOR: Six months later...

BORIS: Hello, Boris the Balagoola, Mayor of Chelm. To whom I got the pleasure?

GITLITZ: Mayor Boris, this is Gitlitz! I call to complain! I asked for first class, I got first class. I received your letter describing the beautiful funeral for dear cousin Shpilkas. The plot, the stone, the music, the choir, the flowers, the tuxedo-- everything. But these "additional funeral expenses," every month! Why do I continue to receive a monthly bill of forty-seven kopecks?

BORIS: Listen, Mr. Gitlitz. What you asked for you got. Every single request met, every detail honored. But, after all, you have to pay for the rental of Shpilkas's tuxedo!

TICKET, PLEASE (Script Version)

By Mel Powell

BORIS: Ticket, please!

LABEL: Ah, yes, good *yuntif*, Boris! You see, it's like this. I must get a message to Berel the Beadle! May I please enter the synagogue?

BORIS: Good *yuntif*, Label! Welcome to Yom Kippur services here at the Great Synagogue of Chelm. You look terrific! Have you lost a little weight? Ticket, please.

LABEL: Boris, I haven't got a ticket! But I must get a message to Berel! Please, you must let me in!

RIVKA: Ah, good morning, Label! Boris, what seems to be the trouble? The line outside is getting long.

BORIS: Label doesn't have a ticket! But he says he must get a message to the good beadle!

RIVKA: Berel? He's sitting in his customary seat in the front row. But, Label, you know you must have a ticket!

LABEL: Rivka, please help me! It wasn't my fault! I got the news from Mendel the Messenger that the High Holy Days were approaching, but I didn't realize that they were coming so soon! I forgot to order my ticket!

RIVKA: (sigh) Dear Label, today is the Day of Atonement. It is the day when we cleanse ourselves of our sins. So...for the sin you have sinned by forgetting to buy your ticket...we absolve you, and we trust that The Almighty will do the same.

LABEL: Oh, thank you, thank you! As soon as I balance my checking account, I will make a nice donation!

BORIS: So...you may go into the Synagogue, even though you have no ticket. And you may give your message to Berel the Beadle. However...

LABEL: Yes?

BORIS: Don't let me catch you praying!

TINK BEFORE YOU TALK (Script Version)

(A Passover Parable)

by Mel Powell from the CMP story

TEITLEBAUM: Teitlebaum's Tel Aviv Tink Tank, Teitlebaum talking. To whom I got the pleasure?

GENERAL: Tink tank?

TEITLEBAUM: Tink Tank. T-Haitch-I-N-K, Tink. We tink of everything. You got a problem, we got a solution. If the solution don't vork, you don't pay, and we tink again.

GENERAL: Tank you--excuse me, thank you. I am Brigadier General Thomas, and I am calling you from the Pentagon in Washington. You may be our last hope.

TEITLEBAUM: Now you're talking. So what's the problem?

GENERAL: The problem is that when one of our brand-new supersonic fighter jets gets up to 3,000 miles per hour, the wings snap off. We've tried everything. Nothing works.

TEITLEBAUM: You ain't tried everytink yet, buddy. You ain't tried us. You'll give me a call on Tuesday, or maybe Toisday, and we'll have for you a solution.

GENERAL: Tuesday? Or even Tois--Thursday? I'll have you know that the government has been working on this problem for years. The best minds from M.I.T., Cal Tech--even the Germans' best engineers can't solve the problem of the wings breaking off.

TEITLEBAUM: Not to worry. You'll call Tuesday. If it don't vork, you don't pay.

NARRATOR: On the next Tuesday...

TEITLEBAUM: Teitlebaum's Tel Aviv Tink Tank, Teitlebaum talking. To whom I got the pleasure?

GENERAL: It's General Thomas and our top people on the line. We don't suppose you've got a solution yet?

TEITLEBAUM: Today's your lucky day, Brigadoon General. Of course we got for you the answer. First you take an airplane. Then you need a knoll punch.

GENERAL: A what?

TEITLEBAUM: A knoll punch. Something you can punch a knoll with.

GENERAL: Oh, you mean a hole punch. Yes, I'm sure we can find one.

TEITLEBAUM: Good. You'll punch a knoll every six inches where the wings meet the plane. That'll do it.

GENERAL: The problem, Teitlebaum, is one of stress! Drilling holes at the point of stress can only make it worse!

TEITLEBAUM: You got a better idea?

GENERAL: Well…no.

TEITLEBAUM: You got remote control, so if the idea don't vork, no one gets hurt?

GENERAL: Yes.

TEITLEBAUM: So you'll try. If it vorks, send money. If not, not.

NARRATOR: Three weeks later…

TEITLEBAUM: Teitlebaum's Tel Aviv Tink Tank, Teitlebaum talking. To whom I got the pleasure?

GENERAL: It worked, Teitlebaum! It worked! How did you know? The best engineers in the world couldn't figure it out, but you did! Payment is on the way. How did you do it, Teitlebaum?

TEITLEBAUM: It was easy, Your Generalship--if you happen to be Jewish. You see, we Jews have a similar problem on one of our sacred holidays, Passover. We eat this cardboard that we call Matzah. It comes in sheets, with perforations. Did you *ever* try to break a piece of matzah at the perforations?

WHAT I DID ON MY VACATION (Script Version)

By Mel Powell from the CMP story

RIVKA: Berel! Berel, wake up already!

BEREL: Oyyyy. Why do I hear Rivka the Baker's voice? Why am I in this tiny boat, on a river, with a headache? Wait--I remember. It's my summer vacation and I paid three rubles to take the Chelm River Cruise.

RIVKA: Exactly. My first time trying this cruise, too, which is also why I am in this other tiny boat. Look over there at that third boat. Boris is waking up. Boris!

BORIS: Oy, what a headache. Berel? Rivka? You also paid three rubles for the Chelm River Cruise?

BEREL: Yes, Balagoola. But I don't remember anything after I paid the cruise director the three rubles and saw him swing a stick at my head.

RIVKA: I think that's what I remember from when I paid the cruise director! But nothing else until I woke up ten minutes ago in this boat, with a headache.

BORIS: And I also have a bump on the head. But a summer vacation is a summer vacation!

BEREL: I don't see any other boats floating on the river with us. I wonder if the cruise director will catch up to us with some cruise activities.

BORIS: Activities would be nice.

RIVKA: And maybe an umbrella or a hat to protect us from the sun!

BORIS: An umbrella would be nice.

BEREL: This is the worst three rubles I've ever spent! They knock you on the head and put you in a boat! I won't do this again ever!

RIVKA: Some Chelm River Cruise! They won't fool me again, either! Boris, do you think they at least serve breakfast?

BORIS: They didn't last year!

THE WOODCUTTER (Script Version)
By Mel Powell from the JP story

BEREL: Meyer? What are you doing out here in the overgrown forest? I'm interviewing for a new Town Woodcutter.

MEYER: What, you think I'm here for a sandwich? I'm applying for the job.

BEREL: Meyer, you're our dear retired Mohel Emeritus. You're 87 years old! You're barely five feet three inches tall! How could you possibly chop down even a twig, let alone a tree?

MEYER: Berel, my boy, don't you know that when was a young man I was the world's greatest woodcutter? It was only twenty years ago that I decided I didn't want to work so hard anymore and I retired from that job and became a mohel. I figured that with all my experience I could do something in the same field that would be easier. After all, cutting is cutting.

BEREL: Impossible! If you even try to lift the axe, you'll hurt yourself.

MEYER: What have you got to lose? Gimme already a test!

BEREL: OK, try this tiny sapling if you must try something.

MEYER: You are insulting me…but fine…here, done.

BEREL: Not bad. But, well…maybe you can cut down those three big trees for next year's sukkah. If we had the money, we would have rented the cutting equipment from Minsk. But I guess you're all we've got, Meyer.

MEYER: Equipment? You're dealing with the world's greatest woodcutter. …There you go.

BEREL: Fantastic! You're hired! Meyer, where did you learn how to do this?

MEYER: Well, for many years I was the Chief Woodcutter in the Sahara Forest.

BEREL: Sahara Forest? Don't you mean Sahara Desert?

MEYER: Sure…NOW!

Printed in Great Britain
by Amazon